Ravinder Randhawa was born in India and ⏤
her childhood. She went on to found the Asian women writers ⏤
which she co-ordinated for some years. She is the author of two previous
novels and numerous short stories including 'Normal Times' which has
been short-listed for the 2001 Wong Award. She is currently working on
her next novel, *The Snake Charmer's Daughter*. She is a frequent speaker
at universities both in the United Kingdom and abroad, is a member of
International Pen, and in March 2001, took up a fellowship with the Royal
Literary Fund, based at Toynbee Hall. She lives in London.

THE CORAL STRAND

Ravinder Randhawa

Copyright © 2001 Ravinder Randhawa

This edition published in 2001 by House of Stratus, an imprint of Stratus Holdings plc, 24c Old Burlington Street, London, W1X 1RL, UK.

www.houseofstratus.com

Typeset, printed and bound by House of Stratus.

A catalogue record for this book is available from the British Library.

ISBN 0-7551-0344-0

To my parents,
Pakhar Singh and Kartar Kaur Randhawa,
with my love, gratitude and admiration

Acknowledgements

I would like to thank the following people and organisations for their help: Rohan Armstrong, Devika Bannerjee, Lloyd Gee, Indra Khanna, Meena Thakor, Sushma Mehta; my agent Jane Bradish-Ellames for 'recognising' this novel, Euan Thorneycroft for seeing it to the end, my editor Jenny Rayner for her meticulous attention to detail; The K Blundell Trust for their help, many years ago; The Royal Literary Fund for their invaluable support; Pukka Palace. Most especially Rukhsana and Rahila.

Chapter One

London, January 1997. Early morning

'Afraid? No fear. Not me!' chanting her early morning litany into the tiny mirror that only has space for a fragment of her face – Sita/Ferret's daily dose of Dutch courage!

Sita the Ferret had kept and taken into herself these names that Emily and Champa had given her: Sita from Champa, Ferret from Emily. She had joined them up, and would murmur them to herself. Sita/Ferret. Syllables of the self.

Taking the bottle of Old Spice from the shelf, she removes the top and dabs drops onto her clothes, wrists, the base of her neck; breathing in deeply, inhaling the pungent, spicy scents!

The history of a scent! More than twenty years earlier, Emily had caught the child Sita/Ferret at her dressing table trying to open a silver perfume bottle. The young girl had flinched and immediately moved away waiting for Emily's hand to rise and crack across her face. Instead, Emily had done something unusual: she opened the carved doors of an almirah and searched inside. The child had stood still, waiting. She wouldn't move till she was given permission, their last fight still vivid inside her when she'd shouted back at Emily and tried to run out of the kitchen. Emily, furious with rage had caught her by the arm: '*Gutter ki batchi*, vermin of the sewers, thinks she can talk back to a memsahib!'

'Mutant Memsahib!' Sita/Ferret had retorted recklessly.

'Disobedient worm!' Emily had said, spitting the words. 'A servant is not her master's equal. I was too lax with her.' Who *her?* 'Even bringing her here. Great Britain itself! You,' finger pointing like a knife at Sita/Ferret's heart, 'you're living off me and I won't have you getting uppity.'

1

Closing the almirah, Emily had held out a bottle. 'This is for girls like you, from Over There. Look, it says "spice" on it, so it's especially for you.' Emily opened the bottle of Old Spice and sprinkled drops over her hair, shoulders and face; suddenly the air was filled with a sharp, sweet, peppery perfume. The child clamped her mouth shut and held her body tight, determined not to breathe in Emily's scents from Over There. 'As obstinate and stubborn as her,' Emily commented acidly, 'it won't do any good.'

Will and flesh are enemies! Sita/Ferret had held on till her chest and throat were burning, but then her mouth burst open with a gasp, the aromatic sting hitting her tongue. Emily held out the bottle. Even if it had been a burning coal, the child could not have refused it. Sita/Ferret put her fingers around the bottle and held it away from her body. 'No geniis in there to jump out and eat you up!' Emily knew about fear, not only that, Emily knew about the frailties of the flesh too. 'Stop snivelling!' Emily had once commanded. 'If I'd done that I'd have rotted on the dung heap.' Sita/Ferret had rushed upstairs to her room, driven by relief that no worse punishment had been visited upon her. Her room was at the top of the Victorian house, with a sloping ceiling, a small fireplace, and a window through which she could watch the street below. Leaning out, Sita/Ferret would watch the ebb and flow of people: those on their own, couples, families, groups, cats and dogs. In the dark winter evenings, street lamps would transform the street into a distant, mysterious place. Pulling a box from under her bed, Sita/Ferret had carefully placed the bottle of Old Spice in it. She hadn't thought to throw it away. She possessed so little of her own that every odd object she'd managed to pick up was carefully hoarded. Each one helped to give her some weight in the world.

Since those early years Sita the Ferret had grown up and run away from Emily the Mutant Memsahib and Champa the Dumpa. After her 'great escape', she'd spent many an hour browsing among the perfume counters of the city, as fascinated by the crystal, gilded containers as the precious contents themselves, contents which promised passionate pleasures and liquid dreams. She would look, linger, and indulge in experimental dabs, but at the end, she always moved to the men's counter, and out of a perverse stubbornness, bought the one that Emily had said was for girls like her, from Over There!

Coming out of her bathroom into her rented attic room, Sita/Ferret opens the curtains and rubs at the condensation on the old window pane, the one that Mrs Sangeeta Rayit, her new landlady, had pointed out as being original, as old as the house. Freezing glass against her palm! Darkness outside. Sita/Ferret has never complained about the English winter, neither has she admitted to the heresy of enjoying the bitter-sweetness of its grey embrace. In the block of flats across the road a few windows are also lit, early risers providing her with a distant sense of camaraderie. She wonders if, like her, they have a special reason for their dawn start this morning, or if this is their habitual time. Are they part of that secret army whose work starts in the dark, lonely hours?

Picking up her heavy, thick-soled boots, she pushes in her feet, pulls and tugs the laces into a hard knot. Emily and Champa would have a fit if they saw them. Tip-tapping ladies' shoes with thin heels were their style. Her boots are hardwearing and dependable. Sita/Ferret has to provide her own certainties.

Taking a dark, woollen coat out of the wardrobe, she first puts it on the bed, checks the hem, makes sure all the stitches are securely in place, then picks it up and urgently pushes her arms through the sleeves.

Only now is she ready for her annual pilgrimage. To peek and spy at the house in which still lived Champa the Dumpa, and Emily the Mutant Memsahib. The house that Sita/Ferret had called the Mausoleum. That Emily had named 'Simla Sunshine'.

Coincidence – the mysterious hand of fate!
Symmetry – a poetic balance.
Calculation – the logic of mathematics.

Sita/Ferret wants them to unlock their hidden power and answer all the questions simmering inside her. She cannot beg, she cannot ask, she can only utilise the past, and it is for this that she arranges her secret visits on the anniversary of the day she left, setting herself up for a bruise with the past. She has argued with herself that she could cut the connection, save her money, and the wear and tear on her emotions; she could use the day for indulgences, relaxation, pampering; or put in extra time at work and improve her prospects and her pension. But year after year, when the day comes, Sita/Ferret sets her alarm clock extra early.

Her boots tread lightly down the stairs. She doesn't produce unnecessary noise. 'Are you an elephant or a donkey?' Champa's voice would spiral through the Mausoleum, 'no need to walk on my head.'

Swinging open the front door Sita/Ferret steps out, and silently closes it behind her. Just as she had done when she left the Mausoleum. The sleeping occupants wouldn't even know that someone had made an exit. She turns into the dark, freezing cold of the early morning. Street lamps shed a yellow glow, icy air hanging like a veil; her breath puffing into little clouds in front of her, the sound of her boots dispersing into the darkness. Occasionally, other solitary shapes pass her, enveloped in anonymity. For her, these are the symphonies of winter.

The weight of a coat, the protection of gloves, the softness of a scarf: the imagined love of a family.

Emily had taught her the techniques of survival in a cold climate. And more. Not that she had ever known any other. Her skin had never darkened under the heat of a faraway sun. It was dark all by itself. The young Sita/Ferret had taken a chart of paint colours and compared her pigmentation with the little squares on the sheet, the back of her hand sliding backwards and forwards, halting at a pink rosiness. At a wish? Or a consideration of the difference? The hand had moved on to the colours that deepened and darkened. The child had decided that she and bronze brown must be first cousins.

But it was Champa who had taught her the techniques of survival in a hostile environment. And more. Love was not a word prettily sprinkled among the sentences uttered in that house.

'The Lies of Human Bondage!' she scribbles into the grime of the train window, then rubs out 'Lies' and writes in 'Ties', unable to remember the exact wording. Still dissatisfied, she rubs out 'Ties' and replaces with 'Lives'. Which again she erases, for human bondage is made up of many ingredients, and she doesn't know how to convey the complexity. There is no one else in the compartment to watch her hands become dirty rubbing and re-writing. In the end she erases it all, leaving a clean patch on the dirty window. Greasy grime will soon cover that blank space, ready for the next graffiti guru.

4

The train was rushing her nearer. It would rush her away just as fast. The promise of a quick departure excused the foolishness of this journey. She'd be able to return three hours before the opening of the exhibition. An hour to revise the information in the catalogue, an hour to get ready and an hour to get there. Symmetry!

Outside, the world was flashing past: long rows of damp gardens, the backs of terraced houses, large factories, zigzagging fire escapes, car parks, and numerous derelict buildings. As if London was falling apart at the edges. She has a few more stations to go and then a bus to catch, for Emily and Champa live in the wide avenues of suburbia.

Sita/Ferret opens her newspaper, and concentrates deeply on the main article – but finds she cannot read a word. Normally she looked forward to her newspapers and magazines. She found the printed stories far more potent than any doings in Soapland, for here was actuality, dirty and sinister, treacherous and corrupt; powered by greed, anger, revenge or scorned love. She was still astounded by what people did to each other.

Eventually she gives up her pretence, puts away her newspaper, and folds her arms tight around herself. When recognisable landmarks hit her eyes, her heart starts to beat faster. The high roof and tall chimneys of the school come into view. A part of her still lives there, standing against the wall, watching the other children, but that little girl's world had only ever extended as far as her fingertips. Sita/Ferret feels piercing pity for the child self that she once was. She has more territory inside her now; more names and experiences filling her memory, but her world still begins in her head and ends at her fingertips. For all her travelling, she hasn't moved so very far. How Emily would laugh if she knew, how Champa would shake her head.

Sita/Ferret hands in her ticket and pauses at the exit to take change from her pockets and put it in the charity box. Across the road from the station, sits the Palm Court Hotel, with its old-fashioned tearooms, where Emily would ensconce herself and, lifting her chin, order tea and pretty cream cakes. Sita/Ferret had watched her through the windows once. Delicately pouring and sipping. Sitting alone.

The external face of a place is forever changing. Old buildings are torn down, new ones go up in their place, shops change names and styles, businesses rise and fall, people come and go. But the arteries of the town, the roads and streets, rarely alter. Sita/Ferret doesn't need to re-orientate herself; she's never forgotten. She looks at her watch. On this day, twelve months ago, the rest of the journey had taken forty-five minutes. She pulled down her hat and waited at the bus stop.

'Hats look silly on Indian women,' Emily had once said, 'get yourself a headscarf like Champa.' Sita/Ferret had gone bareheaded.

As she steps off the bus and turns left, ghosts begin to greet her, ghosts of her childhood selves. There are the hurried, harried ones that dash from school back to the Mausoleum, for chores and duties awaited. There is the thief in the park, the one that steals rides on the swings when she should be in the kitchen, brewing their afternoon tea. A line of schoolchildren walk by and she sees the sulky ghost, the one who walks at the end of the class crocodile, for when there are odd numbers, there is always one child who can't be paired up. The two Indian children in the class look back and giggle.

Turning the corner, Sita/Ferret sees the shop and realises the shop ghost will be waiting for her too, so she quickly crosses the road, hoping to evade it. Spooky fingers follow her. She remembers hurtling out of the shop, running out on the precious Saturday job for which she'd begged, pleaded and bargained. She'd refused to go back, or give Emily and Champa an explanation. Emily had sniffed, perhaps the girl had no staying power, and perhaps Emily would have to support her forever: 'In which case someone...' A pause to get her breath back? 'Someone had better look lively and put in her tuppence worth.'

A thin, fine rain has begun, casting a flickering mist over everything. Taking off her hat Sita/Ferret lifts her face. She likes this rain that falls so silently, secretly. Stopping by the postbox on the corner, she prepares herself for the tall Victorian house, double fronted, with an enclosed veranda, a low hedge and an iron gate. Even in winter, Emily and Champa had liked to sit on the veranda, Kashmiri shawls around their shoulders, lamps lit against the early dark. Sita/Ferret would bring up the tea and snacks from the basement kitchen.

The builder had said, 'Most people have conservatories at the back.'

'I'm the one who's paying,' Emily had snapped back. She liked people to know that she was the one with the wallet. Sita/Ferret had learnt about the power of money and the abilities of its possessor to arrange the world to her wishes.

Sita/Ferret reaches the tree opposite the house, under which a person can stand, as if waiting for the rain to pass. The house looks asleep, the curtains in the upper windows still closed, the colouring faded and patchy. She wonders why Emily, appearance proud, appearance obsessed, had allowed it to get tatty. Perhaps age was finally working its depredations upon Emily's steely abrasiveness.

Sita/Ferret had hated Champa the Dumpa as much as she had hated Emily. She'd worked and reworked the list of Champa's crimes: Champa the mindless and spineless; Champa following Emily like a cowed cat – cooking for Emily, echoing Emily, smiling at Emily. If they'd had to breathe in turns, Champa would always be saying, '*Pehle aap, pehlai aap, after you, after you.*' Neither would ever die: Emily plain refused to do so, and Champa couldn't, because it would always be a case of 'first you, first you.' Could it be true that Emily had magical powers? She had whispered into a child's ears, 'You don't know all the things I know from Over There.' That unknown, yet omnipresent land across the oceans! 'I can see you when you think I'm not looking. Even when I'm not here. I can do *Kali* magic!' she'd finished, smiling into the child's frightened eyes. The child Sita/Ferret had been so rattled by the idea of this *Kali* magic she had risked asking Champa about it. Instead of receiving a proper explanation, or being told it was all rubbish, Champa had said something else entirely, 'Life is very hard. You are not as strong as life. Don't run away with your ideas.' Sita/Ferret had followed the advice and hadn't run away with her ideas.

She'd run away with the family jewels. Not that she knew if she were family or not.

Sita/Ferret steps out from the tree to cross the road for a closer inspection. She will stand at the edge of the hedge and peer around, over the gate. After this she can go away for another twelve months. Halfway across the road, she sees the double doors of the house opening and a wheelchair being pushed out. Frantically, she rushes back to the tree, heart pounding. She reminds herself that she's a grown woman, and there is no need to act like a petrified rabbit, but she is also filled with revengeful glee, exultant with righteousness. So, the Grande Dame of Simla Sunshine doesn't have the gift of everlasting life, after all. She doesn't possess magical powers, *Kali* or otherwise. She's merely a frail old woman who can't even walk on her own two legs. Hubris has finally arrived for Emily. Sita/Ferret has a mad impulse to go over and gloat. But then hubris will arrive for her. 'Thief! Thief!' Champa will shout, alerting the neighbourhood and setting off a spate of 999 calls.

Sita/Ferret hears the clang of the gate and carefully slides her head around the tree. The sight of an orange border flapping at the feet of the one in the wheelchair suddenly extinguishes her glee. Emily bends down and tucks a blanket more securely around the legs. Sita/Ferret stares, her eyes glued to them as they start down the road. As if a divine order had been overturned!

She digs her hands into her pockets and stands tight against the tree, but in the end she can't resist the temptation to follow them, to dawdle up behind, and examine at close range this calamity in the haughty house of Emily, who forever talked of inferiors and superiors, of those who should know their place and be suitably grateful. Emily is wearing the Astrakhan coat that Sita/Ferret, as a young girl, had once dared to try on, and fallen, sprawling onto the floor, unbalanced by the weight of it. Emily is opening an umbrella and placing it in Champa's hands. From where she is, Sita/Ferret can't see if Champa is wearing the purple coat with the plate size buttons that she'd always loved. Emily's body bows with effort as she pushes the wheelchair along the uneven pavement. Theirs is a slow progress along that street. Sita/Ferret lessens her pace, quietens her steps. No scraps of casual conversation float back towards her.

Sita/Ferret calculated her own age at thirty approaching a thousand. If three decades were hers, how many decades belonged to the two in front? How much of their lives had they spent together and why?

A crack across the old ways!

Quickening her steps, she gains upon the labouring Emily, taking in the thickened legs with bulging veins, hearing the loud noise of her breathing. She comes abreast, looks down, catches a glimpse of sagging cheek and glinting nose stud, and suddenly they're behind her. The coincidence of place and time. They had walked side by side. Fabric must have brushed against fabric.

Trains are neutral. They stay on the rails. It's the living cargo, the passengers, who ricochet from one emotion to another. She'd always wanted damnation to make a house call on them. But hadn't guessed that when it did, she too would be affected. Sita/Ferret had made her annual visits without being able to give herself any good reason; 'because I bloody well want to,' she'd justified to herself once. She'd traipsed there, year after year, had a good look, and left, reassured that nothing had changed.

Therefore she needn't change. So she was the one who had wanted time to stand still!

Chapter Two

Mirror, mirror on the wall. Who isn't the fairest of them all? Sita/Ferret was back in front of her tiny mirror. 'The Mutant Memsahib? Champa the Dumpa? Or...' folding back the dog-eared pages of a magazine 'me, myself, the Sita/Ferret?' She was still at war with them, she always would be, but today the enmities had taken a twist.

Propping the magazine *Asian Woman* on the ledge, she opened a bag and took out an array of cosmetics, all new and pristine. After Mr Kalyan's hint, she knew what she had to do, but hadn't known how to do it. Sita/Ferret had never known how to dress for an Asian occasion. *Asian Woman* had become her bible and she'd spent several weekends, painstakingly gathering together the various parts for the engineering of an image.

Eyes flicking between the magazine and her reflection, she followed the instructions for this month's 'Sizzling Glamour Look'. Make believe that all believed! In the Mausoleum, she'd learned how to follow instructions meticulously, to work fast and work hard. Essential survival skills. Perhaps she should be grateful to them. 'You're living in a gilded palace here,' Emily had declared once, 'too good for the likes of you. Over There...' (*Over There!* Sita/Ferret had come to hate Over There) '...you'd be searching for scraps in the gutter! Or dead!' Emily had stated cuttingly, guillotine fashion! So she must be thankful to Emily for her very life and demonstrate it by unending servitude.

Carefully reading the last instruction, she picked up the lipstick. Emily and Champa had adorned themselves every day, rubbing in rouge, patting their faces with powder puffs, whooshing hairspray over their hair. As if they lived on the catwalk! In the glare of the paparazzi! Sita/Ferret swivelled the lipstick, a rich gleaming column of colour rose up, the slanted top like a pure, untouched mountain peak. Such must be the allure of virginity! She leaned towards the mirror. 'Too much looking, too much cooking,' Champa had once said, catching the teenage Sita/Ferret in front of the large mirror with the ivory pattern, bequeathing admonition and conundrum. Ignoring these echoes from the past, Sita/Ferret moved right up close to her mirror, room enough for her lips to be reflected: to part them, pout them, paint them!

And yet, she was not done. Taking the last packet from the windowsill, she extracts a glittering, tear-shaped little thing that she balances on the tip of her finger. The *bindi!* Subject of tradition, fashion fads and Bollywood movies. Eyes darting back and forth between the page and mirror, Sita/Ferret concentrates on a spot on her forehead, steadies her finger, quickly presses the *bindi* into place.

It falls off. She manages to catch it in her hand and looks at it, puzzled. Strangely, *bindis* had never been worn in Emily's house. Champa had never adorned herself with a red dot or a sparkling itty-bitty little thing picked from a packet. Turning it over in her hand, she eventually realised something had to make it stick, and kicked herself for her ignorance. She moistened the back with a drop from the tap. Others may have licked it, but not Sita/Ferret, Champa's disgust deep inside her. Some things can't be dug out. Finally, after great deliberation and holding her breath, she lifted her hand, pressed it on, and waited.

Success! The tear did not fall. Today must be her lucky day! Then corrected herself quickly – she needed to be precise. *Unknown* was this day. Wheelchair tracks across her mind, Sita/Ferret examined parts of her face in turn. Almost as if she'd become someone else. To be different, must mean possessing a different knowledge?

Sita/Ferret sighed, she was only halfway through this engineering project. Taking the magazine, and flicking the pages, she moved into the bedroom, and propped it on the pillow; the picture of the languid, bejewelled model had become as familiar as herself. Opening the wardrobe door, she brought out the first item, laid the silky cream-coloured kameez on the bed; 'Cream – The Colour of Dreams', the headline announced on the page.

Trekking backwards and forwards between the wardrobe and bed, she brought out all the other pieces, all except the chunky jewellery the model was wearing. She couldn't afford that.

Sita/Ferret assembled herself, item by item; from the kameez to the shalwar, from the *dupatta* to the green platform sandals. She'd been horrified at the amount of money she'd had to fork out, from the tiniest of make-up brushes, to the pots of colour, to the clothes, to the sandals on her feet. Fitting into an image didn't come cheap. Standing up, she closed her eyes and ran her hands down her body, feeling the shape and texture of the fabric. She had nowhere to check her appearance, so had to place her trust in the very act of imitation. But it was the subtler, inner transformations that she was attempting to capture. Can there be a flow from the garments into the wearer? Making the wearer something else? When she takes them off, at the end of the day, will an effect remain through other days?

Mr Kalyan, her employer, the man who paid her wages, had approached the matter delicately. Coming down to her basement, sitting by her desk, he had talked about the fact that this was to be his first 'Indian Arts Exhibition' – for the first time they were 'going pubalik' – and stated how important the event was for the business. Mr Kalyan was a stocky man, always suitably dressed, always on top of every detail. He had recognised Sita/Ferret's worth to him; he didn't know that she had recognised him as one who walked a tightrope each day. 'We must make a good impression,' Mr Kalyan had continued, 'or people will think we're a laughing stock, and they will laugh and laugh. I know people,' nodding his head, confirming his knowledge of this derisive world. 'Because it is the evening, many people will be coming in evening clothes,' he had added. Sita/Ferret had been kneeling on the floor, cleaning out a cabinet in which they were to store the figures from the current consignment. The unopened crates were piled along the wall. Sita/Ferret had listened to him, but continued with her work, rinsing the cleaning cloth in the bowl of water, rubbing at stains. 'The ladies will be dressed in saris or suits. Is that the right word?' he had said, furrowing his forehead. 'For an Indian occasion, of course, they will be dressed in Indian clothes.' Sita/Ferret had sat back on her heels and looked at him. It was only polite to do so, since the words were so indirectly directed at her. Sita/Ferret came to work dressed in old tracksuits, or jeans and T-shirts, some with ingrained stains, others with shiny, worn patches. In her previous jobs, all with charity organisations, the pay had hardly been extravagant or the other workers Armani clad. 'And the ladies will have all the jewellery that women like to pile on themselves,' Mr Kalyan had added, with an indulgent laugh. 'My wife is always complaining that in this country she hardly has the chance to wear her best clothes and jewellery. You must also have wedding clothes and jewellery that you don't get much chance to wear?' Sita/Ferret had smiled and nodded. Having started with him as Mrs Pandey, she could hardly have disagreed.

Now she deviates from the magazine. Taking her coat and a pair of scissors, she smoothes the hem of her coat, then immensely carefully, snips the stitches halfway to the back; she leaves the other half of the hem intact. Sliding her fingers underneath, she opens out the folds. They lie dull and fluff covered, held by their stitches. She hesitates. Is she being needlessly reckless? The first time in ten years can hardly be foolish. Their weight, patterns and colours are as familiar to her as her own face; they are her daily companions. And as strange, as unknown! People look at themselves in photographs and ask, 'Is that really me?' She looks at them and wonders, 'Are they truly so fabulous?'

She had reasoned and negotiated with herself. Who was to know they were not wedding gifts? Furthermore, would it not be more surprising if she did not possess the requisite amount? Deeper, and removed from reason, was an underground emotion, a desire to be different for one night, to indulge after all the years of abstinence. Quickly she snapped the scissors, cut the threads, and took them out!

Later that night, when she returns, she will place them back; hide them away perhaps for another ten years. A necklace, bangles, and earrings. Then threading a needle, she securely sews up the hem, again double-checking the parts she hasn't opened. Quickly and swiftly, buffing each item with a velvety brush and barely looking at them, she hurriedly places the necklace around her neck; cold metal and stone against her skin making her shiver. The bangles are for a much smaller hand than hers, but with unrelenting determination she massages the bones of her hand, pushing at the knuckles, working the bangles over them, scraping her skin, till they finally chinkle on her wrists. Had Emily been slender boned in her youth? The earrings have thick curved stems that she knows will be skin tearing murder to hook through her ears, but having broken the denial of years she isn't to be defeated now. Closing her eyes, and stretching her earlobe with one hand she works the stem into the hole, gently persuading it in. No amount of gentle prodding will work here. Taking a deep breath, she holds the stem steady and pushes. A sharp pain flashes through her. Taking a tissue she dabs at her ear. Blood. That's what happens when you deck yourself out in stolen feathers! She had meant to take them. To take her revenge.

She could have left the Mausoleum without the packet that had nestled against her skin. The appropriation had been pre-calculated, the act pre-planned. However it was not till a few days later, installed behind a door with a lock, that she had opened it out, spilled the contents onto the table and been startled at the amount, at the number of things that had glinted and glimmered up at her. To touch a white ball and tell herself that this must be a pearl, to smooth the shine of a white stone and tell herself this must be a diamond, to have a finger hovering over green and red: *precious* stones.

Awesome beauty! In her possession. She had told herself that she could convert all this into paper cash and organise a fully enjoyable life for herself. Somehow the appropriate time to arrange the conversion had never arrived. In the meantime, she had been taking her revenge.

And had found that revenge was not sweet or even bitter, but hard and demanding. The safeguarding of its fruit exercised untold ingenuity, burdened her movements, and placed a tax on the new life. Serious alternatives had often been considered. She could sneak back to the Mausoleum and pop them through the doorway. She could pawn them and never redeem them. She could walk into Hatton Garden, enter a shop and sell the lot. She could have been free. And rich! Instead, she became adept at hiding them, inside her clothes or sewn into a belt and tied underneath. She did not dare leave them behind, for she could never know how many people knew the nooks and crannies of a rented room. Besides, she'd miss them if she weren't wearing them.

Going down the stairs, she halted on the landing. Not looking. Not looking into the full-length mirror on the wall in which she must surely be reflected.

Outside, she saw a taxi and on an impulse, hailed it. Sita/Ferret never travelled in taxis. They were the luxury of the weak-willed and weak-limbed. Perhaps she had become heavily weighted – by something from the morning and something from the evening.

Chapter Three

At Grand Central Station I Sat Down and Wept. At London's Paddington station Sita/Ferret sat down and choked back her tears, shocked by what she had done, unexpectedly assaulted by grief and guilt.

She had imagined herself getting off the train, totally happy and free, ready to embark on a new life. Horizons would beckon, opportunities invite. Sita/Ferret and her life would be transformed. Perhaps even one day to become Sita, and banish the Ferret forever.

She sat on a bench, cradling her bag in her arms, unable to understand why she had this strange wrenching feeling inside her. After all, no ties of affection existed between her and them, and no other connection that she knew about. Her days had been spent in doing their bidding, doing her duties, and doing them well. 'Because that's WHAT YOU ARE,' Emily had declared once, putting pay to a bout of rebellion. Emily and Champa had hated her going out of the house; even shopping trips had been carefully monitored. The first time she'd been sent to the Asian shop, she'd gone up to the young girl at the counter and, mindful of her diction, had carefully enunciated her requests in Hindi. The girl had heard her out, her eyes opening wider and wider, then opened her mouth and yelled 'Daaaaaad,' at the top of her voice. Sita/Ferret had gone hot with embarrassment and fear, wondering if the E & C had played a monumental trick on her and taught her a lingo that no one could understand. The father had emerged from a backroom carrying a box of cans of baked beans, but Sita/Ferret had switched to English and the girl had said, 'Why didn't you say so before.' After each shopping trip, totals were carefully calculated and change handed over. Sita/Ferret came to know the prices of household goods and groceries, and could easily have computed their annual budget. Not that the E & C didn't have the same knowledge. Money was controlled to the last penny. Even though Champa paid her share, the awesome power of decision-making rested with Emily. The effect on Sita/Ferret was to circumscribe, control and deny. Emily defined the world and the nature of their lives.

'Life is work. For a woman.' Champa had stated once, in the middle of a cooking session. 'Not so much salt,' stopping Sita/Ferret who had poured a large mound of salt into her hand, for Champa was teaching her measurement the Indian way; no fiddling around with teaspoons, tablespoons or ounces. You measure with the eye, and if you get it wrong, then God help you.

They wouldn't know till that evening that she had gone, when she failed to return from her job. That morning she had risen early, after a sleepless night, and had done the cooking in the morning, questioning all the while why she was bothering. 'They won't suspect so soon,' she had reasoned with herself, as she quickly chopped vegetables, stirred the masala, and cleared up, loathe to admit that guilt or some other emotional connection could be playing a part.

She slipped a hand under her coat to check the improvised belt, checking for the bulge of its contents. 'If you can't be trusted, then you're no good for nothing, a piece of shit in the gutter.' Emily had her pretty ways of talking. Should Sita/Ferret make a symbolic offering of purification to the Fates of Life, and abandon the belt or even redistribute its contents to the needy? Sita/Ferret looked to the future and didn't know if she could trust herself.

At London's Paddington station, a young woman's tears turned towards fears; and the fears turned towards the years of the future. Dare she ask of life now, whether it would endow her or disown her? Would her days end in brittle bitterness, or would she be contented, fulfilled? Always the choice between opposites. Or dare she ask, what will Sita/Ferret do to herself? The good, the bad or the ugly? Take a wrong turning and she could end up on skid row; take a wrong turning and she could end up in a place called self-loathing. A cold wind pushed at her. People hurried past, intent on their destinations, towards home, work or pleasure. Her eyes travelled up to the high arched roof, with its transparent panels, and she felt like a nothing in this vastness. She bought a cup of hot tea and cradling her hands around it, sipped the strong, bitter liquid. She alone had the responsibility of keeping herself alive now. Sita/Ferret watched trains coming and going, people alighting or boarding, greeting or bidding farewell, watched embraces that clutched and embraces that pushed away, watched foreign arrivals with an excess of baggage, some with unsuitable clothing for a cold climate, some with only a few words to serve their needs. But all of them beginning anew, driven by a belief that what they can do here must yield them something greater than what they could do from wherever they came. They would work, perhaps take any rotten, disgusting job, in expectation of a greater yield, which could then be put to the use of creating possibilities. That most magical of words.

But it was probability, that most prosaic of words, that took over. A man approached Sita/Ferret. 'New in town love,' were his opening words, 'need a place to stay? There's a place just round the corner from here. Lovely, clean rooms. Nice people, who'll look after you. And cheap. Come along, I'll take you,' bending towards her bag. Sita/Ferret quickly moved it away. Out of the frying pan and into the jaws of a shark!

'Bugger off you disgusting old bastard, before I call the police and have you arrested for pestering.' Emily's tones came ringing through her voice. Emily was here, right inside her. The man mumbled that he was only trying to help and moved off. Sita/Ferret threw away the polystyrene cup and slung her bag on her shoulder. She had had her first inkling of the future – the predators in the city and the E & C in her head. She'd have to put more than geography between them! She determined to live the opposite of their lives and their beliefs, carve her days into a different idea. And thus create a vast distance between them and her. She wanted a moral victory over them. Or so she thought as she left Paddington station.

Chapter Four

London, January 1997. Evening

The Pomegranate Gallery was all beige and red and brightly lit. Tonight, before entering, Sita/Ferret straightened her spine and balanced on her platform heels, trying to push away her nervousness. This was the first time in her life that she would be in an 'Asian Situation', with those who were so 'well-established' that they knew the 'Over There and Over Here' of everything. Inside herself she felt rootless and fraudulent, barely held together by need, deed and thought. The only part of herself that she could hold onto with certainty was the 'gutter child,' as Emily had always called her. The gutter child had nothing, deserved nothing, was nothing. '*Gutter ki bachi, where are you?*' The call would lasso through the house. '*Gutter ki bitch yourself,*' Sita/Ferret would mutter back. But the gutter child had eyes that saw through the wallets of the rich, and knew their power to suffocate. She considered money as something tawdry, even ignoble.

Sita/Ferret took a deep breath, decided that she would look carefully at the Buddha displayed in the window and then go in and 'actress' to the hilt. The catalogue entry for the Buddha read thus: '*...standing with his left leg slightly advanced, wearing a sanghati falling in delicate sweeping folds over his body, his face with majestic countenance, protruding chin, slender bow-shaped mouth, delicately lidded almond-shaped eyes, his hair swept back from his forehead in finely carved wavy strands...£500.*'

Mr Kalyan had given her a Sotheby's catalogue and suggested the descriptions be done in the same style. She hadn't objected, grateful for any crutch, though she suspected a disparity between Mr Kalyan's 'art products' and those sold at Sotheby's. However, her suspicions were mollified when she noticed that there was a big gap also between the prices. Pretensions there may be, but it seemed no deliberate intent to con people. She could rest easy. She wasn't in a morally corrupt environment, although she was now working purely for the sake of her pocket.

Perhaps her moral purpose was all worked out. Or else she was having a fallow period, having been over-zealous in the last job. There she had given the boss a ferocious tongue-lashing for the way that he treated the residents of the charity hostel. A gutter child has nothing to lose! A gutter child can speak where others will stay silent. This gutter child had found herself out on the street, dismissal notice in her hand. After this she had decided to take a break from charity jobs; a decision which sometimes left her worried that she would lose her moral victory over Emily and Champa. So she had given herself a deadline – a full twelve months, and no more. The symmetry of the four seasons! She had begun in October and would end in September, when autumn leaves spin down from trees, when the dark comes early to rush people home to warmth and welcome, or to put a veil over those who walk alone to empty rooms.

She had answered an advertisement for a saleswoman who would visit Asian homes and shops to 'introduce' them to Mr Kalyan's Indian Arts Products. Sita/Ferret had salivated at the idea of stepping into others' lives, getting glimpses into homes where regular Indian life happened, of eavesdropping on tradition and culture, brushing against the real stuff! She had been afraid that she wouldn't be good enough, wouldn't get the job. Afterwards, she discovered she'd been the only applicant, and that the work began and ended in the basement.

Mr Kalyan had been surprised by her comments on certain items. He was not to know that she had grown up in a house crammed full of old and ornate Indian furniture, carved marble, wooden and metal artefacts, chests, statuettes; a house where even the kitchen utensils were made of bronze and copper, complete with etched designs. All of which Emily must have brought over in shiploads. But then Emily could never let go of anything, neither objects, money nor people. When Mr Kalyan had questioned Sita/Ferret further, she had been evasive, disowning any real knowledge.

When he had informed her of his 'Indian Arts Exhibition,' pronouncing the words as if made of gold, she had addressed him as, 'Mr Kalyan, sir,' for he liked differentials, and asked, 'who is the clientele you're aiming for?'

His hands had folded tight, 'You must know the type. The first, second, third generation. The grocery-store owners who want to impress the relatives, the doctors and dentists who need to make investments, the small factory owners who can now afford to buy culture, the younger generation who need to learn about their traditions, the English who are in love with India…and so on and so on. There is a big, big, big market out there,' arms opening out. 'When people have left their own country,' leaning forward, 'they have to have a bit of it with them. It is like the blood in your body. You can't live without it!' Sita/Ferret had remembered the pouch, lifted from its hiding place. 'When the English went to India, they took their English things with them. When they came back, they brought their Indian things back with them. You see!' Mr Kalyan had finished triumphantly.

'Most people bring things back from their visits,' she had replied, 'purchased in rupees.' The immigrant's endemic preoccupation with conversion! Emily would refuse to buy anything from India – every time she converted the price from pounds to rupees, she'd have a heart attack.

'Tourist rubbish,' waving his hand disdainfully, 'they don't know the difference.'

But they know what they can afford and what they can't with money that they've laboured and sweated for. In the mornings, when she came to work she passed the muffled thunder of machines behind walls, or walked over sections of pavement that vibrated under her feet. Once she had paused by a tiny open window, looking into a room crowded with heat and the clamour of machines; at bent heads, hands moving swiftly backwards and forwards. A thin, young man, already worn old, had glanced up, their eyes grazed across each other's, then his bent back to their work.

Escape hovers on the horizon!

'I escaped,' she tried to assure herself, knowing that it wasn't merely the exit through the door.

She opened the door of the Pomegranate Gallery and went in. The sparkle of arrayed wineglasses greeted her. 'Libations to liberate the purse!' she thought. She was glad to see that she was early, as she had intended, and as was expected, till she spotted a figure moving at the far end of the gallery. Sita/Ferret was mortified. She hadn't reckoned on anyone's desire to arrive so ahead of time. Pinning on her badge she approached to offer assistance. The guest was earnestly consulting the catalogue, as he moved from piece to piece, making notes as he went along.

'Steven Singh,' he introduced himself, shaking her hand firmly and looking intently at her face. She knew he would recognise her, even if he met her twenty years from then. A pony-tail snaked down his back, a gold band glinted in his ear, and an intense lined face made him into another young/old man. 'Pretty, all these things,' he said, waving his hand, 'now all I wonder is, why this? Rather than some other way of making money. Then I think to myself. This is damned clever. This is definitely being one step ahead of your market. And you, Mrs Pandey, are a find in a million, I hear.'

'Thank you,' she replied.

He smiled, his skin folded, his eyes lightened, and then it was over, as if he didn't have time for more. 'I keep my ear to the ground, and my nose to the grindstone, and grind stones, grind exceeding small. How much d'you reckon he'll make tonight?' She noticed the accent on the 'he'. Must be the 'he' in Steven Singh's grindstone.

'I'm sure the exhibition will go very well. Many of these are original pieces, specially commissioned, of great cultural and traditional value. For instance, this Ganesh…'

Steven Singh held up his hand, 'No, no, don't give me the patter. These artists that he commissions, that his in-laws in India rip off… Blimey, there I go, putting my foot in it already. Let's start again. These artists, that are *commissioned*,' lifting the word, as if to look underneath it, 'must think the sun shines out of his arse. Oh,' holding up his hand, 'no offence meant. But I am very impressed with the entre-pren-eur-ship. That's the word, right? And you've got a job lot,' bringing out his East-End accent, 'sorry, sorry. I mean, *an extensive range*,' making a big show of reading from the catalogue, 'back at the shop. I'll have to come and have a dekko won't I? You know what?' He paused, and closing the catalogue, 'Looks like a thieves' market to me. Those *antiques* and whatnots, ripped off from some poor villagers; the 'Modern Art' is all paint and no talent; but those sculpture pieces, just…' He looked at her, hand on his heart, voice filling out, '…are just too utterly beautiful. They speak to my soul.'

She giggled, and immediately tried to cover up. 'Are you interested in any particular pieces, sir?'

'Call me Steven. And I can't afford your smallest, cheapest little doo-dah.' That smile again, a flash of sun on a rainy day. 'Are you a loyal employee, Mrs Pandey?'

Loyalty! The lock that keeps out poachers.

'I do my job, Mr Singh.'

'I wouldn't expect anything else. I'll shove off now, before the wallet-wallahs rush through your doors and snap up your…' He stopped, was he searching for a word? '…your wares. Anyway it's a long walk back home and toffs bring me out in a rash.'

He was halfway to the door when Mr Kalyan, his daughter Poonum, and madam wife made their entrance. They seemed as surprised to see him as he was dismayed, for he made a quick movement as if to turn away, but stopped. Then Mrs Kalyan said something, and he nodded his head, Poonum shrugged her shoulders and looked away, Mr Kalyan stepped forward and gave him a hug. Steven Singh didn't seem to enjoy it.

Poonum Kalyan came towards Sita/Ferret, her eyes an advance scouting party. For a shaky moment, Sita/Ferret wondered if Poonum had perused the same magazine and recognised the theft of an image.

'How diligent of you to be so early, but then *the early bird catches the worm*. Which seems to be just leaving,' she said, as the door closed behind Steven Singh. 'You know, I've nearly finished that godforsaken trainee managerial stint I've been doing. Can't wait to get stuck into the business, I'll really turn things around.'

Sita/Ferret saw her basement being invaded. 'Shouldn't you be doing higher studies?' she asked hopefully. 'An MBA seems to be an essential survival tool these days.' Judging by its frequency in the Asian matrimonial columns which she perused with a vicarious interest!

'Business is buying and selling, isn't it? You buy some; you sell some, and so on. Forever. You gotta buy at a good price, sell at a better one. Get it wrong and you're in the shit. No such thing as a free chapatti. Hubby here?'

'Who?'

'Hubby! Husband! *Mister?*'

'He's dead.' Taken by surprise, her prepared statement rushed out in indecent haste. When making up her CV for Mr Kalyan, she'd practised the break in the voice, the sob in the throat. She'd blown that one, as Poonum immediately pointed out.

'Looking to hook another one then, are we?' Poonum asked. 'Glammed up to the nines. Do let me know if you want introductions, though we mustn't let people think you're the main exhibit.' Smiling sweetly she moved off. Poonum must have been hard-boiled in the womb! Sita/Ferret was left wondering when she should hand in her resignation, for who knew what hot winds might rise up when Poonum took her rightful place in the family firm. Poonum was one of those for whom the world was an entity to pull, force, manipulate into whatever shape she wanted. Whereas Sita/Ferret was one who wanted to know the meaning, the purpose, the essence of the world. Sita/Ferret could hear Emily in her head, hooting with laughter, 'baby-brain!'

'Good evening, Mrs Pandey.' Mrs Kalyan had now materialised in front of her. It seemed Sita/Ferret was being granted an audience with each member of the family. Like the pieces on display, Mrs Kalyan was a carefully constructed artefact too: body adorned in a smooth silky sari, face immaculate in its presentation, black shoulder-length hair (not a grey one in sight) held back with a gilt clip. For all her politeness Mrs Kalyan carried an undeniable hauteur. Sita/Ferret preferred the cutting arrogance of Emily, who wouldn't consider it beneath her to engage in hand-to-hand combat.

'How nice to meet you.' Mrs Kalyan's enunciation was as carefully applied as her lipstick. 'Are you enjoying working at Uni...' Even she couldn't get it out. The first time Sita/Ferret had seen Mr Kalyan's company sign, 'Universal Enterprises,' complete with drawings of the earth and planets, she'd been awe-struck. One either laughed, or admired the audacity. Clearly Mr Kalyan didn't believe in subtlety. Sita/Ferret wondered how the sophisticated creature in front of her had got herself married to that hustling merchant of a man. '...I mean, at the business?'

'Yes, indeed,' Sita/Ferret nodded her enthusiasm. And if the Kalyan women left her alone, she'd be even happier.

'That's very good. Perhaps I will see you later in the evening then.' Mrs Kalyan nodded and moved away, duty duly performed. After the women came Mr Kalyan. He complimented her effusively, 'Looking very charming and Indian,' but his eyes were striped with anxiety, already looking towards the door.

He could have saved himself the heartache. Enough bodies came through the doors to satisfy his predictions. They came in batches: the 'before-dinner' group who looked, chatted and left, the after-work professionals, holding onto their briefcases, a few actually bringing out their chequebooks; the arty crowd, whom Sita/Ferret recognised by the fact they were all dressed in black, only talked to each other and constantly spouted the word 'project'; plus a small sprinkling of students who were torn between wanting to be radical and dismissive, and paying reverence to 'roots 'n' kulcha'. The after-dinner group came late in the evening when Sita/Ferret's throat was sore from answering endless questions, and her lips tired from stretching out smiles. Mr Kalyan was very pleased with her unstinting efforts, until he overheard her commit a sin. When asked about the investment value of a piece, she had replied, 'I don't know.' Mr Kalyan had taken over, but she could see him keeping a watchful ear on her after that. Perhaps she wouldn't need to resign. Mr Kalyan might be having second thoughts about his wonderful employee.

Sita/Ferret had been occupied for a while with Mrs Bhatia, an egg-merchant's wife, who had launched into a story about the hijacking of an egg-truck. 'Making omelettes on the motorway,' she said, laughing at her own wit. Mrs Bhatia was a cumbersome storyteller.

Anyone else would have sidled off, or fixed a polite smile on their faces and endured the situation in the hope of making a sale. Not so Sita/Ferret. She listened with avarice, extracting from the words greedy glimpses into another's life. Ordinary lives of husband/wife/children/mortgage/bills/pain/passion/habit/boredom were a mystery to her. If she hadn't been concentrating so fully she might have missed the passing of an expression on Mrs Bhatia's face. If only she could have grabbed it with her hands! She looked in the direction she thought Mrs Bhatia had glanced and saw Poonum with a man. In the catalogue Sita/Ferret would have written him up as: *a stunningly beautiful male figure, luminous grey eyes, seeming to flash across the viewer. Thick wavy hair, allowing for finger-furrowing luxuriance, sculpted lips inviting closer examination, an oval chin to bring the lines of the face into a sumptuous whole. The figure is medium sized, right foot slightly advanced in front of the other, one hand hidden from view, the other holding a wine glass, wearing a black jacket over a dark shirt. Circa late twentieth century. Provenance unknown. Present owner: Poonum Kalyan (to be confirmed).*

He must carry a strange fate! Though people glanced, and some covertly stared, a little space, the size of a hyphen, stood between him and the others. Mrs Bhatia unconsciously paused, her eyes going back to Poonum and her companion.

'Is that Poonum's fiancé?' Sita/Ferret asked, a question that indicated her adherence to the proprieties. To have asked if he was Poonum's boyfriend might have landed her in sticky waters, and to have asked directly his identity might have indicated a vested interest.

'Fiancé?' echoed Mrs Bhatia. 'Oh no. That girl's not engaged.'

Sita/Ferret tried another tack. 'He's trying so hard to pretend he's a real lady-killer.'

'He doesn't have to pretend!' If there was any stoning to be done, Mrs Bhatia would be first in the queue.

Sita/Ferret had moved on from Mrs Bhatia to a young Asian woman with a pure Welsh accent. The woman must have thought Sita/Ferret was particularly brain deficient, for she had to repeat each question before she got an answer. Sita/Ferret, for her part, was struggling heroically not to mimic back.

'Have you just come from India?' she asked Sita/Ferret at one point, sing-song Welshness lacing every syllable.

'No. British born, British bred, British something or other.'

'You've got a really thick Indian accent you know,' she commented.

'Noo. You doon't saay,' replied Sita/Ferret. The woman looked at her suspiciously, but finally made her purchase, and Sita/Ferret took it off for wrapping. Poonum and her friend, Mr Stunningly Good-looking, were standing on the left-hand side. Sita/Ferret could just as well have gone to the right, but didn't.

'Oh, where are you taking that?' asked the All-India Handsome-Hero type, as she drew level with them. Sita/Ferret stopped in her tracks and looked at him in surprise. She'd wanted a closer view, but hadn't expected contact. 'May I?' he asked, holding out his hands for the figure in her arms. His voice had the cadence of Indian English, it spoke of privilege and class, and another kind of Over There. As he examined the 'Ascetic with a Broken Begging Bowl', her eyes roved over him, not examining, but as a kind of introduction. A few times, those silver-grey eyes lifted, glancing at her, weighted with seriousness. Poonum watched.

'A for Ascetic,' murmured Prince Charming. 'B for bowl and C for cash or was it card? Quite a beautiful piece.'

'B for beautiful?' asked Sita/Ferret.

He laughed a little apologetically. 'The price could keep an ascetic going for a lifetime.'

'Our pricing is extremely reasonable sir,' Sita/Ferret replied.

'He has a houseful of the best stuff, so you don't need to pitch.' Had Poonum been gifted with a barbed tongue or had she sharpened it on life's anvil?

'I grew up in a house full of the best stuff too!' Sita/Ferret could play tit-for-tat as well as the next immature adult. Emily would have been delighted to hear this praise of her possessions. 'Perhaps that's why I like our collection.'

'Our?' pounced Poonum.

Before Sita/Ferret could reply, Mr Good-looking interrupted, 'in which case you're very lucky to have Miss…'

'Mrs Pandey. The merry widow!' Poonum announced, and then suddenly said, 'Oh, so sorry. Daddy's always praising her dedication,' she added. Poonum didn't appear to be the toadying kind, this turnabout was a suspicious surprise. Sita/Ferret sensed a withdrawal by the Unknown.

The leaf-shaped hand on the clock had gone past the midnight hour. Gradually the crowd had thinned and departed. Mr Beautiful must have left without Sita/Ferret noticing. Had she really expected him to come and say goodbye?

Sita/Ferret pulled out boxes from under the cloth-covered tables and started packing. Mr Kalyan totalled the amounts for the evening and professed himself satisfied, though she knew his expectations had been rather grander, 'People have to learn about the higher things in life. I can predict we will have more customers coming to the shop in future. Perhaps we will have to get you an assistant, Mrs Pandey, and then you can spend more time upstairs.' Sita/Ferret was alarmed. Her immediate reaction was to refuse absolutely, but Champa's voice came drumming into her head: 'there is no need to show everything on your face, no need to say everything in your mind. Push back those silly tears.' Then, the child had gulped and struggled, but the tears had continued to seep out. 'You will be squashed, flat.' Thwack! Palm hitting palm. 'Kaput-ed!' Some of her best vocabulary came from the fifties movies. 'Sometimes you have to pretend a little. Even do a little actressing.' With this had come a twist of the wrist, a tilt of the head, a little flourish of the hand. 'Give yourself time to think! To use what is in there.' And then, a little slap on the head to drive home her lesson. 'It is necessary in this world. If you give in to everything that happens, then it's *bye bye baby*.' Champa says control the emotions, 'or you have no chance, not in this house, not anywhere.' Strange lessons came from Champa, attended by her constant counsel: 'You are only a girl, only a woman.'

Mr Kalyan said, 'Pack the most expensive items, and leave the rest for tomorrow. You will make sure they double-check the security alarms before you go?' She nodded assent as she continued with her work. Mr Kalyan hesitated, then opened his wallet and held out some money advising her to get a cab and a receipt. Sita/Ferret couldn't extend her hand and take it. Emily had made her beg even for bus-fare money and when she did give it, she'd make sure that Sita/Ferret appreciated Emily's generosity: 'Gutter children don't go to school! What do they need it for? You're lucky you're here, in Great Britain, where else do they give free schooling to the wretched? And be grateful I'm looking after you.' Miffed, Mr Kalyan put the money on the table, satisfying his pride, and went over to Mrs Kalyan, who was waiting with controlled impatience. Mrs Kalyan twitched her sari when she stood up, though no twitching was necessary.

An hour later Sita/Ferret had made certain that the owner had indeed double-checked the security systems, refused his offer of a lift home, and was waiting outside the gallery, taking in great lungfuls of London's damp, dark air. As she secretly loved English winters, so she secretly loved London: this great heaving, monster of a city, delicate and ugly, beautiful and brutish, containing within it every kind of life form, every kind of idea that could exist. She too was within it, part of it and yet alien to it. Sita/Ferret turned around for another look at the Buddha and saw, with a shock, the flash and glint of her ornaments. She'd forgotten she was wearing them! Turning back to look anxiously up the road for the cab she'd ordered, she saw a set of headlights glow into life and start to move down the road towards her. She stepped back into the doorway. Fear is in the mind! She used to fear Emily. She used to fear Champa. These days she tried not to give houseroom to fear, but she well knew of the existence of the sinister predator within the skin of the city, of those who would seize and devastate body and soul.

There was no one who could be waiting for her. Hers had become an economical life. 'Everywhere you go there are little, little dangers,' Champa used to say. She would not be shackled by Champa's fears! The vehicle was coming towards her, but it would roll on past her, disappear into the dark. She'd be left, waiting for her cab. She'd grow grey, she'd grow old, waiting for her cab. Sita/Ferret smiled at herself. The jeep stopped opposite her. The man inside caught the smile.

She would remember this moment as before and after.

She stared in astonishment as Mr Beautiful leaned out, and lied, 'Hello. Goodness, are you still here? The dedicated worker indeed. I wish I had people like you working for me.' Nothing is done without a reason.

'Then offer me a job,' she replied lightly, keeping back.

'But you don't know what I do,' he replied. His grey eyes flowed over her leaving sensations in their path, his lips were a whisper upon her. She could reach out and touch! Was this how bewitchment began? Drowning merely by looking? He opened the door and came out, keys tinkling in his hands.

'I run a flying club, C for club,' he said. 'I'm a pilot. Well I had to be. After my upbringing.' Past and present together. Why try to give her so much so quickly? 'I've been in Europe, England, for the last ten years.' She'd left Emily and Champa ten years ago, but he was not to know that. A coincidence! The thought stuck in her brain like a burr. 'You must be one of those who has grown up here. A proper Vilayeti!' *Vilyet!* That old-fashioned name for England! Champa would sometimes use it with a sad echo. But what a chatterbox he had turned out to be. He couldn't have been lurking in wait, just to exchange life histories with her. 'It's very late. May I give you a lift home?' Premeditated intent! So that was it! She should tell him to get lost and take his lying offers with him! And lose the unknown... 'Did you enjoy the evening?' he asked, in the silence that followed.

'I was working.'

'Of course. And you worked extremely hard.'

'So you kept an eye on me?'

'Oh no, not at all. I mean whenever I happened to catch a glimpse of you, you were busy, beavering away. B for beavering. Why not let me give you a lift, then we can continue our conversation.'

'C for conversation?' she asked. She was no fatal-attraction femme fatale. He must have women queuing up for him. Opposites!

'Cab! Who ordered a cab here?' came a shout from behind. Given that the first words were the first lie, common sense dictated a quick exit, to take the cab and wave bye-bye to Mr Beautiful. And if she did, she'd never know what this moment had been about. 'Come on. I haven't got all night. Not here for my health you know...' tooting his horn for emphasis. She could have continued to live at the Mausoleum and never known the sharp cut of the world.

To know is to be – ask Eve!

She ran towards the cab and handed over Mr Kalyan's notes. Bridges burnt.

Mr Beautiful opened the door for her. 'What beautiful manners,' she commented.

'If nothing else, I do have inbred breeding.'

'So I'll be safe?'

'Oh? Were you in danger?' (His voice is easy, casual, but she wonders if she heard a little strain in the middle; remembers Mrs Bhatia's expression.)

Street after street passed without a word being spoken, but he was following the recognised route towards her abode. As none of the promised conversation came her way, she pondered on the mystery of beauty, its power to attract and overpower the senses. From Helen of Troy to Cleopatra, from the Mona Lisa to Marilyn Monroe, women are the ones who have possessed its power, and have either used it or been used because of it. Lives have been made by beauty and lives ruined by it. Men are seldom such clear-cut examples of the beautiful face. They're either hunks or heels. What if the man next to her had had looks that were plain and ordinary? Would she be sitting here now, in his passenger seat? She had experienced attraction before, that erotic brew of excitement and lust, but never with this sense of sadness and yearning, mixed with a strand of grieving for all the love that she has never been able to give, for the laughs she could have given and taken. Where could these emotions have come from? Was it true that soul called to soul? And recognised its partner, whatever the outside appearance? In which case she could rest easy. She was no sucker for a pretty face! However, she could be on a one-way street to grief, for the other gave no indication of being affected by any overpowering emotion. His soul must be deaf, dumb and blind!

She hooked her hands together and determinedly looked out of the window. But if she could have done it without loss of dignity, she would have turned in her seat and gazed her fill upon the profile next to her. But she wasn't in an art gallery and hadn't yet bought a ticket into his privacy. Did he know that he possessed this rare gift – and did he trade on it? Beauty is goodness. We are bewitched into believing it so.

And then he spoke. 'Um, I wondered, if I asked you, would you have dinner with me?'

She glared at him, 'If you were to ask me,' voice sharp and cutting, 'then I would remind you of the line, "Fain would I fly, but fearest to fall".'

'Very Elizabethan,' he laughed, 'you can't get me on that one. "If thou fearest to fall, then fly not at all." Were you as diligent a student as a worker?'

'Diligence or death. Story of my life.'

A pause. He was gathering himself to say something. 'I was sorry to hear about the death of your husband.' Lies that come back to haunt! Hers, not his, had been the first. She'd made it up, trying to tie knots around holes, to give herself a background, so she could fit in, to make them think that she was one of them. Camouflage! But a common enough device employed by Asian women living in the West who had to hip-hop between cultures.

'It was an accident,' she replied, looking away. Guilt for murder, even as a fiction, and guilt at her falsehoods.

'I'm sorry,' he said.

Dark streets sped by. Lamps shone like lighthouses through the muffled rain. She had bathed her face in the rain this morning, lifted it and seen the order of her old world turned around.

He broke the silence, startling her and taking their conversation backwards, 'So you won't have dinner with me?'

Did he always use a circuitous route? 'You haven't asked me. Remember!'

'Couldn't take the risk of a rejection.'

He was looking straight ahead, as a good driver should, so she couldn't examine his face and see where that lie of a line was coming from. 'You're so funny. Funny I forgot to laugh,' using the sarcasm picked up from her landlady's daughters. But theirs didn't contain the bitter undertone of hers. He probably didn't know what the word 'rejection,' meant. 'But, if you had asked, conditional tense, then the answer would have been, past future tense, "no".'

'Excellent!' he said, grinning at the look on her face, 'present tense.'

'So glad you're pleased. That's the sod-off tense.'

'Next time, you ask me.'

'Sure. You play safe. I take the risks. Does Poonum know about your extra-curricular activities?'

'What extra-curricular activities?' he asked. Quite true! He hadn't made a single improper suggestion. Then he pulled over, stopped and turned off the engine. She shifted in her seat, towards the door. 'I haven't made any promises to Poonum.' A pause, in which he didn't divulge that he'd implied them by going along with the flow of social activities, the frequency of which classified them as a couple. He'd wanted everyone to see them, to show that nothing was hidden. No secrets.

Then he came out with his question. Afterwards, she realised he had done his pondering too, and at far greater length. 'I wanted to A for ask you,' he said. She waited, one half of her warning that she should be ready to jump out, the other half wanting to hear words that could sink into her, like the milk and honey of life. '...if you'd be interested in doing some work for me.'

'That's supposed to explain the furtive stalking in the middle of the night. I saw you starting off.' The danger of truth mixed with celluloid fiction! He might turn out to be a rabid psychotic and she'd miss next year's pilgrimage to spy on the E & C.

'Oh that? Sorry,' he apologised, with a forgive-me-smile. He could melt the polar ice-caps! 'I didn't think you'd want me to suggest *extra-curricular*,' spicing the word, 'employment in front of your boss. Anyway, it's a private job, I mean, I don't want it talked about because I need to raise some money, and I don't want to broadcast to the whole world that I don't have a penny to my name.' The second poverty-stricken male she'd met tonight. Where were the sugar daddies?

She who practised pretence suspected him of doing the same, and couldn't fathom why he should feel the need. She put her hand on the door handle. Not only was she accustomed to standing on her own two feet, she was used to walking on them too! Sita/Ferret had tried to teach herself that she didn't need to depend on any one. But a wishing had begun inside her. So she turned to practicalities and asked for details.

'I live in a place my family has owned for generations,' he said. 'It's crammed full with stuff. The attic has over a hundred years of the family junk stored in it. I want the good sorted out from the bad. I need to know what needs repairing, what needs to be chucked out and so on. And also, how much it's all worth. I may need to sell it – to save my skin.' And what a luscious delicious skin too, she nearly said! 'Who knows,' he continued, 'you might find something that'll restore the family fortunes, and there's also some jewellery which my grandmother left behind. Actually, A for actually,' creasing his eyes, peering at her adornments, 'in a similar style to yours, I think.' He'd saved the best for last and riveted her attention.

The doorman at reception nodded. The lift doors closed, they stood side by side, silent. The hush of a sleeping corridor in which the sound of their steps on the carpet beat loud in her ears. He unlocked the double doors of number seventeen, and invited her to step in. Adventuring into a man's quarters in the middle of the night, a hint of the forbidden brushed through her.

He had said, 'I work late every evening, it may be difficult to arrange another time. I could show you round the flat now, if you're not absolutely exhausted. Of course I'll run you back afterwards.' He hadn't known that he needn't have bothered with excuses. Disappointed emotions she could have taken home with her, might-have-beens to be held close. But the reference to her jewellery, the hint at similarity, would have got her running and chasing after him. Similarity spawns stories. Perhaps, she'd learn something; perhaps a chink of the past may be uncovered. Her fingers had strayed over the bangles on her arm. She'd seen Emily and Champa today, seen what a mere twelve months had done to them, but never seen any of their past, and therefore none of her own.

She stepped into a circular hall, a high ceiling rising above her, and a chandelier sparkling as he switched on the light. He opened doors into rooms, she followed. High windows of stained glass spread along walls. He quickly drew thick, tasselled curtains across. The first action upon entering each room. What prying eyes was he afraid of?

Sita/Ferret wandered like an intoxicated tourist, running her hand along statues, the curves of bowls and vases, bending down to trace the patterns on chairs and table legs, examining decorated portrait frames; she browsed from room to room, followed the hall till it turned a corner, and was suddenly startled to be surrounded by jungle foliage, with a tiger roaring out. Someone had possessed a dramatic streak! Painted directly onto the wall, the colours were faded and patchy, and would require a deal of money to bring them back to glowing life. The jungle scenes gave way to hunting ones, and right at the end, with only one door remaining, to scenes of ladies and gentlemen 'en flagrante delicto'. Abruptly cut short by a blank space. Had someone's prudery caused an artistic calamity? The fascination of unfinished signatures!

'No,' he exclaimed quickly, moving in front of her, as she started to open the last door. 'Just my bedroom. It won't be necessary for you to go in there. At all.' Being assured of honourable intentions is respect; being told to keep out is rejection. She nodded her compliance. He wouldn't find her storming the doors.

She watched as he built a pyramid of coals, lit a piece of paper and fanned the flames. 'I haven't introduced myself have I?' he said. 'They call me Kala,' holding up his hands, black with coal dust.

'That's a strange name. Kala. Black.'

'Ah, truly a well-educated girl,' nodding his head and putting on the pukka Indian accent, 'so you are knowing your Hindi, *han*? That is verry good. Actually,' dropping his dramatics, 'my grandmother's always called me that...' Pause. '...to "keep away the evil eye".'

'Did it work?'

He seemed intent on brushing up the debris of wood and coal. A man who tidied up after himself! Then he looked up with those grey eyes, 'You can't expect me to admit to superstition.' He excused himself to go and wash his hands. She got up and going to the wall paced the room to the folding doors, counting. Five paces larger than Emily's reception room. She put her hands on the doors and pushed, they gave way to reveal the next room; two huge chandeliers swung from the ceiling and a wooden floor stretched from one end to the other; the room was bare, except for a long dining table and chairs. This room must have been filled with music, dance, gossip, sarcasm, bitchiness, all the play and power play that people revel in; did women glide between the rooms, swathed in long ropes of pearls, carrying cigarette holders? Were there any that were sari-clad, who shot back their whiskey, and cancanned with the best of them?

'Wine?' The voice came from behind her. He held out a glass, 'I think you prefer white?' She'd only had one glass of wine at the exhibition. Was he just extra observant? And how long had he been standing behind her just now?

'Do you use your real name, Mrs Pandey?' he asked. Coming out of nowhere the question was a hit in the dark. Others might have taken it as a joke or even an insult, but Mrs Pandey was immediately on the alert, wondering what he suspected. Danger always looms when you gamble. If you live in a house of cards, don't play with dice.

'Oh, well, you know how it is here,' she replied casually, sipping her wine, ambling back to the fire, 'everyone has nick-names, abbreviations, Anglicisations...' A name can be obtained by flicking open a telephone directory and taking the first Asian name the eye alights on. When the E & C had been forced to send her to school, 'because of a nosy-parker busy-body social-worker neighbour,' Emily had complained bitterly, and Champa had said her name was Sita Bombay; the child had asked why her surname was different from both Emily and Champa's. Champa had said, 'It does not matter.' 'My name's Sita,' she said, prising it away from its other half, pronouncing it the English way with a hard T.

'Very nice name,' he complimented. He must have pulled it out from the blandest part of himself. If they were going to spend the evening exchanging inanities, she'd certainly made a mistake in coming.

'You mentioned some jewellery,' she reminded him. If questioned about hers, she could deny all knowledge and still remain ninety-nine percent honest.

'Certainly, C for certainly,' he said, as if suddenly reminded of his duties. He went out, she moved nearer to the fire, holding her hands against the flame, watching the red glow through her fingers.

He returned and placed a cloth-wrapped parcel on the table, 'My grandmother must have taken the jewellery back with her, last time she was here,' he said, not looking at her, busy with the unwrapping of bundles. He took out three rectangular boxes. 'But I have photographs.'

'If they're not here to be valued, there's really not much point in looking at photographs.' The first deviation from the promise that had lured her here!

'Perhaps,' he said, angling the lamp downwards. 'Come and sit here,' he invited, opening two of the boxes for her.

Side by side at the table. The light pouring down on two old black and white photographs of a couple. In the first, they stood beside an ornamental tree, the man in western dress, and the woman in a full skirted, heavily embroidered outfit, a *dupatta* trailing over her head and shoulders. The second photograph was a close-up of the same couple, the head and shoulders more clearly delineated. The man and Kala bridged the gap of time by the similarity of their looks. The woman was a dainty, delicate young girl. But she sported a collection of hair ornaments, earrings, necklaces, bangles and rings that would have made a diamond dealer envious. Sita/Ferret imagined that the feet too must have been adorned with anklets, toe rings, and whatnots. Over the years of hiding, spending fascinated hours examining and marvelling at her stolen loot, Sita/Ferret could replicate them in her mind. The grandmother must have had quite a hoard for there were a few that Sita/Ferret did not recognise, and others that sat in the hem of a coat which weren't in the photograph. A girl has to choose!

How had Emily come to possess them? Surely a woman as richly endowed as the one in the photograph wouldn't have sold them?

She looked up and saw Kala watching her. He must have observed every flicker and shade of expression as she perused the photographs, and now waited to see what she would do, what story she would spin. Waited to see what she was.

She felt like throwing them at his face. His charm had all run out. She unclasped the necklace and placed it on the table. Unhooked the earrings, wincing as she pulled them out, dried blood on the stems; stretching her fingers and forcing her hand into its thinnest shape, she worked the bracelets off with bruising effort. Not a word from him as he watched her strip herself.

Kala moved at last and, opening the third box, took out a magnifying glass. A possession that told the tale of an obsession! Furiously, she pushed back her chair and went to sit by the fire. He had waited for her to lie!

He must have watched her all evening. Sita/Ferret's anger grew as she thought back over the evening's events. Taking a big gulp of wine, she looked at him, bent over the photographs and the jewellery.

'Your grandmother wasn't ever here,' she accused, breaking the silence, like a rock shattering still water. 'You made that up about her taking the jewellery back. You lied.'

That wide-eyed sombre grey look slid across her. 'Yes,' he confessed. And to her confusion she found she could forgive him anything. She could have gone over and smoothed those weighted eyes, comforted the unsmiling lips. 'I had to get you back here, B for back, so I could compare them. I imagine you don't wear them every day. Not that you needed a great deal of persuading,' he finished, a grin on his face.

Sharp anger sparked inside her; she was somersaulting from one emotion to another. 'Don't flatter yourself, kerb-crawler!' She would have liked to have left now, marched out and slammed the door hard behind her. In a whole decade she and they had never been separated; either they had nestled against her body or been only a few yards away, within close reach. They had become part of her sense of self. Now she felt shorn.

She put her arms tight around herself. She couldn't blame him entirely, he may have thrown her a line, but she'd jumped at it like a starving fish at a hook. Her dark areas of unknowing bugged her blood too. If the pieces of jewellery were the same then he would have to tell her the history that went with them, and perhaps she'd at last learn something about the hidden past of Emily and Champa, and if she learnt about them, then she might learn something about herself. Thus she calculated, while he compared.

He put the magnifying glass down with a bang.

'You'll break it,' she informed him with revengeful smugness. He glared at her then, pushing back his chair, went out of the room, returning with a more powerful desk lamp. Moving and angling it with finicky exactitude till he had the light in just the right place, he started all over again.

Questions breed questions! What would he ask of her? Perhaps he would be content with the dazzling beauties that lay before him. Or would he also ask for the knowledge imbued in them? The spirit of the substance? Restlessly, Sita/Ferret moved over to the window and, parting the curtains to look at the night, found an embrasure. She walked in. The curtains fell closed behind her. She felt the delight of a child, in this soft secret place. She rubbed the glass to clear it, as she had done that morning, and found it was just as cold to her hand. Outside street lamps cast their glow, just as they had done that morning. But it was still dark. No dawn in sight yet. She'd thought it must be so much later. She couldn't look out over any roofs as she could from her attic room, the buildings here stood high and imposing.

'I thought you'd disappeared,' he said behind her.

'You hoped.'

'No.' She hadn't seen the momentary alarm on his face, else she might have believed him. 'Would you like to come out or are you going to stay here?' he asked.

'These are jolly nice curtains.'

'Worth something?'

'Did you find anything, "worth something"?' she couldn't help asking.

'I don't know. It's jolly cold here,' mimicking her.

'And I'll be catching my death of a cold.'

He put his hand on her arm. It was too familiar a gesture. Involuntarily, she moved her arm away. He put his hand in his pocket. 'Let's not get dramatic. The drama's over there actually.' Moving the curtain away, she saw colours sparkling under the lamp. 'By the way, how did you come by them?'

She ignored his question. 'Do you always get women to take off their jewellery for you?' she asked, going through the curtain and back to sitting at the table. She shivered as the room's heat warmed her chilled body.

'It's only an interest of mine,' he replied, sitting down next to her. Liar, she thought, folding her arms. If she didn't get some truth soon, she'd leave. And take her goodies with her. 'Actually, the first thing I look at is a woman's jewellery.' Now he changed his mind! Had he heard her thoughts, or had his conscience suddenly activated? 'Many times I thought I saw resemblances. So I'd go for a closer look. C for closer. Something which made other things happen.' She didn't miss the secret smile.

'Poor you.' How long had it taken him to pin his eyes on her ornamentation? She'd thought herself clever plotting a path to his proximity. And all the time he'd been the one watching and waiting.

'Are they the ones you wanted?' she asked.

'They bloody well are, and you'd better get going while the going's good, or I'll have the law on you for possession of stolen goods.' This is what most people would have said, looking forward to the life that could be enjoyed once these darling little rocks had been converted into cash.

He said, 'I don't know.'

'Oh,' she said, 'I'd better take them back then.'

'C for Certainly,' he replied. But both knew that a shift had occurred. They couldn't go backwards.

'What's this ABC thing?' she asked.

Did she imagine a shiver pass through his body? Or was it just a cold draught?

He shrugged his shoulders, 'Just a habit. My turn. Who are you?' Such a simple question.

She couldn't even begin to answer it, so she told him the truth. 'Insufficient data,' she replied, 'that's who I am.'

'That's so funny. Funny I forgot to laugh,' he chanted, repeating her childish sarcasm from the jeep back to her.

'Your fire's dying out,' she informed him tartly.

Not believing her, he looked round to check, then pushing back his chair, went to put more coal on. She watched him as he came back to the table, his shirt dark on her retina; a shirt held together only by buttons –

which could be undone. She looked away, and harvested a question inside herself. And after this question nothing would ever be the same again.

'Tell me about them,' she asked, a hand brushing across the glittering beauties on the table.

When at last he spoke, his voice came from some deep trouble, 'If something comes to you with a label, then you know what it is, don't you? You know where it's come from and what you should do with it. But if something turns up, right out of the blue, how do you know what it is? It could be a forgery. A deception. A trap?' His voice had become lower and lower, almost to a whisper. 'Perhaps it's better to leave things exactly as they are.'

'They're worth a lot of money, an enormous amount of money in fact,' Sita/Ferret stated. 'You could sell these, and live comfy for the rest of your life, buy your luxuries, oodles of your favourite goodies, anything.'

'Why didn't you sell them?'

'Me?' As he couldn't admit to superstition, so she couldn't admit to being possessed by her possessions. 'Oh, I was waiting for a good home for them. Bless their stony little hearts.'

'So cool!'

'And C for cool?' she added. He was offended. That silence between them, again. She had relinquished, without hesitation, and thereby created an IOU. Wouldn't he honour it?

He picked up a bangle, turning it round and round in his hand; eventually he spoke into the silence. 'My grandmother brought me up. My mother was there too of course, but I was my grandmother's little *ladla*. Her pet, her darling.

> '*Dadima* had a little *ladla*
> Whose face was black as coal
> And everywhere *Dadima* went
> Her little *ladla* was sure to go!

'She fed me, not on almond milk and cajoling dishes, but stories of our past glories. Once we were rich and proud. Then we were poor. And covered in shame. And so on. To be truthful,' a look up at her, sombre grey, 'the stories change from one retelling to the next, or one story becomes mixed up with another, and so on. And so on. She's rather obsessed with it. In fact, she's a bit crazy. C for crazy.' Admissions that come in stages. Was this a habit of long standing? Quietly putting the bangle down on the table, he picked up the necklace, and draped it over his hand. Like a story with many folds, this was a necklace of many layers: from the inner rim, across the broad collar containing flowers, petals and leaves, to the outer rim, from where crescents dangled, each of which branched out into dangling clusters of pearls, emeralds and coral.

'Each gem has a meaning,' explained Kala, 'the coral is the odd one out. Pearls are supposed to calm a hot disposition, help the wearer to chill out. Emeralds are a protection against devils, and an antidote to poison. Diamonds are supposed to bring good fortune. They sure make a good investment. People used to believe that ornaments with gems brought the wearer respect, fame, wealth, strength, happiness, and so on. That sounds logical! If you have a few of these, the rest follows naturally. The coral is out of place here, among these heavyweight gems. But it has the most significance. Coral is supposed to give protection against spells, to calm storms, to enable the wearer to cross rivers, to staunch the flow of blood and impart wisdom. It's also supposed to help the wearer to overcome fear.' Sita/Ferret thinks she needn't have bothered with her daily 'I ain't afraid' routine – the coral was doing it all for her.

'To be really effective,' Kala was saying, 'the coral had to be worn conspicuously.' Phew! Thank God she was the type who talked to herself after all! 'Apparently, when she was a child, an astrologer, A for astrologer, said that my grandmother needed the protection of coral and should always wear it, so it was always included in her jewellery.' One by one, he picked up the pieces and pointed out the coral in each. 'Coral comes from the flesh of Bala.' He was silent. He placed the necklace back on the table. Was this one of his habitual pauses while he considered whether to carry on with the next instalment, or had he stopped?

She was impatient and couldn't wait. 'Tell me,' she urged. For this night of breaking patterns will not occur again. She dare not let it stop now.

'B for Bala. Bala was a demon. Top-dog type. Sumo wrestler number one of the underworld. He decided to go up to heaven and conquer Indra, who was god number one, the top guy up there. When he got to heaven, the gods, being the clever chaps legends say they are, spun him a line about being the guardian, or is it the beast?' He hesitated, '...the beast in their sanctuary. Big honour stuff and all that. Bala fell for it. The illustrious gods say to him big bad Bala must go through a sacrifice, to be purified, in order to enter his new employment. Well it was curtains for bad boy Bala. The gods killed him and cut up his body. Each grabbing a piece. But, you know these celestial heavens, anything can happen. As each grabbed a piece of his body, it turned into precious stones. His blood became rubies, his teeth pearls, his bile, now there's one to remember, emeralds, his bones diamonds, and his flesh, that became coral. His life was never so great as his...' She waited for him to continue, but he didn't. Instead he asked her the pertinent question, couching it in his own fashion, 'What's your *rishta* to these?'

Rishta! Relationship! She couldn't deny they'd been part of the family; if the strange configuration of Emily, Champa, herself and the jewels could be graced by that name. Cogitating thus, the words flew out before she could stop them.

'I stole them!' If they had been point scoring, this would have scooped the jackpot for stunning him flat.

He couldn't stop the reflex action of his eyes flicking around the room, checking. 'Um, do you do that professionally?' He might want to search her as she left. A dubious delight. Then he'd find the rest, tucked away in their little hiding places, and know her for a liar as well as a thief.

'I'm learning,' she replied modestly.

'An apprentice thief! Is this a government scheme? One of these job training projects?'

'It's the alternative kind of thing,' she said, lowering her voice and talking with actressed intensity. 'You know, take from the rich, give to the poor. You said you were poor.'

'Thank you. So where did you...' He hesitated, searching for a word that meant the same, but didn't carry the criminality. She waited; wondering if he'd manage to alight on one. '...take them from?' Was this the best he could come up with?

Hours ago, as if in another world, she'd jumped at a hint, reading her own questions into it. Perhaps there was nothing more here than a similarity of styles, a coincidence without substance.

'First, let's get the facts,' she said, more sharply than she had intended. 'How did they "leave" your family? If indeed they came from there.'

'I asked first,' he countered. 'We'll forget about your methods of obtaining possession. By the way, is that how you do your shopping?'

Ungrateful idiot! She slapped a hand, hard, onto the table! It was either the table or his face; the poor table copped it. 'I've been wearing them all night, in full view of the "general pubalik," I can pick them up and walk right out of here,' she warned. A deep and distant part of her cried its protest at this threatened separation. How many selves does a person have?

'Yes,' he replied, seeming to agree with her. He couldn't mess up this opportunity either. 'My grandmother lost them,' he said eventually.

'Left them at the *dhobi's?* Tut! Tut!'

'I'm glad you find it funny.' The grey eyes flared their full force at her. 'Too late in the night for you? Brain cells gone to sleep?'

'If I hadn't used my brains, B for brains,' she interrupted him hotly, 'you wouldn't be sitting here with a fortune lying in front of you. You'd still be making moves on women in glass beads, if I hadn't had the guts to take them.'

'Steal them.'

'You wanna return them? You'd have died without ever seeing them,' she hurtled on, 'those old stories scrambling your mind. Ignorance isn't bliss, it's a screwdriver in the brain. The least you can do is thank me, instead you insult me.'

Times were when she'd existed on the minimum and counted each penny; times when she'd eat the cheapest food, dress only in functional clothes, and all the while carried a fortune on her. Sitting in a dingy café, she'd look around and think to herself that she could buy it ten times over. If she wanted. Now Sita/Ferret glanced towards the curtains, but their thickness blocked any light from the outside. She couldn't tell if dawn had begun or if they were still in the blackness of night. She wasn't wearing her watch; out of homage to her new adornments, she'd left it off. She waited...and shivered, perhaps there was a cold wind passing.

'I'm sorry,' he apologised, 'you're cold, let's sit by the fire.'

Sinking into the broad, deep armchair by the red glowing warmth of the fire, she takes a cushion and hugs it to herself. He follows her, tops up their wineglasses, like mini-fireworks sparks refract from the crystal of the glasses.

He sits opposite, across the length of the fireplace, far apart. 'These things aren't much talked about. I'm probably the only one who has them sitting in his head. This is what I've gathered from all the different versions. It seems my grandfather was part of the fun-loving, good-time crowd. Man-about-town type. They had a social life together too, he and my grandmother being modern young things. She stopped wearing the coral. Then...' A long, long pause. '...at some point, things happened, my grandfather went missing, disappeared.'

Disappearing people! The *She* in Emily and Champa's words, even herself, who had disappeared from the Mausoleum.

'There were ransom notes, etc.' Kala continued, rushing, 'money, those,' waving his hands at the glittering objects on the table, 'everything went. And then some kind of scandal.' And no grandfather! 'By the way,' Kala asked brightly, 'do you know where the rest are?'

Sitting in the hem of her coat, which was hanging in his hall, but she saw no need to rush into a reply. A moral crusade was all well and good, and she'd acted according to her puritan conscience, not according to the rites of the late 1990s, where a little fibbing, a little fraud makes you a smart operator. But she was not going to surrender the rest without being sure he was properly entitled. The true owners could even be Emily and Champa. Emily could have paid 'good money' for them. Emily never paid bad money. Which would make Sita/Ferret the real thief. If she was, she reasoned, then she was entitled to hang onto the spoils by virtue of being the one who had committed the crime. Patience is also a commendable quality. Let him feel its beneficial effects. Furthermore she may wish to wander, once or twice more, towards this address.

Not getting an answer to his question he repeated a previous one, 'Who are you?'

The tunnel of the past, the well of the self!

Because she hadn't given him the rest, she gave him this: '*Ferret ki bachi!* Ferret is what I am.' First in the Mausoleum, now here, no other place had heard this name. 'And that's nothing! Wait till you see the rest of...' She stopped abruptly, as if the sound had been cut off. She had been about to say the word 'family'. She didn't know if she had the right. She'd already given him enough, the loss was starting to ache inside her.

She changed tack. 'You were right, I am a well-educated girl,' imitating his stylised Indian accent, 'mostly self-educated, you understand. So lo and behold, I'm reading a book on India, and I come across the caste system, which makes me think of my "place". It is either the lowest of the low, or so low as not to make any difference. That's who I am. Perhaps you should move a little further back,' she said. 'Do not come too near us low-caste people.'

'The lowest of the low don't carry fortunes on them.'

'Nope. They make other people's fortunes. Just a few hours ago, you said you didn't have a penny to your name, now look what you've got. If it's yours.'

'It is. They are.'

'Prove it.'

'I know.'

'A man's instinct?'

'It's late, perhaps it's time to leave it for now,' he suggested.

'You mean it's time to leave my belongings with you, and say bye-bye?'

'You can stay here and say goodnight.'

She'd been warned off his bedroom, so she could hardly mistrust his invitation. Neither could he say they're mine now, you can go. They were both caught. Wimps! thought Sita/Ferret. For she couldn't scoop them up and leave, *them that had been her next of skin.* There was enough unknowing to make them his; enough of her had been shed these last hours to make her want to stay close. 'If I promise,' holding up her hand in Scout's honour, 'not to interrupt, will you tell me one thing more, anything, to do with these,' sweeping her hand towards the items on the table, 'perhaps something about your grandmother.' As usual he takes his time, is he choosing answers, or trying to decide between truth and euphemisms? 'She's a ruined woman. I don't just mean money, or the jewellery and so on, she's ruined on the inside.'

He showed her to a spare room. From somewhere he brought sheets and pillowcases edged with old lace, embroidered in delicate pastels. Solemnly standing on either side, they spread sheets on the bed, covered pillows, and pulled up the heavy Indian quilt. He showed her the bathroom, said goodnight and disappeared round the corner.

She examined everything in the room. Stood and learnt, by heart as it were, a sketch of a lady with tumbling curls and a choker round her throat; a scribble in the corner stated the name 'Henrietta'; was that the artist or the sitter? In the space between the windows, hung a painting of a crumbling temple with the setting sun behind it. On the bedside table, a lamp with a beaded fringe, and below it, an old burn mark. She ran her fingers over the mark, which had become part of the wood, smooth and polished. Sita/Ferret climbed into bed, loosened the curtains and enclosed herself. *In India, they sleep under mosquito nets; or lie on the streets and get bitten to death.* Many times, she'd played this game, using knowledge culled from books, overheard conversations, Emily and Champa's exhortations that she be thankful she hadn't been born there, for if she had, she'd be in the gutter, or slaving away for a few paise, or dead, or worse. What could be worse than dead. She'd imagine the opposite.

The idea of another life, of the self being another self in another place had rooted. She'd look at pictures of village girls, with unkempt hair, herding animals and think, 'That could be me'; or smart city women, in crisp saris, and think, 'That could be me...' Always carrying the possibilities of other destinies!

What if the E & C disappeared?

He had folded everything in tissue paper, put them in a box and asked, 'What shall we do?'

'Why don't you just say thank you!'

'When I'm sure.' Generous man. He had put them away in a safe. Finders keepers! Losers weepers! She'd carried them around like a baby. Or if she left them behind, she'd hurry back to make sure they were safe. They'd forced a restriction on her life. Perhaps they'd kept her on the straight and narrow. 'Why are you just handing them over?' he had asked, suspicion entering the picture now that he had them safely locked away.

'Afraid I might steal them back?'

'You could have sold them and made yourself extremely wealthy.'

'I can make do on chips and chapattis.'

'Really?' He could be so very English. 'Are they hot? I mean are gangsters going to be breaking down the door?'

Emily and Champa? If they knew they would!

This morning she'd gone on her annual pilgrimage. This night she'd parted with half the possessions she'd guarded so carefully for ten years. He hadn't even had to ask. Was it truly her moral conscience or just female gullibility, the weakness of women throughout the ages? Perhaps she wasn't so very different. Seduced by a pair of pretty eyes! Sita/Ferret turned around, drew the quilt tight around herself, recognising the comforting heaviness of the packed cotton inside. Duvets were too light. The last time she had slept under an Indian quilt had been ten years ago, at the Mausoleum. She drew up her knees, and put her hands around her stomach to hold in the ache that troubled her there. She'd had plenty practice at voyaging through times of unhappiness, pains and troubles, but today it was as if she'd become extra sensitive, as if a layer of her had been stripped away.

Chapter Five

Gravesend and Bombay, 1935–42

The last adventure! Before adventures became extinct.
The last frontier! Before frontiers closed.

They'd called him foolish. Foolhardy and reckless! Prophesied that he'd never return. Predicted that the natives would get him with their alien magic; foresaw terrible fates, gruesome deaths; warned of flesh-eating cannibals, and how they love white flesh as a particular delicacy; swore he would be lost forever in some far-off place, never to return. But his ambition was adamant and he laughed at their doom and gloom stories. He taunted those in whom the glint of envy shone clear: 'some have wings on their heels and some have shackles on their ankles.'

Stories of another kind, hot, erotic and lusting also came his way. When the men were alone, they regaled each other with tales of tropical climates breeding hot women. Removing all restraint from their tongues, they indulged in pornographic fantasies, talked of lands where the girls matured early and were ready for a man when English girls were still in pinafores. They talked of dusky beauties driven by animalistic desires who had been trained to please men, who knew all the pleasures of the flesh, and could take a man to paradise. The words became sweaty and sticky as each man's lewd imaginings vied with his neighbour's. Thomas Miller's eyes shone at the thought of sensual pleasures awaiting those who dared to chase after them.

Thomas Miller had been working for the Brothers Pottinger, Merchants of the East, hauling boxes of cloth of silk, bales of cotton and sacks of spices. And while the Brothers Pottinger lived in luxury and riches, he had sweated and laboured day after day. He saw the flow of goods into their yards, and imagined the flow of riches into their coffers. Fortune was depositing its goodness into the laps of the Brothers Pottinger, bringing cargo-laden ships across the oceans for the enrichment of the Brothers Pottinger. He had heard all the stories, retold as if they were myths, of the first Brother Pottinger to venture east and found the family fortune.

As a child, he had heard other tales, told as truths, tales of divine rights over the Eastern lands. He had been shown photographs of a queen being made into an empress; and just this year had seen, through glowing newspaper reports, how the Silver Jubilee celebrations of George V had reached even unto the far corners of the empire; had read of 'white helmets and red feathers, gold braid, jingling spurs, spats and silk hats...'[1] He might have subsisted on these dreams for the rest of his life, transmuting yearning into sentimentality, if gossip had not turned a screw inside him. He was hardly privy to the worried talk of changes and upheavals in the offices of the Brothers, but words leak out like water, and enhanced versions came to him in excited gossip.

A guillotine descended upon his horizon!

Fears of missing the last opportunity haunted him. He must pack and travel at once, carve out a niche for himself before the locks were in place. Thomas Miller boarded a ship and saw the land fall away and the sea take over. He travelled as a hunter, dreaming of rich killings on the other side.

Seven years later, he returned, to a country in the midst of a war. And showed those who lived on rationing how he had made good; displaying the rings on his fingers, the presents he had brought for family and friends and talking of the grand life to be had out there. He didn't tell of the bad times, of the humiliations, the wilful wrecking of his own goodness, the wilful wrecking of other lives, the continual, desperate maintenance of pride. A newcomer makes many mistakes, imagines that he is entering virgin territory, imagines that markets haven't already been appropriated, imagines that he's free to do as he likes. Free to become the proud conqueror, walking in the steps of conquering heroes, when in fact the 'conquerors' were a deceitful, violent and murderous bunch. But he learnt and he copied.

The busybodies who ran the rumour mill soon put out the word that he must be looking for a bride. He wasn't seriously bride-hunting. But he had been happy to let the rumour exist for it provided a convenient cover for his journey – which was to have a temporary separation between his history and his future, for he had been too desperate, some would say too greedy, and had trespassed into areas he shouldn't have. The wiser decision may have been for him to have stayed permanently in his England, but that was not a choice he could make, for that land of heat and light, deserts and rivers was in his blood, and his mind was still full of what he could take from it.

However, would-be brides hunted him down. Women, whose days were spent toiling in factories, bakeries, shops and homes, who dreamt of knights in shining armour whisking them away to a life of luxury and glamour, saw him as a modern-day substitute. Including a young woman called Emily. Except that Emily was cleverer than the others at playing this game of lure and allure. She took risks that others wouldn't. She blew hot and cold, risked quarrels, risked his patience, risked losing everything. A sign of her success was that he embarked on a revenge tactic, singling out Maureen for special attention, the one who pampered him and smiled at him most.

Emily took this in her stride! They both knew that it was an act, but so impressive was the performance that he started appreciating the qualities of character behind it, and decided that if any woman was going to survive as a wife of his, then it had to be one who could grit her teeth, dig her nails into her palms and smile as if the world was pure perfection. His mind started calculating the benefits of having a wife; of the changed appearance it would give him, and the doors it could open. A married man gains the mantle of respectability; a married couple can associate with other married couples; a married man can move out of the risky world of single men.

Even before he had arrived on the scene behaving like a nabob, Emily had attempted to change her life. Others may have moaned, complained and grumbled about their lot, but they accepted it. Some deemed it a betrayal to want to be like a nob. Not Emily! Emily, who lived in tight desperation, who knew there must be another life, who longed to escape her dreary, work-worn, shabby surroundings; Emily, who had already turned down two proposals of the 'I love you, marry me' kind because all they were offering was more of the same; Emily knew, in her bones, there was a different life beyond their terraced houses, but she didn't know how to reach it. She had tried to find a route to that other life and had received only humiliation for it. Emily had plucked her eyebrows, washed and curled her hair, begged the use of Annie's lipstick, borrowed Sandra's best coat, and with a nervous heart, gone along to apply for a job in one of the Services.

The lady sitting behind the desk, had looked her over and condescended to ask her a few questions. 'Are you a typist?' Receiving a shake of the head she'd continued, 'Telephonist? Dental assistant? Teleprinter operator?' She'd sighed at each shake of the head, impatience sharpening her voice, 'Motor-car driver?' Emily had left the office before she got to clerk and cook.

On a cold smoggy evening, they had gathered in the pub. Thomas was the local boy made good; they had taken to calling him the Indian Rajah. Maureen and Emily were there too, Emily keeping her distance. He bought drinks for everyone in the group, and regaled them with stories of that faraway land. 'India is the land of opportunity,' he said. 'There's gold all over the place, in the land itself.' He paused, waited for their exclamations to die down. 'Bangles as thick as your arm, necklaces you could use to weigh pounds of potatoes.' They shook their heads, and told each other not to believe a word of it. Maureen excused herself for the powder room. Emily moved a step nearer to him, begged him to carry on. 'The natives dress in rags, live in huts, with their animals mark you, share and share alike, eh? They work all year long, ploughing, sowing, seeding, then bang comes the harvest! It's a sight to see. Fields of corn as far as the sky, fields of wheat like gold, going on and on and on. A man gets dizzy looking at them. And what do these poor ignorant savages do when they've harvested, sold their crops and collected their money? Build themselves a decent house? Buy new clothes? Not on your Nellie! They buy gold. Chunks of it. Then,' he said, taking a drink from his glass, 'they bury it!'

He delivered his punch-line, and watched Emily and the others, grinning at the look of horror on their faces. 'They bury it all over their land. Not for some superstition or mumbo-jumbo, because,' shaking his finger, 'they don't trust banks and officials. And I don't blame them either. Half of them don't know how to read and write.' Emily was transfixed by this description of a land in which even the poor hoarded treasures. She had a vision of gold peeping out from the soil, glinting in the sun. 'When they need money for some big do, like a wedding or more land, they dig some up, sell it, and Bob's your uncle, they've got it in their hand.'

'How do you know all this?' she'd breathed in awe. His words fell into her as naturally as a seed falling into soil. She curled her fingers into her palms, hiding the rough dry skin. This man had been across the oceans, broken the boundaries of their ordinary lives, adventured further than they could even imagine. He had transmuted himself, lifted himself into a higher class. 'I met a man who needed to sell some,' he replied. He didn't tell her of the violence used on a man to betray the family. For a father must tell a son where the family wealth is hidden, else an accidental death may take the knowledge with the life. And if the son is vulnerable, then a door of opportunity can be forced by another.

Emily didn't know how carefully he had calculated the benefits of being a married man before he went down on his knees and begged for her hand. 'Marry me,' he proposed, 'and I will build you a palace with servants and peacocks in the garden.' She didn't know then that palaces with peacock gardens were not as easily come by as the words of dreams. But he had the ring of confidence in his voice and the knowledge of that distant place. And she had the desperation of the condemned, with the icy nerves of those who know how to go for the long shot. Emily feigned reluctance, complaining that the words of a man who courted two women couldn't be trusted.

She didn't know what he had said to Maureen, but one day, after the last siren had whistled and the factory women were going home, Maureen waited for her outside the gates, with murder in her eyes. Emily had the habit of trailing behind the others, never wanting to rush home to the chores waiting for her there; she'd listen to the laughter of some and wonder what it was that kept their voices ringing, she'd watch the determined trudging of others, and wonder what kept them going. Word must have got around, for a little group lingered behind Maureen. Others looked and passed quickly by. When Emily saw Maureen and the waiting spectators, she knew she'd won and couldn't keep the triumphant smile off her face.

'Whore. Slag. Bitch, bitch, bitch.' Years later these words would burn into Emily as an evil spell.

'Run out of words have you?' taunted Emily. 'Never did have brains in that potato head of yours.' She must have been right, for the next attack was physical and brutal, a vicious punch into her stomach that doubled her over and left her gasping, a fist to the head, hands in her hair pulling and twisting, a foot landing bang on her shin sparking splinters of pain, her face rubbed into the ground, grit in her skin and mouth.

'Not so hoity-toity now, are we?' gloated Maureen from above.

'You're still an ugly slag!'

A fist to the head and deliberate blows on her breasts brought explosions of agony. No matter how she struggled, she couldn't get the upper hand, Maureen was not only heavier but also determined to inflict punishment on a thief. 'He's mine, mine, mine!'

'He made a fool of you! A laughing stock!' Emily got a kick in the back that made her scream. The watching spectators, who knew the boundaries of such fights, pulled and dragged at Maureen till they'd managed to prise her off.

'Bleeding bitch, I hope you die in a ditch,' Maureen's last words as her friends hauled her away. And another sentence that would come back to haunt Emily. She was left alone, with bruises, blood, and throbbing pain. Spitting blood and grit, Emily tasted victory.

Years later, this public punishment would outweigh all the others in her accusations against him. She'd think that Maureen had had a lucky escape.

He told her of the grand life enjoyed by those of their race in that land of the East; for all they had to do was command, and the commands would be fulfilled. He told of servants bowing and scraping at every step. He painted pictures in the brightest colours, spoke of fabulous animals, vast jungles, fantastic rivers, a huge land harnessed to serve their needs, riches waiting to be taken. He could not have been accused of telling deliberate untruths, only of withholding other truths. He did indeed make a concession to reality, and admitted that he did not have a house to take her to, but in the same breath promised he would build her one bigger than her whole terrace put together. From her side, Emily defended her position, and told him how, if she went, she would also be making sacrifices, that she might die of homesickness, that she would be afraid of the heathens that belonged there, of the terrible things they may do to her. Perhaps she should stay where it was safe and normal. He took her hand and promised that he would always look after her, and assured her that there were many English women there who enjoyed wonderful lives; they were called 'memsahibs'.

Memsahib! When alone, Emily rolled that word round and round her tongue.

These essential skirmishes over, they set a date, and she began her preparations. He gave her white silk for the wedding day. She made herself a promise to love him, and imagined Mrs Thomas Miller having hands as soft and beautiful as the silk.

Wedding Bells! A reception for which Emily and her mother had worked themselves to the bone, begging, borrowing, cooking, baking, to put on a show. To show off the grand match that Emily was making.

Emily's only moment of hesitation came when it was time to board the ship, and she saw the swaying ramp, the dark waters underneath. She didn't know then that the Indians called it *kala pani*, the black waters. Thomas gave her his hand and encouraged her, she smiled thanks up at him, and her hesitation turned to anticipation. She'd done it!

Early morning is the best time to shop in the market, before the day becomes too hot. Two women, shopping for various goods, at different parts of the market, saw the stir created by the English couple emerging from a tonga, otherwise known as a Victoria coach, the snorting of the horses, the unloading of suitcases, and the effusive welcome of the boarding house owner. After a suitable interval, each approached the owner of the building; and after asking a question received an answer.

They couldn't wait to tell Champa!

The Acid Eyed one arrived at the same time as Telegram, who had been honoured with that nickname for her particular abilities. Neither of course was pleased to see the other, but it was not their way to display inner feelings. Both greeted the other with a great show of affection and charm, and hiding their disappointment at having to share the newsflash, mounted the open stairs to Champa's modest rooms.

Champa welcomed them enthusiastically, hugging each in turn, her still-wet hair a damp caress across their faces. Champa remarked how wonderful it was to see them, so early in the day. As they settled themselves, she realised this was to be an extended visit and offered refreshment. When both opted for tea, her heart sank a little, arousing her suspicions about this prompt conviviality. Determined not to be outdone, she went behind the partition curtain and told The Girl not only to prepare tea but to fetch sweetmeats also, putting a few coins into her hand.

'What're they after?' whispered The Girl, but she climbed out of the window, ran across the roof and down the stairs of the adjoining building, rushing to return for she didn't want to miss whatever was to be targeted Champa's way.

To fully milk the enjoyment of the event, suspense must be created, with hints and teases strewn along the path. Acid Eyes and Telegram sipped the tea and complimented Champa not only on her sweetmeats but her glowing beauty also. Champa laughed, returned the compliments and complained of her grievous imperfections, alluding to another who must surely be reckoned as the reigning queen.

The Girl stood behind the curtain, waiting.

'But she has not been able to keep a sahib the way you have,' remarked Acid Eyes.

'In fact,' added Telegram, the two now joined in a double act, 'she hasn't had a single sahib come to her. What magic do you use to keep yours?'

He had come to her on the wings of his first success, money snug in his pocket, ambition still a clear ball of promise. In her actressing, Champa had entered his enthusiasm and happiness, and in mirroring it back to him, she increased it so that it seemed to him ever after that she was a source of happiness for him. Plump Champa with the dimpled cheeks still possessed the secret of joy! She would launch their evenings in delight, smiling into his eyes, lifting her moist lips to his. Thus she became the reservoir of good times and good feelings for him; and he returned time after time – much to the envy and chagrin of others. Many a time they accused Champa of having done *jadu* on the poor man. Airy in her confidence Champa advised them to try their *jadu* too. He came in the good times and bad times, always meeting his obligations to her even if he didn't have enough for a meal. Champa received him with pleasure and admiration, treating him like a rising star. To accommodate and compliment his constancy she bought herself English lessons, and practised her new-found knowledge on him. Cleverly, with a dash of mischievousness, she'd mispronounce words and jumble up her sentences, greatly entertaining him with her efforts. He in turn greatly entertained her with his attempts at Hindustani. They laughed at each other and together. They were yet young. They established a linguistic exchange, the lessons always occurring in the backroom, in the tender period after sex. Eventually their echoed phrases turned into a kind of talking. He asked questions of her land, she asked questions of his. She explained the ways and means of hers for his usage; he described the glories of Great Britain for her admiration.

This morning, her visitors casually threw out pertinent questions to see how much knowledge or ignorance she may reveal. Did she know that he had returned? To which she can reply smilingly in the negative; she is not so obsessed that she needs to keep tabs on his activities.

'Do you know when he is coming for his little visit with you?' they asked.

Champa flipped the end of her *dupatta* to cool herself, 'But really, I am so very busy,' silently sending up a prayer to propitiate fate in case it were angered by this ungrateful attitude, 'these bothersome men never give one any peace!' The others laughed and agreed, wondering how many of them went home and then bothered their wives also.

'Speaking of wives...' Acid Eyes got it in first, greatly annoying Telegram who immediately hijacked the story and ran away with it. Gossip has to be like a dish for a feast, richly spiced, stirred, and served piping hot. Emily was never to know how much she owed Telegram, for after her description of Emily, Champa never did quite manage to shed the image and information she was first fed.

In Telegram's version, Emily started off as being pretty, graduated to beautiful, and ended up as being so blindingly, stunningly gorgeous that men fainted at the very sight of her! On top of which, elaborated Telegram, it was said that she came from a very rich family. 'In fact,' added Telegram, 'from the nobility itself.' Acid Eyes smiled and spurred her on. 'Almost related,' Telegram's voice lowering confidentially, 'to the Highest, the Royalty itself.'

Behind the curtain, The Girl listened in wide-eyed awe. She slipped through the window and away across the roofs.

Champa received the news with the proper exclamations of surprise and amazement, eagerly imbibing this tabloid feature about the new girl on the block. She appeared delighted with every aspect of the description, asking for details, elaborations, and repetition. None could fault her stance, for wives were wives and they were what they were. Acid Eyes and Telegram had come seeking evidence of a weakness, for a relationship of regularity such as the sahib had established with dimpled Champa must surely betoken an entanglement of the emotions. Champa basked in reflected glory – of course her sahib would bring a wife like that, she had expected it.

Champa saw them off with hugs. Neither was disappointed that Champa hadn't betrayed a quiver or a cry. That was to be expected, for they were all experts at actressing. Champa had achieved a certain cachet by the possession and constancy of her sahib; if she were to fall from her perch it would be to the accompaniment of an ironic amusement. Acid Eyes and Telegram went away satisfied. The virgin glory of the encounter had been theirs, they possessed the event and now they possessed the story of its telling to Champa.

The Girl waited outside the boarding house for a long time. But there were no more appearances that day.

The paeans of praise to Emily's beauty and riches had left their mark in Champa. Any other woman and she would have known the exaggerations for what they were. But the story that had been delivered to her fitted in with a whole series of promulgated myths about the rulers of their land. She didn't know how to separate the facts from the fiction since it was the fiction that underpinned all their existences.

The Girl had staked out the boarding house. A few days later, she returned from one of her forays and debunked the myth of beauty and ethereality. She received a slap in the face for her troubles. Thus began The Girl's relationship with Emily.

Champa preferred the original version. In the age-old struggle between wife and prostitute, the wife was recognised as the one with the legitimate claim. There was no pride lost in losing to a wife; and losing to a stunning creation like Emily, one who was of his own people, was not only logical, but downright glorious. Perhaps in time to come, she herself would boast of the beauties of her ex's wife.

But before that time came, and after three long weeks had worked themselves out, she decided to go shopping in a certain quarter, in a certain market. With a veil across her face, she browsed from vendor to vendor, deliberating at length on pieces of lace for a blouse, ribbons to thread through her hair, or glass bangles for her wrists. Occasionally she'd glance obliquely at the only boarding house, and then all around, to ensure that today of all days, the accomplices of her profession were not on shopping sprees themselves. After a tedious second tour of the stalls and shops, she'd risked a closer perambulation to the boarding house, and was on the verge of giving up when a car behind her tooted its horn. Startled, and quickly stepping out of the way, Champa glimpsed his smiling face and a flash of blond hair and red lipstick before the car disappeared.

She walked heavily back to her rooms, hoping that at least one of her regulars would come to her tonight, for it did not seem that the sahib would ever again be bending his steps towards her little corner. Her unhappiness was not the result of confirmation or otherwise of Emily's beauty and allurements, but the evidence of a new life for the sahib. Champa, who had never sat in a car, associated those who did with a high and superior status. It was obvious that her sahib had moved up and away from her. Underneath the externals, a private secret also gnawed at her, one that was to do with emotions and not one that she would want known by any other; one belonging to that feeling in which tenderness is found. No matter the face that she projected, her life contained little of this nourishment.

As if magicked by a wish, that very night he was smiling into her startled eyes. 'Why didn't you send me word,' she complained, 'that you were coming. I would have made myself ready for you.'

'But I like you as you are,' hand on her plump throat, brushing down across her breasts.

Afterwards when there was not even a sheet to cover her, he took a little box from his clothes and opening her fingers placed it within them.

'For me! From Great England!' Champa gasped with incredulity. Velvet covered and brought all the way across the oceans! She was as taken with the box as its contents. Bringing out the locket and chain he twirled it in front of her. Then he cut off a lock of his hair and a lock of her hair and placed them entwined inside. Neither knew whether it was love, an excess of romanticism or an attack of sentimentality. The chain and locket shone upon Champa's plump darkness. He couldn't wait to taste its effect on her.

The next day, as the Soiree Sisters, the sisters of the profession, gathered for one of their afternoon sessions of gossip and chit-chat, Champa's smiles couldn't be hidden and the locket couldn't be mistaken. The trinket, passed from hand to hand, was examined and acclaimed by all. They saw that the chain was a very light, slight little artefact, but none would criticise it for that; this chain and locket carried the glamour of power – it came from the ruler's land itself, and were they not the arbiters of quality and perfection? Champa had slipped badly in the ratings at the apparent defection of her sahib. Now she was number one again.

The Girl squatted by a wall playing a game of five stones. Occasionally she'd glance up at the windows of the boarding house. Once she saw Emily, a cigarette in her hand, looking down upon the market below. Emily took a leisurely drag, lifted her head, showing the creamy line of her throat, and blew the smoke out through puckered lips. The Girl did not stare at Emily for too long, she'd slide her gaze away, for fear that Emily might feel the weight of watching eyes upon her.

Chapter Six

London, January 1997. The next day

Sita/Ferret awoke in a fright. Something was wrong! In the first uncomprehending moments it seemed she was back in her attic at the Mausoleum, but when she put up her hand to touch the ceiling, there was nothing there. 'There was nothing there,' had always been a fear, ever since leaving the E & C, as if she had hacked off what little past she had, and now, 'there was nothing there.' Her annual visits to the Mausoleum had begun all because she had been afraid that 'there had been nothing there.'

Loss and desolation swamped her. Complete darkness pressed upon her. She sat up and searched for a glow or reflection from somewhere – no rooms were light-proof.

Over the years of being on her own, she had worked out a system to counter the unfamiliarity of new places, to soften that first moment of waking in a strange room. Before sleeping, she would memorise the address, and then, one by one, the places of all the things in the room: the table, the chair, the wardrobe, then the colour of the walls, curtains and carpets so that on waking she would know exactly what to expect, and could cheat those first terrible, forlorn moments. Occasionally, perhaps when she'd moved too quickly from one place to another, she failed to keep up with herself. Like now. Pulling up the quilt, she held herself very still, waiting for memory to return.

Rip! The sound of rushing cloth through the air. She switched on the lamp and swung her legs out. She didn't know how long she'd slept but it felt as though some great age had passed. Dressing in yesterday's crumpled glamour, she opened the door and stepped into the corridor.

The quiet brooding of an unknown place. The stranger never knows if it means enmity or friendship.

'Keeping guard?' she asked, leaning against the doorway of the lounge.

He looked up from where he was sitting, reading by the fire. 'Good morning.'

'I don't know about that,' she replied tartly.

'You're awake early,' he remarked, closing his book.

'Not as early as the "master of the house",' dragging at the words. 'If you had Dobermans would you have put them outside my door?'

'I've just locked them back in their kennels.'

'Relax. I can't crack safes.'

'Your training behind schedule?'

'Aren't you being rather ungrateful?'

'But I was just about to offer you breakfast. B for breakfast.'

He made a pot of coffee, toast, eggs and put a variety of Indian *achars* on the table. Neither spoke. He worked efficiently and methodically, everything cooked to perfection, tidying and clearing away as he went along. She recognised the pattern. *Take care of yourself and your business and you don't need to go to no one with a begging bowl.*

Sita/Ferret wriggled her toes on the cool marble floor, which must have been as old as the building, and passed her hand over the wooden kitchen cupboards, feeling the many places where the wood was warped and the doors didn't close properly. She ran her finger over the tiles, which had a raised pattern of flowers and butterflies in shades of blue and yellow. These tiles were from another age, long before she was born, and were carrying the signs of their past: cracks, chips and stains. It would be impossible to buy them now. They no longer existed. Crossing over to the window, she looked down on the street below. A white van sped through, followed after a few moments by a solitary cyclist, a backpack on his shoulders. Coming or going? So early in the morning! Had he been working in a factory, or was he a doctor going on duty?

'You like windows,' Kala remarked, breaking her reverie.

'Yes,' she replied, remembering all those years at the Mausoleum when all she had were windows to watch the world going by. Like a fucking Lady of Shalott. 'You have to like windows in my trade.'

'Ever been caught?' Neither knew which was the more serious.

'Once.' A child hadn't been able to resist rummaging in an open trunk. Emily had caught her, and given her the thrashing of her life, thinking to teach her a lesson. Instead Sita/Ferret had learnt about brooding on revenge.

'And what happened?' *Meaning did you get chucked into the slammer, and have you got a criminal conviction?*

'I got a warning.' *Ever do that again and I'll chop your thieving hands off.*
'But it didn't stop you in your wicked ways.'

'You know what they say about bad apples!'

She winced as he spread mango *achar* on his toast. 'How can you eat that so early in the morning?'

'A for *achar*. It's the only way to start the day. Gets the nerves up and jumping. But of course, you're a proper Vilayeti. Memsahib needs her jam and marmalade!'

'I hate that word. How did your grandmother come to lose her loot?'

'Where did you obtain it from?' he asked, ignoring her question.

'I don't remember addresses.'

'Of course not. That would be incriminating, wouldn't it? They came flying into your pockets?' She remained silent. 'So what's the deal?' he asked. It was no idle question. He'd been waiting all night to ask her. What was the *quid pro quo*? What could he possess that could possibly be greater than the value of those jewels? 'Beware,' his grandmother had taught him, 'always look behind you.' In case something took him. *Disappeared* him.

He waited for her reply. Sita/Ferret was silent, concentrating on cutting her toast into tiny pieces like a well-bred English miss should. Trying to get the words up from her throat, past the privacy notice, past the fear barrier, she forced them out, knowing that no matter what she said, he would ricochet back with questions.

'The deal is that you have to tell me about everyone connected with those little beauties you have under your lock and key.'

'Why do you want to know?' *And when you know, what will you do with that knowledge?* This was the question underneath his words. And, beneath it all – *who is it that you want?*

'OK. You don't have to,' she said, shrugging her shoulders.

'Pardon?'

'It doesn't matter,' she replied, 'you say, you're the rightful owner. If it's true then so be it. Congratulations!' And then, putting on an American accent, ' "It's your lucky day. Man and Stones reunited! What a touching scene folks! Tune in tomorrow for more stories of Man and Mineral." But,' reverting to her pukka-Londoner voice, 'if you're not, and you've lied to me, then you'll have to sort it out with your conscience.' Like his conscience was going to give him a hard time!

'And you don't think I have one?' Said so bitterly, she looked at him in surprise. 'I don't know what happened. My grandmother's stories don't make sense. And,' picking up the coffee pot and topping up their cups, quite unnecessarily, as if the action would aid the flow of his words, 'I

don't know why we are what we are. The pariahs of our family! That's it.'
He ended with a smile. Had he practised that smile since childhood? Used
it to fend off the taunts of cousins, the whisperings of uncles and aunts?
But then, as if he'd said more than he should have, the smile went and he
changed direction, 'Was it difficult *acquiring* the goods?'

The question fell on deaf ears as she was still longing to ask what he
meant by 'family pariahs,' and wondering if that was behind the strange
reception he had received the previous evening. Or whether he was
making it all up to get her sympathy and make himself deserving of the
fortune sitting in his safe. 'By the way they looked fabulous on you,' he
said. Another change of strategy; this time stooping to compliments.

'Bullshit.'

'I mean it,' piling more mango and chilli *achar* onto his toast. 'They'd
look fabulous on anyone,' allowing himself a little grin.

'That stuff's pickled your brains!'

'Vat a verry English retort,' he countered, bringing out his Indian
accent. 'But, we lived on this stuff, sometimes it was all we had.' A little
flick of the eyes – those grey orbs that she could have touched in an
intimate gesture whose descriptive word is a kiss. Was it her scepticism or
gullibility he was testing?

'So did I, mate. I had to make do with lemon *achar*, mangoes being a
luxury in this fair isle of Albion where the darling buds of May do not
stretch to tropical treats. Now, however, you can expand your culinary
horizons.'

'Are you giving them to me?'

'Are you refusing them?'

Neither answered the other. 'How do you like working at Mr Kalyan's?'
he asked. So now he was off on yet another track! She told him she
enjoyed it very much. 'Better than your previous job?' She nodded her
head enthusiastically. 'But that must have been very different?' She
nodded again. 'So what was your previous job?'

'Working in a charity hostel.'

His toast stopped halfway to his mouth. 'Indeed. How very worthy of
you,' not bothering to hide his disbelief. She'd damn well show him! She
launched into an exhaustive description, going into minute detail about
the daily work, the staff, residents, management committee, social
workers, even the milkman who delivered the daily pints, regaling him
with some of the funnier anecdotes. He laughed, and then said, in a
puzzled way, 'But they would have nothing for you to...' another one of
his pauses, '...appropriate,' his eyes carefully on her.

'Yeah. It was a dead loss.'

'What did you do before this charity hostel?'

'You mean previous to the previous? Next you'll be asking me what I did before I was born.'

'Nope,' shaking his head, 'I wouldn't bother. You wouldn't answer. It'd be giving too much away.'

She should be leaving, returning to her attic room, to get changed and get to work. For work was the staple food of life. But she couldn't just up and leave. She'd never get back what she'd given over. Like a package tossed into a river, they'd moved far away from her, out of her life and into someone else's. Once she left she may never come back. So she talked, stretching the moment till she would have to go. Telling him about all her other jobs, the hopelessness, the brutality, the degradation, and the mercy and pride of people too.

'Why,' he asked, 'this kind of work?'

She still wasn't ready to tell him about Emily and Champa. 'Because I wanted work with a purpose, to do some kind of good.'

'Odd work for a thief!'

Now was the time for her to leave.

A strange atmosphere between them. He stood watching her as she put on her coat, as if he was expecting to be hit any moment. Did he expect her to demand her goods back, pull out a gun and march him to the safe? She was otherwise engrossed, listening to the sounds of the flat. Was she expecting something to call out to her?

He said, 'I'll call you.' That meaningless mantra that men chant when they say goodbye the morning after! Only this morning after was different.

'Rather than calling your bank?' She adjusted her coat, distributing its weight across her shoulders. He wasn't that much taller than her, another inch and they'd be eyeball to eyeball. 'By the way, about the work,' she said. 'When would you like me to start?' She enjoyed the look of incomprehension before realisation caught up with him.

'Did you find anything interesting here, anything that you might like to put somewhere else, geographically speaking?' he retaliated.

'It's my goods you've put under your lock and key; geographically speaking, yours are where they were. Want to check?' holding out her arms, tempting fate.

'Maybe I should give you the keys and you could examine at your leisure.' Sarcasm and anger mingled, perhaps a bruise to the pride?

This woman was preparing to walk out, having shed valuables that men would have killed for. He hadn't known what to expect when she looked up from the photographs; but her actions had crumbled his nerves. He would have preferred an outright assertion of ownership, or at the very least some kind of hard bargaining. He opened a drawer and picked out a set of keys. Looking at them a moment, he held them out to her.

She didn't know what thoughts had initiated this act. Did he think that this action would balance hers? And why did he need to balance when all he had to do was bid a polite farewell?

She was always first into work, but not this morning. First she had to make the trek across London to her rented attic.

Sita/Ferret opened the door to Mrs Sangeeta Rayit's house, quietly closed it and was about to run quickly upstairs when she bumped into the two raised eyebrows of her landlady.

'What a lovely outfit!' Mrs Sangeeta Rayit complimented. 'Stayed over at a friend's house? Missed the last tube home?' Mrs Rayit was a thirty-something, with a well-tended perm, shoulder pads, two daughters and a divorce, who worked assiduously at her estate agent's job, her part-time solicitor's course, housekeeping, mothering and cultural transmission.

'Yes,' replied Sita/Ferret quickly to both questions, unable to control the flush that whipped across her face. Guilty by implication. Mumbling something about being in a hurry, she rushed upstairs.

'Room alright?' Mrs Rayit shouted after her.

'Fine. Thank you.'

You take the rough with the smooth. She was experienced enough in the world of bedsits and flatlets to know that seldom is anything perfect, that landlords and landladies remain strangely oblivious to broken equipment, cracks, gaps and holes – like the cold draught that had gushed through the gaps in the window frames. Sita/Ferret had bought a few lengths of material from the charity shop and tucked them into the gaps. These windows had survived not only the depredations of age, but also the shattering bomb blasts of the war years. They'd survive Sita/Ferret long after she was dust and ashes. When Sita/Ferret had come to see the room, Mrs Rayit had proudly pointed out that one window still contained the original glass. 'How fascinating,' Sita/Ferret had gushed, and going heavy on the plummy accent, 'I shall be able to look through the glass of history.'

'This here's the East End of London!' Mrs Sangeeta Rayit had replied, going heavy on her cockney accent.

Sita/Ferret had lived here nearly a month and not once had this landlady, unlike other landladies, raised the subject of Sita/Ferret's background, family ties or lack of them. So she hadn't needed to call on her fictional reserves to put together a patchwork Sita/Ferret. There had been another landlady whose thoughts ran on a different track, and she had asked Sita/Ferret why she didn't buy a place of her own? 'A woman needs her own roof, her own key and her own bank account. I am a married woman but I make my husband put money in my bank account each month. In this country is independence. The women here waste it. Independence needs a strong wall around it.'

'No,' Sita/Ferret had answered, 'no property for me,' and had horrified this woman. Emily had worshipped her house; Champa had counted each penny she had earned, having kept every payslip over the decades, and translated them into rupees. 'Better this way,' she had said once, 'I was bird of paradise when I was young. I am a wealthy woman now I am old. I can still make them jealous.' Sita/Ferret would have licked her boots for an explanation.

Removing her designer clothes, now falling like yesterday's ideas, she wondered if she'd ever wear them again. Hastily she washed and put on her work clothes, the anxiety of being late driving her. Within twenty minutes she was back on the road, her boots thumping on the pavement, her thoughts thumping in her head, 'I've given them away, I've given them away, I've given them away to the man with The Face.'

Her interest in men had been erratic and infrequent; the confused legacy of Emily and Champa. Champa had had ambitions of a traditional marriage for the girl and had enforced modesty and separation from men, had guarded her like a jealous matron whose family virtue is vested in the girl's chastity. Champa had talked at length on the honourable institution of marriage – 'respect, and a respected place. Nothing else in life gives it.' She had embroidered the romance, glitter and glamour of marriage. It would be Champa's reward, for a job well done, 'but *She* must do the necessaries. That is her duty.' If Champa was referring to Emily, then Sita/Ferret could rest assured she was safe from any arranged marriage. Emily's approach to men was hate, scorn and sarcasm. 'A man is a woman's downfall,' Emily had declared, 'their tongues do their lying, their wallets do their buying and their willies do their cheating.' Between ambition and loathing Sita/Ferret had been as closely controlled as any Asian girl from a zealously traditional household.

Even after she left the Mausoleum, several years elapsed before Sita/Ferret had been able to bring herself to explore the unknown territory of the opposite sex; telling herself that people did it all the time, that, at her age, and in this age in which she lived, men and women were free to indulge their interests, in fact, free to indulge their obsessions and passions within each other. Sita/Ferret didn't know it, but she was as typical of the Asian females of her age as any other.

So when the time came, as if diving into the deep end, she responded to overtures, and got herself, dreaded word, a boyfriend. She could see Champa's face crinkling in disgust, could feel Emily's scorn. The second boyfriend turned into the first lover. She could see Champa turn from her at this immoral behaviour – she had become a fallen woman. She could feel Emily's mockery, she had become a *gutter ki bitch*.

Sita/Ferret had been afraid that if she indulged in sex, her emotions would spiral out of control, that she would lose her grip on life. But found, to her disappointment, that delirious excitement and passionate obsession never came her way. Her flesh participated, but her emotions remained virginal.

This particular revelation was Sita/Ferret's loss of innocence. The demolition of a twentieth-century fairy tale, that oh-so familiar tale where sex is the act that promises love and happiness. She felt betrayed. She realised that so many were surviving just by hanging onto the surface; living dull, emotionless lives where the sexual act came out of social or financial need, out of habit or possessiveness, out of bodily need, even if the earth didn't move each time. Biology didn't give up.

Some of her 'encounters', as she now called them, had been pleasant, but soon exhausted, some had been difficult and better left behind. All had been English. For the very first time differences between her and them had been thrown into stark contrast. She had lived with Emily and Champa and grown up thinking that the English and Indian ways were intermingled, that the differences didn't cancel each other out, but cohabited; sometimes with difficulty, sometimes like a seamless joining.

However the 'Byofriends', as she came to call them, thought otherwise and examined her colour, compared, commented, and asked endless questions about culture, religion and tradition. Sometimes, just to satisfy them, she'd give them made-up stories of an Asian home, sometimes putting in drama, sometimes playing ordinary and dull, sometimes all they got was the 'Englishness' running through her. But she was just as avaricious on her side, and dug hard for her share of English family information, for the memories, secrets and everyday dramas. What she didn't relish was when some showed her off as their 'Asian babe'; at which point, though she hated to admit it, many of Emily's bitter words about men started to make sense. No Asian man ever came her way. If she saw any, they were often with English women, and would look at her with the same suspicion with which she looked at them, wary of what the mixtures of different beliefs, pasts, accommodations and contradictions may have produced. But there was in her a deep-seated curiosity, a yearning even to have a 'close encounter of the Asian kind'; not a desire she would reveal to another. That would be giving too much away. Last night, she'd been generous to a fault.

Sita/Ferret was an employer's dream come true: she liked to start early and work late. Her childhood days of duties, of serving your elders, working till a task was completed had ingrained the habit of hard graft. It was one that served her well in her schooldays, but brought suspicion and accusations in her days of working for charity groups. Idealism and a hard-work drive smack of ambition and empire-building. Sita/Ferret had put all her energy and passion into her work but soon learnt that in the real world, it's necessary to hold back a little. Else others get frightened. That was the beginning of her disillusionment with her work and the world. The Mausoleum may not have been wonderful, but it seemed the outside world wasn't perfect either.

Now she was glad she hadn't taken her first revenge. When she was old enough, she was told to bring them their early morning tea. Although the house was equipped with central heating, Emily had seen no reason to switch it on regularly. Sita/Ferret would therefore wake up on deadly cold mornings and fall out of bed, landing with a thud on the lino floor. It was the only way. She'd tried the more traditional method of sitting up before getting up, but an icy blast would hit her and she'd dive back under the quilt. Pulling on jumpers over her nightclothes, she'd run, quietly of course, down to the basement kitchen where she boiled water, chucked in fennel and cardamoms, and stood at the kitchen window as they simmered. A time of stillness. She'd take in the E & C's tea and light their gas fires.

One day she had curtsied to Emily who fully appreciated the mockery for what it was. 'That school's no good for you,' she'd said, but Emily couldn't stop her. School was the law. Thank God for laws! Emily didn't know that she'd been saved from a fate worse than sarcastic curtsies. Sita/Ferret had read that Negro slaves would serve beautifully cooked food, with the addition of a revengeful spit. On a particularly cold and bitter morning when snow had shimmered on the ground, and she had had a clutch of grievances boiling inside her, she had filled her mouth and taking careful aim, shot her hidden assault into the cups; only to find herself paralysed at Champa's door. If it had been Emily she doubted she would have been so cowardly. But Champa had drilled the etiquette of food hygiene into her with admonitions and sharp slaps that made her ears sting. The purity of food was akin to the act of worship! Sita/Ferret had seen the shudder of revulsion when Champa, watching a cookery programme, had seen the chef lift a spoon to his lips, taste, and put the spoon back into the food. Champa had been sick with revulsion. And, as Sita/Ferret had stood outside Champa's door with the doctored cups of tea, no feelings of glee or triumph had bubbled inside her. Instead she had felt as soiled as they would if they knew. This was a sordid trick. Revenge should deliver satisfaction! It should be grand, daring, glorious! She had rushed back down, made more tea at express speed, putting in too much sugar, not enough milk, and had got told off for being slow and incompetent.

Sita/Ferret walked quickly on, armed with her newspapers and drinks, passing by 'Bhagwan's', the shop of heavenly goods where gods and goddesses could be bought for a few pounds and a lifetime's help. Today was different, today there was no lingering to admire the divine Sita displayed in the window: Sita who had been banished into the jungle! How terrified she must have been, alone and lonely, in a dangerous, dark place. What had she thought of the man who had put her there? There should be no forgiveness. Sita/Ferret knows what it is to be alone and lonely all your life. There should be no forgiveness for the women who had put her there; and in that she included the woman who must have given birth to her.

'Universal Enterprises,' glowed a deep blue above the door. From one cosmic arrangement to another! A figure was peering intently into the unlit window as she approached. An unusual event, for they seldom had callers at the shop. This person must have a very particular reason for being such an early bird. As she came nearer she saw the pony-tail, the glinting earrings. The young/old man! 'Good morning Mr Steven Singh. Did you walk here or did you splash out on a bus ticket?'

'I heard you were very busy last night.' A little smile on an intense face.

'Me? Oh no.' How could he have known? Had he been lurking in the shadows too? Waiting to lay claim to something else she might have been sporting.

'I heard you were packed out with the social elite.' Distaste underlined the last two words. He was still to learn that she was no admirer of the moneyed brigade either.

Unlocking the door she swung it open, 'Would you like to come in?' Mr Steven Singh's interest must have had some weighty reason behind it, for he had barely waited the requisite period of night and dawn. 'Mr Kalyan isn't here yet I'm afraid.'

'No problem. I'll just look around. OK?' he asked, taking something out of his pocket. For a foolish moment Sita/Ferret suspected it to be a wallet. When he opened it and switched it on, she saw it was a palm top. Mr Singh was here on business!

She went downstairs and started work; she'd have a short break later because she'd come in late. She made her rules and tried to stick to them. If she didn't she'd be sucked into chaos. A word that had journeyed with her from the Mausoleum. 'Chaos! When the world breaks,' Champa had said once. 'Chaos! That's when you've got to be knife sharp,' Emily had said. In her break Sita/Ferret would dive into her newspaper and finish it off later in the day. Once, a few years earlier, when her idealism was more innocent, she had joined a small political group that discussed each week's events, political or social, by role-playing, taking on the identities of politicians and participants. On rare occasions, it might enhance understanding of an event or a decision but mostly it left a sour taste. If anything came up concerning ethnic issues, it would always, eventually, find its way into her lap. 'I don't know a thing about that,' she'd told them. 'I'm the bastard child of Imperialism, Independence, and Immigration,' paraphrasing a French philosopher. In those days she liked to talk in words with ultimate meanings.

She lifted the broom from the corner and wondered what the grey-eyed man was doing with his loot. Was he gloating over it like Scrooge, or had he already hiked off to some dealer to discover the conversion rate from gems to pounds? She started sweeping, pushing together the litter of dust, woodchips, paper and wrappings. She knew what it was to clean a house from top to bottom, including windows, doors, nooks and crannies. Sita/Ferret had never had time to be bored. For that she should thank the E & C.

'I'd never have a valuable worker of mine doing that,' declared Mr Steven Singh from the steps. 'I'd do it myself.'

'You obviously don't own a business.'

'I have an interest in one.' He watched her collect the dust into a dustpan, empty it into a bag, tie it and place it in the bin. 'Very meticulous,' he complimented.

'I had a good, old-fashioned upbringing.'

'And where was that?' he asked.

'South London.'

'Blimey. There's a coincidence. I'm from East London. Shake.' They shook hands with the solemnity of children.

'But, where are you really from? Originally.' *Originally! Origin! Which part of the earth's soil did you spring from?* The question that demanded a blood connection that stretched over oceans, mountain ranges and forests; that swept across the sky in a loop connecting the here and now with the past and foreign. But she was not of the group that criss-crossed the globe, from western municipalities to village courtyards, the group that lived the present in terms of the past and dedicated it to the future.

'We've lost touch with the past,' she told him. 'We're the gypsies of the jet age.' She'd heard this from someone else, and if he'd heard it before too, then it would confirm her status as being part of an historical movement. 'It's globalisation, innit?'

'And you've never been back,' he guessed. 'And you don't have anything left there.'

'Yes we have.' She lied. Perhaps it wasn't a complete lie. Perhaps Emily, the Mutant Memsahib, had houses, tea plantations, businesses, whatever! Champa had memories. They were a possession too. She wouldn't let him erase a connection even if it only existed in the words Over There. She'd given away parts of herself the previous night; she wouldn't agree to surrendering any more. 'We're from Over There and Over Here.' That was telling him. Stretching up, she put her arms around a crate and started to lift it down.

'Here, let me help you,' said Mr Singh, quickly coming over and trying to take the crate. Her hands lost their grip and the crate landed on the floor with a sickening thud.

She felt the crash in her bones. Bang went her chances of winning this year's Best Worker Gold Medal Award.

'What d'you want here Mr Singh?'

'Call me Steven. And all I want is what belongs to me, including the contents of this crate.'

Property! Possession! Passion! The three pillars of society.

'The contents are probably in a million pieces by now,' she complained, kneeling down and beginning to undo the screws on the lid.

'You're working for a bloodsucking, ruthless and evil man,' Steven Singh informed her.

'*Is duniya mein teen kasai – pisu, khatmal, Brahman bhai!*' she answered him.

'What?'

' "Bloodsuckers three on earth there be – the bug, the Brahman and the flea".' Champa's sayings stuck deep in her mind.

'My God! That's bloody well true!' Steven Singh thumped the wall in his excitement. '*Mr Kalyan*,' sarcasm ringing through his voice, 'has been trading on the Brahman purity and social fucking superiority bit all his life. Say it again,' he asked, squatting beside her while she repeated the line. Once more and he'd chiselled it into his brain.

She lifted the lid off the crate and started removing the packing of newspaper, sacking and cloth. Smoothing out the pieces of newspaper she arranged them in a pile. Later she'd go through them, poring over the pictures, picking out the English words. Her spoken Hindi was perfect. Perfectly fifty years old, as Champa had taught her. But Champa had never forced her to learn the written version that Emily had flaunted in her flourishes. Lastly Sita/Ferret removed the layers of unbleached cloth, unconsciously lifting it and smelling deeply; imagining the white heat of the sun, courtyard fires and private women, painted trucks and Bollywood billboards. Suddenly aware of an audience, she opened her eyes and clenched her face to prevent a blush. 'Try it,' holding out the cloth to him, 'not mothballs, something different.'

'Did you grow up with mothballs too?' he asked, taking the cloth and smelling it.

Emily would throw open a steel trunk, vivid colours jumping into the eye, embroidery and textures marking them as the refinements of another world. Sometimes she'd be allowed to touch, even hold, marvelling at the glowing colour, the sheer, elusive material sliding over her fingers, holding them in front of her face: if there were a line between the visible and invisible then this would be it. And always the accompanying smell of mothballs, the smell of locked treasures.

'Thank God,' lifting the first figure from the crate. 'I won't lose my head. Not today anyway.'

'Do you always live with the threat of decapitation?'

'Don't we all?'

'Some deserve to have the sword of justice hanging over them. I know where these little goodies come from, and now I know the mark-up.' He paused, and then, 'I was hoping you might help me.'

She looked at him sharply, suddenly remembering the previous night's question about loyalty, 'You mean spy?'

'I mean just fill me in on some things, occasionally.'

Last night's guy had wanted her razzle-dazzle adornments; this morning's guy wanted her treachery and deceit. 'No.'

'Alright.' The other man had said, 'A for alright'. Steven Singh didn't try a single persuading argument, leaving her nobility hanging with nowhere to go. 'I'll tell you what happened. So that when things change, you'll know why.'

'There's no need,' she replied, 'I'm only an employee.' Other people's stories were her entrée into private worlds, but no matter how much she relished gossip, eavesdropping and the thrill of being taken into someone's confidence, his story threatened complications.

'No, no, no,' Steven Singh said, 'I'll need you afterwards. That's why I want you to know.'

Declarations of impending change! First Poonum, then Steven Singh. And she thought she'd come into a quiet, dull job! 'As long as I'm left alone to get on with my work,' she informed him severely, starting to check the contents of the crate against a list in her hand.

'Sure. You go right ahead. Your employer, *Uncle K*,' he had difficulty with that word, 'was a *pardia/likhia* young man, knowing his reading and writing. Not only did he know the lingo from over there; he also knew the lingo from over here. In the early days, there were very few like him. It's like they were the sighted in a blind world. You know, this world runs on *dokument*,' slipping into a working-class Indian accent, 'paiper, faarms, cer-ti-ffi-cuts, and so on, and the young man was helpful with his skills. Filled in other people's forms, wrote their letters, did interpreting. And those old men had a sense of honour, obligation. They made sure they repaid him with free dinners, drinks, whatever. They worked their guts out, in dirty, filthy factories; days, nights, any fucking hour. They were treated like dirt, but, in their heads, they had dreams, ambitions. They dreamt of building fortunes, changing their children's destinies. They reckoned if they worked hard, broke their backs, anything was possible. Except,' holding up his finger and drawing a line with it across the floor, 'the K. He was too good for their kind of shit work. He thought he should have people doing shit work for him. He borrowed money off my old man, and some of the others, on the *bhai-bhai* basis of money borrowing. Of course, the stock market never got to hear about it. Then he borrowed more dosh off my old man, and again, and again. Now,' holding his hands apart, 'what happened there? I mean why did he home in on my Dad and not the others? Perhaps my old man was the softest touch? Perhaps they got to be mates? Perhaps the K saw how fucking stupid my old man was? Maybe they had some karma to sort out, maybe we deserved it, maybe we didn't and fate dealt us a rotten hand. Fate, meaning K the *Korrupt*.'

She took two figures from the crate, and cradling them in her arm, stood up and moved over to the desk. He rose and followed, sitting on the stairs again, waiting for her to settle down before he continued. She took soft brushes and velvet cloths from a bag, and began to clean one of the figures. Steven Singh went on, 'My Dad slaved and slaved. But he knew he had to do something different, to make the leap, to make the dream come true. You have to get money to work for you – money makes money. The K... (We call him "K the knife," my sisters and me. We think it's downright funny. We say "K the knife" and fall around laughing.) Then K the Korrupt, not paying back a penny, comes up with another one of his brilliant ideas. Joint business ventures: buy old houses, do them up, rent them out and you're making a mint. Got my old man to do the dog's work, seeing as he was so good at DIY, as well as bankrolling the business. Then one day,' Steven Singh paused, 'he keeled over and died.' She looked up at him, at the shadows on his face. 'And we were out on the street. Even the house we lived in had been mortgaged to the last penny.' Steven Singh moved, came over, sat on the chair by her desk. Picked up the other figure, a warrior on a horse, and continued, 'Mum asked "K the knife" about the money. He said, no, no, the old man did the work, and got paid for it. And that was that, the everyday story of a common or garden bloodsucker.'

She'd heard every word; they'd fallen into her like stones, thudding against each other. Either he was lying, monumentally, or there had been treachery. And if it was true, she should leave, separate herself from Mr Kalyan's soiled dosh; dosh that had paid for the beautiful figure in her hands, a dancer with her skirts swirling out, her feet beating the floor.

'But I'm on his tail, I'll get him, and get what we're owed. Then I'm planning a fucking empire!' suddenly jumping up and swirling around. Perhaps the dancing girl had affected him. 'Actually,' sitting back down, smiling that rainy-day smile, 'I don't know anything beyond tomorrow. It's a bleedin' mess it is. But don't you let me put you off doing your job and duty. "Thank you Father for our daily bread, roti and dhal." Roti and dhal are the cheapest meal you can make y'know.'

'I thought it was roti and *achar*?'

'Luxuries darlin'! A jar of Indian *achar* cuts a black hole in the budget if you're trying to make do on the social.'

'Why are you called Steven?'

'After my Dad's mate, Uncle Steve. They worked together. Uncle Steve calls the K the Jackal; he wants to know what happened to all the thousands my Dad earned. Like an idiot I asked the K for the documents. Wouldn't you know it, they all had his name, and his name alone. Know what he said to me?' Steven Singh drew in his breath, 'He said, "your old man liked to talk big".'

Upstairs the door pinged and Steven Singh looked as if a cobra had entered. 'I'm not letting up. No way! I'm busy turning over every little rock and stone from the past. Don't you ever wonder what he does when he's not here? Those houses are falling down now. Hasn't had free labour or money for years. And this arty business must be costing him a bomb. You know why he got into this?' Leaning towards her, his face close to hers, he whispered, 'He wants to climb the social ladder, leave his dirty-dealing days behind him; let's hope he falls off and breaks his precious social status. Wants to impress the wife and the in-laws, got married above himself. Poonum's not his real daughter, you know, the wife was a widow, else that family of hers wouldn't have given him a second glance. They do the Indian bit of the business, not much bother to them; they've got employees, agents, and so on. He wants a respectable front for his old age.

But not if I can help it. First he broke my Dad, then my Mum.' Taking a card from his inner pocket he put it on the desk, 'Keep it for reference. Don't let him work you too hard.' Before he climbed the stairs, he stood a moment, organising himself.

She heard voices, then the slamming of the door.

Chapter Seven

Bombay, 1942

A miracle is to be gifted with one's desires; to be lifted from a lowly into a higher place. Emily was dazzled. No more trudging in the early morning bitterness to the factory, no more cooking, washing, cleaning; no more scrimping, saving, penny-pinching. To live the life of ladies in stories, sitting at pretty tables, embroidering prettiness; to choose food or clothes without enduring the endless calculations of subtraction, division and make do.

On a shopping trip he bought her a gown in pink slipper satin threaded with sequins, a cascade of fuchsia roses trailing from waist to hem. Emily smiled and thanked him prettily, but her bones were locked together with fear that nothing this good could happen to her, that perhaps in an instant it would all evaporate and Maureen would stand there, laughing at her. They passed the Bokhara Palace, and he steered her in to try on a few fur coats. Emily hid her gasp behind her hand. She tried on a dozen different coats, she walked and twirled for him and posed in front of the mirrors. He couldn't make up his mind, and if he couldn't, then neither could Emily. They decided to defer making a purchase until they went to Simla; however he insisted on buying her a fur stole in the meantime, for evening wear. Back in their rooms, Emily wrapped it in cloth and locked it away in a suitcase – but brought it out a week later to wear with her gown when they went to watch 'Bridal Suit' at the Eros, which advertised itself as 'India's most hygienic theatre'. Afterwards, he took her to Green's nightclub where she met three of his friends and, for the first time, was introduced to a lady acquaintance, Mrs Linda Wiggins, who greeted her with great formality, immediately intimidating her. Linda Wiggins complimented her fulsomely on the gown and stole. Emily suspected Linda was putting her down, intimating that she had overdressed.

She didn't care! She was so happy, Linda Wiggins' sarcasm was wasted. 'Thank you,' she replied to Linda with her happiest smile, clapping her hands for 'Theodore and His Boys'. Nothing could dent Emily's contentment – contentment which brimmed to overflowing when Linda asked her if she would be watching the state drive tomorrow along Hornby Road, by the Viceroy and Lady Linlithgow.

'Of course she will,' Thomas declared, turning to put his arm around Emily.

They moved from the boarding house to rooms of their own. Emily moved from being a poor factory worker to a lady commanding two servants. Mrs Linda Wiggins came to give her advice: 'Servants are very wasteful,' she declared, shaking her head, 'I'm afraid you'll have to make regular visits to the kitchen. You'll save your annas and make sure their minds are kept in the right direction.' Emily agreed to do so, she would be a perfect housewife. 'After all, we are in the middle of a war,' Linda Wiggins added, 'even if we are six thousand miles from the front. Have you started donating to the anna fund yet?' she asked. Emily admitted she hadn't heard of it. 'For the war effort of course. But you are a little out of the way here, perhaps it is not so organised in this area.'

'I don't think there are many English people here,' Emily explained.

'The anna fund is for everyone. The Indian troops are fighting too. Donald has just managed to sell...' Linda Wiggins coughed a little. Emily waited politely for her to finish her sentence. Thomas had told Emily that Mrs Wiggins was a widow so she was curious as to what was to follow. Linda Wiggins' attention had however moved on to other subjects – DDT in fact. 'Never buy it locally,' she advised authoritatively, 'these little shops water it down so much it wouldn't kill a sick flea. Get Thomas to buy it in tins, from the reputable shops. Oh, and something most important for us ladies,' coy and smiling, 'your stockings. Keep them in a jar. With a glass top or a very tight-fitting lid. That will keep out the insects and the monsoon damp,' she added, delivering her words with the panache of an oracle. Emily was deeply impressed. These were the secrets of the initiated, the exclusive knowledge of a coterie. She begged her for more information about life in India. What Emily really wanted to know, was how to be a memsahib.

'You are rather out of the way here,' Linda Wiggins repeated again, 'otherwise, normally, we go to the bazaar in the mornings,' lifting her eyes at the arduousness of such a task, 'then to the club in the afternoon, for tennis, badminton, swimming, that kind of thing,' waving her hand airily, 'and of course dinner and dancing in the evening.' Emily bit her lip to hide her excitement – she didn't think she was out of the way at all. It was obvious that Linda Wiggins liked to put on a snooty air.

However when she asked Thomas about the club business, he was not at all enthusiastic. 'We'll do that when we have our own house.' (House not palace!) 'No point in joining a club, won't be suitable for us.' He had his own ideas about how she should occupy her days, and told her he'd arranged for two people to assist her: one to help her improve her diction and learn the way of doing 'English things' in India – 'learn the ways everyone likes to speak,' (he had thought long and hard about how to say she needed to jump the class divide) – and one to give her Hindustani lessons. 'Don't,' putting his finger to his lips, 'tell anyone about it. You need to have a few hidden cards.'

A while later three of his gentlemen friends were invited to tea. Emily was surprised to find they were a mixture of nationalities: an Italian and a French gentleman as well as Donald, the one who had caused a little coughing fit in Mrs Wiggins. The men all said they were charmed to meet her and welcomed her to India. A great politeness occurred in that little apartment. Thomas explained that Mr Donelli, the Italian gentleman, managed a hosiery mill in Gamari, owned by some wealthy Indians, and posited the idea that he and Emily might settle there. Mr Donelli agreed that it would be a good choice, Gamari was a beautiful place with a good-sized European community. Emily would find many friends among the other wives there, and he had just remembered that the Greek, Yiannoukas, was selling his house, a house that Thomas had always liked.

'It sounds wonderful,' said Emily, imagining a huge house, busy social whirl, status and wealth. 'Why don't we, Thomas?'

'*Jeni chador ho utne paun pasaro!*' was Thomas' strange reply.

'Well done, old man,' applauded Donald. 'I'm sure it means something terribly worthy and boring.'

'The English version is, "cut your coat according to your cloth." '

'When have you ever done that, my friend,' laughed Monsieur Savauge.

'I'm a respectable married man now,' Thomas replied gravely.

The tea party had been organised for the express purpose of establishing this fact, and planting the idea of the next step. Thomas would need the help of someone like Donelli who had lived for years in Gameri and who was married to an English woman.

If Emily had known more about Gameri she would not have been overjoyed. An outpost of the empire, it was a place that was stable yet contained movement and flux. Away from the heat of a major city, it attracted people of many nationalities who came to sell yarn, cheap *dhotis*, and machinery; or to buy hides, skins and other choice goods. Gameri also granted a man distance from the authorities, the stability of a domestic home, and the opportunity to travel when he needed to.

Emily thought to herself that Thomas' social circle seemed to be rather limited. Other than Linda Wiggins, she had not yet met any other ladies with whom she could talk, chit-chat and exchange invitations. However she did see ladies of another kind when they went to the races: a Hooray-Henry male group, obviously of the moneyed class, but thoroughly Indian, had English ladies on their arms. Emily had tugged at his sleeve and asked him how this could be. Thomas had put his arm protectively around her, and moved her away, whispering, 'Those who can't find other buyers have to take what they can get.' Buying and selling was his business too.

The first time he had to go away on business he went for several days, later he would be away for weeks, and then, forever. That first time he went away, he was very anxious about making arrangements for her comfort. He bought her an English language magazine with which to pass her time and told the female servant to sleep in the room; but Emily said it wouldn't be necessary, she wouldn't be scared, then, suspecting she might have made a mistake, modified her statement, 'I'll try not to be scared.'

'That's the spirit,' he said approvingly, thinking that all in all, he'd made a good choice. Emily delighted in whatever he gave her and didn't, yet, ask for more. But he knew that time had already started its work, and that one day the dazzle would fall from her eyes.

Emily was faithful to her promise. She had a quiet meal, she watched the sun showing off its flamboyant colours against the evening sky, wrote a letter to her mother, describing again her delicious new life, knowing that the news would travel up and down the street, in and out of the houses and round the corner, into the envious ears of Maureen. After she had finished the letter, she moved to the cane chair with the plump cushions and, curling up, she opened the magazine Thomas had bought for her. Emily read about hunt balls in Quetta, a cocktail supper dance at the Imperial Hotel in New Delhi, military weddings, best-dog competitions in Simla, a Girl Guides' rally at the vice-regal lodge, a description of Chateau Mapurthala, a palace owned by Rani Jyoti Jasada. Emily felt that she was in the midst of a high-class social life. She had arrived! She would name their house Chateau- something too. 'Chateau

Miller' didn't sound quite right. She would think about it. She passed over the photograph of Mr Gandhi selling *khadi*, the homespun material he was telling all Indians to wear, she also flipped over the article on the 'Quit India' movement – 'Traitorous Rebels' declared the headline. An advertisement for Macleans toothpaste – 'British to the Teeth' – seemed to underline the good life to be had here by them all. She determined to buy only Macleans.

Later, Emily closed the shutters and went to bed under the mosquito netting. She adored the fall of the net around the bed, imagining the net to be lace curtains around a four-poster, like in the old fairy tales. For the first time in her life, she was alone in a bed. She stretched her arms and rolled across the bed, his smell still in the sheets on his side. If love could be produced by effort and gratitude, then Emily had come up with the goods. She wanted to enjoy the luxury of a bed to herself but first she fulfilled the obligations of a wife on her first night alone. She went through the ritual of missing him: imagined his body, the smooth skin under her hand, the rise and fall of his chest, the muscles of his arms, replayed his kisses and compliments. She didn't know of the difference between compliments and endearments, and that while he lavished one on her, he kept the other for the one across the roofs. She thought of all he had done for her, and said 'thank you' out loud. The obligations of loyalty fulfilled, she could now enjoy being alone in her bed, an unprecedented luxury.

Afterwards she felt she should have been frightened on this, her first night alone. Perhaps that would have prepared her for what was to come. He had duped her into a sense of security.

The next afternoon, Donald came by to inquire after her welfare, and solicit requests for anything she might require. He was all gentlemanly courtesy and concern. She felt cocooned in silk.

When Thomas returned, he took her out for lunch at the Grand Hotel. She marvelled at the fountain in the middle of the room, the ornately dressed waiters and the marble on the floor. Afterwards they took a ride in a horse-driven, open carriage, enjoying the clip-clop of the horses' hooves; they passed along a tree-lined street where the houses sat far back behind gates and gardens. 'Choose one of these,' he offered munificently, 'and we'll have one like it.'

'Let's get out and walk,' she said, taking him seriously and wanting a closer look. So far he hadn't failed her. Later she would haunt this particular street, his promise a macabre echo in her head.

Champa sat in the sun with The Girl massaging oil into her hair, the circular soothings of the fingertips relaxing her whole body. Champa was content with her lot. She had her steady flow of customers, and her sahib. She knew that this situation wouldn't last forever. As it was she had fewer customers than in her first years when the bloom of youth gave her a sparkle. Now the future hovered over the present as a dark unknown. Champa saved what she could and knew that she was doing as much as she was able. She closed her eyes, the morning sun warm upon her face, and drifted off into a semi-doze as The Girl massaged her head.

Today The Girl was languid in her movements also, the act of massaging slowing her into a lassitude where she could just float in the amber moment. An unusual surrender for The Girl, for she was one of those whose mind never stops working; watching, listening, thinking, absorbing the life around her. No one suspected the knowledge she carried inside her of the private and secret doings of many in the area. The Girl knew that if she let anything slip, she would be the one broken first, and that Champa would suffer the consequences too. Dipping her fingers into the bowl of oil, she ran them through Champa's hair, careful not to wake her. In the human chain of relationships, her only link was with Champa. She had distant and vague memories of a family and a mother, but she had long-since consigned them to the section under dreams. The mother had not only given her away, but most probably sold her for money itself.

The Girl had been a gift, a love-token, to Champa when Champa was fresh in her beauty. A young man had wondered what unusual gift he could make to impress her and liven their romance. The Girl had been brought to Champa, overdressed in frills, ribbons and laces. She had been old enough to fetch and carry little trays of sweetmeats, retrieve forgotten objects like fans or handkerchiefs, and carry messages. Champa had delighted in dressing the child in pretty frocks, putting ornaments in her hair, bangles on her wrists and making her as cute as cute could be; she was young enough to be a pet and be petted, to submit to fondling and caressing when emotion overwhelmed the youthful Champa, or when Champa simply wished to enhance her 'personality' by creating a pretty picture. The lover and Champa would teach The Girl snatches of popular love-songs and lines from poetry, applauding her efforts as she performed them in her little-girl voice. They had made a home-grown Shirley Temple! The lover particularly enjoyed teaching The Girl political slogans, going into hoots of laughter as The Girl marched up and down, damning and denouncing the English. Champa would look nervously around her and make sure the windows were closed.

As the good times shifted a gear downwards, and as The Girl grew, so also her role. Now clothed in Champa's cut and sized hand-me-downs, she took on the work of the servants that Champa could no longer afford. Fed and housed by her, there was no question of wages, for within the scheme of existence what possible use could The Girl have for them? Neither could wages have financed a separate existence or funded a future. Champa would never sack her, and The Girl would never leave. Champa was The Girl's home, and The Girl was Champa's shock absorber for the rough and hard patches in her life. If Emily hadn't landed in their midst, their lives may have proceeded in this same manner into their old age.

The Girl hadn't forgotten her days of glory. She remembered the pretty dresses and the attentions lavished upon her, but they were purely a part of memory, not to be used for comparison with her present circumstances, or as fodder for longings and yearnings. The Girl understood the absoluteness of change, and the limits that were her life.

Chapter Eight

Invoices! When what is desired becomes that which is owed – an invoice to fate. When what is earned becomes that which is another's – an invoice to hate. Invoices to families and friends, lovers and enemies, wives and mistresses, husbands and strangers. Everyone in the world thinks they are owed something by someone. The world does not have enough paper to write out these invoices.

Steven Singh's words had lodged permanently in Sita/Ferret's mind – just as her wages from a Saturday job had lodged permanently in Emily's pocket. Sita/Ferret had at first requested permission, then begged, and finally raged, ranted and nearly walked out of the door till Champa had stopped her. All this passion for the sake of a Saturday job at the local shop.

Normally it would never have occurred to her to even think about it. But she had seen the notice on a day in which she'd had two fights at school, and was spoiling for a third. Sita/Ferret was an only child, a lonely child. The few Asian girls at school would look at her, make faces, and keep their distance. But on that day, they had pinned her in a corner and questioned her about her domestic arrangements in the way that only children can.

'Aunts,' she'd declared, when questioned about Emily and Champa.

'Why's one English and the other Indian?'

'Why shouldn't they be?' she'd retaliated, trying to push through the bodies ringed around her.

'My mum says they're bad women,' one jeered, the others sniggered.

'Where's your dad then?' asked another.

81

A scream of helplessness and rage burst out of her, and before she knew it, she was shoving fists into stomachs and kicking shins; the others retaliated with fists and kicks of their own. She would have been pulped if a teacher hadn't come along and stopped the fight, declaring that she was 'surprised at them all'. And that hadn't been the end of it. Sita/Ferret learnt that some days are more fateful than others, for in the afternoon, as if looking for punishment, she had had a second fight. Dobs was the playground bully who especially liked to pick on the 'wig-wogs' as she called them. Dobs liked to throw out insults and abuse first, the real fun lay in taunting her victims, verbally cowing them. Dobs didn't know that Sita/Ferret was always cowed at home, and that today she'd not only found her claws but bloodied them too. Dobs had hardly begun on her before Sita/Ferret lunged with a growl that came from anger and aching guts. A crowd had quickly gathered around them, some watching in morbid fascination, others egging them on – till a teacher's voice had cut through and the crowd evaporated as quickly as it had formed. Dobs and Sita/Ferret were hauled off to the headmistress' office, who also said, 'I'm surprised at you,' looking at Sita/Ferret, the quiet, withdrawn student who always got high marks, and gave them a week's detention. They had both grinned, and the headmistress felt like doubling it. Dobs grinned because it added to her dangerous reputation, and Sita/Ferret grinned because it seemed to be the stamp of an initiation.

So when she was going home, late, and rehearsing an explanation which would include all the blood and gore of the day, she saw the advertisement for a Saturday job at the corner shop and went right in and asked about it.

'It's a case of *jaldi, jaldi*,' Mr Saunders said heartily, having already informed her of his army days in India; *jaldi, jaldi* must have been a favourite ex-pat phrase, one of Emily's rare visitors had also used it. 'I've got many others interested in this job.' Mr Saunders added competition as an extra incentive.

'I'll have to ask my aunty for permission.'

'The Indian lady?' asked Mr Saunders. Sita/Ferret nodded, moving towards the door, sensing the next question to come. She didn't make it. 'What's the English lady to you then?'

'She's Indian too,' she had replied breathlessly, dashing out, delighted with her reply.

'No!' Emily had declared. For once Champa had taken Sita/Ferret's side and tried to persuade Emily. 'She'll get money in her hand, ideas in her head, and that's a bloody dangerous mix. Have you forgotten what *She* did?' Emily had demanded. Sita/Ferret had latched onto Emily's words. If the mysterious *She* had done something dangerous with money and a job, then so would Sita/Ferret.

Sita/Ferret had embarked on a relentless campaign of demands for pocket money, clothes, shoes, and every other need she could think of, as well as the Saturday job, remembering Mr Saunders '*jaldi jaldi*,' afraid that it may already be too late. Emily had been outraged. 'You're dressed a hundred times better than the ones Over There.'

'I'm not Over There, I'm sick of Over There. I'm sick of your hand-me-downs, sick of your second-hand clothes.'

'That's the way it's done. For the likes of you.'

Sita/Ferret had wanted to scream, hit and punch, but remembered the *She* who had done a dangerous thing, and held herself in.

'Then give me the money.'

Emily shook with anger as if Sita/Ferret had actually hit her. 'First one, then the other. Devil spawn. The money's mine. I worked for it. Get your own!'

'Then let me work.'

'You've got your work. You belong here.'

Belonging was being Emily's. 'No I don't.'

'Then walk out and starve.'

'All right then.' She'd run to the door and tried to open it. Champa had stopped her. Emily had punished her.

Champa the Dumpa hadn't been one to make waves. Sita/Ferret never knew why or how, but Champa had finally persuaded Emily to let her have her precious Saturday job. Emily, however, stipulated a condition to which Sita/Ferret had shouted 'No, no, no,' but eventually agreed, though it was like having her wings chopped, tearing apart the combination of money and ideas that Emily had said was so dangerous. At the end of each Saturday, Emily would come to collect her from the shop. And collect her day's earnings. These would be popped into Emily's purse. Sita/Ferret had accepted the arrangement, had reasoned that half of something was better than nothing, and this way she might get other opportunities, learn something about the world. Till the day she received a pay rise of fifty pence, and saw that also land in Emily's purse. She had a vision of bondage. But she had continued to work, and Emily had continued to collect – till the day she came running home at midday, hot and breathless, announcing she'd left, refusing to give a reason.

Mr Saunders had gone on holiday that week, and left his sister, Mrs Cuthbert, in charge. Business had been slow so Mrs Cuthbert said there was nothing wrong in having an extended tea break. She had opened a packet of cakes and shared them out between her and Sita/Ferret, talking about her daughter's forthcoming wedding. Sita/Ferret had listened entranced, and had asked for exact details of the wedding dress, reception, trousseau, bridegroom, flower arrangements, drinking in every detail of Mrs Cuthbert's description. With such a rapt audience, Mrs Cuthbert hadn't been able to resist the temptation to indulge in some exaggeration, and getting carried away, had said of course she would love to invite Sita/Ferret, if it wasn't for Emily. After which she had stopped talking, looking guilty. Sita/Ferret had shrugged her shoulders and said that she was right, for Emily would never have allowed her anyway. Mrs Cuthbert had looked relieved and nodded. A pause as Mrs Cuthbert had poured more tea into their cups; Mrs Cuthbert moved a cake from her plate onto Sita/Ferret's, declaring that she must watch her weight. And, as if this sacrifice had permitted her to indulge in another way, she had lowered her tone confidentially and asked if it was true that Emily had kept a house. Sita/Ferret had nodded, her mouth full of cake. Suspecting that she may have been misunderstood and intent on confirming her query, Mrs Cuthbert had elaborated a little, leaning towards Sita/Ferret and whispering, 'A house where men came, Indian men!' Had she become oblivious to the widening eyes and growing colour of the girl sitting in front of her? Mrs Cuthbert didn't see the flush rise to the girl's cheeks, for she was thinking of forbidden bodies entwined in exotic pleasures. Mrs Cuthbert enjoyed her marriage bed and in the secret places of desire wished she'd enjoyed a few more. Sexual curiosity, more than social calumny, fed her questions else she would have seen the shock on the girl's face sooner. Sita/Ferret fled and Mrs Cuthbert said 'Oh dear.'

Secret knowledge! She had looked at Emily and hadn't been able to believe it. She couldn't possibly have asked, so she had started searching. Whenever she could. In Emily's drawers, cupboards, open bags and locked cases. She didn't find any stacks of old letters, or notebooks that revealed the past; but in one case, tucked into a side pocket, she did discover a gold cigarette case. Emily didn't smoke, perhaps she used to and this was the clue to the unknown Emily. The top lid had an engraving of the Taj Mahal, with 'Taj Agra' inscribed on it; the back of the bottom lid had a map. Sita/Ferret had held it to the light so that she could see it clearly. The map went from Baluchistan on the left to Sikang and China on the right-hand side, bordered by the 'Himalaya Mts.' on the top. She had puzzled over some of the other places for which only initials were given: 'NWP' in the north-western section, 'UP', 'BN', 'CP' in the middle, and right on the other side, 'F. Indo China'. 'Rajputana' snaked down from the Punjab, bordered Sind, Bombay and down to 'HYD'. Sita/Ferret had opened the cigarette case, hoping to find something vital, at least some kind of clue. But the inside had been empty except for the two pieces of elastic that ran across each side, and which must have been used to hold the cigarettes. The inside was engraved as beautifully as the outside; a border ran around each side with a pattern of discs in the middle. Closing it, she had glanced at the map again, and with a shock had realised there was no Pakistan. This cigarette case had been pre-Pakistan, pre-Independence. Carefully she had put it back in its place. A token from another era. When the world had been a different shape.

What did it take to change the maps of the world? Sita/Ferret, the only child, the lonely child, used to be the only one reading in the school library during the long lunch breaks. She had read of Partition, of millions dying, of millions on the move, of families broken, of women captured and raped, of a land soaked in blood.

Blood is what changes the maps of the world.

Sita/Ferret read other books on other countries; read about tumultuous battles, ghastly wars, of countries captured and countries that have disappeared. Blood at the beginning and blood at the end! Leafing through the newspapers, she read of Palestine and Israel, of Ireland and the IRA, of bomb blasts in the world's cities, of gun-toting men marauding through towns. It was going on all around her. Sita/Ferret, the only child, the lonely child, heard gunshots as she ground spices for their evening meal, saw blood as she chopped vegetables, felt the heat of fierce fires as she made chapattis. She ventured to ask Champa about Partition. At first Champ didn't seem to understand, then she had shaken her head violently and said, 'No, no, no. Not to talk about.' Sita/Ferret had continued with her furtive searching and her lonely reading, gradually seeing an inkling of a truth: a truth that says no one has a fixed place in the world. Calamities of all kinds maim, destroy and scatter. Some are natural, like earthquakes and nothing can be done about them; but others are political ones, man-made ones, and these are the most grievous for they could have been averted. The possibility was always there, if only the intelligence and humanity had been there too. Through her reading she also discovered that the one thing that people hang on to most is their family name, their family place, even if that place has just joined the dust of history.

She hadn't found anything more hidden among Emily's trunks, or anything that filled the gaps of her own life, but she did discover something else, something which left her incredulous. Sita/Ferret had been particularly ordered to polish Emily's bed. The bed was made of wood and brass, the headboard tiled with oval tiles, each set in its own space and painted with pictures of peacocks. Having cleaned and polished the whole bed, Sita/Ferret had been exhausted and, like a tired animal, she had lain down on the floor and closed her eyes. When she had opened them again, she had found herself looking at the broad beam running under the middle of the bed, and she had groaned in despair. If she left it, Emily would notice and get her to do it twice over. But if she hadn't lain on the floor, she would never have seen it and wouldn't have done it anyway. Just in case, to save trouble later she decided she'd do it in five minutes flat and damn Emily. Sita/Ferret had picked up a big wodge of polish with her cloth, and lying on her back, had wiggled under and worked as hard as she could, putting on more pressure than she ever would normally. Something gave a little. Sita/Ferret had gulped, thinking she must have broken something; after all, the wood must have been hundreds of years old. She had put down the cloth, felt with her fingers. And thus discovered Emily's secret, and the route to her revenge.

Just over a week had passed since the night of Mr Kalyan's 'Indian Arts Exhibition'. A week in which she felt that her coat wasn't as warm as it used to be, a week in which she'd examine the jewellery of any woman near her; a week in which her wishing went from gems to grey eyes, from stoicism to longings, from desolation to hope, from denial to desire. A week since her reckless abandonment of certain dazzling items. She wished she'd worn them more, enjoyed their sheen on her skin, like a love that could have been.

At work Sita/Ferret did her best to keep to her old standards, but if Mr Kalyan had checked he would have been surprised to find that mistakes were being made and that the quantity of work had sagged a little.

Her eyes would often wander across to the telephone. No, it hadn't even tinkled with a thank-you call. Uncouth man!

She only had one telephone number in her memory. She called it.

'Good afternoon, Flotsam,' said the voice at the other end, immediately recognising Sita/Ferret's and showing no surprise at getting this call after an interval of many months.

'Good afternoon, Jetsam,' replied Sita/Ferret, too warmly, too enthusiastically. She always reacted like this to Jetsam's coolness, wanting to drag her out of her iceberg centre. They did not call it a friendship, both being wary of relationship words. They had met whilst working for the same charity organisation and instantly been intrigued by each other. Two Asians on a do-gooding stint! Paying for their karmic crimes? Gradually they had started socialising together, each counting the pennies all the while. They'd gone through a phase of going to children's movies: *Snow White and the Seven Dwarves, Beauty and the Beast, Aladdin*, and *The Little Mermaid*, and it was from *The Little Mermaid* that they adopted the names of Flotsam and Jetsam, the two eels who serve the Wicked Black Witch of the Sea. Sita/Ferret took Flotsam, saying that she had known two witches.

'I know a black witch, too,' Jeevan had said, and appropriated Jetsam.

Sita/Ferret and Jeevan never indulged in female exchanges of Asian-ness, Englishness, family-ness, the famines of the heart, the toils and troubles of precarious love. Sita/Ferret hadn't been ready to unzip herself and start the talking; Jeevan's words always had a safety guard around them.

And on the phone neither did they engage in small talk. Jeevan immediately launched into an arrangement, 'There's a new club, called *Sala-Sali*, dress code: Sari to Seductive, Lacy to Lascivious.'

'I don't know how to do Indian dancing,' replied Sita/Ferrret.

An exasperated sigh came from the other end. 'Look,' said Jeevan, patiently, 'it's not the place for classical Kathak or Ye Olde Harvest Dance from the *Pind*. It's House, Techno, Garage, Drum and Bass, whatever. With some Indian stuff thrown in. Like chucking in a few spices. Coming?'

'Sure.' She'd just have to take time out from her dizzy social whirl! They arranged to meet first, for a coffee. Neither could afford to eat out.

Jeevan was waiting for her, sitting at the table outside the café, her dark coat buttoned to her chin, red beret on her head, rolling herself a cigarette.

'It's an art, Flotsam,' she said, 'rolling your own,' as she gingerly licked the edge of the cigarette paper. The steam rose from their cups, Jeevan lit up, and Sita/Ferret became surprised by Jeevan talking. 'Look,' pointed

Jeevan at the people coming and going from the tube station. 'Have you ever seen so many Asians, all prettified in pinstripes and briefcases? Or the young women in high-powered suits. They're the new *babus*. The first *babus* serviced the Indian Civil Service, this lot are servicing the new empire. Shall we call the women, *babu babes*? And where are the new *babus* in the pecking order I ask you? Exactly where they were two hundred and fifty years ago!' Jeevan finished, not looking at Sita/Ferret, instead busying herself with relighting her roll-up. She had said too much. Too many words had rolled off her tongue.

Sita/Ferret risked a question of the personal kind. 'Were you born here?'

'Depends what you mean?'

'Biology and geography, did they combine? You damn well know what I...' Sita/Ferret began hotly but, and for the first time ever, Jeevan interrupted her.

'Stop. I'll tell you. But don't ever add biology and geography for me again. Agreed?' She waited till Sita/Ferret nodded. 'I grew up in a proper Indian home. In England-land. Here. In Englistan.' And then she hurtled on, as if she had an ending to get to. 'And when something happens, then homes can break up, can't they? Like, if a Black Witch comes along. And then, if it is...'

She stopped, and Sita/Ferret thought she'd stopped in mid-sentence. When she restarted it was as if from a different place.

'...it is said the Black Witch is not to be blamed, then what do you do? I used to think we shouldn't have come here; because if we'd stayed back home, it couldn't have happened. But then if a Black Witch is going to come, she'll come anyway. The fault is in the heart. Whether it's living in Hindustan, Englistan, the same heart, has the same weakness.'

Snapshot of the soul! The details would take a long time coming – if ever.

' "Door locked, against the tempest, I missed the summer",' Sita/Ferret quoted. Strike while the iron's hot, as they say, even if it were to take advantage of a vulnerable moment. 'Who's the Black Witch?' she asked Jeevan.

'Now, look at that,' Jeevan exclaimed, pointing her roll-up towards a young Asian man waiting by the tube entrance. 'I wouldn't mind some of that candy.' Jeevan meant it. She practised 'consenting lust', but never invited them back home, never allowed a relationship.

'You'd better be careful,' warned Sita/Ferret, eyes on Jeevan. 'He might be waiting for mummyji and if she saw you,' putting on an Indian accent, ' "good-hearted girl, working for the charity, helping the poor you know," she might decide to rush you both off to the temple. Seven times round the fire and you're done, Missus.' Still watching Jeevan.

'Then I'll have to "Hie me to an ashram," won't I?'

'How very traditional!' commented Sita/Ferret.

'Tradition and culture, Flotsam,' Jeevan replied with more cut in her voice than was ever there before, 'are no shield against the accidents of life. And accidents start long before they happen. Ten hours before or ten years before...' her voice like dry ice, '...or even two thousand, three hundred and twenty-three years ago. That's when India's accident began,' Jeevan hurtled on, '2-3-2-3 years ago. How's that for some snappy digits? That's when that cocky brat Alexander the Great came, saw, stole – and went back to the West to blab about the goodies in *Hindoostan*. You know, Hegel said, "India as a land of desire" formed an essential strand in the history of the West...'

'So what's it to you?' asked Sita/Ferret, interrupting her crudely. *And what're the E & C to me*, came the thought. She pulled her coat tighter around her; it just didn't keep her warm like it used to.

'Nothing,' Jeevan replied coolly. 'We're getting late. Let's go.'

'Answer my question!' Sita/Ferret's voice whipped at her, startling Jeevan. 'You go around like the fucking Mona Lisa, mystery woman with secrets to hide. Well I've got things to hide too, only half actually 'cos I've given half away. No one answers my questions. But no one gets away with that now. I won't let them.' *I'm coming to you, E & C.*

Jeevan had been staring at Sita/Ferret; she didn't know her hands had curled up, turning in upon themselves. Something had happened to Sita/Ferret too, perhaps another one of life's 'accidents'?

'It means that India was a strand of their history long before they ruled it. They were at each other's throats for it, and when England got it she stripped it bare. Then England became the Land of Desire.' Sita/Ferret was still looking mutinously at her. Jeevan slowly uncurled her hands.

'It's about poison, about what happens when you take something you shouldn't. I've got a quote for you too. "The truth, the whole truth and nothing but the truth." The purest, most abused words in history. But you have to go backwards to get it, you see?'

She'd have to go back to the Mausoleum to get it, you see.

'Now,' Jeevan was on her feet, slinging her bag onto her shoulder, 'let's go. Want to have the pick of the male merchandise, don't we?' She was off, Sita/Ferret running to catch up with her.

Jeevan's arms were honey-gold against her thin white dress. 'Lacy to lascivious,' she had said. Her springy, curly black hair had been tied back. The ambience of the club was high-tech orient, chrome and orange, glass and green, screen and image, from Birmingham to Bombay, from Ashrams to Aspirins, from Madonna to Madhuri. Jeevan and Sita/Ferret hovered on the sidelines watching, absorbing, and psyching themselves up. The crowd was mostly Asian, but many others were mixed in too, dressed in all the range from men in shalwar-kameez to women in belly tops and Doc Martens. As she looked, Sita/Ferret wondered at the history of each, and was jealous. They all had a background, whether they bucked against it or not.

The music was the hard, driving mix that Jeevan had said it would be, with a few filmi-fusion songs thrown in. When the hot rave favourites came on, the crowd became one mass of pumping energy. Jetsam and Flotsam were lost in that sea.

Hours later, sweat dripping off her, Sita/Ferret glugged water, and saw Jeevan come back in, her hair floating round her shoulders.

'Seen anything you want?' Jeevan shouted in her ear. Sita/Ferret shook her head. 'No need to be picky, it's not for the rest of your life.'

'Why not?' asked Sita/Ferret directly, breaking all their taboos. Jeevan would have to answer with a reason that could only come from inside herself.

'Because,' replied Jeevan, and moved away, plunging back into the mad, heaving crowd. Sita/Ferret followed her. She too had evaded Jeevan's question, unwilling to admit to promiscuous lust, to admit that she too had observed arms and shoulders, thighs and crotches in tactile desire, had imagined the choosing and coupling. But left it there. Sita/Ferret was not used to letting go.

Wiped out, wrung out like rags, they left as the screen flashed Nehru up with his immortal words: '…tonight we keep a tryst with destiny…'

'Rather early,' remarked Jeevan. 'Independence Day is a little way off.'

'You know, "August is a Wicked Month",' remarked Sita/Ferret, remembering a book with that title, and saw Jeevan staring back at her, a streak of grief across her. Jeevan turned and quickly climbed the stairs; Sita/Ferret followed, not knowing what she had unlocked. Outside, the streets were wet with rain. They walked in silence to the bus stop to wait for late-night buses. Their budgets did not run to taxis.

'I took a taxi last week,' admitted Sita/Ferret, and then couldn't resist prodding further. 'The Partition happened in August…'

'Shut up. If I ever tell you, you won't like it, you'll hate it, so just shut up.'

'So what? You think I'm a delicate little thing brought up in a fucking silk cocoon?'

Empty taxis passed by, cars with clouded windows, buses that were going to destinations other than theirs; they moved back, away from the kerb, so as not to get splashed. 'Alright then,' Jeevan said, as if making a momentous resolution. 'A for alright,' the man had said too.

Jeevan began, 'If you want to know so desperately, I'll make a bargain with you. You go on a little visit for me, and I tell you. Agreed?' Sita/Ferret hesitated. She should learn where the lines are drawn and not hover over Jeevan like a vulture. Then Jeevan spoke again, 'But you'll never look at me with the same eyes again. You'll always see something else.'

See what Jeevan saw? Kala had watched her, waited to see what she was; Jeevan it seems, had already made a patent of her; yet Sita/Ferret was the one who thought she didn't know herself. 'Agreed!' replied Sita/Ferret.

'You'll need to take the day off work,' Jeevan told her. 'For the visit. That's how the world changes, minute by minute.'

The next evening must have been affected by the night before, the dye of desire running through. The shift in Jeevan causing a reaction in her, the music still pumping in her head, the mad energy of the previous night still coursing in her blood, propelled her into the madness of paying Mr Gorgeous a visit. Since one had not yet been requested by him, she could only assume he must be extremely busy. He naturally must want her to start on her work for him straightaway. And since she didn't have any pressing social engagements, that very evening would appear the perfect time. She could always use the excuse of passing by. Any excuse.

It was a bitterly cold evening. Locking the door of Universal Enterprises, she belted her coat closer around her, checking the weight of the items in the hem. She couldn't afford to lose any more.

At the outer door to the mansion block, she craned her neck to look up, but being unfamiliar with the building, she couldn't possibly tell if any of the lighted windows belonged to his flat. Tempted to turn and go, she almost did, then chided herself for cowardice, her morning litany coming back to her. Sita/Ferret extracted her notebook and pen, tried to look casual, as well as efficient, and pressed the bell. No answer. She could leave. Her pride had been saved. Her stubborn finger pressed on the button again. The speaker remained silent, conveying the image of an empty flat. Disappointment spiked sharp. All the desire and nervous energy which had brought her here, lay rejected and flattened. Putting away the notebook and pen, she saw the keys in the inside pocket. Temptation into intimacy. What greater way to know someone than to explore their home in their absence? To see clothes tossed carelessly onto chairs, perhaps a letter lying open on a table, perhaps the bed still rumpled? Taking out the keys she glanced up.

She didn't take the lift, instead choosing to inflict a minor punishment upon herself. Following signs, wending through the warren of corridors, she came to number seventeen and quickly opening the door, squeezed through. Leaning against it, she waited for her breathing to slow, and for the feeling of being a thief to evaporate. Whether the accusation came from the flat or her mind, it still questioned her presence in his home behind his back. She shook her head, although there was nobody to answer. No matter how it looked, she wouldn't turn back now. Keeping on her coat, and again taking out her notebook and pen, she put herself in motion to do a job.

If she had gone into the reception room, the dining room, or any of the spare bedrooms, she would have had enough to occupy her. Instead she decided to work her way down the hall which ended at the door of the forbidden bedroom. Conscience is a gate, not a wall, and is susceptible to dishonourable reasoning. She reasoned. Her eyes would leave no trace, her footsteps no marks. She would neither disturb, nor steal. Carefully she turned the knob. A click and the door opened. If she did not step over the threshold could she still be accused of entering? She pushed the door wider and then to its full extent, hearing a faint thud as it hit the wall. A Spartan scene was laid out in front of her. An enormous old bed with a wooden headboard, covered by a beige spread, was against the opposite wall, and beside it a grandly carved cabinet with glinting metal worked into it. Not even Emily possessed anything so magnificent. An alarm clock, table lamp and a row of books lay on the top, some in Hindi and some in English. An image of solitary nights! She couldn't believe it.

She stepped over the threshold, glancing quickly around. At one end of the room, square-paned windows ran across the wall, heavy curtains, rug-like in their thickness, hung at the sides. They must be decades old. She touched them delicately, with a fingertip. They made her feel too young, too new, too flimsy. Her flesh and bones would turn to dust, but these curtains would still hang here, almost like sentinels. On the other side, an open door led into another room. She went through; telling herself she would glance around, fill in the spaces in her mind, and then quickly leave.

Only the air would know she'd trespassed. Only she would know that she had a little more of him inside her than before. The second room contained a massive old wardrobe, dressing table, and chest of drawers. Everything was closed, tidy, as if he wanted to know exactly what to expect when he returned. A door from this room led into a bathroom. She turned back to go out.

'Namaste!' He didn't fold his hands in the traditional greeting. Her heart went cold. There was nothing she could say to excuse this breach of privacy. 'Find anything interesting?' he asked.

'I'm sorry.'

'Only because you've been discovered. My keys,' holding out his hand. Her reply was odd. Shrugging off her coat, she held it out to him.

'You'll find the rest in the hem.'

'More stolen property!' He made no move to take it. 'Shall we move out of here.'

She followed him to the door.

'I need my keys, or I'll have to have the locks changed,' he said.

She took them out of her bag, slipped them into a pocket of the coat, placed the coat on his arm and left. The door slammed behind her.

At the tube station she paid the busker. Sita/Ferret always paid the busker. She arrived home with a shiver running through her body. She couldn't tell whether it was from the cold or the absence of the protective stones.

Chapter Nine

Bombay, 1943

And what is hell?

Hell, Emily would have told you, is the opposite of a miracle. She would also have said, if I'd known about the second, I would have done without the first.

Donald came to tell her. At first speaking in a roundabout way, trying to tell her without using the dreadful words, but seeing that he wasn't getting anywhere, sat down opposite her and spilled out the awful truth. Thomas had been found dead in a godown of cotton waste and oil in an area near the docks. Donald sighed and took her hand to comfort her. These were bad times, he told her, and no respectable Englishman was safe. Rebels were spreading dangerous ideas, and weak-minded fools followed them.

'How?' she asked, barely able to move her tongue, her whole body frozen. Her world come to a standstill – from security to danger in an instant.

'You don't need to know that, my dear.'

She stood up and screamed at him, her hands balled into fists, 'Tell me the truth! Now!'

Donald didn't know what to do. He had expected sobs and tears, expected to impart gentle comfort. He hadn't expected this white-hot rage. But then the husband had never run true to form either. He should have sent Linda and kept out of these women's affairs.

'He was stabbed. Very bad business! But we will do our best to look after you.'

'Why?' Emily shot back at him. Why did it have to be him whose promises were still unfulfilled. Why did it have to be her who was left abandoned? She had hardly tasted anything. Emily wailed inside herself.

Donald shook his head sadly, 'Hard to say, my dear. Thugs and dacoits roam the city pretending to be freedom fighters.'

'What was he doing there?' Why hadn't he been sitting in a decent office? Why had he been in a place where death was waiting for him?

Linda Wiggins came to visit her every day. His friends took care of the arrangements. An Englishman must be given a decent burial!

Emily went through the motions with a ghostly calm. At other times she'd be churning with fury. She swung from one extreme to the other. When the coffin was lowered into the ground, Emily couldn't help the sobs that tore out of her. That was her life being buried. Linda Wiggins put a hand on her arm.

Two weeks passed, some of his friends, and there weren't that many, came and gave condolences, offering their help. Monsieur Sauvage hinted that if funds were required for the return journey to England, he would be happy to help a lady in distress. They all took it for granted that she would be returning.

One day, as a grieving widow, Emily felt able to ask Linda Wiggins a personal question.

'Oh no, Donald's not going to marry me,' she replied, 'he'll get himself an unplucked rose from back home if he wants to. You'd better be getting yourself ready to go the other way, before we're all thrown out. Maybe we'll be rushing to catch up with you, things being as they are. Some of them have really got a bee in their bonnet about getting us out. But I've got nothing to go back to.'

Thomas had hated any mention of the word, 'Independence'. 'They'll never get rid of us,' he'd say. 'They know they can't manage without us. They'll go back to being a rabble of heathens. What about those of us who came late? We've got three hundred years to make up.' He didn't have to worry about time anymore. He had eternity!

After three weeks, Donald asked her plainly what arrangements he should make for her return. She shook her head, 'I don't know yet. It's too soon.'

England loomed like a black hole waiting to swallow her once and for all. Her enemies would be delighted at her downfall. She'd never have another chance to escape.

Emily did think about packing and leaving when the police inspector came to question her. Indian and not English as she would have expected; delivering his vowels with perfect ease, he questioned her about her husband's work. She denied any knowledge and evaded all questions about the names of friends and acquaintances, unwilling to cede anything to a native, arrogance and the snobbery of the new arriviste marking her manner. He had his revenge as he left, remarking that she should be thinking about returning for those from the English lower class could never hope to succeed here. She could see that he'd meant to say worse, but had changed the ending of his sentence. His eyes said it for him.

The news went round that she'd been visited by the police. Not Donald, but another whom she'd first met at Green's nightclub came and offered to fund her passage back. She shook her head again. He paid a month's wages to the servants and left. The visits of the others tailed off.

Linda Wiggins came to visit and looked at her with knife-sharp eyes saying, 'Don't imagine you're going to dig riches out of the ground! Don't go thinking you're a real memsahib!'

Emily spent all her nights alone now, but the luxury of the extra bed-space was no longer the pleasure it had been. She'd look at the other side, where he had been, and remember his face, the glowing eyes and the smiling lips, which had promised so much. She too had made promises, and had kept her side of the bargain. His promises became her charge sheet against him, her first accusation against him being his death. She had learnt enough now to know that he'd worked the wrong side of the law. He had probably thought his skin made him immune. What a surprise it must have been when the knife slid in and sliced breath from body. He was responsible for the dire circumstances she was in. If he had never promised, she would never have listened. The corrosion of promises unfulfilled!

Lying in bed, she listened to the night sounds of a foreign land. A dog bayed far away. Its yowls were no immediate threat, but Emily knew they might be yet, for she had no defence – there was no one to filter the outside. No one to stand by her side.

She could go back to England. No loss of prestige in a widow returning home. But Emily's hands were empty. No fortune, not even a small nest egg from her husband to see her through her days; she would be back where she had started, and she had hated where she had started. Her ears picked up the sound of distant thunder. Getting out of bed, she opened the shutters. Black clouds hung in the sky. Her eyes travelled to the horizon, seeing the far-away rip of lightning.

When Thomas had taken her out on excursions or to watch the evening sunsets, she'd had to force her eyes to travel the distances in front of her, the space and breadth overwhelming her. Accustomed to a world bounded by walls and terraced houses, the open expanse created a strange feeling, as if she would dissolve in this limitless space, and the tiny speck that was her would be blown away by the wind. She'd stand by him holding his hand and see that he had no such fear. He saw something else in the scene in front of him.

Tonight she trained her eyes on the thunderous horizon, turning the gold band round and round her finger. This, thought Emily, is the cause of all my troubles. Sliding the ring off, a huge blast of thunder crashed above her; startling and shaking her, the ring fell out of her hand and rolled away. Trying to follow its sound, she crawled across the floor on her hands and knees. Sheets of rain suddenly poured down, hitting flat roofs, tin sheeting, and blowing into the room. She moved back to close the shutters, just in time to see the white knife of lightning splitting the dark.

Pulling the shutters forward, but not completely closing them, she crouched by the window, becoming damp with the rain that fell through, watching the street turn into a river, someone's stall overturn, and dogs bark madly somewhere.

Thunder rampages through the sky, but its real arena is inside the skull, where every crack reverberates, mixes fear with guilt, and threatens retribution. Emily's mind telegraphed a defence to the heavens, pleading that she was a foreigner caught in a foreign storm; its threatening must not be visited upon her. The answering roar seemed to dive straight towards her, she who had journeyed here for the sake of vanity and greed, whose heart had bartered false promises of love for equally false promises of earthly rewards. The punishing zigzag split the sky again, and Emily didn't know that she whimpered.

The world is a broken bowl.

The lightning did kill. The next day she learnt from her servant woman that a brother and sister, young innocents in their teens, returning from some journey had been struck down.

Throwing a shawl over her shoulders, demurely covering her head, and taking her servant woman with her, Emily went to take a look. The two lay side by side, their skin horribly blistered and burnt. The grieving group around them moved to give her space, or perhaps to keep away from her. All courtesy double-edged! She lowered her eyes, knelt, intending to say a prayer. To look on merely as a tragedy tourist would have made her days even more precarious. As she put her hands together she became aware of the glaring omission on her finger. None of the prayers from godfearing childhood days came to give meaning to the movement of her lips.

On her return she went down on her hands and knees and painstakingly searched the whole room, and eventually discovered the ring lodged in a hole in the floor. If the hole had been a fraction wider she would have lost it. Slipping it back on didn't bring the expected nostalgia for that day aeons ago, when she had stood in a church, a veil over her eyes, and watched the ring travel along her finger; she had thought of it as a harbinger, a gilded barge, a golden door, and been overwhelmingly grateful to him.

Thunderbolts that she had thought destined for her had struck down others. Emily decided that lives hung on sheer chance. You could be destroyed either by people or the elements. Or you could get off scot-free. There was no right and wrong, no fate dishing out rewards and punishments. Your only chance came from what you could do.

Each morning Emily awoke with immediate rememberings of what had been done to her. He had duped her, tricked her, made a fool of her and ruined her life. What greater damage can a person do to another?

Three days after the storm, Emily dressed neatly and went to St Christopher's Mission School, enquiring as to the possibilities of a position. The headmistress, a nun with busy practical eyes, listened to her story, expressed her deepest sympathy and advised her to return home: 'These are changing times. Who knows what turmoil will come our way.'

Thomas used to say, when he was alive, 'The gates are starting to move, you've got to work hard and you've got to work fast. You've got to take what you can.'

On the way back she took a detour around Winchester Colony, stopping to stare and glare at the moneyed houses and gardens beyond the gates. These people didn't have to worry about gates clanging shut, they'd been here for generations; long enough to have property and spoils here, and property and spoils Over There. Emily had a vision of loaded ships sailing away carrying their goods to give them as good a life Over There as over here.

The next day Emily dressed neatly but more attractively, making sure her face powder and lipstick were in place, and went to Mademoiselles, 'the exclusive dress shop for ladies of fashion!' The owner of Mademoiselles listened to Emily's request, inquired into her circumstances, and in words of plummy diction declined the offer of her services. Emily understood the intended comparison. Embarrassment and hate rose within her. This rigidly coifed and *maquillaged* woman had been happy enough to take their money when Thomas had brought Emily here for purchases.

Her anger shimmered as fiercely as the sun, blazing down on all. Dismissing the rickshaw she had come in, she started to walk back to her rooms, laying claim to the earth she walked on with each step. Stopping at a cheap roadside stall, she bought a plate of food, and ate it standing at the side. Passers-by looked curiously at her, some doubling back for a better look, unable to believe what they were seeing; ragged children pointed and giggled; women looked at her and glanced quickly away, embarrassed for her, astonished that an unaccompanied memsahib should be standing on the road like a vulgar person, and eating from one of these stalls where the food is full of dirt. Emily's tongue burnt with the unadulterated spices and chillies, but she continued to put portion after portion into her mouth, breaking the puris, scooping up the chana, turmeric staining her fingers. Unaccustomed to eating with her hands, some dropped onto her clothes and Emily's rage grew. A car worked its way through the jumble of traffic. As it drew abreast, the cool Englishwoman inside stared at Emily. Didn't she know it was rude to stare? Emily stared back, counting each item: the driver at the wheel, the Indian servant in the front, the children in the back, the woman's haughty eyes, the shiny gloss on the car, and the deference. Emily totted them all up. She was owed!

The next day Emily rearranged her speaking tones and wended her way to 'Clara's London Designs'. The manageress wore black with a brooch on the shoulder, and pretended that she wasn't Anglo-Indian. With practised charm and courtesy, she listened to Emily's sentences. Emily kept her back straight, her hands in her lap, and enunciated her words with care.

'You are looking for a position until you can find another man to marry?' the woman asked her.

'No,' declared Emily, half truthfully. Marriage had left a bitter taste in her mouth, and she wasn't keen to rush into matrimony again. On the other hand, it was the only option open to her.

'There's no need to pretend,' replied the manageress, 'what else are you to do? There are many like you. Some give tuition, pretending to be very high-class ladies, pretending they are only doing it because they have so much time on their hands and they get terribly bored,' acting out ennui. 'For those positions an introduction is absolutely necessary.' Emily could polish her speaking manner, but she had no access to the networks of introductions. No doubt they had been here for generations too and had their webs well in place. The manageress continued, 'Some become seamstresses. Do not imagine that garments actually...and some,' quickly switching to another topic, 'some find other ways of maintaining themselves.' A pause to let that sink in. She didn't offer Emily a job, but the same advice as all the others. Return home, for her own good.

They'd given her such a send-off, as they would remember all their lives! If she was really lucky, she might get her job back at the factory. Perhaps even be working next to Maureen. She had come halfway round the world and had less than when she'd started off.

Leaving 'Clara's' she walked through the crowded streets. People either stepped out of her way or commented quietly as she passed. To those that stared at her, she stared boldly back, beating them down with the aggression in her eyes. She turned into a narrower street where people, bicycles and animals jostled each other, and traders looked out from cubby-hole openings, their wares displayed on poles hung out across the street. A thin man, composed merely of bones and dark flesh, was selling *bhajia* in a tiny niche he had established for himself. He sat cross-legged behind a bubbling vat, dropping in balls of mixture, spooning out the cooked ones, putting cooked portions in newspaper cones, pouring chilli chutney on top, taking payment, dropping in more mixture and so on. A continuous circle of endeavour. Emily counted him into her tally. Emily knew the words and asked for a cone. The long lashes on the thin face lifted and lowered at her request, a cone came into her hand, his freed hand automatically opening to take payment, while the other continued with its work. A break in the circle suddenly registered with him as his outstretched hand remained empty. His eyes shot up and met Emily's burning blue ones before she turned away, clutching the cone tight in her hand. He shouted after her, but Emily continued without a backward glance. He sprang up and ran after her, words hurtling out of his mouth. Emily stopped and screeched back at him. His voice rose higher and higher too, neither understanding a word of the other. A crowd gathered around them, puzzled by the unusual sight of a memsahib engaged in a public row. The man made a grab for the cone; others sprang forward to hold him back while one tried to talk to Emily in English, trying to explain the obvious.

'India's fucking mine,' Emily retorted, clutching the cone to her, the red chutney seeping out and staining her dress. The hissed warning of 'polise, polise,' snaked through the crowd who quickly dispersed. The English-speaking one took Emily's arm to move her away, then suddenly dropped his hand, mindful of the penalties of touching a white woman. The *bhajia* man's friends forcibly moved him away, trying to din into him the inevitable repercussions to livelihood, family and future. He allowed himself to be led away, complaining grievously of the theft; back at his niche, burnt *bhajia* sizzled in the fat, while his pan of mixture had been overturned, a creamy pool soaking into the ground.

Emily had moved off in the opposite direction, not hearing voices lower or cease altogether as she passed, clutching the remnants of a cone smeared with chutney and crumbs.

That evening Emily counted the days she could survive. They amounted to less than a month. Taking a shawl and calling the woman servant, she went out for a walk though it was already dark. The small shops and stalls were still doing business, *laltens*, small lamps, hanging at the sides. Emily walked the streets and narrow alleys, yet her mind went further, encompassing the vastness of the land that stretched away, horizon upon horizon. In this magnitude, there had to be something for her; she was insignificant in comparison to all the others, so whatever she took would also be insignificant, and only important to her. One day, she too would send cargo in ships sailing back to Over There, and herself return in style! The servant woman whispered that they should turn back, that it was very late. Emily complied, opening and shutting her hands, her mind worrying at ways, means, casting about for the raw material.

There came a point, when she realised there is no such thing as raw material.

Champa unhooked the little necklace and locket, and carefully put them back in their box marked 'London, England'. This she placed in a little metal box, and locked the box away in a steel trunk. Dressed for the evening, her thick hair coiled into a bun, she carefully applied lipstick to the full contours of her lips. Then she took a little brass pot, decorated and fashioned in the shape of a vase; the little stick that went into it had a fan-shaped top with tiny little bells that dangled from it. Every time Champa used it, tinkling sounds accompanied her movements. Withdrawing the stick and shaking off the excess black powder, Champa placed it on her lower eyelid, and closing her eyes, drew the stick across, quickly blinking as she dipped it again and drew it through the other eye. Grains always got onto the eyeball itself, filling her eyes with water. She dabbed at them.

The Girl had brought the news to her, words tumbling out in a rush. Champa had slapped her hard across her face and told her to have respect.

Late morning was the time for visits by the 'Soiree Sisters'. Champa had endured the visit about his death. Knowing they would come, she had steeled herself beforehand. Resignation and astonishment was the tone Champa adopted: resignation to the twists of fate, 'always hard to lose a valuable customer'; astonishment that a gentlemanly sahib like him could have met with such a fate.

Today the Soiree Sisters came in ones and twos and threes. The system of visiting worked on some unspoken principle. Today it was Champa, tomorrow someone else, and on a third day perhaps no one. The Girl was kept busy bringing drinks, tea and snacks. When she wasn't needed, she sat behind the curtain, listening.

At the moment, the topic was Emily and her continued residence. None could understand why she was still hanging around. Life in England, the rulers' land, must be so much better than here, so much grander and luxurious, so why didn't she pack her bags and go?

'Perhaps she's looking around for another husband,' suggested one. 'She didn't have the first one for very long, she needs her "entertainment",' arousing titters from the others.

'Then why did he come to our plumpy chumpy Champa? *Hai*, look at her,' in sorrowful tones, running a finger along Champa's cheek, 'here is the one missing him. So pale she is growing.'

'It's my pocket that's missing him,' replied Champa. Cynicism was de rigeur.

'So, tell us, Champa,' asked another, moving a little closer, winding a strand of Champa's hair round her finger. 'What did he like? Any especial specialities?'

'They don't have the imagination,' she answered back, inviting their smiles, forcing down the feeling of disloyalty. 'Cold land, cold heart, cold everything.'

'So he needed a lot of heating up?' teased another.

'But what is his beautiful *bibi* needing now?' Champa asked of them, attempting to change the course of the conversation.

'She's alone!' This stark truth came from Acid Eyes. English ladies are never alone. There must be something strange about Emily.

The Girl hovered invisibly around Emily. Waiting for her to demonstrate her power. Emily was of the ruling class, the ones that had the power; therefore each one of them was powerful. The Girl assumed that Emily must be waiting for something to happen, for one of her male relations to arrive and escort her back. Emily would ride away in a car. Once she followed Emily's servant, hung around to hear her talk as she purchased vegetables for the day, heard her complaining of her mistress' stingy ways. The Girl could hardly believe it.

The Girl was there when an Indian gentleman drove Emily back to her rooms one day. Like an addict of a soap opera, The Girl was also there when the servants left – and when the bags came out, with Emily following, and travelled to a cheap boarding house. The Girl was in the shadows and about to leave when the same Indian gentleman went up to Emily's room, and stayed.

She felt a shock, as if she had been betrayed. But her busy mind started working at this new information, and eventually comprehension dawned, and spawned an attitude. However she didn't tell Champa. It hurt The Girl to have to keep something from Champa. Up to now, every scrap of news, gossip and information had been served up to her. But for reasons of her own, Champa had placed Emily on a pedestal.

Chapter Ten

London, February 1997

'Afraid? No fear! Not me – I'm gonna go see Emily.'

With nothing left to lose it was the only route to choose. Two weeks had passed and not even a thank-you note from a particular person. Such bad manners! Just as well she was never going to see him again! What a relief!

As usual she was busy with her chores, her reading and her work. She spent even longer at work than usual, being meticulously perfectionist. She'd bought a new cheap coat for herself and hated wearing it. She waited for Jeevan to announce the date for the visit, for the bargain to be fulfilled. She could have agreed to do the visit out of her so carefully nurtured morality. So she was as shabby as anyone else! There were no saints these days, and heroes had to be certified by history. Sita/Ferret felt that she was nothing more than shreds of feeling, mourning for what she had given away, grieving for the magical hopes that had sprung up and wilted. *You must have one thing on the outside and yourself on the inside, or they will eat you up*: Champa's lessons to the child who had screamed, 'I want...' Not good enough, raged Sita/Ferret twenty years later. There has to be some kind of truth in the world. Perhaps she should ask Jeevan, but Jeevan had only just begun. She'd have to wait. In the meantime Sita/Ferret's focus had become enlarged and sensitised, as if looking at life through a magnifying glass: unhappiness and suffering swilled through the world, ninety-nine per cent man-made. Why should she think herself special? And now there was something new that had come up; the future stood in front of her demanding its dues. No more sheltering behind glittering stones.

'Mrs Pandey.' Mr Kalyan had come down to the basement. There was a cut above his left eye. 'Come sit, we must have a talk.' Her heart quailed. Talks were dangerous! They held meanings, changes.

She sat down by the desk, a black ceramic figure of Krishna in her hand; Krishna the seductive, Krishna the lover. Dipping the corner of a cloth in oil, she started cleaning the figure with it. 'I am negotiating to move into premises in...' Mr Kalyan's voice filled with pride, '...in Mayfair! Poonum will be in overall charge, but you will be in everyday charge.' The beauties of language. Poonum would crack the whip, and she'd have to jump to her orders.

'Actually, Mr Kalyan, back-room work suits me. So I'll carry on with this end of the work.'

Mr Kalyan looked as taken aback as if she'd just turned down a million. 'But Mrs Pandey, you cannot spend your whole life hidden in a basement.' Then she nearly jumped as he patted her on the shoulder. 'Sorrows come in every life. Sad, sad time for you.' Dead right! One day she's carrying round a coat full of glittering goodies, the next day, she can't even afford a paste ring from Woolworths. 'You have had a tragedy in your life.' He nodded his head in sympathy.

Sita/Liar! Poonum must have told Daddy about the hubby who had died an untimely death. Sita/Ferret sighed, dipped her cloth in the oil again, and concentrated on polishing the figure of Krishna. Krishna, the one who had been brought up by a woman who wasn't his mother; the same story gets spun round a thousand times, but the heart still hurts.

The sigh had reached Mr Kalyan. He said, 'Life has many troubles.' This promotion of pretence was no good. She'd better think about leaving. Though she didn't yet know what her next step should be. She had removed herself from her do-gooding days.

'And now you are alone,' continued Mr Kalyan. (*Which makes for a perfect employee* was what he really meant.) 'You must remember we are always here to help you, Mrs Pandey.' She nodded her thanks, as if too overcome to speak. 'There is another area we must explore,' Mr Kalyan announced, he was full of plans and projects today. Did he need to make a quick move? Was Steven Singh on his tail? 'Here I am, bringing things from India, paying for shipping, packing, paying taxes at every step, when there is no need! England is already full of Indian art, furniture, antiques. There are English houses full of everything Indian,' moving his head from side to side, practically waggling it – he donned this Peter Sellers Indian persona occasionally, English people loved it. 'Did you not say this once?' Sita/Ferret shook her head quickly, not looking up. 'I would like you to investigate, Mrs Pandey. And then we can expand our work.' She could start with the Mausoleum. Its contents would keep Mr Kalyan going longer than the contents of a hundred crates. 'You are spending too much time in this basement. This will be a chance for you to get out, visit many different places. We will start...'

'No thank you, Mr Kalyan. I'd like to stay here. I'm really best at back-room work.'

Mr Kalyan's temperature rose, but he pushed it back down. 'Mrs Pandey, if something needs to be done, I expect it to be done. We can discuss this again.' She guessed he was rethinking his plans without the wonderful Mrs Pandey as his prime employee. He rubbed his hands, 'There is another idea which is very, very interesting. Something new. Rajesh is selling his club...'

'Rajesh?' she echoed.

'Perhaps you were introduced to him as Kala. He should be using his proper name now. He is selling and going to India. I am wondering...' The figure in her hands, Krishna the kala, slipped, fell all the way to the floor and crashed. Broken pieces shivered and juddered on the floor till they were still.

Accidents happen long before they happen. Her eyes travelled up from the floor to Mr Kalyan. His hands were in his coat pockets; she remembered that this was a man who walked a tightrope. His voice came out like spliced wire, 'That's why I'm sinking into the sewer. You're destroying me from behind. People who hide in basements have something to hide.'

A is for accusation. Everyone points the finger at each other over mistakes, broken dreams, missing pennies; entire families tear each other apart; entire countries accuse each other. The world bubbles like a cauldron with this word.

'I can't trust anyone,' Mr Kalyan was shouting. 'I pay for everything, I pay for everyone, I pay for you,' finger jabbing at her, 'you take my money and hate me...'

'No, Mr Kalyan...' but her voice hardly came out. Once only, had she broken a plate in Emily's house. Emily's anger had made her bones shiver: 'trying to destroy me? Nasty little brat! *She* wanted to put her filthy low-class claws on my goods. You don't even have the brains to do that.'

'...you are all like this,' Mr Kalyan's voice brought her back; she'd missed half his indictment, '...wanting fur coats, wanting money all the time. You women, dancing naked in the street!' His hand banged on the table. 'I can't trust anyone. How much of my property have you destroyed?

Or. do you give to others to sell? Stealing from me!' Suddenly, as if something had been cut, he stopped, quickly turned and went upstairs.

Kneeling down, Sita/Ferret started to collect the pieces, making a pile in one hand, when the ringing of the phone cut through her raw nerves and the whole lot fell on the floor again.

'Good evening!' Jeevan! 'Working to the last minute? Your employer should give you a pay rise.'

'My employer's ready to kick me out.' *Thief! Traitor!* Was that Emily's voice or Mr Kalyan's?

Jeevan didn't pick up on it and demand an explanation. Complete self-sufficiency was what she aimed for, filling her days with work and activities, from karate to weight training, from psychology to history classes. 'Can you do the visit next week?'

'And that's when you'll tell me?' Shylock Sita/Ferret!

'It's not always good to know,' Jeevan replied. 'Vultures only get dead pickings.'

'That'll do me.'

Jeevan gave her the details and rang off. Sita/Ferret tried to pick up the pieces of the broken Krishna again. Once broken forever gone. Once dead forever silent. She'd given up asking her questions, especially when she got older, for then she felt embarrassed to do so, because they would reveal a foolish childishness within herself. She was too old for questions like, 'Who is my mummy?', 'Where is my mummy?', 'Who is my daddy?', 'Who am I?'. She imagined herself putting a finger on the doorbell of the Mausoleum. Emily would have to be the one to open it now. Sita/Ferret could also imagine a Black Maria come to fetch her double quick.

Suitable recompense is required. The words echoed in her mind. She could only have heard it at the Mausoleum, and it could only have come from Emily. Perhaps there was a meeting point between her and Emily after all. She was feeling as fragmented as the broken Krishna. In the shifting of a second, in the utterance of a word, your world can change its face. Mr Kalyan was not to know that since leaving the Mausoleum she had promised herself to be truthful, decent and honest. Poonum would have told her that's one promise broken for starters.

She wrote her resignation letter and decided to leave early while he was still upstairs at his desk so she could hand it to him personally.

'No, no, Mrs Pandey,' Mr Kalyan exclaimed. 'You must not get upset over a little thing. I will not accept this. The problem is, I am too busy, too many things to look after. I think it is that modern thing. Stress,' nodding his head sagely. 'When I came from India, we worked like dogs, like animals, we said "yes sir", "no sir"...' Sita/Ferret noticed a faraway feeling in his voice. '...But we did not have stress. So Mrs Pandey, we will put this here,' throwing the letter in the bin. 'You can pay for the broken article and order another one. Nothing more to say.'

'You said, Sir, that you couldn't trust me.'

'I am sorry. I apologise.'

But trust can't be given or retracted in cycles. 'Perhaps you're right,' she replied, 'and maybe it is time for me to come out of the basement. Goodbye, Sir.'

She decided she would go shopping, and then back to the quiet house of Mrs Rayit to rest her weary bones. She felt like she was a hundred years old. Perhaps on the way she'd buy herself a treat. *Treats are for failures!* came Emily's voice. 'Go to hell,' came Sita/Ferret's reply.

'Are you talking to me?' asked a belligerent voice next to her. He was a professional-looking gentleman, all suit-boot and tie, with an aggression level in the red-hot zone. The dangers of the city come in many guises! Sita/Ferret apologised profusely and walked fast to outstrip him. Machete maniacs, gun-toting murderers, knife-wielding killers roam the streets of the metropolis. She had learned it was no foolishness to look at someone and wonder how dangerous they may be.

Sita/Ferret got off at her tube station, and was nearly flattened on the stairs as a group of teeny-boppers in shiny dresses and sparkly shoes rushed past her. Friday night fever! Sita/Ferret felt like a pious nun whose faith had gone missing. She shopped for her essentials, going in and out of the Asian shops, hovering behind people, eavesdropping on snatches of stories or complaints about 'him', or 'them' or 'her'. She sniffed the aromas in each shop, eyed the shopkeepers and wondered what they had been through to have come to this point. Where had they first been born? Why and how far had they travelled?

Ghetto was not a word much used to describe this area. Poverty had been kept at bay by a single-minded concentration on earning money and saving it. The people had their small terraced houses with central heating, the good-quality second-hand cars, food in the fridge, a VCR in the lounge, gold jewellery in its hiding place, and ambitions of every kind. 'Faith will see you through!' promised the poster on the church wall as she went further up the road and spied Mr Steven Singh unloading sacks of onions from a van.

'Hi,' she greeted brightly.

He turned round startled, a sack over his shoulder and sweat running down his face.

'The first-class worker!' he beamed at her. ' 'ang on, let me get rid of this,' he said, dumping the sack onto a trolley. Wisps of onionskin hung in his hair; damp patches stained his T-shirt, his pony-tail hung limp behind him. 'You live round here then?' he asked. She told him the name of the street. 'My mate and his missus live down there, number twenty-six. Give them a shout if you need anything. I'm working here for a while; it's my friend Sukey's shop. How's your boss?'

'Fine,' she lied.

'That won't last for long,' retorted Steven Singh, emphatically. 'I'm going up north to see some of the old boys who used to be around at that time. A couple have gone to India and if I have to, I'll go there too. Hey, what d'ya like?' suddenly changing his tone. 'Cauliflower? Cabbage?' She laughed and said goodbye, but he picked up a cauliflower and walked with her until she took it. One took her jewels; the other gave her a cauliflower.

Sita/Ferret was covered in confetti. A couple were on the run, laughing and holding hands, others chased after them, throwing showers of confetti. She watched them drive away. Love and belonging! Possessing and being possessed! Marriage was still the bank into which people deposited their love. And the whole world queued up to participate. Sita/Ferret had tried to join the queue too.

Two years earlier, she had taken herself off to an Asian marriage bureau. In the process of taking the details, the lady had asked Sita/Ferret about her material situation. Did madam 'possess a house, a car, a good salary?' Sita/Ferret had been astonished and said shouldn't the man be providing this? Mrs Desai had stopped and turning to face her, had explained this was the twentieth century, soon to be the twenty-first century, that these days everyone must contribute their share to an arrangement; if she thought that was wrong, then, Mrs Desai had smiled and said, 'There is always love, which is blind, knows no barriers, and wouldn't dream of asking material questions. Until afterwards!' Mrs Desai's Modern Marriage Bureau had given her two introductions. The first was a man in computers who had immediately told her of his house, earnings, Porsche and said that previously all his girlfriends had been English, but he'd like to meet a nice Asian girl. 'What if she isn't nice?' Sita/Ferret had asked. 'That will be even more interesting,' he had replied. Dislike had formed at those words. If Sita/Ferret had been better versed in the flora and fauna of the British-Asian world, she would have been able to place him with fine precision in his particular niche.

The second introduction had been a teacher who had said that the permissive society was all very well for the middle classes: 'they have jobs, property, cars, and even trust funds. When they change husbands or wives, they just re-organise a few things like addresses or telephone numbers. The working classes copy them and end up in grief.' Sita/Ferret had been very keen on him, thinking that here was an ordinary, down-to-earth man. She had assured him that she possessed all the domestic virtues, 'I can do cooking, cleaning and boot polish.' The meeting had been going very well, till he had asked about her family and she had said, 'I don't know.'

She was longing to be at home now, looking forward to closing Sangeeta Rayit's door and enjoying the peace and safety of that orderly house. Sangeeta Rayit was a stickler for cultural exactitude, discipline, and hard work. She got up at five o'clock every morning to put in two hours' study on her law course, as well as working late into the night. At the breakfast table, she practised times-tables and spellings with her daughters, insisted they call Sita/Ferret 'Auntyji,' in time-honoured Indian tradition, and took them to religious and Hindi classes. Sangeeta Rayit fulfilled all her responsibilities. She was an essential piece in the jigsaw that makes up community and culture.

Looking forward to a hot bath and bed, a sleep that would last forever, she opened the front door carefully and closed it gently, in case the girls woke up, and was greeted by a gale of laughter from the kitchen. Eight or so men and women were crowded into the kitchen, some gathered around the table, others leaning against the worktops or the walls. Mrs Sangeeta Rayit, dressed in a silky top and long skirt, was stirring a bowl of liquid while someone else poured from a bottle. Oranges and apples floated on the top.

Sita/Ferret stood at the door, clutching her shopping.

'Come and join us,' invited Sangeeta. 'Everyone, this is my new lodger, Mrs Pandey. Now be respectful.' 'Hello's, 'hi's and nods came her way.

'Forget the cooking,' said Sangeeta, 'and drink this up.' Sita/Ferret put down her bags, and taking the drink held out to her, indulged in a dainty sip. If the empty bottles on the table were any indication, this concoction had more spirit in it than the temple and church in the market. Sangeeta reeled off names: Akshay, Vijay, Nisha, Raman, Leena, Sukhi and Jas. All Asian thirty-somethings. It wasn't clear if these were couples who'd

110

already paired off, or if they were cool about connections. Sita/Ferret looked for wedding rings and found them on the fingers of most. The one called Jas was busy with a tobacco and paper job, lining up his carefully-rolled efforts on a plate.

'Are the girls sleeping?' asked Sita/Ferret, the prude in her worried about the effect of this unbridled partying on young minds.

'Girls! Children!' Mrs Sangeeta Rayit shivered with horror. 'Don't mention those words again.'

'She's locked them in the cellar,' answered Akshay of the checked shirt. 'Good riddance to the brats!'

Nisha, in the spangled T-shirt, handed out glasses. Everyone held them up as she counted out, 'One, two, three…go!' Glasses turned up, throats gulped. Sita/Ferret watched in a mixture of surprise and disapproval. Leena, in the tight black skirt, banged hers down first. 'One!'

'Two!' shouted Sukhi, whose rounded stomach testified to well-established drinking patterns. The others followed suit, shouting out their number, till Jas' glass joined the rest.

'Number eight, you are a disgrace,' admonished Sangeeta, refilling his glass.

'He's always slow,' complained Leena.

'Better than being too fast,' Raman replied. Giggles and laughter came from the women. Sangeeta refilled Jas' glass and handed it back to him.

'One, two, three…' the rest chanted till he had drained it to the bottom, and ended with a round of applause. Jas shook his head, and taking one of his rolled creations, lit it and inhaled deeply. Sangeeta punctiliously refilled glasses, then looked suspiciously over at Sita/Ferret.

'You a teetotaller or something?' Sita/Ferret shook her head and demonstrated her enthusiasm for alcohol by taking a few more sips.

'Wow!' Sangeeta expressed her admiration. 'Cards, everyone, in the other room.' Sangeeta and most of the posse moved off. Jas offered her his smoke. She took it, but it was obvious that she was an amateur at inhaling. The puffs coming straight back out.

'Ever had this before?' he asked, taking it back from her.

'Of course,' she replied. Inexperience is the eighth deadly sin.

'Do you all have children?' she asked, fishing.

'We have our quota.' A wave of laughter and arguing from the lounge pulled at them. She stood, undecided whether to stay or absent herself.

'Do you have these parties often?' she asked.

'Meaning, do I come here often?' He laughed. She hadn't meant that at all. 'Yes we do. Drink up; you're not going to enjoy yourself if you don't join in. One, two, three…' She emptied half her glass. She often held back from the brink. There was only her to look after her. 'You won't catch up that way,' he informed her.

An hour later, she was doing her very best to catch up, and was draining her third glass. But the others were way ahead of her. This was a group that drank, smoked, and pursued their pleasures with determination. The alcohol had begun its intoxicating changes, her vision had deepened, as if the world had taken on extra colour, her body felt sweet and soft, willing for one desire to lead to another.

'Who's married to who?' she asked Raman, through her haze, and received a little shock to her melting state.

'We don't ask those kinds of questions,' Raman replied sharply. 'Whatever you're thinking, keep it to yourself. We're adults. We work ourselves ragged, we obey our mothers-in-law, and once in a while we do exactly as we damn well please. And if you don't like it, go sit in your room and feel superior.'

No fun in feeling superior. What she needed was a refill. She gingerly made her way to the kitchen, she had to be careful because the world had lost some of its gravity and was not quite so fixed anymore. Akshay of the checked shirt was just coming out. They met in the doorway of the kitchen. Neither moved back or aside. She lifted a finger, 'One, two, three…' counting the buttons on his shirt, '…seven! And one hidden away, or is it two?'

'You'll have to find out,' said Akshay. Putting her hand round his neck she pulled him down. The barriers inside her shivered at this intimacy with another's flesh while the fear of surrender rose within. She quashed it with determination; she had relinquished the goods. She was free. Moving closer against him as his hand roved up and down her back, she tasted drink and smoke, felt the stubble on his chin, the slope of his shoulders.

The doorbell pealed. Akshay lifted his head, blinking. Sangeeta came out and took a good look at them. 'Enjoying yourself are you?' she asked dryly. Akshay's hands pulled on her again, and she closed her eyes to swim into the honey darkness.

'Someone to see you, Mrs Pandey,' Sangeeta came back with Kala behind her. 'Didn't know you were expecting company.'

'No. Hello.' Had she conjured him through an alcoholic alchemy? Putting her hand to her head to help her focus, hot embarrassment washed through her – he had witnessed the privacy of lust.

'I'm sorry,' he apologised, 'I needed to talk to you.'

'I'm all out of hidden fortunes,' leaning against the wall to steady herself.

'We'll leave you to it,' said Sangeeta, pulling Akshay away, her eyes mocking the quiet Mrs Sita Pandey.

Kala looked thinner and tired, dark shadows had formed under his eyes. Hardly the face of a man rejoicing in a load of dosh!

'What a surprise. Never thought I'd see *you* again,' she accused.

'Sorry to disappoint you. How drunk are you?'

'Not enough,' she retaliated.

'We can't talk here. We'd better go to my place.'

'I was told to get out last time.'

'You deserved it. We'll drive with the windows open...'

'So I can catch pneumonia.'

'And then I'll make lots of B for black, coffee.'

'And C for coffee? How about B for boring? How come you never get to D?'

He winced. 'Does alcohol always bring out the sweet side of you? I'll sprinkle some *ganga-pani* to soothe that savage breast. Shall we go?'

'What an irresistible invitation,' she replied sarcastically, the only way she could defend herself. If he'd invited her to look at his fish tank she would have gone crawling.

He opened every window: not a word as they drove through the cold night air; not a word till he'd lit the fire. Some men drink, some men gamble, some men watch TV; he lit his coal fire. The tips of his fingers were covered in black. She could have licked them clean. Not a word till he put a cup of coffee in her hand, and then asked, 'Who was the bloke?'

'Who?' Pretending.

'Your East-End Rom-e-o.'

'Oh, him! Someone's husband.'

'More stolen goods!' Bastard!

'How did you get my address?' she asked.

'You told me the first time.' He must have burnt it into his brain.

'I heard you were selling up and going to India,' she challenged him. Of all the bad news in the world, would this be the worst?

'Correct.'

'Why?' she asked, as if she didn't know.

'Because I'm losing money. No matter how hard I work, how many hours I put in, it doesn't work. This country's falling apart, businesses are going bankrupt and everyone's busy having drinking parties.'

'When they could be having flying lessons?'

He brought out large jewellery boxes and a long brown envelope with Indian stamps. Opening the boxes, he set them out side by side, as if organising a display. Where she had bundled them up in a bag, a pouch, or a hem, tangled and jumbled, he had laid them against dark blue velvet, each item in its own space.

'Why didn't you come back for these?' he asked.

'And tarnish a grand gesture?'

'Why didn't you sell them?'

She didn't know the answer. Perhaps they had become a remnant of the only home she had known. Perhaps they had become companions and protectors?

They sat at the table. He turned the boxes of jewellery towards her, as if they were evidence in a trial.

'Who is Emily?' His words came out slowly and were carefully enunciated, as if too heavy to be casually thrown to her.

She wasn't ready to answer him. The past is part of the flesh, the weave of the skin. 'Why didn't you shoot off and sell them?' she asked back.

His finger ran up and down over the patterns, his lips closed tight together, guardians of pain? 'The money could save your business,' she suggested.

He had been looking down, and now he looked up, long lashes lifting over grey eyes, darkly sombre. A finger could run underneath, follow the curve. 'I was brought up with three rules: one, never betray anyone; two, never trust anyone; three, never depend on anyone.' Each time he uncurled a finger till three fingers stood straight. 'So I stand on my own two feet. Or fall. Right now I'm tottering,' a dry laugh, 'and it's not drink. But enough about me. Tell me all about yourself,' lowering his voice, smouldering his eyes.

'I've done with one fake Romeo today, I don't need another one.' A sharp put-down that had its effect. He looked abashed, and she felt rotten. There are women who fall in love with thieves and crooks, who marry them, defend them, and forgive them everything. For them love is blind and a bind. He'd hardly done anything outrageous, and she'd slapped him down because of her own turmoil.

114

Guilt and the wish to make up to him started her off, slowly, tentatively. When to give of oneself and when to withhold was something that had never been clear to her. Other people seemed to move smoothly through life, unfazed by situations that, for her, presented dilemmas and difficulties.

She put the Mausoleum into words, told him of Emily, the Mutant Memsahib, and of Champa the Dumpa, of how it had been for her, and why she had done what she had. She couldn't tell him what Emily and Champa had been because she didn't know. She was looking down at her hands, or at the jewellery in front of her. The perfection of colours and patterns made her feel like damaged goods from a reject shop. 'It's as if they stole me from myself. If you're not anchored by a family tag, if there are no details of the past, you don't know what you are. At Sangeeta's house,' for the first time glancing at him, 'they knew who they were, what they were doing and why.'

'Crap. C for crap,' was what he said. Sita/Ferret felt herself starting to shake. Had she revealed herself only to be ridiculed? 'All you lot, who live here,' he continued, 'including the "guests" at your landlady's bash are completely and totally fucked up. But it's no big deal.'

'At least they know their names,' she retorted.

'And can't pronounce them properly. Or they shorten them to ridiculous abbreviations. All your Pavs, Kams, Ravs and the like. If that's not proof of colonial arse-licking I don't know what is. Give them a French or German name and they'll go through fucking contortions to get that right. Then they bleat about how difficult it is to be in two cultures. Crap.'

'You're repeating yourself.'

'So? You and your friends are all urbanised westerners, with a touch of the exotic, clinging on for dear life to anything that'll add drama to your lives.'

'They're not my friends,' she flung back at him.

'Yes. I'm sorry. I interrupted the introductions. They'll live and die here, but they want to hark back to some golden homeland which never existed. If they're that desperate they can buy a one-way ticket. You know what all Indians love, wherever they are, they love to beat their breasts about this, that and the other. "Woe is me" should be the national anthem.'

'You didn't grow up here, you don't know what it's like,' she replied angrily.

'No, I grew up in India and it was goddam fucking awful.'

'Well, I grew up here and it was goddam fucking awful for me too. So don't you go feeling sorry for yourself,' she shouted back at him.

'Only you're allowed to do that are you?' he mocked.

'Should we take it in turns?'

Silence, like a vacuum.

He speaks first, 'A is for apologise. I didn't mean you. After all...' a smile that slipped out, 'it would be very ungracious of me to...'

'Bad-mouth your benefactress?' she suggests.

'Exactly,' pouncing on her words. His face falls, 'I've said the wrong thing again, haven't I?'

'Don't try the innocent-little-boy act with me,' she warns sternly; knowing he could try any act and she'd fall for it, hook, line, and sinker.

'I went off at a tangent,' he confesses. 'This strange breed called *British-Asian* gets under my skin. I didn't mean to offend you. Truly.' He holds out his hand. She looks at it. Like a work of art! A map of the future and the past, with lifelines and heart lines. She puts her hand in his hand. A little clasp from one to the other. Forgiveness. Togetherness. The hands part.

His hand passed over the jewellery, not touching, as if afraid of the energy that may be contained in them. 'This is the first evidence I've ever had that the past happened, because...' He picked up the brown envelope and taking out a few crackly papers, put them in front of her. 'I wanted you to read them. No one outside our family even knows about these papers. It's all we've ever had. I don't know if there were others, maybe there were and they were lost. There must have been I think. If someone's memory becomes,' a Kala pause, '...unreliable, then you just don't know.' A canyon of unknowing; this she understood. 'My grandmother doesn't let them out of her possession. My mother had to get them away, quickly get them photocopied. A is for ask; ask me if you can't make out anything. I know them by heart.'

To know something by heart! To have it inside you. Ticking away.

'We've never known what happened to him,' Kala says. Sita/Ferret has never known about the *She* embedded in the sentences at the Mausoleum?

Photocopies are unreal, giving the impression of belonging to the present while carrying contents that are decades old. Someone, who was long dead, had left a slice of himself. The handwriting started off in practised copperplate, with curls, loops and flourishes – evidence of a rich education – then deteriorated into scribbles, disjointed sentences, odd words, and what looked like a code. Now she saw where Kala's habit of alphabet-speak had come from. Macabre imitation. And she realised with shame, why he never got to D.

Sheet one:

> *Sarojini,*
> *Is this bloody fool chaprassi doing his job? I told him you would pay him well. Why am I not out of here yet? That idiot chaprassi said he would give you all the information. Why has nothing happened? Now he says I should write to you. Apparently I am being held as a "traitorous revolutionary". Damned ridiculous, false and base! I assume you have contacted all the top people. Get me out! If they want bribes, give them bribes. You do not know what this hell-hole is like. I hear screaming that turns the blood to ice. Get Prakrit to come immediately from Delhi. Perhaps a man can get things moving faster than a woman. Have you spoken to the Superintendent of Police? Go also to my uncle, he is always boasting of his legal successes. And Judge Browning, he has long been acquainted with our family.*
> *I am waiting to see you. And touch your soft arm.*

Sheet two:

> *At the beginning the chaprassi said, 'these people are* Beimaan *Sahib. Do not trust them. I will help you. No replies. No relief. No help.*

Sheet three:

This dung heap of a chaprassi has had me fooled. When he brought food I threw the disgusting mess back at him. The fool laughs like a cockroach. They say sahib will be doing a Ghandi fast.

A gap, then more writing:

No window to show the passing of the days or months.

A visitor came. A long thin man with a stick. He said I must learn my ABCs. I assured him I was already proficient, and made a great commotion telling him they had made a mistake, telling him who I was, my wealth, and connections. He is an Englishman who likes to show off his Hindustani. He asked me how I liked my home. I do not frequent dungeons or associate with low-class people I told him.

Sheet four:

Today they dragged someone past my door. I cannot see anything but I could hear the blood in the man's moans. I have not been one to think of these things.

The long thin one came again. I asked him his name. He laughed, said if I learnt my ABCs then I would know his name. "What pretty pretty eyes you have," he said. A is for Ask. B is for Baksheesh. *C is for cash. I have been given more paper and ink. I am to write to Sarojini.*

Sheet five:

A is for alone. B is for betrayed. C is for captive.

I should have guessed. They stick together. It is we who are the trusting fools.

A agony
B batter
C chained
tried E...

The long thin one came. 'Not so pretty now,' he said. 'We know what to do with pimps.'

Sheet six:

The ABCs have begun:
a abomination
b back
c carnal

a abject
b bent
c carrion

Sheet seven was blank except for a few words in a corner, in tiny writing as if the words were a secret between the writer and the page:

a apparatus
b butchery
c castrato...
...where is d?

She looked up at Kala. He was staring into the fire. *What pretty, pretty eyes you have.* She leaned forward and touched his face, a quick fleeting contact.

'Pimps and murderers,' he said. 'Welcome to the family!'

She carefully lined up the papers, folded them along the creases, and gently slid them back into the envelope. The helplessness of a person when in the power of others! How much cruelty can a person dole out? And how much cruelty can the other endure? The equation will never balance.

She curled herself up in the big four-poster bed, hands folded and tucked under her head, knees drawn up, body curved over itself. *A for ache, B for bent, C for contained.* Protected so that none may touch her; none who are relentless, cruel, evil. They are there, too, in the everyday world; tortured and murdered bodies tell of their existence. *Evil is as Evil does!* She'd never understood that before, and still could not comprehend what it was that made for evil. The abandonment of conscience? The shedding of human feeling? It required a choice; the choice to wreak havoc upon another. But what in the world could be so valuable? A country? A desire? No, thought Sita/Ferret. Nothing. Sita/Ferret had used to think that Emily was evil. She hadn't known what real evil could be. She had left the Mausoleum with body and soul intact, and could return. As could the *She*.

Sita/Ferret sits up with a jolt! She has no right to conjecture anything. She knows less than Kala. He knows 'by heart'.

Throwing back the covers she padded out to the kitchen. She filled a glass with water, drank half and then held the cool glass against her face. Emily hugged her material possessions to herself, her spirit fed off them; how had Emily come to be the mistress of all she surveyed, including a pouch of jewels? Carrying the glass of water, Sita/Ferret walked carefully back to her room, the long way round (she must be in dire need of exercise), past Kala's door. Light glowed underneath. She paused, tempted to break his rules a second time. If he had been so exhausted, why couldn't he sleep? He had said the room was full of ghosts. Was he communing with them?

She was back in her bed when he opened the door.
   'Why didn't you come in?'
   'It's too late to get thrown out.'
   'I wouldn't have.'

He holds out his hand. A fresh promise? She takes it and goes with him, seemingly acquiescing. He does not know that she is examining herself to find out at which point she will say stop, and at which point she will allow her wants to take her wherever the flow goes. Her hand rests in a consolation of comfort, an unusual experience for the hand to be so long nestling in another. In the days of yore, when she had explored the territory of man and woman togetherness, she hadn't indulged in sustained hand-holding. A tender act, it would have been too corrupt to fake. As they go through the open door of his room, he switches off the light. She stands in the dark, suddenly alone. He's moved away. A jingling of metal curtain rings, and pale dawn light seeps through the window.

The poignancy of early morning when the world appears creamy and new! He moves to the bed, lifts a pillow up against the headboard, turns the covers and invites her in. 'You'll be cold,' he says. The act in itself is solicitous, the consequences unknown, like stepping off a cliff, perhaps into an abyss? She climbs in, he tucks the covers around her. Then he moves over to sit in the armchair.

He says he should tell her of the woman; of himself and the woman. 'Anyway, I'd better tell you before someone else spills the beans.' Mustn't be too serious. Mustn't show how deep the dagger goes? This is late nineteen-nineties London where style and surface is everything. 'She was the last woman to be in that bed,' he tells her, indicating where Sita/Ferret is now. 'Afterwards, if you want, you can leave.'

He starts at the beginning. She flinches with jealousy. She bunches the bedclothes and hugs them, like a child clutching a teddy bear.

Never once does he use the name of the woman. Maintaining anonymity, the respect of privacy. So he talks about Her and Him. Sita/Ferret is the outsider.

She had called, wanting to book lessons for her son. She was the one who had pressed the buttons to make the connection. He had not been slow in responding. She should not have punctured her well-organised life for the sake of an adventure. 'Once,' she had said, 'just once, I'll indulge in temptation. An affair. Then no more will this convent girl stray.' He knew the gossipmongers had built him up as a must-have; he hadn't been high-mindedly oblivious, he had enjoyed his whispered reputation, seen it as an adjunct to his business success. His phones were busy, his books full, and his bank accounts healthy. He could send home cheques with numbers and happily rounded zeros. He had arrived! Money and success, women and charm – the joys of life were at his disposal. His cup runneth over.

It had been an empty, cracked cup for all his life. The family passions had been focused on regaining the time when they had abundance, status and respect. His father had tried, and failed, losing what little they'd had left. He was to be the next one. He must create wealth, and place the family back in its rightful position. Lift the curse.

When he met her, she was wearing a double row of pearls round her neck, and basked in an affluent, successful marriage. Why had she, who organised her household and social duties with faultless administration, allowed herself to be overwhelmed? And what was he that he had loved, but kept himself intact? 'Love and let live,' had been the implicit contract between them; but swept aside when love's possessiveness grew and demanded exclusivity? 'Faithful?' he had once laughed at her, '*quid pro quo*. How can you demand a one-sided faithfulness. Let her who is without sin, cast the first stone.' A cruel jibe! By her virtues and duties she had measured her life; a real Shakespearean heroine.

She had made her last arrangements with her usual precision for organisation. She wrote instructions and, together with keys, pinned them to his pillow. With housewifely efficiency, she had ground the white tablets to a powder for she had read that it could become difficult to swallow the requisite amount. She then proceeded to finish off his brandy and her bag of powder.

He blamed her bitterly. Her forethought, her intelligence should have told her that all pain passes, the passage of time shaves at its layers till the day you look back in surprise, and ask yourself if you were really that person so distraught? What had been unleashed within her, by this 'adventuring' from her regular life?

He had followed each item of instruction on her list: slipped the keys into his pocket, wrapped her in the sheet, carried her down to his car, laid her on the back seat, put his jumper under her head, driven slowly through dark streets.

She had written she was happy. Vicious word!

He had slipped her into her own bed, pulled the duvet over her to keep her warm, placed the note for the husband on the other pillow. Then gazed at her face. He didn't know for how long. The odd chirping of the birds in her garden at last drove him away, throwing her keys in the gutter as she had requested. Back in his flat, he had wandered from room to room, finally curling up in an armchair, imagining over and over again her last actions, her last despair. Not till much later did he drift into that bedroom.

An overturned bottle and glass lay on the floor, dark liquid stained the carpet, a pillow dangled off the bed, a sheet – missing. He flung himself out, down the stairs, into his car, and bang into the middle of the morning rush hour. He took side turnings, he doubled round, he drove through red lights, he overtook waiting traffic, he mounted the pavement and he prayed, sweat beading his face. The house help would get there first, the husband was due back later in the day. He'd bribe the help as much as she wanted, appeal to her, beg her, whatever, so as not to ruin her last plan.

On her street, a few yards from her house, the police booked him for speeding. Two police cars and an ambulance were parked in front of her home.

Sita/Ferret had wanted a history of her own; he had given her a slice of his. Perhaps to tell her that this territory had already been occupied and was no vacant lot? Or that there was danger here, beware! He slipped in at the other end of the bed. They faced each other, space between them.

'At the exhibition,' he reminded her, 'you were talking to a woman, d'you remember? Her face curdled. As if the devil's spawn had walked in. And you turned around, flashing your hardware.' She nodded. It had been the egg-merchant's wife. 'There was no scandal. No public flogging. But whispers did the rounds, and whispers can cut through steel. A is for attrition. B is for brand, C is for crime...'

'Stop it!' she told him sharply.

'A is for afterwards. B is for bankruptcy...'

'Don't do that.' To Sita/Ferret it sounded like an evil mantra.

'I've always done it,' shrugging his shoulders. 'But if madam is displeased, I'll desist.' A pause, and then he continued, 'There were fewer invitations, fewer business favours and so on. Not only have I fallen on hard times, I'm also a fallen man.' *Catch me!* He didn't say it.

After the depths of two tales, the words that whipped out were entirely selfish. 'Poonum rescued you,' she accused. He was silent, then he nodded. 'And what does she get...?' hating herself for asking.

'I'm very fond of her. We're good friends.'

'And grateful?'

'Yes,' he agreed.

'Gratitude and fondness have worked miracles for many a...person.' She had been about to say 'woman', to be bitchy and beastly. B words – had the ABCs taken up residence inside her too?

There was no forgetfulness in the snatches of sleep that came their way; they huddled against each other, like children, forming a pact against the space around them.

In the morning, he grinned at her. 'How was it for you?' Mischief-maker!

'It wasn't.'

'Well then,' he replied seriously, 'you'll just have to try harder.'

'Don't hold your breath!'

Chapter Eleven

Bombay, 1943–4

Suitable recompense is required! A cry that coursed through Emily's blood.

Calamity stalked her at every turn. Emily had to have a plan!

Any day now, the roof would fall in on her, the ground give way, and she'd be buried alive. She kept fingering her wedding ring. It had brought her thus far and then abandoned her. What curse lay trapped within it? Perhaps one of Maureen's wicked spells had got into it! She'd push it up and down her finger, but never to the point where it might slide off. Ring and respectability went together.

She had to do something!

She could invest in a sewing machine and spend her days stooped over it, growing old and grey, poor and bitter, all for the sake of the circle on her finger and the few rupees she could earn. She had gone back to Mademoiselles, and enquired about the 'remuneration to be expected by seamstresses?' The manageress had made a big song and dance about it, blabbing on about the quality of their clients who would only take the best. When she did mention a figure, pretending that it was just a guess, Emily had left her shop.

She had to have a plan! She could wish for something to fall in her lap, or she could use her brains. Later, that was how Emily always thought of it: using her brains. *For suitable recompense was required!*

Emily invited Linda Wiggins to tea. She pinned up her hair and carefully painted her lips; set the table with dainty crockery and English biscuits. When Linda arrived, she exclaimed at the prettiness of the arrangements.

Tea was poured and spoons tinkled against the cups. As they sipped, Linda waited for Emily to begin.

'Pity this isn't England,' said Linda, 'you can get rid of the first ten minutes by talking about the weather.' Emily offered her some biscuits, wondering when she'd ever be able to buy more.

'Can I ask you a few questions?' Emily tentatively began.

Linda eyed the biscuit in her fingers and then took a dainty little bite, 'You won't like the answers.'

'Do you get enough money for what you do?'

'How dare you!' Linda exclaimed, glaring furiously at her. 'That's what you'd get from someone else. They'd have marched out in high dudgeon by now. There are polite ways of asking rude questions. You need to learn the soft touch, my girl. Now, d'you mean do I get paid every week or month? A regular sum for my services, with Sundays off. Don't be daft! They think they're doing enough for you by giving you bed and board.'

Linda Wiggins settled back in her chair, popped the biscuit into her mouth and licked her fingers. 'If that's where you're thinking of heading, I'll buy you a ticket back, with my own money. I can tell where you're from, but don't imagine it's going to be any better here. And they're not all like Donald. Some don't give a damn how they treat you. When they've had enough, they give the woman a few rupees and it's bye-bye darling. I know a girl whose man left town without even that. She got so desperate she went to Maggie at the Blue Bowl, but Maggie wouldn't have her, she likes to offer dusky beauties to her clients. "Exotic Orchids of the Orient!" no less – not that her customers would recognise an orchid from a weed. It's the ordinary soldier that goes there and what's he got to spend? Happy with your answer?'

'Why didn't you go back then?'

Linda fiddled with the spoon on her saucer. 'For one thing, my mother was dead by then, and I didn't fancy living with my sister and her husband.'

'Didn't you have anything of your own to take back, to set you up?'

'That husband of yours spoilt you. I could see it. I thought, "she's heading for a mighty great fall." They're not all like that, but then they don't all end up like him. No need to look daggers at me,' objected Linda, 'I'm only speaking plain words. By the way, if you should ever wish to,' changing her tones, 'to tidy your wardrobe, I may be able to assist. Certain persons, I know, may be interested in certain items.'

'Never!' exploded Emily. She knew that Linda was thinking of the fur stole and satin gown that she had worn to Green's nightclub the first time she had met Linda. 'Never,' she repeated. They were the only symbols of what she had been promised. She'd die in them if she had to. 'Didn't your husband leave you anything?' she asked Linda again.

'He was only a soldier. What d'you think he earned? A bloody fortune? It's them others who take bags stuffed full of gold – the churchmen, the officers, the high-up ones. I thought about becoming a nun. Why not? A nun in the sun can have a lot of fun,' she said, laughing at the look on Emily's face. 'The church is everywhere here. But then I met Donald.'

'And what're you going to do when he doesn't want you anymore?'

'You've got a cheek!' cried Linda, pushing away her cup and saucer. 'Don't think he's going to be interested in you. He's going. Not back to England, he says it's too grim there. He's going to set himself up in southern Rhodesia. That's where they're all heading, the ones who haven't got a country place in the Home Counties. The agent said,' puffing out her chest and putting on a pompous air, ' "The people and social conditions are outstandingly British in both character and outlook!".' Both giggled like little girls. 'Donald's already got himself set up. He thinks you're mad, hanging around here, with what's likely to happen. England's a hard place for the likes of you and me, but you'll be better off there than here. No knowing what could happen here.'

'Perhaps I'll go to southern Rhodesia with him,' said Emily, and watched Linda's temperature rise. Linda's reactions gave her far more information than a hundred questions and answers would have.

'I hear the Kamal Circus are looking for performers,' Linda bit back.

Emily laughed and soothed Linda's ruffled petals, assuring her she was only teasing, vowing to herself never to be caught in such a predicament as hers. 'Of course,' said Linda, 'you could always hook yourself a rich nawab who'll set you up in a "dahling little place" of your own. The only problem being they're few and far between; you're not likely to meet one, and even if you did, he'd be bound to have half a dozen others chasing him already.'

'How do they manage?' asked Emily, pouring another cup of tea for her. 'These other wo...ladies,' remembering the polite way of asking rude questions.

'What all women do, married or not. Make sure they wheedle lots of teensy, little presents from lover-boy, inflate the housekeeping, get him to buy them dresses and then return them and so on. Female ingenuity is the only thing keeping the female race going. And don't imagine I'm about to be left with nothing. It happened once and I don't intend to let it happen again.'

Emily listened.

Emily visited the Blue Bowl – she wasn't asking for work, but pretending to do so was no crime – and came out thinking that anything would be better than this. It was the kind of place that would make her run gratefully to the factory back home for this was a factory of another kind. Emily had envisaged a French bordello, red drapes, velvet sofas, and beautiful languid women: images handed down through women's gossip. The Blue Bowl went for a fast turnover, for quantity rather than quality.

A trade in flesh! A trade in promises! Hadn't she engaged in that transaction also!

'The times have changed,' Maggie Salford, owner of the Blue Bowl, had advised. 'Go back while you can.'

Time running out! Her promises shivered on the horizon; so tangible Emily could taste them! If only she could stretch herself a bit further she'd be able to grab them. To go back to the world she had left would be to turn herself hollow, when all she had wanted was to turn herself into something else. The only bridges to this other self were marriage or money. She'd tried the first, and fallen lower than when she had started off.

Emily walked back from the Blue Bowl, the sun beating hard on her head, sweat dampening her whole body and no pretty frilly parasol to lend her shade. She'd had a few of course; he'd bought them for her. One evening she'd gathered them up and given them to the astounded servant woman. Emily had smiled grimly. 'Just so,' she had muttered. Frilly parasols didn't make up for the fact that she didn't have a roof over her head. Even that swanky snob Maureen could boast her own now: '…*small*,' her mother had written, '*hardly room to swing a cat, but she's gone all posh, swathed her windows in yards of lacy net, with ribbon bows at the bottom! Who does she think she is? Dear, can you send me some pale blue silk. Your cousin Joan's wedding is coming up. It'll make their eyes pop out. And some pink silk for your sister. Your granny has been a bit poorly, but we've been having terrible*

*weather here, and I can't afford to light a fire for her everyday. Your father and
brother send their love. We're glad to know you're getting on so well.'*

Baptism by the heat of the sun! Defiantly she stopped and looked directly
into the sun. People climbed mountains so she could bloody well climb an
idea! Black circles whizzing in front of her eyes, she stumbled towards a
low wall, cradling her head in her hands.

Visiting her one day, and seeing her desperate face, Linda said to her,
'You'd better take what help you can. Donald would still buy you a ticket
back. But not for long.' *Not for long!* Emily shook her head, but begged
Linda's help.

The next day Linda took her to the Crystal Tea-rooms. Cigarette
smoke, music and talk swirled around the room; the band sweated under
the whirling fans; the crooner sang his love's praises into the microphone.
Emily and Linda were invited to join a table and offered drinks.

Emily knew exactly how few were the rupees hidden in her room. In
the old days she would hardly have thought they were worth the bother.
Now, they were her last, thin barricade against the world. She'd taken to
only eating tiny amounts of food and keeping the rest under lock and key;
she still had the servants, her remnants of pride. She would have to do
something soon; borrowing money would be the first step, but as soon as
she did that she would start sinking. Degradation where she had been
promised elevation! She looked at the hot, flushed faces of the men
around her, and calculated their potential to lead her into disaster rather
than happiness. They worked for others and were at the mercy of their
masters, accidents and disasters. At least he, the one who had adorned her
finger, had blazed a trail of his own. Not that she had benefited much, but
his glowing eyes, his desire to grab the world in his hands had lifted him
out of the ordinary.

From now on she would check a man's worth first. Emily was becoming
steel. She would not be destroyed! She could see there was no one at the
table who could match her requirements. But she smiled brightly at the
one nearest to her. Stepping stones? Perhaps that was the way she would
have to go. She'd have a look round the rest of the room first. Emily
excused herself for the powder room. She passed a group of men, intent
on their card game, and a pair of European girls being romanced by
misquotations from Shakespeare: 'Julie, my Julie...' declared her swain,
'wilt thou be forever a Calcutta maid...' The girls laughed in delight at this
display of wit, and lingering for half a second Emily realised they were

actually Anglo-Indian. She'd been told how difficult it was to distinguish sometimes, but crucial to do so. Turning round to continue on her way, she bumped into glorious grey eyes and a perfectly beautiful face.

'Madam, I'm so sorry. I do apologise.' His English was very good; his race was very Indian. 'I hope you are not hurt?'

'No. Thank you.' Emily assured him, never having been in such close proximity to one who belonged to this land. Her husband had taken care not to bring any of his native friends home. 'Quite unsuitable,' he had stated, but that may have been for reasons other than social propriety. The grey eyes smiled and moved to let her pass.

She went through the motions of patting powder on her face, retouching her lipstick and tidying her hair, unreasonably piqued that he had let her go so easily. They were supposed to be wild for English women; or so she'd been told. Wasn't that why the ladies always had to maintain their distance?

Back in the room, she glanced around for a sight of him and saw him with a group of men and women near the band. Amid their cheers and claps he climbed onto the stage and took the microphone:

> *Don't make me wait,*
> *Oh, honey dear,*
> *This heart's longing and living just for you,*
> *Don't make me wait,*
> *Oh, honey dear,*
> *This man's going craaaazy over you...*

At first Emily smiled with derision: a poor crooner wasn't worth a paisa in this land. Then she watched as he played up to his pals in the audience, the aura of money surrounding them. The love-sick crooner was directing his heart-rending lines to one black-haired woman in particular. At the end of his song, exaggerated applause and sarcasm greeted his efforts. He bowed off the stage as the original singer came back on.

The madness of calamity must have propelled Emily. She set a course that would pass his table, halted near it and looked lost, a frown on her forehead, a hand over her mouth. Eventually he noticed, but didn't immediately rush to her side. She bit her lip, wondering how long before she would have to give up and move on. Sliding her worried glance from left to right, she met his grey glance midway. How had he inherited that colour?

'Oh, hello,' she faltered. Damn him! Couldn't he make the first move?

'Is something troubling you, madam?'

'I've lost my friends. I can't see them anywhere,' fluttering her hands a little.

'Well perhaps you should look further around the room,' he suggested, unhelpfully. The full stop after a sentence.

'Darling, help the lady,' drawled the Indian woman, blowing out a puff of smoke, a smile hovering on her lips.

He kept a polite distance as they circled the crowded room, working a passage through the gaps created by shifting bodies; she gasped as they almost stumbled over Linda's table and quickly turned her back. Linda would understand. But not the men. 'So hot in here,' she whispered, fanning herself.

'Perhaps you'd like to go back home. I'm sure we can get you a taxi or rickshaw outside.' She knew she'd never be able to pay for either of them.

'I think I just need some fresh air.'

'Well, there is a garden at the back. It's very nice. If you'd like to spend a few minutes there?'

The green coolness of spreading trees met them as they stepped outside. She dipped her fingers in the little fountain, and apologised for keeping him from his friends. He smiled politely, and declared that she need not concern herself. But what was she going to do about her lost friends? Perhaps she would like the singer to make a request to them to meet her in the garden?

The sun slanted through the tree overhead, diamond spots glinting on the water. How many more days could she survive as she was? If starvation came to visit her how long would she survive then? What use politeness and respectability then? She pushed her hand into the water, shaking the reflections of sunlight and leaves, splashing water onto her dress and shoes.

'Please be careful,' he warned.

Time was gathering behind her, ready to bury her. The mini-storm in the fountain died away, the water settled back, the reflections floated again. Thoughts don't leave a trace on the body; private acts stay within the body.

'You speak very good English,' she said to him, not knowing it was the wrong thing to say, revealing more about herself than conferring a compliment upon him. He didn't answer immediately.

'My family have a home in London; I've visited a few times, spent a few years there off and on. You know how it is.' She didn't know how it was. So there was a group that rubbed shoulders, hobnobbed with each other and bought houses in each other's countries.

'We really should do something about finding these friends of yours. Would you like to go back in and have another look?'

She shook her head. If he wished to go, he would have to remove himself voluntarily, and she doubted that the demands of courtesy would allow him. But she knew that to create a connection, she would have to feed something into this moment. She'd managed to swing one man towards her and come half way round the world. Hesitation, not action would defeat her!

'My husband is dead!' she cried, starting on the story of their marriage and her widowhood, her plight in a foreign land. She didn't look to see how he was receiving it; the various hurts still raw in her, her voice faltered, her eyes shed tears, and he had to give her a handkerchief.

'I'm terribly sorry,' he said when she had finished. 'Look, I hope you don't mind, but perhaps you'll allow me to help a little,' taking out his wallet and extracting notes.

'No!'

'Please do. It may help somewhat.'

'I don't want charity.'

'What are you going to do then?' he asked, the notes still in his hand.

'Something. It's just that there's no one to help me.'

'I'm sure your friends will do so. Shall we go in now?' Forever trying to move away from her!

'Everyone here knows each other, and they all help each other, but I'm just a newcomer. I don't have their connections. I'm just a simple girl on her own. I don't come from a fancy background.' Truth may work where pretty pretences had failed. 'Would you happen to know of any jobs that I may apply for?'

'I'll do my best to enquire for you.'

How are the ingredients of attraction compounded to propel one person unto another? Or to repel one person from another? She should have had a foothold in his interest by now; he couldn't be oblivious to the message. Closing her eyes, she put a hand to her head – the time-worn ruses! 'I'm not feeling at all well. I would be terribly grateful if you would see me home.' She'd had to do the asking.

And yet he hesitated. Having flings with ladies in England was one thing; being with an English woman in India was quite another. He was a man who carried both prudence and recklessness within him. So far his recklessness had been confined to having too much fun, overdrinking and singing his amours in public. He knew how it would look to be seen with Emily...and decided he wasn't going to be cowed by convention, particularly for a woman in distress.

His friends expressed their sympathy as he went to say goodbye. 'Our Golden Gopal,' laughed one, 'ever to the rescue!'

'Do be careful not to do the Midas touch on the lady,' advised the black-haired woman. Emily wondered if she was imagining the streak of disdain in her voice. 'I'm sure she wouldn't wish to turn into a statue of gold.'

The luxury of sitting in a car with a uniformed driver at the front! Emily felt light-headed, as if she had moved out of ordinary time, out of the ordinary world. He opened a gold cigarette case and held it out to her.

'Why did your friend call you golden?' she asked, taking one.

He laughed, 'They like to joke.'

'What did she,' Emily persisted, 'the lady,' she added for the sake of politeness, 'mean by Midas?'

'I'm afraid I'm the butt of their jokes. A couple of my companies have done rather well. So of course they have to make me suffer for it.'

'I don't see what's wrong with success,' objected Emily hotly.

'Oh please don't take it seriously. They're only ragging me.'

All the while Emily had kept touching her wedding ring. 'Do you know where I may sell this?' she asked, holding up her hand. 'Somewhere where they won't cheat me.'

'Good heavens,' he exclaimed, shocked. 'You mustn't do that. Please let me help you,' hand fishing for his wallet again.

'Never,' declared Emily, forcing him to really look at her. 'If you want to help me, I'll tell you what I need. But not yet, I can't do it yet.' She didn't know what she would want from him yet, but handouts of money wouldn't see her very far; though his conscience would be satisfied, he'd say goodbye and forget her. 'Say that you will give it to me then.'

'I should be pleased to render whatever little help I may be able to.' A careful sentence, he wasn't lavish with his promises.

When they arrived at her home, he got out, opened the door for her personally, and began to take his leave. She asked him to escort her to her apartment. He hesitated, then said that he would be charmed to do so. It was clear that he was someone who was prepared to deviate from the straight and narrow, to take a risk.

Inside her rooms she prepared him a cool drink, without stopping to ask him, all the while talking about her fears, letting him know that she didn't really have any friends who could help her. Gopal promised to scout for 'suitable positions for her', told her to be brave and strong, and left her his office address. As she saw the car drive off, she knew that today's sympathy was tomorrow's forgetfulness. Well, she wouldn't let him forget her. Gopal the Golden! She turned the name on her tongue, tasting gold dust.

Before she had to leave the apartment, she sent a message to Donald. No one would be able to say she hadn't asked her own kind first, tried every possibility – like the hanged man's last kick for life. When Donald arrived, she explained that she wanted to set up something. He listened to her and stood up in shock.

'You can't do that. They won't let you. Why, you're as wild as he was. Go home, and everything will turn out fine. You'll find a nice man to marry, have children and live to a good old age.'

'I won't live to a good old age,' Emily raged back at him in white heat. She had nothing left to lose. 'I'll die in childbirth, or from overwork. Or pneumonia. I'm not going back into that hell-hole of a factory, to be ordered around by others. I should be the one giving orders. That was the plan. That's what he promised!'

Donald was a man looking forward to making a new start; he washed his hands of her.

When she moved to a cheap room in the poorer part of town, the ground shifted beneath her feet, became swampy, dangerous. She sent a message to the grey-eyed crooner.

That night, as she waited for him, she was afire with fear and fright, pacing up and down, her fierce energy willing the day to turn around and move her upwards, away from the threatening descent into poverty, destruction. When he arrived he was met by an Emily whose eyes burned and whose words crashed through barriers.

She was the one who touched his skin first. Her fire set him ablaze.

His flesh. Her flesh. One flesh. Heresy!

The talking came afterwards. He also said no immediately and emphatically to her proposal, instead offering to 'help' her regularly.

'I'll still die in the gutter,' she stated calmly. After the storm, she was all icy calm. 'I want money to start. No one need know. Anyway everything you touch turns to gold.'

'A joke,' he protested.

'So you won't be setting up any other businesses, companies?' she asked him, a snake look in her eyes.

'Indeed I want to,' he answered enthusiastically. 'I'm going to start an airline company.' His eyes were glowing, his voice as eager as a child's. 'It'll be a huge enterprise. Tata have already begun. Air Services of India are flying twenty-one seaters, but India is an enormous country,' stretching his arms out, 'the airplane is perfect for it.' And then, looking mournful, 'But, pauper that I am, I don't have the capital.'

'That makes two of us, doesn't it.'

'But I am working towards it,' he assured her earnestly, engrossed in his own vision. 'Everything that I do, my investments, companies, will be used to set up Golden Arrow Airlines.'

'I have a name too,' she said, leaning over his shoulder, kissing it. He had the sweetest skin. All constraints had fallen away, as if a lock had been taken off her mind, an iron suit removed from her body. She had to touch him, talk to him, turn him in every way towards her. Had danger made her mad?

'My "company" is going to be called The English Rose Garden. And it'll be a success, the first of its kind. I'll make sure it's a success; if I have to sell my blood I'll do it. No one needs to know that Gopal the Golden has anything to do with it, and Golden Arrow Airlines will come that much quicker. Lend me the money, that's all I'm asking, and you'll get it back with profit. I spit on charity, it'll see me into a madhouse. Haven't you ever lent money to anyone?'

He wouldn't agree. Emily badgered and argued with steely determination, but he wouldn't change his mind. Then Emily heard about Gandhi going on a fast, protesting against some action of the English. She was in India, why shouldn't she copy the natives? As it was, time had almost run out. She was already an outcast from her world. Emily went on a fast. At first Gopal laughed, then he got angry, then he said her behaviour was ridiculous, then he said this was no way to discuss business.

Vices and virtues? Versions of a world that is always turning.

She was using her brains, that's how Emily always thought of it. In the end the world worked to its own convenience. After all, if it was convenient to overrun another country then it was considered a positive virtue to do it.

A grand but ruined old house on the outskirts of town; Emily moved in immediately, no matter the holes in the roof, the crumbling walls. Desire starts at the beginning not at the end.

Champa felt that she knew Emily, so when The Girl had rushed home, panting and sweating, scarcely able to get the words out, Champa had refused to believe her. Again! The Girl had kept the first item of news, the Indian gentleman, to herself, but knew that the second was of an urgent importance. Champa had done exactly the same as before and, 'slap', whacked her around the face. The Girl had a lot to thank Emily for. The next day Champa had asked her to find out more.

So when Champa was at the bangle stall, admiring the effects of different colours on her plump wrists, and was hailed by two others on their way to a visit, she was prepared. Shock and consternation ran through the group. No one was ever happy with new competition, but this was unprecedented. How could they be expected to compete with these English mems? The allure of the forbidden was a far stronger attraction than their accomplishments, no matter how proficient.

'See,' declared Acid Eyes, 'what's the difference? When it comes to it, they've only got one thing to sell too. Now we know why she's been hanging around.'

One laughed and suggested they all dress up as mems and do the same thing. 'Faking it is the same in any language isn't it?'

The group exploded into hysterics.

'No, no, no,' said another. 'You have to learn how to say "darling, darling, d-a-r-ling",' swooning back, '...as they do their business.'

'Or they do it drinking tea,' suggested another. 'Standing up straight and saying "How do you do?",' acting it out for a delighted audience.

'Idiots!' reprimanded Acid Eyes. 'You can laugh about it now, but that's the best money in town, and where is it going to go? Not into your pockets. Supposing another Daisy or Jane or Susan decides to do the same? They'll mop up all the business? What are you going to do then, huh? Rely on your one-paisa, two-paisa customers?'

The room fell into a disquieted silence.

'But how many mems are ready to do this work? It's only the one's who can't get anything else,' replied the one who'd started it all, cracking a nut between her teeth, piqued at the whole situation.

'If there's enough money in it,' stated the inexorable voice of logic, 'they'll come flocking, they'll materialise out of thin air,' clicking her fingers as she spoke. 'Since when have any of them asked if this is right or wrong? Theirs or ours? When those mems fill their purses with money, is the money going to look any different?'

Champa felt responsible by association; she'd spent the whole night trying to visualise Emily in her new occupation, and had come up with two rationalisations: firstly, that it must be a very superior set-up if Emily was involved; secondly that if Englishmen came to Indian women, then why shouldn't it be the other way round? However she knew better than to parade these ideas in front of the others.

'All we need is a spy,' she announced brightly. 'Someone to go in there with dress, hat, tripping on high, high heels,' walking on tip-toe like an English lady, looking down her nose at the world, 'and calling herself...' She paused, inviting audience participation, and names came flying at her, 'Daisy', 'Maisi...', 'Lucy'. Champa quietened them with a sweep of her hand, '...calling herself Daisy,' emphasising the name, 'and work there. Then this Daaiissyy,' dragging out the name, 'will learn the secrets,' voice dropping low, 'of what these mems do and how they do it!'

'There is the little matter of language and colour,' pointed out the voice of reason; in another age this woman would have been a business executive, or a top administrator.

'So, so, so?' enquired Champa, hands on hips. 'Acting! Drama! Do we not do it every day? Smiling like this for this one,' coy and fluttering lashes, 'smiling like this for another,' brazen bedroom eyes. 'We can all go to the English hairdresser, the English dress shop, do the English make-up, and start our own English...'

'...Thorn Garden,' the cynic finished off for her.

'Thorn Garden is the perfect name for the variety of thorns: little thorns...'

'Big thorns...' others took up the idea to smiles and giggles.

'Limp thorns...'

'Smelly thorns...'

'Oh God!' complained one. 'Do you have to bring that up? Just because your regulars are like that!'

'And what about yours?' retorted the other. 'All rajahs and nawabs are they?'

'Even if they were,' spoke the rationalist, fast becoming the most unpopular woman in the room, 'they'll all be going off to that English Rose Garden now.'

That put an end to the afternoon's fun and frolics.

The Girl had been haunting Emily like a shadow. She was there when Emily moved out of the boarding house and into a huge old house with a garden all around it. The Girl was in awe of Emily's powers of transformation. She slipped through the broken gate, zigzagged between the bushes, taking care to avoid the thorny weeds, for though her bare feet were hard and toughened, they couldn't withstand everything.

She saw the square building with the crumbling shallow steps leading up to the wide double doors, one of which hung loose, the windows with only shards of glass remaining in them, and the old urns round the sides that were either broken or filled with weeds. The Girl traversed a semi-circle that took her to the side of the building where windows came down to the floor and doors opened out. Hearing a voice she quickly ducked behind a chipped, grimy statue; there she made out the sound of footsteps, but no one came out. The Girl ran, like a little monkey, knees bent, hands almost touching the ground, to the side of a window. Peering in, she saw Emily with scraps of paper that she held up to the walls as she talked to someone out of her sight. This was the closest The Girl had ever been to Emily, and the first time she had heard her voice. She couldn't understand what was being said, but the timbre of Emily's tones settled into her mind, so that hearing them, she would recognise them anywhere. The Girl saw Emily writing in a book, and wondered at the skill that could do so. A man's footsteps became louder, moving towards the window; the Girl scuttled back to the statue.

One hand in a trouser pocket, the other holding a cigarette, the man sauntered out, turned and surveyed the building. The Girl recognised him as the Indian man who had visited Emily in the boarding house. After a few minutes, Emily followed him out. He took a drag of his cigarette and turning, handed it to Emily, using his freed hands to open the buttons on her dress.

The Girl cannot move and watches with wide-open eyes. She knows about the act, but not its details. Has spied on bodies in dimmed rooms, but has never seen anyone dare to enact it in the open, in blazing daylight.

The man's clothes and Emily's dress lie crushed.

The Girl will remember them like this.

Three months! Three months in which Emily stalked the workers like a tigress, hardly slept and fashioned a version of the promises promised to her so long ago...

A colour scheme of pink and gold; sparkling chandeliers dangling from ceilings, French sofas and chairs adorning the rooms, new urns filled with fresh plants and flowers, a smooth shiny forecourt, a wall around the property, huge gleaming black gates and a gateman... The night before the opening!

Gopal was visiting. He had come in the night, as he had been doing in the past few months. No one was to know of his part in this English Rose Garden, that was the deal with Emily. He and Emily were sitting on the little balcony outside her room. Emily was as tense as a bomb! What if everything exploded? What if a great disaster came and knocked it all away? Gopal poured her a glass of his favourite whisky and didn't bother telling her to calm down. He knew the words wouldn't do any good. So he lit a cigarette, slowly drank his whisky and watched the moon and stars. Gopal lived with a fluid ease, enjoying all the pleasurable things that life had to offer, from good food to expensive clothes, to lots of fun. Instinctively he worked on the principle of live and let live, never seeing a need to force anyone or allow himself to be forced. The only time he had departed from this principle was in agreeing to Emily's plan. Gopal wasn't exactly worried, but for once he was a little disquieted. Apart from the fact that he hadn't wanted to be connected to The English Rose Garden, he'd had to put in far more capital than he originally budgeted for.

As he looked at Emily, saw her deadlocked concentration on herself and moneymoneymoney, his mischievous streak bubbled up, tempting him into teasing her. Instead, he decided it would be safer to leave; her mood was too deep and grim.

The first night Emily dressed herself in shimmering silver. She now had a rail of gowns and matching shoes yet to be worn. Giving herself a final look in the long mirror, she imagined herself as a destitute woman out on the street, the butt of anyone's kicks. Emily knew the threat was still there. Her hand fingered the gold band and slipped it off, like taking off a skin.

138

Downstairs they were hammering at big blocks of ice, making them splinter into cascades of diamonds. Emily picked up a piece and placed it on her tongue – the freezing bite of ice! A luxury of the rich!

Champa had Emily in her head like a knot in her brain.

Six months on and The English Rose Garden effect had trickled down. There was only a finite amount of business in the town, and if the best, as the voice of logic had predicted, went elsewhere, then the rest had to make do with what was left. Prices started dropping: Champa, who had been in the comfortable middle range, found her clients being lured by those who prided themselves on being the best and who wouldn't be seen dead in her alleyways; not that they hunted in person, they sent their minions to whip up business and re-route it their way. Champa was forced to entertain men who normally found her 'too busy' to accommodate them.

The Soiree Sisters jibbed and jibed at Emily, but there was nothing that anyone could do. They were aghast at the stories coming out of Emily's house – that the women did wild western dances, that they wore transparent clothes and did certain kinds of 'actressing', both as a group and singly. 'Shows' they were called.

'How can they be so shameless? Brazen?' asked one in scandalised tones.

'Did you hear,' said another in an incredulous voice, 'they drink wine from the women's slippers?'

'*Chi chi chi.* Disgusting.'

'And the men prance around like monkeys.'

'It is called dancing,' volunteered Champa.

'*Hain, hain.* If you know so much about it, why don't you go join them?' Voice lowered, 'I heard that the women dance on a table, to show, you know, everything...' Her voice expired at the very idea of such wantonness.

'They'll corrupt our men.'

Champa unlocked her steel trunk. Carefully removing treasured garments, she took the small metal box from the middle. Unlocking it, she took out the packets at the top and laid them in a neat row by her garments. They contained little bits of jewellery and carefully hoarded money: her defences against emergencies; the riches of the poor. To The Girl, these would be the riches of the rich. Champa unwrapped a packet, extracted the red box with 'London, England' emblazoned on it; opened it and lifted the chain and locket, holding it up to the light.

While Champa brooded, The Girl made contact…with the back of Emily's hand. The Girl had been dying to see the inside of The English Rose Garden. She couldn't have come in the evenings; Champa's work and the dangers of the dark held her back. She decided on an early morning foray; the chill cut through her clothes as she climbed out of the kitchen window.

When she reached The English Rose Garden, she found the gates securely locked, but no watchful gatekeeper nearby. The workers of the night slept late! She debated whether to try climbing up the gate, the sharp spikes at the top would have to be carefully negotiated, or to find a foothold in the wall. She went around the entire circumference of the wall looking for toeholds, or cracks where her fingers could get a grip. The wall had been well repaired; it would take some time for cracks to appear, perhaps after the rains. The Girl couldn't wait that long. Back at the gate, she stretched her paper-thin body, gripped with her feet and hauled herself up; at the top, she held on with her toes and manoeuvred her body over the sharp spikes, her thin arms shaking with the extraordinary effort, almost wishing she hadn't attempted this, perhaps there was a line that she couldn't cross.

She found the hairslide among the grass, glinting in the morning sun. The French doors at the side, where she'd first spied on Emily and Gopal, were open. The Girl sidled in, sticking to the walls, brushing by the drapes, running for the corners. The silence of the house tempted her to the stairs. As one foot followed another, she mounted higher. Gold-framed prints of English beauties hung on the walls. The Girl paused before them, admiring the blonde curls, creamy complexions, the backgrounds of Greek temples, rivers and woodlands, but shocked by the display of bursting cleavages. Upstairs, the house spread out in every direction. The Girl slipped along the corridors, picking up lost ribbons and scarves, fingering them, enchanted by the silky texture of the material, leaving them where she found them; but when she picked up an earring that glinted as brightly as a diamond, she placed it in an inside pocket.

The Girl glanced into bedrooms where the doors were half-open and bodies slept under rumpled covers. She wriggled her toes in the rugs, unable to believe that such thick luxuriance was for walking on, passed her hand over the wallpaper; the first time she had seen anything like this, The Girl thought that the intricate flower patterns had been painted straight onto the walls, and was awed by the power that could buy such skills. In all her wanderings and spying, The Girl had never been inside a building as opulent and rich as this. Another flight of stairs led up. Curiosity propelled and common sense did not hold her back, for she felt she were a ghost flitting through a sleeping town. She didn't know that her doom awaited her upstairs. She stepped on a broken wineglass, and though her feet were hardened and tough, the thin sharp shard pierced straight through, and she couldn't suppress the cry that burst out, breaking the silence and alerting a cleaner.

She was hauled struggling and resisting in front of Emily, depositing patches of blood behind her. Emily would have been terrifying if The Girl didn't have a memory of a naked Emily and a man in the grass; she was defiant rather than scared out of her wits which incensed Emily even more. Thus the backhanders. Slap! went her hands across The Girl's face. Emily wanted to see her snivelling and grovelling, and The Girl duly obliged when her head started spinning. Emily ordered one of the servants, male as it happened, to search her thoroughly. His hard fingers went under her clothes, over her skin, opportunistically delving into her body, making The Girl shake with shame. He discovered booty, the hairclip and earring, that he triumphantly handed over to Emily.

'Thieving little Ferret, thinks she can creep around my house, helping herself to my property does she?' Emily declared. 'Do you want me to call the police?' The Girl understood the last word and real fear flooded her eyes. In fact it was the last thing Emily wanted to do. So far the authorities had kept away from her establishment, and if they were turning a blind eye, it would hardly serve her to invite them through the gates.

'Don't let me see you again, or you know what!' Emily ordered the servant to drag her to the gates and throw her out.

Chapter Twelve

London, March 1997

The day for Jeevan's visit had arrived. But first the phone rang, and it was Mr Kalyan asking her if she'd come in to despatch an urgent order. She looked at her watch, calculated time, grabbed her coat and ran. Outside, a hard, relentless rain was falling, the kind that makes the bones shiver with damp and cold.

Minutes ticking away in her head, she was busily packing items, addressing labels and taping up boxes, when down the stairs came Poonum, equipped with briefcase, ambition and barbs.

'Good morning, Mrs Pandey.' She sat down and, taking a notebook, asked Sita/Ferret to explain precisely what she was doing. 'I want to build a profile of what happens here so that we can streamline.'

Words colliding against each other in her hurry, Sita/Ferret worked and explained, and Poonum took notes. And then there was silence.

'You met Kala last week. Why?' asked Poonum. Personal business!

'Couldn't keep my hands off him.' Sita/Ferret had never before had a cat fight over a man.

'I'm so glad for you,' Poonum smiled. 'You must have been desperate. Hubby long dead and all that. I know quite a few Pandeys and none of them know of one who ran off, married and then copped it.' Some stories follow you like a skunk.

The door upstairs pinged and steps came straight towards the basement. Both women waited, watching the stairs. Was a coincidence about to occur wondered Sita/Ferret? Had their words pulled Kala here?

The feet, body and the young/old face of Mr Steven Singh descended. 'Do you always entertain your gentlemen friends here?' Poonum asked. Then, turning to Steven Singh, 'Why don't you stop hounding us? You're just making yourself into a laughing stock. No one believes you.' Poonum

142

stood up, picked up her briefcase, and delivered her parting shot. 'It's your life. Chuck it down the drain if you want to. Well, goodbye, Mrs Pandey. Don't let anyone distract you from your work. I'll start full time next week.' With that, she marched up the steps and was gone.

Sita/Ferret shoved her arms into her coat, the image of a wet shivering Jeevan on her brain, picked up the boxes and said, 'I've got to run.'

'Why? What've you done?' he asked.

The phone shrilled. She dumped the boxes in his arms, and grabbed the receiver.

'Good morning.' Kala's voice. Delight darted through her. The first phone call.

'I'm in a rush,' she said. 'I have to make a visit for a friend.'

'Then visit me too,' he invited. She was silent. She knew his invitations by now and wondered at the reason for this latest one. 'How about it?' he asked. How about wearing a hair-shirt? How about grief and heartache?

'Yes, bye.' Damn. She'd chosen the scorched soul route. She rushed Steven Singh upstairs and out the door: 'Walk with me to the Post Office.'

Steven Singh carried some of her boxes. Rain-soaked words fell into her as they hurried. 'I went up north. Those blokes are worn and old now. The K looks thirty years younger; he didn't go in for back-breaking work. Parasite! Some of those guys are well set up now. Two or three properties to their names, pensions, money in the bank, kids who've gone professional. They got their dreams come true! Others...' shaking his head, thumbs down, 'kids gone from bad to worse. And how's this for betrayal? One idiot and his brother decided to build a hotel back home in Jallandhar town – first-class hotel, western toilets, all modern conveniences! The idiot brother stays back here to earn the money to keep the extended family going, the smart brother goes over there, builds the hotel, and lo and behold, everything ends up in his name. I thought I'd seen bitterness and betrayal. Not till I met this bloke.'

'B words,' adds Sita/Ferret.

'One tiny detail – in those early days, they had a shift system for bed space. The blokes who worked nights used them during the day, and those that worked in the day used them at night. They also had their own support system. The last guy to come from back home helped the next guy who came and so on. My old man and the K were room-mates. They might have even shared the same bed. That's where it began!' Steven Singh stopped dead. 'The K sized him up, saw through to his weak and trusting mind. And so began his calculations. The two went and got themselves girlfriends too. They were only lads then. Two German girls – semi-nurses or something. Seems a lot of German girls came over at that time. Saturday nights were pub nights for the men. The more daring ones went dancing.'

They'd arrived at the post office. 'Where there's a wrong, there's got to be a right,' concluded Steven Singh, handing her parcels back to her. 'I'll write his life history I will. It'll be X-rated too. How was the *gobi*?' Sita/Ferret looked at him, flummoxed. 'The cauliflower?' he reminded her. 'Did you cook it?' *Or did you waste it* was the implication. Mr Steven Singh did not like waste. She assured him that she'd cooked it with ginger, green chillies, and fresh coriander. He'd remember that.

Out of the tube station, she walked towards the park where Jeevan had arranged to meet her. The rain was still steadily falling, eroding brick and stone, filling drains and darkening the day. On such days when the Mausoleum was in a quiet, somnolent mood, Sita/Ferret the child would drag the old chair to the window, put the Indian quilt on it, and then snuggle in with a book and stolen snacks from the kitchen. She'd often fallen asleep like that, the heavens keeping her company.

Jeevan was sitting on a bench, coat collar turned up, a closed travelling bag by her side, the bottoms of her shalwar wet through, drops of water dribbling from her hair, trailing over her face.

'Let's go somewhere dry,' Sita/Ferret suggested, looking around for a park hut or shelter.

'No need,' replied Jeevan briskly, 'we've got to get going. I'll show you where you have to make your visit. We have to walk through the park. And then a couple of streets will take us there. You'll see the wall when we get near.' Jeevan slung the bag over her shoulder and started walking quickly up the path. Sita/Ferret had to run to catch up with her.

'What's the hurry?' she asked.

'Got to get back to work, doing the evening shift. But I'll wait for you. See how you are when you come out. Right, you want your explanation?'

Your pound of flesh? 'Yes,' replied Sita/Ferret emphatically.

'Fine,' accepted Jeevan. 'This is how it goes then: you're going to visit the man who is my paternal parent. First I'll tell you about him; secondly I'll tell you why he's there; thirdly I'll tell you about my mother and myself. That'll be the end. No questions.' Jeevan had already drafted it, subheadings and paragraphs. How hard had she worked at it, how much had she rehearsed so that it would come out pat, like a newspaper report, and without the emotional angle?

'He's in the slammer, over there,' she began. 'You can't see anything yet. I don't meet him. They, his fellow inmates, drubbed him for growing his hair, for getting religious. He's in the hospital wing at the moment. He was given a sentence of seven years. There was a trial. "The wheels of the law grind slow, but exceeding small." Our lives were dissected for all to see. The case was proved beyond doubt. It got into the newspapers. You probably read about it. End of first part.' She stopped, perhaps waiting for Sita/Ferret to admit to having read it, so she wouldn't have to talk any more. But Sita/Ferret is silent, thinking of the *She* in the E & C's sentences: Is *She* old and wrinkled now? Is *She* banged up somewhere?

'He committed,' Jeevan speeded up, 'the usual male crime.' Her feet splashed through a puddle, water flooding her shoes. Jeevan was silent, and when she did speak, she made a huge effort to say the words normally, but they came out squeezed, as if they'd been locked away under high pressure. 'The offence was: having carnal knowledge of a woman without her consent. The woman was known to us – a friend of my mother's, living on her own. "Fair game" goes the thinking in many minds. End of second part.' Jeevan stopped and, taking a bottle of water out of her bag, gulped it down.

'Third part: my mother and me, our lives were shipwrecked! We weren't social outcasts, but the world had changed. Nothing was different, yet everything had distorted. Not many daughters are given the chance to hear about their father's sexual exploits in anatomical detail – and in public. My mother worried about my marriage chances. I have removed that worry. I shall not marry. She normally does the visiting, but she's not well, and insists that these things need to be taken to him: clothes, home-made delicacies, forgiveness, loyalty and faithfulness. All the Indian wifely virtues are in this bag. My mother insists that he was led astray. I don't go for that. Two rules are absolute: taking personal responsibility and never taking anything by force.'

They came out of the park and walked across the road. 'And I'm doing my duty. He did bad and he's in there doing time. He did bad and I'm out here, doing good. Both paying off the family debt. This matter is now concluded.'

'No, it's not,' replied Sita/Ferret.

'Tough shit. That's your lot.' Then unable to stop herself, Jeevan asked, 'What else would you want?'

'Dunno,' Sita/Ferret replied, unable to say it was like desert sand in the eyes, and how about some tear water to dampen it?

'We're here,' Jeevan stated, coming to a stop by a high wall that seemed to be yards thick and miles long, curving away. Sita/Ferret felt dizzy looking up to the barbed wire on top. She'd escaped the Mausoleum, was she going to walk voluntarily into a prison?

'They're expecting you,' said Jeevan. 'I've made the arrangements. The papers are in the side pocket.' Sita/Ferret put her hand to the wall, as if she could feel the vibrations from inside.

'I'm going to go see Emily and Champa,' Sita/Ferret told Jeevan, shocked at herself as the words came from her, 'going-back' words. 'I grew up in their house. Emily's house really. I'm going to ask them about the woman who must have given birth to me.'

'Saying mother takes half the time.'

'Say father.'

Jeevan wiped the rain off her face. 'I've got to get to work on time. Susi's on duty today. So it'll be chaos when I get there. Time's short.' *But not for all*, was the unspoken sentence in both their minds. Behind the thick reinforced walls of that place, chameleon time changed its nature, became slow, never ending.

> *Abhorrence for the crime;*
> *Punishment for the guilty;*
> *Pity for the broken.*

Grey-black hair fanned out against white hospital pillows, framing a battered, scarred face. His eyes had looked away from her as she explained who she was, in this instance his daughter's friend, speaking in Hindi, bringing out the formal phrases of polite address. She became silent. A broken jaw had saved him from having to search for words with which to speak to her. She had sat for a few minutes longer, unable to inflict the brutality of an abrupt departure. Was he deserving of mercy and forgiveness? Everyone is deserving of mercy, but forgiveness is a different act altogether, implying the acceptance of guilt and reconciliation with the perpetrator.

From which part of ourselves do we bring out evil? From which part love? From which barbaric part do we crush others and from which sublime part do we cherish them?

Theft is a criminal offence too. People get banged up for stealing a plastic toy from Woolworths; she'd stolen a damned fortune. Why hadn't Emily put the police on to her? As the victim had done in this man's case. Sita/Ferret said goodbye, and left with these thoughts.

Outside, Jeevan is shivering; her clothes are completely damp. They do not speak. Sita/Ferret understands more than a thousand explanations; is now privy to the riddling incomprehension, the horror. They walk off in different directions.

Evening-time: time to walk towards the station, to journey to her next visit, the one that also holds the fear of the unknown. Are people always unknown? Her steps are fast, purposeful. She used to stalk people! Watch the way they walked, the bags they carried, the clothes they wore; eavesdrop on conversations. Thus the streets became hers. Now she walks behind a group of Asian girls, dark hair flipping round their shoulders, clothes ranging from the latest fashions to home-sewn shalwar-kameez with ingenious mixing and matching along the way, bags on their shoulders, platform heels on their feet, and the patter of mixed lingoes on their tongues. They started looking back, suspicious of the woman stalking their footsteps. She ducked into an Indian café, ordered a coffee she didn't need and became fascinated by the tender Asian romance two tables away. Judging by the elaborate arrangement of her dress, the woman must be a bridal arrival: henna-patterned hands, red wedding bangles chinkling on her arms, gold-fringed *dupatta* on her head, *fresh from the pind! Culturally organic.* Several plates of food lay before the couple: the woman delicately gathered portions with her fingertips and tenderly popped them into the man's mouth. That's why he'd gone all the way back, for a home-grown girl!

By the time she reached his street, darkness had come, street lamps lit the road, and curtains were drawn against glowing windows, intimating private comfort and familial togetherness.

She collected the envelope from the caretaker, with the key inside! Such trust being placed in her. Closing the door of his flat behind her, she leaned against it and listened. The fourth visit. They were still strangers to each other; 'I woz 'ere' hadn't yet been etched into the air. Putting her hand on the wall she progressed along the hallway, her hand gathering a sense of the patterns, bumps and bulges – did the murals have a coolness of their own? She hesitated before going into the bedroom. His injunction no longer applied.

'*Do not tempt fate!*' Champa's voice admonished. Then she remembered the fire. Loading her fingertip, she closed her eyes and placed a dot of ash onto her forehead. Now she could enter the bedroom.

Looking but not touching, she ended up in the bathroom and found herself opening the large cupboard, examining shaving foam, deodorants, the paraphernalia of keeping clean and smelling good. At the back were bottles of cough medicines, cold cures and a stack of Paracetamol packets. Was there a perennial headache problem here? She took a packet, opened it and found it to be empty, the same with the second packet and the rest. Quickly restacking them she closed the cupboard. A door banged shut in the hallway.

Awkwardness stayed any embrace of greeting.

'You've got a smudge on your forehead,' he remarked. She rubbed at it with her fingers. 'Now you've smeared it all over. Let me...' one hand at the side of her head, the other rubbing with a tissue. Proximity!

He had planned a dinner evening.

'Can you cook?' he asked.

'Depends,' she replied guardedly, empty Paracetamol packets now stacked in her brain.

'Oh, right,' he said, 'in that case, can you wash the lettuce?'

'Will I have to get my hands wet?' She was sulky and sullen. Old loves can't be evicted, especially if they willed a legacy of guilt.

'Indian *khana* tonight,' he said, busily taking out packets and vegetables from his freezer. 'You know the old joke, "eating Indian food with a knife and fork is like making love through an interpreter".'

Love again! That poor, much maligned word. 'Do you still want me to do the "work" here or was that just a lie and a fabrication?' she asked, and accused.

'No,' jerking his head back as he slid his ingredients into a pan and hot oil spluttered up. 'I mean, yes to the former and no to the latter.'

'Don't do that,' almost stamping her foot. 'I hate this former latter, latter former business. Takes me ages to work out which is which.'

'So sorry. Didn't realise I was going to be overtaxing your brain.'

'Is this enough lettuce?' she asked coldly, holding up two leaves.

'Excellent. Great choice of lettuce leaves.'

148

'How come there are Seven Deadly Sins but Ten Commandments?' she asked. 'I mean if the Ten Commandments are broken, then ten deadly sins will have been committed. Are there three missing Deadly Sins?' He didn't look at her puzzled and uncomprehending as others might have. He was concentrating on emptying his cooking into serving bowls. 'It doesn't balance...' she was about to continue and then shut up. *Thou shalt not covet thy neighbour's wife.*

'This isn't supermarket food,' she remarked as she helped herself.

'I had to learn how to look after myself. A is for...' A warning look stopped him.

They sat in front of the fire. He in one armchair, she in the other, space between them, as on the first night. She excused herself, and took off her boots, tucked her feet under her, snuggled into the armchair. Her visits to this flat must be numbered by now. Soon there wouldn't be anything left he would want from her.

'I'll give you Emily's address,' she said into their silence. He went and fetched a notebook; her eyes slid over his body as he came back, from the shoulders to the tender stomach, down to the glinting belt buckle.

'Is that buckle gold?' she asked.

He laughed, 'Nothing misses those sharp eyes.' Not even stacks of empty Paracetamol packets! 'It is,' then he continued without one of his pauses. Was he becoming accustomed to talking to her without having to first examine his thoughts. 'It used to belong to my grandfather.'

She spelled out Emily's address. A feeling of betrayal pervaded her. That address had been knitted to her since she left; its sounds had never passed her lips.

He put on a tape, and the haunting notes of a flute filled the room. He started talking. *Quid pro quo?* Matching what she had given him with what he could give? 'I lived under the threat of theft,' he began. In the end, it had been an American girl who had stolen him, seduced him, and planted rebellion in him. 'She didn't give a damn, about anyone or anything. She was a barbarian!' But she'd evidently lit a slow-burning fuse.

'As soon as my training finished, I came to England and didn't see them, the mother, the father, the grandmother, for three years. I punished them. Then my father died. I chucked in my job and took a train,' one of his pauses, 'in the opposite direction. But it didn't work. Running away never does, does it?'

'Bloody well does,' she answered. She'd force open that creaky gate if she had to. 'It's just that you have to go back for the things that got left behind.'

'I ended up returning on the next train,' said Kala, picking up from where he'd left off. 'B for borrow, borrowing the money for the plane ticket. That was a lesson.' A stained-glass lamp threw shades of colour upon them, velvety darkness surrounded them. 'There's complete confusion over the past. My grandmother changes what she's said, perhaps she's telling different parts of it, I don't know. This is what I've pieced together. After my grandfather disappeared, my grandmother didn't go straight to the police. I don't know why. Then there were ransom demands. There's confusion here too. At first she refused to pay. It was coming up to Independence, a time of meltdown, turmoil, terror. She did hire private detectives.' He was staring into his wine glass. 'I visited their office once, and talked to the son; they thought it was a gang of blackmailers. Apparently my grandfather had been involved in…something he shouldn't have been involved in.' Kala wouldn't use a descriptive word; wouldn't say 'bad', 'wicked', 'criminal'; wouldn't speak ill of the *disappeared*.

'They wouldn't tell me. "Only your grandmother can tell you," they said.' He shook his head, 'She never has, there are still secrets she carries. At some point she received the C for communications, demands. And, an item,' his hand a little unsteady. 'An item of the male body, you understand.' Sita/Ferret goes cold and looks away from those *pretty pretty eyes*. 'She sold everything, gathering cash, paying up. She has guilt to make her mad too! For not doing it first time, for not going to the police. The last letter was different from the others. Demanded her jewellery, mentioned specific items. This was odd. Cash and gold were the currency; cash can be converted, gold can be sold anywhere in the world, but jewellery is more difficult to exchange. After that, silence.' He closed his eyes. A semi-circle of black on his cheeks, then the grey eyes opened to look at her.

'The country was drenched in blood. Murder, killing, rape, looting… The Seven Deadly Sins ran rampant. My grandmother waited and waited, but no more C for communications. Eventually she dragged herself to the police. What could they do? They were in the middle of a battle themselves, an unofficial civil war, or perhaps official – who knows? – raged around them. They didn't have time for her sorry tale. She was no longer the rich haughty woman who could command power. They reprimanded her for dealing with thugs, and told her that her husband was probably long dead. She should say her prayers for him. "Not till I've seen his body," came the reply; she still hasn't said those prayers. The last rites have not been performed. So I think,' he said, leaning forward, those dark fringed grey eyes that much closer, 'if your Emily can throw some light on this business, my grandmother can do the necessary, and the past can finally be history.' She didn't answer him. Emily's house was a house of secrets. Emily herself was a secret.

They lie against each other, neither inviting nor rejecting, to be both in themselves and next to each other. Sometime late in the night, through the dark, her fingers travel over his face, a fluttering butterfly path, alighting and lifting, gradually settling; exploring the texture of skin, learning the hidden shape from forehead to cheek, moving down to the chin, then wandering up again, smoothing the eyebrows, feeling the flicker of a ladybird's wings; fingers following the curved lines of lips, hovering; and descending, tracing the distance from corner to corner, discovering tiny movements, brushed by warm breath. She places her five fingers over the lips, simulation of sealing; he withholds his breath, and her fingers grow cold with a waiting fear. Here was the fear of loss. She was familiar with fears of loss; the loss of security, the loss of home, the loss of gems secreted in a coat. She'd shed them and found that she had survived, but bruised, more vulnerable. This was a new breed of fear; the fear of losing something that had not yet been possessed, the cancellation of a journey not yet planned. She removes her fingers and bends her head to catch the rush of air, dipping lower...

Having thieved the taste of him, her lips draw back, her fingers retreat. Having foraged into another, do you remain the same or does the simple act create a new version of you? The old tales tell of a kiss stealing a soul, a kiss waking the sleeping beauty, a kiss betraying Jesus. The kiss of death! The kiss of life!

A shudder runs through her as searching lips comb their way from neck to eyelids, fashioning a path across the brow, travelling down the other side: skin upon skin, touch upon touch, a conversation without words.

He stops and moves back, but not away. The differing shades of black in a darkened room come into focus. Is this destiny? Where engaging in one act creates other acts that create the pattern of a life? Faith and future placed into the hands of another? *Broken faith never mends. Once committed, forever condemned.* She lies on the side where a previous one, in such recent memory, had mixed her love into powder, and made herself into ash.

Hadn't she known that the age of tragic love is long past? These days, love is the diluted dose served in soaps on the TV screen.

Sita/Ferret woke up, shaking with fright. Emily and Champa were visiting her. Emily talked of blood on the streets, 'You're a vicious people, you like to do down your own. There was a girl,' Emily had whispered, 'the men took her off.' Sita/Ferret slid out of bed, crouching by the side. Emily used to tell this story to the little girl, winding the girl's plait round her finger, pulling slightly, 'You know what they do to little girls?' she'd asked. The child Sita/Ferret had shaken her head. 'You'll learn,' Emily had declared, as if pronouncing sentence. 'I was out with F...with *She*. A mob of men suddenly appeared in front of us. I pushed myself into a corner. *She, gutter wali* held onto me with her filthy hands. She's lucky I didn't push her away. The little girl the men had taken,' Emily had breathed in deeply, 'screamed her head off. Not that they cared. The screams added to their blood lust.'

Emily had relived it, she knew the perforations of the act; somehow it had evened out the score to witness its affliction on another. 'One of their own, they did it to their own. When they'd done what they wanted, they cut her screaming. Knives cut screams,' her finger across the child's throat. The act had settled in Emily. If they could do this kind of cannibalism to each other, whatever she had done or may do was insignificant. 'It happens here too.' She'd nodded her head warningly. 'Men on their own or in gangs. Gangbangs, they call it. Men doing it to women. That's what you'll get if you leave this house. Be glad I look after you. You don't want to end up like that little girl, with blood in your eyes.'

Sita/Ferret slipped away, out of the room so as not to disturb Kala with memories of Emily. He might hear them doing their nightmare work in her mind. *Look a cobra in the eyes and you'll never be afraid again.* Sita/Ferret had tried to imagine a cobra and practise, but always failed. Emily had stoked her head with grisly tales, always ending with, 'This is what you do to your own.'

She went into the reception room and curled up in the chair by the cold fire.

'What are you doing?' He was standing at the door, anxiety on his face. He had woken up and found the place next to him empty. Old fears had come hurtling back.

'So,' she said, as if concluding a conversation, 'you're going back to India?'

He looked taken aback, 'Yes, when I can,' moving around her to sit on the settee, running his hand over her shoulders as he passed, reassuring himself of her solidity.

'I can't,' she replied, though he hadn't invited her. 'Haven't got a passport. I could apply for one.' Adding a thin laugh, 'Can you imagine what the Home Office would make of me?'

'They'd declare you illegal and deport you. But the Indians wouldn't have you: "Madam has no proper documentation for return entry",' mimicking officialiese Indo-English. 'They could say to you, "go back where you came from",' he paused to add the relish of an ironic smile, 'but the English would say, "we concur entirely, madam should go back where she came from." You'd be in a right pickle.'

'Fuck off!' she shouted, jumping out of her chair and stamping her foot in a childish rage. The words hurtled out of pain and rage. She shouted them at him, as long ago she had shouted them at Emily. In her teenage years, with hormones causing havoc inside her, she had asked for permission to go to a school disco. Champa had delivered a straight 'No,' and lectured her on the unsuitability of such events for young Indian women whose reputations might be put at risk if they were to be seen disporting themselves at such nefarious events.

'Reputation?' Sita/Ferret had repeated incredulously, and stomped off to ask Emily who was English and would understand. For once she had been confident of Emily's support.

'No,' Emily had declared also. 'These affairs are not for Indian girls.'

It was a sentence which had thrown the teenage Ferret into a screaming fit. 'How do you know what's good for us?' she'd shouted back at her, dangerous, raging shouts against Emily. Champa had hauled herself up the stairs as fast as she could, her breath coming in short gasps by the time she had reached them.

'What are you going to do there?' Emily had asked sarcastically. 'Sit against the wall. Stupid little wallflower! Or go off with English boys? Come back with a bun in the oven? A little half-caste bastard. Not here you don't.'

'I'll do whatever I want!' Sita/Ferret had replied recklessly.

'You stupid little girl,' Emily had said, levering herself up from her chair, 'getting stupid ideas into your head. That was what ruined *her*. You're not like us. You're like the ones back there,' stick pointing through the wall.

'You're going to arrange a marriage for me are you?' Sita/Ferret had spat at her.

'A deaf, dumb and blind cripple wouldn't have you.'
'Fuck off!' Sita/Ferret had yelled, inviting retribution.

She had thrown those words at Emily and now at him, a century in between. On her planned trip, when she got to the Mausoleum, she knew Emily wouldn't tell her a thing, and Sita/Ferret had no key with which to unlock that tongue. She'd given away the only thing she might have bartered. She'd return from the Mausoleum, empty-handed and humiliated – if she was lucky. Emily could always dial a three-digit number and get the boys in blue to cart her off for good.

Bristling with her anger, Sita/Ferret asked him about Poonum. She had asked him last time too. Jealousy gorges on repetition.

'There's only one hen in this coop that I can see. At the moment.'

'How very romantic,' she commented.

'That's the last thing you want.'

'The last thing you want,' she threw back at him.

'It doesn't last – or do you know different?' he asked, coming up, hands tight on her shoulder, scratching her neck with his teeth. She didn't know any different. She pushed herself into him, hands on his buttocks.

'If I asked you,' she said to him, echoing a sentence of his. 'If I asked you politely,' reneging on herself, 'would you return the...goods to me?'

'Can't. They belong to my grandmother.'

'How do you know?'

'With my brain, heart and history! The only way.' Hand pushing between her legs, through her clothes, his clothes, in fact, for he didn't allow an undressed state in his bed. She grabbed his hair as his fingers plunged into her and they tumbled to the floor. They looked at each other warily, appraisingly, assessing the dangers in front. How much grief would one visit upon the other?

She's over his face, her hands on either side; his hand goes round her head and they meet in a hard, severe kissing where flesh and feeling tumble in circles, from resistance to attack, from defence to aggression; their bodies roll, tussle and wrestle, hands roam, hold, grip, bruise. Clothes remain intact, flesh remains hidden. If a button comes undone, it is quickly refastened; if a pyjama top rides up, it is quickly pulled down. Thinking they are safe, they enter more dangerous territory, and their clothes become wet with the mauling.

Chapter Thirteen

Bombay, 1943–4

Emily was in a state of red alert. The servant had brought up a message that an Indian lady wished to see her. The servant added that the lady had mentioned a name, a name made familiar by marriage.

This was no innocuous social call. The woman and those who had sent her were coming for payment or revenge for something that her husband must have done. So now he was trying to ruin her from the grave.

Emily's first instinct had been to refuse to see her, but then had immediately changed her mind. If she refused to see this woman, who could tell what kind of person they would send next. She sat down at her desk, running her fingers along the raised lattice edge. Contrary to the rest of the house, everything in Emily's rooms was Indian; her bedroom was furnished with carved cupboards, painted screens, a decorated bed with ivory inlay patterns, and various woven settees and chairs. Gopal had laughed at her choices, 'Nobody buys this stuff anymore, only the peasants who can't afford anything else!' The Indians of his ilk were all busy filling their houses with foreign-designed goods. But she'd stared back at him stubbornly; she was building the future she'd been promised.

Emily clenched her fists around a pen and pulled a sheet of paper towards her. She'd reinvented herself. If she hadn't, she'd be dirt in the gutter – or back home and the butt of their scorn: 'Miss hoity-toity didn't know that pride comes before a fall.' At first the twin sisters Sin and Society had haunted her, no matter how often she reminded herself she was only using her brains and if she really had sinned, the devil would take his payment in due course. As long as it wasn't in this life. As long as she could achieve the life she'd longed for.

But that didn't mean she was about to make payments on behalf of her dear deceased, not to anyone. These people must have had cool and calculating heads for they had bided their time, waited till she had dragged herself up and had something in her hands. She heard the chinkling of anklets and bangles long before the woman entered. Dipping her pen in the inkwell, Emily scratched across the paper in front of her, writing his name and scoring it through, writing his name and scoring it through.

When Champa entered all she could see was a halo of blonde curls and the glint of blue eyes. Abashed, she hovered near the door, her confidence seeping away.

'Namaste!' using the rituals of greeting as a steadying post.

'Good afternoon!' replied Emily, cold and stern.

'Forgive me for visiting you.' This was not what Champa had intended to say. She was completely thrown by seeing Emily sitting like an officer behind a desk, pen in hand as if writing a report. A thought came to her mind, twitching a smile out of her lips: were the ladies who worked for Emily required to write reports on their work; did Emily then write reports on the reports and send them on to a higher authority? Perhaps there were to be many establishments like Emily's, properly run and regulated – yet another innovation by the caring, sharing Rajwallahs.

Emily saw the twitching lips, the vain attempts to hide a smile. Flinging aside her resolution to handle this in a cool and calm manner, she marched over to the woman, who was much shorter than her, and glared down.

'What do you want?' she demanded. The startled woman fell back a pace, the peek-a-boo smile utterly erased. 'Well?' demanded Emily, moving a step nearer, 'I haven't got all day!' Champa mumbled an incomprehensible half sentence, which infuriated Emily even further.

'If you can't tell me what you want, then leave.' The look of relief on the woman's face as she turned towards the door goaded Emily into contradicting herself. 'No you don't!' The woman stopped dead in her tracks, her back to Emily. Emily found herself automatically assessing the attractions displayed by the deeply scooped neckline of the blouse, and the luscious display of flesh between sari and blouse; this woman possessed a voluptuousness that would stand her in good stead for a while yet. 'Since you've gone to the trouble of coming here, you'd better come clean, and tell me what you want.'

Being barked at in this way did little for Champa's confidence and composure. She chided herself for coming here on the whim of an idea.

'I used to help your husband with the language, explaining things to him, and advising him much about our people and country. Now that you are in business also, I thought you might be requiring the same kind of help. I would be glad to be of assistance.' That was what she had meant to say. Instead, her hand brought out the velvet jewellery box, and a foot moved towards the door. Emily read the address of the jewellers and examined the contents. Snapping it shut, she put the box on her desk. 'A cheap trinket,' she scorned.

'Your husband gave it to me. It was a present, to me. I was only showing you.' Champa moved a step back into the room, her hand outstretched.

'The wife,' declared Emily in a tightly turned voice, 'is the one who inherits; all I got was debts, disgrace and damnation! This,' clutching the box again, 'is a token of what I should have had, but which he gave you! Did you think I would be pleased to see you? To know that my husband went from me,' blue eyes ablaze, 'to you?' she finished, looking at her in contempt.

Champa hadn't seen it that way. As far as she and all the others were concerned, a wall of unknowing stood between them and the wife. Two parallel worlds.

'There was something wrong with my husband,' said Emily, 'and now I know what it was. He liked the likes of you. But the likes of you killed him, ruined my life and now you think you can come here and try and cheat me again!'

'You can keep the box.' Ever since Champa had first heard of Emily, she had placed her on a pedestal; even after she had learnt that Emily had joined the oldest profession in the world, she had remained there, for Emily's social reach was so far above hers that she may as well have been of another world. Emily's entrepreneurial flourish in setting up her own establishment had impressed Champa even further. Until this moment. Champa turned towards the door.

'Stop!' Emily's voice glued her to the spot. 'Don't you dare move. Look at you, all fat and no shape,' power tripping on jealousy, 'another couple of years and you'll be no good to anyone. Is that why you came? Because you thought I could set you up for life? Did he promise you that? Well he promised me too and look where I am!'

Champa was dying to be out and away, to put this mistake behind her, but Emily's last few sentences proved to be of a fascinating potency. For the first time it occurred to her that life on the other side may not be as rosy as it was made out; that these *bade log*, these higher people, had frailties and futilities of their own, and that Emily was a very disappointed woman.

'There's nothing I can do for you,' snapped Emily. 'You're the wrong colour, the wrong shape, the wrong type.'

'Did you and he have jokes and laugh?' asked Champa.

Emily stopped short, 'I was his wife, not his whore.'

'Of course. It is better to be the wife,' Champa agreed sagaciously.

'Get to the point? What did you come for?' demanded Emily.

'Oh, it was nothing. I only came to give my best wishes for your...for this...' Not knowing such euphemisms, her voice faltered, 'to you!'

'Not good enough!' Emily leaned against her desk, arms crossed.

'But, very best wishes I do give you and I hope God will bless this...' She should have stopped at the end of the first bit, then a memory rose up. 'Good luck!' she declared resoundingly, in precisely the tone that her sahib had taught her. Emily heard his voice in the repetition. 'I go now. Thank you madam.'

'No, you don't. Why did you bring me this box? Did you think you were going to blackmail me?' Champa hadn't been taught that word, or she would have left immediately, horrified at the interpretation put on her visit, and berating herself for being naive and foolish. However she didn't know, and the future began to take shape.

'Introduction. To introduce me. But you are a very busy woman, so I will say goodbye. And if you like, you may keep the box. I will only take the little, little chain inside.' The loss of it was now afflicting Champa as sharply as if she'd handed over a diamond pendant. Never once had it occurred to her that Emily might appropriate it. She'd imagined that Emily had a hoard of jewellery, worth a thousand times more than this little gift; that the man who had lavished this present on her, must have honoured his wife with items of far greater value and beauty. Neither had she thought of jealousy as an ingredient in their encounter; she had imagined Emily secure in her superiority.

'And why on earth did you think it necessary to introduce yourself to me? Did you think I'd be interested in his one-anna whores?'

Champa pulled her sari *palla* around herself. Defence. 'No, it was not necessary. I am sorry. I made a mistake. If you please, give me my chain then I will go.'

'And come back again tomorrow with a trumped-up demand, flaunting another trinket that some man gave you!' Emily accused her.

'I will not be coming again. And please keep everything. Namaste.' The last was a defiant gesture as she opened the door and slipped out. It was no consolation to Champa that Emily had more emotional corrosion lying in wait for her amid the entwined hairs. Champa was grieving the loss of her connection with him.

Feet came running after her. Emily had sent one of the servants to bring her back. The point of choice! Champa could have refused and who knows whether she and Emily would have ever met again. Champa did not, and perhaps could not refuse. One defiant gesture was enough for the day.

The Girl had given up on Emily. Nowadays she lingered on a roof, next to the tiny rooms occupied by the elderly Mr Ram Lal who gave English tuition: 'First class, A class tuition. Most Reasonable Fees.' His voice intoned, 'Aaaai, B, C.' Her lips imitated. 'Pleeze,' he said; 'pleeze,' she said. 'The day is verry hot!' 'The day is verry hot,' she whispered into her hands. Once he had heard her and had come out to investigate. She'd pretended to be picking nits out of her hair. Disgust had wrinkled his face and he had hurried back into his room. Occasionally he would catch glimpses of her, but never bothered to chase her away. He would have been astounded to learn that a linguistic theft was in progress.

Chapter Fourteen

London, March 1997

Beware the Ides of March!

The morning after! And the third time Sita/Ferret had sat at his breakfast table. They were quiet, restricting themselves to a few words, shying from any that might touch on the personal. Kala said he had to go away for a few days.

Separation! An anguish shot through her. Wasn't this the usual, tritest way of saying 'namaste, bye-bye babe.'

'When I come back, I have to see Emily.' Relief zinged through her. He yet had unfinished business. His last goodbyes could wait.

She rushed to the station, thinking she was forever on the run. She had a resignation period to work out, a future to sort out, and an E & C to visit. As she walked, the spring sun lit the world with fresh new sunshine, warm on her skin, the colours of spring flowers stood out vividly bright, and a teasing breeze lifted her hair.

Standing on the escalator, moving down into the depths to travel below the city, her eyes skimmed the passing posters that covered the entire range from books to bras, from West-End shows to sleazy revues, from monuments to money making. Sita/Ferret had walked endless miles of London streets, visited every famous building, browsed in the markets, gone into the museums, wandered through the parks; lived in its squalid council estates, eaten in its cheap cafés, seen the wretched and the rich, the sinners and the saviours. She could reach out, touch a brick and claim kinship. This city of church, palace and parliament, plots and conspiracies, gravitas and nobility, raunchy sex and high-powered commerce – its allure enticed the world.

On the platform, Sita/Ferret ran her hand along the wall; it came away covered in grime. Everything leaves its deposit. The woman who had carried her for nine months must still have Sita/Ferret living in the lining of her brain! She must have to work hard to stop her seeping out into the rest of her, that rest of her called conscience.

Working in her basement, marvelling at the marble or metal figures she worked with, awed by the life and passion contained in them, she was already starting to miss this edge of beauty that she handled each day. The phone rang, disturbing her concentration.

'Good afternoon,' said the voice at the other end.

'Jetsam!' Sita/Ferret exclaimed. This frequency of contact could become addictive.

'How are you?' Jeevan asked – she who didn't normally indulge in these meaningless rituals. Sita/Ferret replied that she was fine, fine and dandy, and waited.

'Are you going to go?' So Jeevan had remembered – and the first time Jeevan had asked a personal question.

'To the Mausoleum? Yes, yes, yes,' answered Sita/Ferret, laying traps for her tomorrows.

'Once something's happened,' Jeevan began, tumbling out her words so she couldn't take them back, 'you can't rub it out. Starts to live right inside you. Like, in the eyes, so you're always seeing it, or in the guts, so when you're feeling something about anything, could be lollipops, or the colour of cornflakes, it kind of floods out.'

Was Jeevan trying to warn her? Emily might not even open the door. Or Champa might say, 'Where have you been, you naughty girl. Have you remembered the things I taught you?' Time might shiver and deposit Sita/Ferret back at their beck and call, as if nothing had happened. Or Champa might go on about her other obsession: Champa the chaste might ask of Sita/Ferret, 'Have you come back "intact?", "respectable?", "marriageable?" ' Did Champa still cherish her dream of seeing Sita/Ferret bedecked and dressed in bridal red, taking those seven sacred steps round the fire, taking her rightful place in society? Sita/Ferret didn't know why Champa was the one so concerned about her matrimonial future; perhaps a sustained ambition that hinted at a connection? Sita/Ferret had shied away from that idea, as if she could pick and choose whichever truth she wanted. This brought the hidden crevices of Emily to mind. The maternal connection could just as well be Emily: an unsuitable liaison at an advanced age, an unwanted product; only tolerated because chucking babies in the bin was considered bad form. A dread weight settled inside Sita/Ferret. Was there any need to trek out to the far borders of suburbia for a dose of blood poisoning?

'Want to meet up?' asked Jeevan.

'Clubbing? Going to a rave?' Sita/Ferret asked eagerly. Dancing, drinking and scoring. The London tribe at its habitual rituals. 'Yeah, I want to shake, stir and sauté my nerves.'

'There are other ways of doing that,' replied Jeevan dryly. 'How about eating?' As if this was the latest fad to hit London town! 'There's a restaurant,' she continued quickly, 'called Chor Bizarre.'

'Shouldn't that be Chor Bazaar? Thieves' Market?' questioned Sita/Ferret.

'It's my birthday,' Jeevan continued quickly, ignoring the interruption. 'Don't,' she added, sharply cutting off the 'Happy Birthday' congratulations. Jeevan had left it to the last minute to issue her invitation. Had she teetered all day, in case it carried consequences greater than she could foresee?

'Did you know India was a Police State?' Jeevan asked, shooting off in her other direction. 'Under the Raj. The Raj functioned as a Police State. "Coercion was the bedrock of British policy." End of quote. Author V B Kulkarni.'

'You know things off by heart, too!'

'No, Flotsam,' replied Jeevan, 'I know it off by memory. A great deal can rest on memory!' A verdict? 'The country was brutalised, barbarised, pauperised. And then the spin-doctors got to work. The Brits pulled off the biggest PR heist in history.'

'And it is history,' argued Sita/Ferret. 'Leave it.'

A pause at the other end, then the voice came, like a slow crack across glass, 'By the end I wanted the untruth, the lie. Afterwards, I thought I should have lied.' Then she started working her voice back up to normal. 'After all, everybody lies, the world is built on lies, isn't it?' Jeevan stopped, and then said, 'History lesson over.'

'I think it's just beginning,' replied Sita/Ferret.

'See you tonight.' Click. The phone went dead.

Flashing neon signs, the bright lights of city bars and floodlit displays of shop windows, the movement of people like electric currents along the streets – the buzz of night-time London! She walked through the crowds in Leicester Square, vibrant with its cinemas, restaurants, and gut-shattering fairground rides, scattering excited screams into the night.

Jeevan had dressed in a long, black, figure-hugging dress, not a centimetre of skin peeping out. She'd taken a table, poured wine into glasses, and opened a pack of cigarettes.

'No roll-ups?' queried Sita/Ferret.

'I've been saving up for these,' explained Jeevan. Then waving her hand at the jumble of artefacts, she declared, 'Welcome to Chor Bizarre, Thieves' Market. And lifting her glass, added, 'Thieves R Us...'

'A meeting of thieves!' contributed Sita/Ferret.

'The Tory Party,' translated Jeevan.

'Let's keep this clean shall we?' admonished Sita/Ferret. 'Criminals Incorporated.'

'That could be any one of the multinationals. Let's be specific shall we?' rebuked Jeevan, lighting their cigarettes, telling the waitress they weren't ready to order yet.

'Breaking and Entering, Burglary with Intent,' Jeevan announced.

'That's the whole of colonialism, what's specific about that?' argued Sita/Ferret, taking a careful puff of her cigarette. If it rushed too quickly down her throat, she'd splutter and cough. 'How about Disturbance of the Peace, Battery and Assault?'

'That's all the wars that have ever been, and there's nothing clean about war,' stated Jeevan categorically. A mixed group of people, men and women, Asian and English, had settled at the table next to them; one of them, an Asian guy, was casting his eye around the room. A predator!

'OK. Robber's Retreat! How's that?' Sita/Ferret's glance crossed that of the predator and did not look away.

'It'll do,' conceded Jeevan. 'So we're back to square one. Don't do that!' Her voice cut across Sita/Ferret like a whip. 'If you're not going to follow through, don't start.'

Sita/Ferret was not in a mood to be preached to. 'I'll do what I bloody well want.'

'He thinks,' Jeevan leaned towards her, 'you'll bloody well do what he wants. India was prey to the predator. Do you know how much money was transferred to England from 1757 onwards? Over seventeen million pounds a year. Figures by William Digby. Work it out to 1947, add in extra taxes for wars, plus men and materials, loans that were never repaid, the loss of industries, inflation etc. I'll write it out for you, the figures will make your eyes go dizzy...'

'A for accounts, B for billions, C for cash. How about some more wine?' asked Sita/Ferret, quickly draining her glass and filling it again, tanking up for the history lessons that were becoming the essence of every conversation with Jeevan.

Jeevan looked at her with desolation in her eyes, 'As soon as something's happened, it becomes history. And we lose the truth of it, so we have to go back to find it,' she continued, looking down at the table, hiding the feelings she couldn't hide in her eyes. 'Truth does balance the world, like a spine running through it. Money isn't the soul of a country, but it damn well is its blood. To steal blood and soul. Hey Flotsam, don't look so worried. We should enjoy Englistan properly now. We paid in advance. Let's drink to that.' Glasses clinked, wine spilt. For once they giggled.

A large, noisy group of women passed by them, settling at one of the bigger tables. Metropolitan women on a night out!

Jeevan continued, 'You know, they used to say living in England was like living in a jail. Let me tell you, there's nothing sweet about... Right! Confession time! I go first. Since we started yesterday, we may as well continue.' Cracking a *papad*, she took a large piece and bit into it. 'It's "happy b'rtday," day today. It's also *his* birthday. Hence the special delivery and so on.' Jeevan kept her eyes down. 'Used to be a great day – father and daughter doing "Happy B'rtday". I can't understand...' At last she looked up, her eyes too red and dry, 'Why? How could...' She stopped to adjust the shaking of her voice. 'It's a sin.' She took a cigarette and lit it. 'So's this,' holding up her red-tipped cigarette, 'according to some people. But real sins are sins beyond doubt. I thought if I could commit a sin, I might find out. But this is as far as I got. Pathetic isn't it? But I can't go any further, can I?'

Jeevan was trying to live in her brain while all the time her heart was hurting.

Sita/Ferret didn't know what to say, and in between a movement, Sita/Ferret saw Poonum staring at her, grim and tight, from another table.

They left Chor Bizarre fairly drunk, but exaggerating wildly, swaying, slurring their speech. Each took a taxi. Jeevan had booked them earlier, leaving nothing to chance. 'Chance can be GBH.'

Sita/Ferret kept her mind tightly bound and on the Sunday morning began a journey that seemed out of place, out of time. Too near to the annual pilgrimage she'd already made, too soon before the next.

At the station she bought a return ticket, a newspaper, and dropped coins in the charity box. The media was the biggest gossipmonger of all. An article about Diana and Camilla occupied the centre pages of the newspaper: one man, two women. An ancient story. Sita/Ferret turned the pages and read about the possibility of an election in the next few weeks. The politicians would saddle up, ride across the land and its TV screens, claiming morality, acumen (she smiled at another A word) and right to be on their side. Could it be that now change would at last come? A turn in the history of the land? Would she be able to get even a hint or clue from Emily, a mere fragment upon which she could build a history of her own. And if she did, would she then want to bury it as deep as the sea?

Outside the station, Sita/Ferret couldn't bring herself to wait for the bus. Her tense, nervous state would take her there just as quickly. Crossing the road she saw her reflection coming towards her from a shop window. Sita/Ferret didn't like looking at herself, she had never indulged in long examinations of her exterior for answers to the interior. If ever she had made the mistake of lingering narcissus-like, the old voices of mockery would fly out: *go on, have a good look, devils live in there. The longer you look, the nearer they'll get, then they'll jump!* Flinging her red-nailed fingers into Sita/Ferret's eyes, Emily had cried, 'Devil eyes, devil child.'

Thus, Sita/Ferret saw no need for a larger mirror in her bathroom.

Now she walked towards her image in the shop window. Had the mother looked like her at her age? Or had the father bequeathed the lineaments of face? Coming eye to eye with her reflection, Sita/Ferret risked an extended, in-depth look, searching for the devils planted there. Emily would no doubt ask how a devil child could see the devil in her own eyes?

'Afraid? No fear. Not me. I'm on my way to see E-m-i-l-y.'

Lifting her hair in her hands, she twisted it into a knot, stretched a hand and measured her face; the delicate place where she and the world met. Within the context of the world, her face was worth less than a grain of sand, but she was the only occupant, and she held a lifelong lease. She moved to erase her reflection and behind it emerged Mr and Miss Smart-Set India, surrounded by an excess of accessories. He was dressed in a black high-necked jacket, red handkerchief decorating his pocket. She, hand on her hip, stared haughtily out at the world.

Jeevan was the one most often dressed in shalwar-kameez: 'Just to show that not everything in a shalwar-kameez is sugar and spice and all things nice,' she'd said, baring her teeth in a tiger smile. Sita/Ferret had only once, since leaving the Mausoleum, decked herself out Asian style. Meanings are given over by clothes and fabrics, and she was sick of Over There, so she wouldn't choose to be like Over There would she?

Forever the shifting sands underneath her: perhaps, possibly, maybe; always the conditional. She couldn't use permanent words because she didn't know anything. Sita/Ferret's only permanence was in Emily's possession. How was she going to wrest it from her? Assuming she didn't get banged in the slammer for theft of Emily's permanence. Sita/Ferret opened the door of the shop. She would purchase an item, just one item with which to add a layer to herself, to use as a weapon against Emily, to act as a shield for herself, to keep her skin warm and subtle.

Chapter Fifteen

Bombay, 1944–6

Addition and subtraction!

First comes addition!
Emily had thought that she was only adding one new person to her life, but a one often comes as a two. The Girl had come trailing after Champa. She'd cringed at the sight of Emily.

'That's right!' Emily had declared.

Champa was to oversee the servants, keep her ears and eyes open, and 'help' Emily. She would continue to live in her own place and see her own clients, coming to the Rose Garden every other day. Emily didn't particularly need her help; the truth was that Emily couldn't let her go. The connection with the husband had created a connection with Emily, and if Champa had served him she could serve Emily too.

Gopal had placed his own man to collect the money and do the accounts, paying him a goodly sum on account of the loyalty and discretion required. And now Emily placed her own woman to look after his own man. Champa took him cool drinks and hot teas, and sometimes came back with the totals for the day or the week. Each time they took Emily's breath away; the amount that she received as her share pitifully small in comparison, ignoring the mountain of capital that had gone into setting up the Rose Garden. She decided she would wait for time to consolidate the business of the Rose Garden before she initiated any action to boost her share. Champa was proving more useful than she could ever have imagined. In fact Champa might turn out to be the one useful thing her husband had left her.

The Girl had lost the momentum of her days. Hanging around The English Rose Garden, she'd be press-ganged into working with the other servants. The Girl didn't like being lumped with the commonality of them all.

The Soiree Sisters were offended and sarcastic at Champa's attachment to The English Rose Garden. They kept away from Champa. And Champa kept away from them, feeling herself a little traitorous.

At that time India was like a land locked into an interminable, slow-rolling earthquake. Gandhi and his satyagrahis, who faced bullets and *lathi* charges with bare heads and folded hands, were a rebuke to all who assisted the English. Champa and the Soiree Sisters were hardly political activists, for they knew that whoever was in power, they would always be where they were and what they were. But they had loyalties to India as a whole, and those amongst them who thought further than themselves knew that the Raj was a parasite upon the people. In the streets and on the market stalls, people were repeating the words of Lady Rama Rao: 'The British will go and go soon, leaving our country in a pool of blood.'[2]

One afternoon a group, who must have become detached from a larger group, ran through the neighbourhood, shouting slogans against the British, swiftly followed by the police. Little damage was done except for some cloth ripped from a pole and a cart overturned. They had come and gone in a second, but had flashed through the street like fire, shocking and frightening everyone. Stall-holders grouped together, householders came out onto the street, voices rose up. Their little neighbourhood had been visited by the turmoil at large. Champa came out onto the stairs leading to her rooms, her *dupatta* held tight around her. From further down the street, a woman waved to her. It was one of the Soiree Sisters.

Three days later, in those limbo hours when the afternoon heat has drifted off, when the body is still full of lassitude, but the mind seeks some distraction, Champa was surprised to be the recipient of a visit by the entire posse of the Soiree Sisters. The group drifted in, in ones and twos and threes, slowly gathering in her room; flicking fans, bangles chinkling, humming a song, deliciously gossipy. With real delight, Champa welcomed them and sent The Girl running off to fetch nuts, savouries and cool drinks. She had missed them sorely. Though none would ever admit it to Champa or each other, they had missed her also. Champa had a certain winsomeness that charmed.

The conversation was desultory at first, but gradually sharpened and fell upon Champa, avid with curiosity about the Rose Garden.

'Becoming a mem now, are you?' asked Telegram.

'Getting more clients?' suggested another.

'Soon becoming a big rich woman!' said a third. 'Getting big, big money *hai.*'

'No, no,' Champa protested, 'I am learning their ways.'

Emily liked to give her a few rupees each month, searching her out so as to be able to pay her, waiting for Champa to stretch out her hand, before handing over the money.

'Is this how my husband paid you?'

'He was a gentleman.' Champa would look misty as she put the money in her blouse and turned away.

'I do not want to learn their ways,' declared another one of the Soiree Sisters, waving a languid, dismissive hand. 'Look what they are doing to our *Jawans*, the flower of Indian manhood.' (She was the one who loved to 'actress' the vamp.) 'What do they need punishment for?' she asked the room. 'Such hot-blooded, brave men should be suitably rewarded,' flicking her eyelashes, brushing her hand across her breasts.

The others laughed and teased her, 'What, all of them?'

'Leave some for us.'

'You'd exhaust the poor men.'

The government had brought charges of treason against the officers and soldiers of the Indian National Army who had joined the Japanese side during the war. Nehru, who was helping with their defence had argued:

'...how did the British Officers behave when they were routed by the Japanese in the jungle? They abandoned their gallant Indians to the enemy and made haste to save their own white skins. The Japanese then promised their prisoners Independence for India if they fought on their side to defeat Britain. To whom were the renegade Indians disloyal? Certainly not to Mother India.'

The soldiers had great public sympathy because people felt they had been courageous and brave, making up for the passive resistance of Gandhi, and proving that Indians were not cowards.

'*Hai*, my Jawans,' sighed the vamp, 'to think of them languishing in jail for years and years.'

'When they could languish in your arms *hain*?' teased one.

'I would not let them, l-a-n-g-u-i-s-h,' the vamp drawled her voice through all the meanings. The room laughed in appreciation.

'The English will hang them,' stated Acid Eyes, shattering the mood.

The months passed, the year changed, moved on a digit and 1945 became 1946. Life carried on for Emily, Champa and The Girl. Emily was busy and engrossed, though still ambitiously looking to what she yet had to achieve. Gopal did not know that The English Rose Garden was so efficiently run that it needed two sets of books. He didn't know that Emily had visited a bank to organise accounts in England, and had started remitting money back home.

Champa and The Girl divided their time between Champa's rooms and The English Rose Garden. The dimple still danced in Champa's cheeks, but that was a trick of her features. The Girl had suddenly, it seemed, grown taller and thinner, budding breasts – which both Champa and The Girl ignored. A dark little scrap of humanity, tied by an old thread to Champa; neither was unhappy, but neither had the untainted contentment of before. Champa and The Girl did not know it, but their hearts would never have the old ease again.

Bombay was burning!

That was what they thought at the time. Later they were to see what real burning was. Now in the early days of 1946, Bombay received a taster of what it would get later. Starting as a mutiny on the ship, *Talwar*, *The Sword*, the anger rolled inward from the harbour and over the city. Driven by simmering resentment at British rule, and angered by the discriminatory treatment and insults of the British officers, the Indian sailors had splashed the 'Quit India' slogan on the ship and the walls of the barracks. This was sacrilege, according to the British authorities, and severe action was taken against them. Sparking a mutiny! The sailors flashed the news over the wireless network to the other ships and the strike spread. Though newspaper reporting was censored, the news spread across the city, arousing rebellion and violence. Trams and property were burnt, grain stores looted, people attacked.

Business at The English Rose Garden dwindled. It was a time to lie low and wait for the storm to pass.

Addition and subtraction!

Emily had drawn Gopal, Champa and The Girl into her orbit: Emily plus three.

Then came Anant: Emily plus four.

Emily should have known that where there is addition, there must also be subtraction.

Anant was dark-haired, brown-eyed, with a lightly browned complexion, tall and thin, apologising effusively for the roughness of his English, explaining that his tongue was more accustomed to Hindi, and that he was a simple ordinary, little-bitty businessman; a modesty belied by his lavish expenditure at the Rose Garden on wines and food. Eschewing Western style, he dressed in silk, with embroidered waistcoats and finely woven shawls. Emily told the girls to pay him special attention. With a city in turmoil, their future was uncertain so any guest who came was a most welcome one, but one who was so generous with his finances was the best of all. Anant came the first night and did not favour any of the girls. He came the second night and left early. On the third night he asked for Emily, who informed him that she was unavailable. He bemoaned his fate and hoped to return another day. A week elapsed without an appearance and Emily wondered if she had let a fat fish slip out of her hands.

When he did arrive, he presented a bouquet of flowers to Emily, professed to be her *ghulam*, her humble slave, together with the recitation of a poem in Urdu. Emily took him upstairs into her private rooms. He kissed the tendrils of her hair, the tips of her fingers, showered fulsome compliments upon her, translating them for her delectation, hesitating over some English words, beautifully grateful for her assistance.

In the bed he roved over her flesh, bending her fingers back, till she winced, immediately letting go; gradually pulling at her hair, till she moaned, immediately letting go; nibbling at her flesh, till teeth sank in, and she tried to move away. This time there was no release. Pinning her arm behind her back, he pushed it up till pain burned and she was begging him to let her go. He parted her legs and brutally pushed in; his Hindi love words turned to English swear words, endearments turned to fishwife insults. Mouthing obscenities and banging into her, he said he'd kick the black shit out of her.

Accusation!

Afterwards, when cold knowledge was in her, she said, 'You're English.' She was sitting in the bed; the sheet wrapped around her, dried tears stiff on her face and bruises on her body. Every time she thought she was secure a deadly knife cut the ground from under her.

'How long did you think we'd let you carry on like this?' he asked, rifling through her almirah and extracting a bottle of American Shenley whiskey, lifting it and examining it. Her heart stopped. Did the bottle carry any clues to tell him whose favoured drink this was? 'Present from a Yankee lover?' he asked.

She smiled weakly, ingratiatingly, 'I'd rather have our sort, but what can a woman who's alone and penniless do here? I thought I was going to die, on the street, like a beggar. It's only for a short time. Then I'm going back. I'll be glad to see the back of this country.'

'Can't have it, you know. Our women are sacred to us,' he declared, pouring himself a drink.

'Even when they're whores!'

'Especially. This trade can't cross the line. Once they've got between a white woman's legs, they'll think they can spit at us.' Rummaging on her table, he picked up Gopal's gold cigarette case. Emily had to bite her hand to stop herself jumping up and grabbing it from him. In her panic she couldn't remember if the case carried an inscription or not. Opening it, he took out a cigarette and lit it. Picking up the glass of whiskey, he came back to the bed. 'Call me Ant,' he said, 'short for Anthony. And you can be my Cleopatra. That's A and C, now all we need is a B in the middle, don't we?' He lifted the glass to her shoulder and, tipping it a little, poured some of the golden liquid over her shoulder, making her shiver. Then with his hand, the one holding the cigarette, he gently rubbed it into her skin. She could feel the heat of the cigarette, going backwards and forwards. He asked how she'd obtained the money to open this 'Palace of Delights'. Who did the profits go to and who were the regulars? Emily stalled and prevaricated, hinted that it was friends of her late husband, friends who wouldn't want their names to be known. Inside her head, her mind was whizzing round trying to find a way out. Ant took a deep drag, the tip of his cigarette glowed red. She thought, if she needed to, she could give Donald's name and if they went to Donald, he would just deny it, which was to be expected, given the nature of the business.

He tapped his cigarette, and hot ash dropped onto her shoulder. 'Don't imagine you're the town's most popular woman. We may not like what you're doing but their lot, the 'India for Indians' rabble, think you're poison! We spend our time trying to keep peace and order in a city where thugs and hooligans rule the streets, and here you are, inciting a riot. If I were you, I'd be very, very careful. There are dangerous men out there, with dangerous ideas, the one's who think they can steal India from us. They think they can drive us out into the sea. Well they don't know we're an island race. But they might just get it into their heads to do some tidying up.' Going behind her, he started to rub her shoulders, with fingers that dug into her flesh, with a cigarette that dipped ever nearer to her skin. The other hand veered towards her throat.

'If anything happens to you, no one's going to ask a single question.' Emily was in despair. Whatever she touched fell apart in her hands. 'Now then, are you going to tell me who's behind this little caper? It can't be that friend of your dead husband, he skirmishes at the edges, but he plays safe. Not like your dear Mr Miller, eh, Mrs Miller? The dear departed who thought he could break age-old rules and cross forbidden lines. Like husband, like wife. Is that how it's going to be?' Razor-sharp knowledge entered Emily, and her startled eyes opened wide with a new fear. A quick flash of heat burnt on her.

Ant's hand ploughed into her hair, gathered it up and pulled. 'I always get to the bottom of things. I can take my time, or I can be quick. Someone's lavished a deal of rupees on this place. Someone's cocking a snook at us. That's not very nice is it? They have their women. We have our women,' a laugh, 'and their women! No one goes short. I can close you down tonight or, if I decide, I could let you carry on. Depends.' A deep drag, smoke blew across her. His hands moved down, around to the front, pushed the sheet away from her body, massaged her breasts, tighter and tighter, the glowing tip dipped up and down. 'Peaches and cream, cherries and berries,' fingers squeezing her nipples. Emily sobbed and cried from genuine pain and despair.

She begged him for his help, for wasn't she just a frail and gentle English woman, misguided in her ways perhaps, but in need of his protection? What could a woman do? He moved around, opened her legs, watched her with the eyes of a wolf, a look that she was to learn.

'There could be an arrangement,' he said. 'Take the profits, arrange a few favours now and then. Tell me!' he pushed her back and climbed on top; inserting himself, he moved unusually gently, but his eyes watched every expression on her face. She'd nearly become a beggar on the street once already. She wouldn't let disaster touch her a second time.

He terrified her with his reaction! 'That pretty little bastard thinks he can sell our women to his cronies and crooks! Make money out of them and pass them around like buttered chapattis!' He was out of her and off the bed with the force of a bullet. Quickly he started dressing himself.

Emily got out of bed. It was the most dangerous place in the room. Ignoring the pain in her body, she put on a silk, floral gown, took a clean glass and poured him another drink from Gopal's whiskey.

'Who are you?' she asked, holding it out to him.

For a moment he looked at her with fierce red eyes as he slipped into his waistcoat and picked up his shawl, then just as suddenly he relaxed, and took the glass. 'Why not?' he said to himself, 'I'm the one who controls the tick tock of the clock.'

Emily took a cigarette from Gopal's cigarette case, lit it and passed it to him. 'What am I to call you?' she asked.

'Ant.' She watched the ash grow on his cigarette and, as he made no move, wondered if he was going to flick it onto her precious carpet. She picked up the heavy marble ashtray and took it over to him, waiting at his side. 'You've picked up a few tricks from here,' he said approvingly, leisurely dipping his cigarette.

'Is Ant an English name or an Indian name?' asked Emily.

'Anthony,' he replied. 'I do believe we haven't been properly introduced. Anthony Bernard Child. Descended from Sir Josiah Child and Sir John Child. How do you do?' Ant inclined his head in formal greeting.

'And what is your full Indian name?' asked Emily. 'So that I know what you want me to use and when.'

Ant stretched his lips a little, 'Anant Bepin Chandra. But that's not important. I use it for work. I'm descended from the Child brothers.'

'I see,' replied Emily, trying to co-operate.

Ant lounged back in his chair, 'No you don't. You haven't the faintest idea who they were.' Ant had a mixed voice, at times lilting to a public-school English accent, then veering into an Indian nuance. He stretched out his legs, drank from the glass of whiskey, his eyes roving over the room and back to Emily. He gathered everything to himself. He was the master. 'Sir Josiah Child,' he informed Emily, 'was Governor of the East India Company. The father of the British Raj.' Looking at her, he waited for her reaction. Emily didn't laugh; she accepted. There were families who had been here for generations. She looked at Ant with a new expression. He must be like British India himself, full of all the power those generations had accumulated – not only huge amounts of property, money, gems, but an internal power of the mind, as if hundreds of years of rule over others, of enslaving a people, had created a power chromosome, so that these people had power packed into their bones. Emily was nearly right. They didn't need a chromosome; they possessed the belief. And had practised it over hundreds of years. Practice makes perfect.

'In 1687,' said Ant, reciting words that he had made his own, 'Sir Josiah Child declared the Company's determination to "establish such a polity…", polity means empire,' he added, with a patronising nod towards Emily, ' "…of civil and military power and create and secure such a large revenue…as may be the foundation of a large, well-grounded, sure English dominion in India For All Time To Come." '[3]

Ant's voice rose a little at the end. No one ever knew if Ant spoke the truth or not about his origins. He bore the Child name and so far no one had contested his ownership of it. He placed his claim so far back in history that no one could accurately argue with him. He could just as well be descended from any one of the many adventurers that the Company had chosen to send to India, adventurers that so often had been morally and physically dissolute. Paid low salaries by the Company, these men had fallen to the temptations of private trading. Riches had been devoured and India's wealth transferred to Europe.

Emily would have been surprised to know that, until recently, Ant hadn't cared overmuch about the extent of his material possessions. He possessed something much more important: the power over others! Over their flesh, will and pride. God-like powers. Power was what Ant cherished.

'What do you do?' Emily asked him, biting her lips, knowing he may not like being asked such a question.

'What do I do?' he repeated, and Emily quailed. 'I do what I'm supposed to do. Look after Company business. I look after John Company Raj.'

'But I was told there is no Company any more,' Emily blurted out, remembering things Thomas had said.

Ant grinned up at her, a wolf grin. She was still standing by his side, holding the marble ashtray, and had wrong stepped. She didn't think he was going to answer her.

'Do you have homes in England too?' she asked, trying to move on, cover her tracks. What she had meant to ask was whether he went to England often, but the other words came out first. Emily words.

Ant drained his whiskey and stood up. 'How do you think,' he asked, expertly throwing his shawl around his shoulders, plunging a hand into a pocket and bringing out a gun, and checking it, 'you can run an empire, rule the whole of India, a bloody sub-continent, and keep control, if you don't have the Company.' He put his hands under her gown, around her hips, rubbing the cold gun against her skin, 'The Company came first. The Company serves. Lord Willingdon was the only one who didn't tolerate idiots. And you know what he did? Dropped bombs on Peshawar during their satyagraha nonsense,' he said, plunging his hand brutally into her, dropping bombs into her.

He replied to her question as he was leaving. 'Yes. A big little something in England, we have that too. Near Hindhead,' picturing the large house, with its slightly un-English look and its dark interior. 'Fruit trees in the back and flowers in the front. But I have to go, my English...' He held back the word 'rose' that should have followed. He prided himself on being a gentleman as well as one of those old adventurers of yore who had founded the Empire. A gentleman and adventurer was how Ant placed himself, somewhere between the present and the past, guarding the future; somewhere between social niceties and private acts, guarding the future.

He left and Emily stood blindly by her window, thinking that an evil witch must have been present at her birth. Every time she dragged herself up, something happened to throw her back down again. A plume of smoke rose far away in the city. The mobs were on the street, the city was under attack. One of the cleaners had come back this morning to say that the sailors who had mutinied had trained their guns on Bombay. Perhaps this is better thought Emily, this unofficial pact with Ant. He would give her unofficial protection. She had been worried that the authorities would one day charge in and close her down. She had heard from one of the women, now working at the Rose Garden, that only one other Englishwoman had ever attempted to set up a 'house' like The English Rose Garden, and she had been closed down and tried in court. Of course they did it the other way round all the time, Indian women for English men; they could set up such 'houses' on every street corner if they wanted.

Street, and street corner, reminded her of The Ferret, 'the thieving little Ferret,' of their first meeting, who had managed to sneak into the Rose Garden, who had hidden a hairslide and earring in her dirty clothes.

Emily scribbled a quick note to Gopal. Asked him to stay away for a while. Betrayal was not a word that entered her mind. She didn't allow it. She called Champa and The Girl. 'Since you're so smart,' she said to The Girl, 'at getting into places where you shouldn't, find out about the man who was here. Next time he comes, follow him, ferret out everything about him. I want to know who he is, what he is, where he goes. But first,' giving her a letter, 'deliver this to the sahib, at this address. As quickly as possible. This is a very important letter. If it doesn't get to him, I'll cut you up into little pieces, fry you and eat you for breakfast, with *garam garam* chutney!'

The Girl didn't understand everything; she thought she could get away with helplessness and looked to Champa for help. Champa, the turncoat, translated and added her own spices to the recipe.

The Girl was back on the streets, her feet flying. Emily's new instructions gave her the run of the city streets again. She didn't have a hope of following Ant today, but she didn't worry too much for she could always try again. The first job was to deliver the letter. When she reached the office building, the watchman told her sahib had already left. Emily would kill her if she didn't get the letter to its destination.

Using her few words of English, she waved the letter in front of him, intending to impress him with her high level of education, but quickly reverted to Hindi and demanded the sahib's home address. The trick must have worked for the watchman told her and gave directions.

She had to walk half way across town; The Girl hadn't been in the rich areas of the town before. She lingered outside the gates of well-to-do homes, watched people as they got out of rickshaws, or drove by in cars, smelled the flowers of an overhanging tree, stopped to stare at two little girls, out with their *ayahs*, wearing crisply ironed dresses, hair tied up with big shiny ribbons. The girls looked back at her as curiously as she looked at them.

At Gopal's house, the servant sniffed when he saw her, and informed her that sahib had not yet returned. Feeling anxious about the letter, she hesitated at the door, wondering what to do, when a female voice from the back asked who it was. The Girl knew enough to know that the letter was not intended for the hands of the sahib's wife, but she was stumped as to what to do next. She was saved from having to search further for a solution, for the wife came forward, and immediately retreated a step at sight of her, not wishing to share the same air. The servant was ordered to take the letter, and The Girl was asked to leave.

Addition and subtraction!

Subtraction!

The one to exit from Emily's life did so on that day. No more of his teasing mischief, no more anger with him, no more gazing on his features, no more of his touch on her, no more jealousy as he deliberately broke all codes and sang the praises of his wife into Emily's unwilling ears. Once, he'd hooked his finger through her first necklace of pearls (bought by herself, with her own money), and had declared that his wife had jewels worth a million times more. 'She has jewels,' he had said, 'even for her little toes, jewelled anklets to tinkle at each step, a dozen rings for each finger, earrings which hang down to her shoulders.' Seeing the effect of his description on Emily, mischievous Gopal had elaborated further, 'Why, she would never consider herself dressed unless she had at least two or three necklaces on, a choker around the throat, a gold and diamond belt around her hips that moves up and down with her walking. Up and down,' he repeated, his hands on Emily's hips. He loved to wind her up, tease her till she fought back with nails and fists. He didn't know that his teasing fell into bitter ground, furrowed by false promises. Emily's anger had incited Gopal into further descriptions of his wife's precious possessions and privileged position. Emily had thought herself the superior, after all she was white and English. Emily had swallowed her bile, and started to hate the wife, sitting like some princess in a silken shell.

In all the time they had been together, Gopal had never brought her a gift. The business venture between them erased the need for the role-play of male and female where the man lavishes little attentions on the woman who, in turn, feigns a child-like delight, out of which rises the thanks from which the man receives his gratification. A pleasant game.

Emily had become stubbornly determined to force a change in the emotional temperature between her and Gopal. She would make him give her a gift, one that would act as a kind of bond between them. She had announced the approach of a birthday, and had looked sideways away, pretending that it really did not matter. She didn't know the reasoning in his head, whether it arose from duty and custom or affection and feeling, but he had arranged for a jeweller to visit her with some of his wares since they had both agreed that they were never to be seen together.

Suspicion! The worm in the gift! The jeweller had arrived with several trays and opened each one with a flourish. The gathered women around her had exclaimed, oohed and aahed, but Emily had wondered, with the acid of jealousy inside her, if he would have chosen these same trays to be shown his wife, or whether he would have picked out other, more expensive ones. However she was prepared to be pleased, and chose a gold choker and earrings for this first gift from him. The rest would come in time. She would outdo the wife! The choker was a little loose on her so the jeweller took it away to be adjusted. That was the last she saw of it.

He exited from her life.

Emily knew several aspects of time: in her factory days, time had stretched into infinity, loaded with the burdens of grinding work and a narrow life; in her days with the man she had married, time had been an expanding horizon of vistas and expectations; in the time after his death, time had been a guillotine waiting to chop off her head; and in the days when she teamed up with Gopal and established The English Rose Garden, time had become a creature of her making.

On the day that Gopal disappeared, time became a mystery, an incomprehensible place where danger lurked. Time was no longer a place where she could deposit her tomorrows.

Chapter Sixteen

London, March 1997

In the dark, a glow on the bedroom curtains – Emily always kept alight the table lamp. Those outside would see the glow, and know that the owner was in residence. This house was not for burning.

Outside, under the street lamps, a white car comes to a stop by Emily's gate. The driver pulls up the handbrake and switches off the engine. She leans her head back against the seat and closes her eyes – to rest them or delay the moment of arrival? She is exhausted, but that's become her way of living. Long hours at work keep thoughts, memories and emotions at bay, though sometimes in the dark, her mind can ambush her into remembering. She resists, guilt and sin like stones inside her.

The Girl opened her eyes and lifted her head. She is many decades older: her hair is white, her skin paler, her face creased with fine wrinkles around the eyes and mouth. She is fettered by names: to the outside world she is Miss T Bombay for that was the name on the papers that brought her here; under her skin she's still Ferret, the name Emily gave her; and in the shady privacy of her mind she's Ancient/Ferret, for 'ancient' is how she feels.

She had never imagined that she could return. Thirty years ago she had left, on a jerky sick woman's hobble, with a few clothes shoved into a plastic bag. And before that, years before, she had been thrown out, spewed out, by the force of Emily's anger. And had vowed never to return. But she had, her swollen belly telling its tale. 'Should have known better,' Emily had snorted.

Should have known better, Ancient/Ferret had echoed, holding onto her head, not knowing that *should have known better* was the history of humankind.

Ancient/Ferret takes her coat and steps out of the car. Her eyes travel the distance from the pavement to the gate, to the house, and to the closed curtains of Emily's room. Emotion begins a surge inside her, but she pulls her coat tight around her, her arms folded across her body. She'll wait.

Time has not been an empty place for Ancient/Ferret. She has travelled the distances between helplessness and knowledge, poverty and profit, loneliness and happiness, grief and endurance. And in between are the things she has kept hidden: the begging when she had first tumbled, stumbled out of Emily's door, the begging for an advance on her wages, and the refusal; the door in her face; the begging for sleeping space on someone's floor; the first dismissal; the terrible feeling she was redundant to all. And below, the separation, the strange homesickness, as if an umbilical cord had been cut. And the nagging worry: how would Champa manage without her? Even Emily?

The curtains were still closed; the lamp still glowed behind them. Ancient/Ferret, the girl whose mind was always working, who had darted like an inquisitive little animal from one place to another, now paced to the end of the street and back; forever accompanied, at the back of the mind, by the man, the prison, and… Ancient/Ferret quickened her steps, burning up her energy as she had always done. At first she'd worked in factories, and in the evenings had gone to English classes. And regularly, every few months, she'd got sacked and kicked out. A weird thing had happened to Ancient/Ferret: she couldn't take orders, though taking orders had been her destiny; she bristled and argued back when supervisors spoke arrogantly or made racist remarks; she'd speak up when other workers kept silent, and she'd speak for newly arrived Asian women whose bridal henna was still fresh on their hands, and who hadn't known that marrying a man in England meant marrying a factory job too. 'Who does she think she is? The bloody Empress of India?' the supervisors would mutter as they sent her packing. Time after time Ancient/Ferret would collect her coat and her cards, leave the only social contacts she had, bury her hurt and pain, grit her teeth and look for another job – until the day she couldn't take any more, and knew the only way left was to go it alone.

The Swinging Sixties, flower power and Eastern mysticism had burst upon Britain; Ancient/Ferret opened a tiny café and called it Eastern Mystique; perhaps she'd have been better off opening a truck drivers' caff. Not that her Eastern Mystique didn't make money; her till tinkled, her cooking was praised, and most astonishingly to Ancient/Ferret, her beauty admired. Ancient/Ferret would shoo them off; no false modesty here, merely disbelief that such a gift could be hers, for she was inferior and soiled with sin. Emily may have given the order and Ancient/Ferret may have been young, but it had still been her hands that had reached out and plucked, all those years ago. And then came the man! Long black hair, kurta and blue jeans, he professed a love deep and undying in lilting Hindi. Constancy and dedication are the sincerest compliments, and on a cold, snowy Christmas day when all others were feasting in their homes, they snapped the thread that held her. Months later when her pleasure-filled body was swelling like a luscious pumpkin, when she thought the gods had forgiven her, it was then that the ruin and damnation came: the police swarming through her café, the man arrested for peddling cannabis, she arrested as an accomplice. She was a 'darkie', a 'wog', of course no one was going to believe her, or the man, when he insisted she was innocent. Prison doors clanged shut through her head. And even then, even after she knew all about him, she had known too that she would miss the man, miss his tender touch and his caring whispers. In the darkness she'd remembered Champa's low, hidden sobs after the sahib had died.

Ancient/Ferret paced back along the street, and checked the window – no changes. She climbed back into her car and opening a laptop, switched it on. The screen glowed into life, and though it showed words and numbers, all Ancient/Ferret could see were the tips of a baby's searching fingers. Danger. Closing the laptop, she got out of the car again and walked along the street at a faster, fiercer pace. Sinful mother, corrupt father. Nothing to give the child. 'Adoption,' she had instructed Champa. Let the child be free of the past.

She hadn't known of the many ways in which her body would punish her. In a dingy bedsitter, she'd squeezed her swollen breasts, collected the milk in a cup, and then, at the sink, tilted the cup: liquid love that's thrown away. Her sin-count had increased.

And so Ancient/Ferret worked; sewing curtains from morning to midnight; collecting customers, collecting work that even she couldn't manage, employing workers and encountering another problem, peculiar to her. As she couldn't take orders, so neither could she give them. When talking to her workers, Ancient/Ferret erased the 'I' and talked about the work as an entity, showed the quality of work expected, and if their work didn't come up to scratch she'd do it herself, showing them how. No authoritarian rages, no impromptu sackings; she practised severe honesty in dealing with customers, and care in looking after the employees. Slowly but surely, Ancient/Ferret's business prospered. But Ancient/Ferret hid from her success. She paid her workers above average, paid large contributions to charitable funds, and paid no heed to luxury goods or extravagant living. She'd locked away too many parts of herself for that.

Ancient/Ferret looks across the front garden to the windows. The lamp has been extinguished. The curtains have been opened.

Hot and humid! The heating was on day and night. Emily sat up in her lacy nightdress and yawned in the warmth. As it should be! The servant should have come in by now with a tray of hot tea and sweet puris. Instead, the machine on her bedside cabinet gurgled into life. She would make-do until she could make-true! Champa had better hurry up, the best was yet to come. She poured herself a cup of steaming tea, her eyes going into the panelled screen opposite, painted with copies of Mogul miniatures: 'Lady Watching the Sun Rising', 'Lady Preparing for Her Bath', 'Lady Feeding the Peacocks,' 'Lady Reclining in her Palanquin'.

Emily finished her cup of tea, and moving back the quilt, put her foot on the bedside stool. This old bed was becoming too high for her; as it was, this bed had betrayed her. When she had discovered Sita/Ferret's treachery, she had first thought of selling it, knowing she would get an excellent price, but then had changed her mind. Just as *suitable recompense had been required*, so now *suitable retribution was required*. Emily had been sorely tempted to rip into Champa, shred her apart: 'See what your meddling has done!' Instead Emily had taken to the bed and drawn the mosquito net down around her to keep out the vile parasites that would prey upon her.

Emily had taken an inventory of everything in the house, and left a blank line at the bottom to be filled by the return of her goods. Then only would the list be complete and Emily made whole. Draping her dressing-gown around her, shiny green silk with fluffy ruffles of lace, she went over to the window and pulled the cord to open the curtains. Sunlight fell upon her, making her blink.

She went downstairs to the kitchen. Even there, in the basement, the temperature was warm and comforting. Emily took out a ready-prepared omelette from the fridge and put it in the microwave. The smell of spices and ginger wafted out. Emily now had an Indian cleaning woman who also cooked and shopped for her. Emily had not always been so lavish with her heating and expenditure. But after that termite, that Ferret-*ki-bachi*, had run off with her hard-earned goods, she had decided that if she didn't live well now, then the riches of her endeavours would pass to others for them to live in luxury, to enjoy the life that had been promised to her. Over her dead body!

The doorbell rang, startling her. Emily wondered who could be ringing so early in the morning and got up to answer. Then suddenly realised who it might be. Because yesterday Emily had been obliged to make a phone call. Champa had insisted. Emily sat back in her seat, her colour rising. The bell pealed through the house again. However Emily did not rush to answer it. How dare she arrive at this ungodly hour? The bell rang again, long and aggressive. Who does she think she is, thought Emily, picking up a gold embroidered shawl and draping it round her shoulders. Does she expect a welcome party with flower garlands?

As Emily reached the door, she glanced around her. Tall ivory candlesticks stood on either side of the stairs, the wooden chest with the carved floral trellis rested against the wall; above it, a mirror shone in its bronze frame. After she had lost the first collection of furniture and goods, Emily had sent over shiploads. She had asked her brother to meet the consignments and to buy her a house – her house, even if she never came back and never even saw it. First loss. Second loss. First the murder; second the flames. Emily had lived as if a knife were held at her throat – which had meant she could hold a knife to the throats of others, or so Emily believed. The brother had done as she asked, but had not boasted to others of his sister's good fortune.

Now, anyone entering her house could see what she was worth; she was no penny-pinching, margarine-scraping pauper. She had style, she had substance, she had status.

Emily straightened herself as she pushed back the top bolt; the bottom one took her longer for she had to bend and that didn't come easily anymore. As she lifted the chain, turned the mortise lock and put her hands to the knob, she examined the shadowy figure through the stained glass. The figure stood still and unmoving.

Emily opens the door. They stare at each other very carefully, as if each were a live bomb.

Eventually Ancient/Ferret spoke, 'Good morning.' She used politeness to other people, now she had brought it home to Emily.

'Well, well, aren't we fancy,' replied Emily, glancing over the haircut, the tiny pearl earrings, down to the good-quality overnight case, the black laptop in its zip-up bag.

Ancient/Ferret did not reply. She knew Emily could solidify like lava. She would be made to ask. Old rebellion stirred inside her. Thirty years and they were still at the same war. But she framed her sentence carefully and spoke slowly. 'Should these bags be brought inside?'

'You were the one who buggered off,' Emily accused.

'You were the one who pushed me out,' she replied.

'Trying to be clever now are we?' Emily jibed.

'I've learnt much since I left you.' The 'I' had come flying back onto her tongue. Emily had pricked it back as surely as Sleeping Beauty had to prick her finger.

'But you came running back, first chance you could.'

Ancient/Ferret opened her mouth to retort, then stopped. Slow! Let the words filter. She tried a peace offering. 'Times change. Sometimes people change.'

'I don't,' asserted Emily.

'True,' she conceded. 'Why the bloody hell did you have to go to India?'

'If I hadn't, you'd be an old hag, sweeping someone's floors for a dry roti,' Emily informed her with relish.

'If you hadn't,' retaliated Ancient/Ferret, 'you'd be living in some dingy hole, not two pennies to rub together.' They were back to the old enmities. 'Your country grinds people like you into dirt. I've seen it.'

'You were happy enough to live off me,' Emily snapped back at her.

'I never lived off you. I worked my,' couldn't stop the next word, 'fucking skin off.'

'Keep your filthy language to yourself, and leave it outside my door! You didn't have the guts to squash a cockroach.'

Ancient/Ferret pushed back her anger. In the past, Emily's scorn used to slam her down. Emily still knew how to reach her raw parts. If she lost control with Emily, she'd break up and Emily would have won.

'I'm shivering here,' Emily said. 'If you're coming in, make sure you lock the door and draw the bolts. And did you have to turn up at dawn when decent people are sleeping?'

'I was working,' Ancient/Ferret replied, picking up her belongings.

The patterned floor tiles of the hall shone, the carpet on the stairs was soft. Ancient Ferret followed Emily, stepping on her steps. They stood upstairs, on the first landing. 'How is Champa?' asked Ancient/Ferret.

'Alright. She wanted you. She was always soppy and soft. Wouldn't give me any peace till I phoned you. The doctors are just fussing. Sending her off to hospital like that! Not enough work to do I should think. Champa's fat as a pig. She wanted *her*, the other one too. But we're not likely to see her,' continued Emily bitterly. 'Living in luxury somewhere and laughing at us.'

A shiver passed along Ancient/Ferret's spine. 'You shouldn't have left a fortune lying around,' she stated coldly, picking up her bags and moving towards the stairs.

'And you should have kept your legs crossed and not dropped your litter all over the place,' Emily shouted at her back. 'But her thieving came as no surprise. A chip off the old block.'

Ancient/Ferret's fury flared and she swung round to retaliate, but immediately bit her tongue. She flattened her voice, 'Without me, you'd have died in an Indian gutter, and no one would have cared a shit.'

'I brought you here, didn't I?' Emily countered. 'Count your blessings and thank your lucky stars.'

'It doesn't work the other way round. You went over there to lord it over us; I came here and I was still the lowest of the low. Nothing changed except scenery. Till I made it change. Back-breakingly hard, you'll be glad to know, and it took me years and years. I worked my guts out. Just as I did over there for you, and here. Except you took all that, and kept it for yourself.'

'It belonged to me,' stated Emily. By God-given right!

'I've admired you,' Ancient/Ferret continued, surprising Emily. 'You kept me going. When it was the end of the road, when I failed yet again, I thought of you. At first it was to keep going in spite of you, then it was to keep going because you had. After that it was to keep going so that I could say I did it by myself.'

Emily had listened in silence, now she said, 'Champa was a hundred times better than you.'

'Because she licked your boots!' retorted the old Ferret, the one who used to snap and snarl at Emily.

'That's what you think. Champa made the best of things. She's got a savings book chock-full of money.'

'You're going to take that too are you?' Ancient/Ferret accused.

'You think you should have a share?' Emily asked. Emily was missing out on her morning routine, a little early siesta after breakfast, before the cleaning woman came, or watching television, lounging in bed. Why should she wear herself out! Emily moved, deliberately turning her back on her. 'You can sleep in your old room.'

'Champa doesn't owe me anything, you do,' Ancient/Ferret replied, picking up her bags again.

'Good,' said Emily, 'because we're going away.' Reaching her bedroom door and looking back.

Ancient/Ferret stretched her lips into a mocking smile. 'Back to India! Fifty years later! Going to join in the Independence-day celebrations are you?'

'So what?' Emily flung open her door, glancing into her room; everything was as it should be. 'I'll live there in style. As promised.'

'Perhaps I'll come with you,' replied the Ancient/Ferret from her bitter side. 'I could go back in style too.' Constantly spar and defend with Emily, mustn't let her get the upper hand, for it was then that she could destroy. 'For now I'll take the spare room.'

Ancient/Ferret went upstairs, passing cupboards and chairs of decorated woodwork, ornaments of brass and silver. Fifty years ago! The words rang like a distant bell; fifty years ago in India, and yet the events sprouted in Ancient/Ferret's mind with newly minted clarity. In the days after The English Rose Garden, Emily had been a woman obsessed, making The English Rose Garden pay even if it had gone. Ancient/Ferret had been sent out to collect little packets from its previous clients; and had become the one who collected the anger of those who thought there was no need to pay for services they were no longer receiving. One man had slapped the young Ancient/Ferret across the face, gripped her arm, and thrown her out of his door, sending her crashing into a wall: 'If that English madam wants more, tell her to come herself.' Some men had given in to Emily the first time, and then given strict orders to their servants that this beggar-looking girl was to be thrown out if she ever came again. Some servants merely did their stern duty and slammed doors in her face, or escorted her out of the gates, holding her at arm's length; others tormented her with taunts and touch. A few of the gentlemen did pay up. They were the ones who had some public connection and therefore the most to lose. One man had said, as he handed over the packet, 'Look at you, thin and bony, a perfect slave; look at me, rich and fat, a perfect slave. The English know how to bugger and beggar us.' More than that, even more than that, there were errands of other kinds.

Ancient/Ferret had led Emily to the places of riot and looting, but it was Emily who told Ancient/Ferret to search the dead, and it was Emily who stood by as the Ancient/Ferret had vomited, then hissed at her to carry on. Emily had worn robes that covered her body so none would know her. But Emily's money-gathering power hadn't erased Ancient/Ferret's memory of that moment of naked flesh and sex in the grass – Emily and the Indian gentleman at the other end of history.

After Emily had come to live in Champa's rooms, The Girl's ownership had changed, a silent transfer. Ancient/Ferret had catalogued Emily's weaknesses, seen behind her boasting, and despised her for her descent into sin. Yet, when murders, looting, raping and terror had convulsed the country, Emily had also judged and said to her, 'You people are disgusting. Barbarians!' Something must have happened to Ancient/Ferret's brain, perhaps the hot wind flaring across the country had scorched it, for she had hissed back at Emily, 'It's my country,' in her own low-class lingo. Did she imagine Emily wouldn't understand? 'No it's not,' Emily had hissed back, 'and even if it were, it shits on you.' The Girl had come raging at her, incoherent sounds erupting from her throat; Emily had raised her hand.

Years later, in England, Ancient/Ferret had started to demand a share in everything that Emily owned, particularly the shiny collection, the special collection. Then the daughter had run off with it.

Ancient/Ferret placed her bags in the spare room, and then quietly sneaked to Emily's door and listened. The sounds of the television seeped out. Emily must be sitting in bed, with another cup of tea, plump pillows behind her. Ancient/Ferret veered away from Emily's door and towards Champa's old room.

Champa's room was dark and silent. Ancient/Ferret cupped her hand around the light switch and very slowly pulled it down. The old green and gold curtains still hung at the window; cheap china ornaments lined the mantelpiece; lipsticks, rouges and powder boxes lay on the dressing-table with its three mirrors. Champa had bought it at an auction decades ago. Emily had told her she'd paid too much for it; Champa hadn't cared. She had become the owner of a dressing-table with three mirrors, just like English ladies! In India she'd done her make-up with a small mirror balanced on top of her trunk.

Ancient/Ferret pulled a tissue from the box and wiped the dust off the mirrors. Three Ancient/Ferrets looked back at her. She sat in front of the mirrors that had housed Champa's face, and imagined her backwards through time, back to the time when she lost her job at the biscuit factory and had to get one in the laundry. That day Champa had gone straight to her room and stayed there. This hiding away had been such an unusual occurrence that Ancient/Ferret had taken up a tray of food for her. She had found Champa huddled in bed and crying.

Ancient/Ferret didn't know how long Emily indulged herself in her morning luxury of bed, tea and television, but knew she would have to work fast. Kneeling by the wardrobe, she pushed her hand into the tiny space at the bottom. Her fingers plunged into a layer of dust, puffs of it flying out, tickling her nose. She covered her mouth and pushed her hand further in, her scrabbling fingers hitting an edge that slid the object further away. Lying flat on the floor and edging her body against the wardrobe, she squeezed in her whole arm, and eventually her fingers caught and pulled out a notebook. Ancient/Ferret blew away the dust and opened it. Only a few pages had been filled with scrawly writing and a few cartoon-like sketches. These were not the rich drawings she had spied in the other books, the ones that had made her gasp in astonishment, and sneak back again and again, like a starving person to a dinner table.

In those drawings their world had been recreated and time recaptured: their old rooms; the market place; the fruit seller; the tailor; the trees outside the temple; The English Rose Garden with Emily in the centre; the shadowy men – Emily's grey-eyed favourite and the tall thin Englishman. Those drawings had glowed with colour and sparkled with sprinkled glitter: the Soiree Sisters; Acid Eyes; Telegram; The Girl as a child; Champa and The Girl walking, sitting on the roof, shopping. And occasionally, there were the quick shady sketches, as if behind a veil, of a man and a woman. This had been the outpouring of all those years when Champa would hide in her room after another hated day at the laundry. Our loves make the marrow run in our bones, else we dry up.

Ancient/Ferret lay on the floor again, and pushing in her arm, swept it from side to side. Nothing but dust. And dust in her mouth. Had illness made Champa afraid for her privacy? Could she have thrown the others out? Ancient/Ferret wouldn't accept it.

Sitting on the bed, she opened the exercise book, running her fingers along the lines, touching Champa's writing. The first two pages contained notes of the doings in the house: of Emily catching a cold, and refusing to see a doctor (Emily does not like 'officer people'); of how Champa had prepared a special drink with cardamoms, cloves, and ginger that had made Emily much better; of the television programmes she and Emily had watched, (it was lucky they didn't argue over programmes); of the Indian films they had seen, and of how Emily wanted the kind of grand house they showed in these films. Emily's aunt had sent an invitation to her son's wedding, and Emily had said, 'If they can't be bothered to come here, I can't be bothered to go to their weddings. Now they think they can come after the money.' Champa didn't know what Emily had been talking about. Champa wrote of how the beautician came every fortnight to do Emily's face and hair. Emily gave her big tips. Emily had an argument with the milkman, now she has to go to the shop to buy the milk.

On the following page, Champa had sellotaped a print of a painting in which a woman hurries through a dark forest, her red *dupatta* flying, glancing fearfully behind her. The print was titled 'Love's Heedless Ways.' Had Champa been thinking of herself or Emily? Underneath, Champa must have copied a story, a story that Ancient/Ferret read and puzzled over.

The Bhooth ran after the woman as she fled through the forest, weaving in and out of the trees; the Bhooth would suck out her soul, fill its ghost-self with it, its wild matted hair springing up like serpents. The woman screamed as the Bhooth came nearer, its cold hands reaching out, clamping onto her shoulders. The black matted locks fell over her face, blinding her, as all her passions and desires, all her beliefs and ideals, her sorrows and her laughter, all that had made her life crimson and electric was being sucked out of her.

'Stop! Stop!' the woman cried, 'I will bargain with you. You can have my soul, but first let me see my lover. After I have seen him, my soul will be richer, more satisfying for you.' The Bhooth stopped and let go of her shoulders. She fled again, the Bhooth following close behind, its coldness upon her. The lover was waiting by the lake. As the woman burst through the trees, she flung herself into his arms. Never had her passion been so strong, never had she given herself so completely. The lover asks what has happened. She tells him of the Bhooth and her bargain and suggests...

Here Champa had stopped. Ancient/Ferret turned the page. More home news: how the English cleaning woman had spilt a bit of bleach over the carpet in the hall, and how Emily had said she would withhold her money to pay for the damage; how the woman had threatened to throw bleach everywhere if she wasn't paid in full. Emily had then said she would call the police. The woman had called Emily a 'wog' and 'nigger-lover'; Emily had shouted back that she hadn't gone there to be a 'nigger-lover', she had gone to make a life, after all, she wasn't the one cleaning other people's floors. The woman had stomped out of the house. Emily had been shaking with anger. Champa had made her sit down on a chair, fetched her a cool drink, and fanned her.

Champa had returned to the story on the next page.

She tells him of the Bhooth and her bargain. She suggests, 'since we are one, and our only desire is to be together, why don't we both surrender to the Bhooth, and be together forever...'

Again Champa had stopped and restarted a few lines down.

She tells him of the Bhooth and her bargain. She suggests, 'I will bargain with it again, and ask that it leave me a tiny portion of my soul, so that I may meet you again, though I will be more ghost than woman...'

When the night is ending, but the sun has not yet come up, the Bhooth, who has waited patiently, comes out from the trees. The woman runs to the Bhooth as fast as she had run to the lover...

After a gap of a few lines, Champa had written another version of the ending.

The lover says that it is an unfair bargain so she doesn't have to keep it. The woman points out that it is a fair bargain, the Bhooth was only doing according to its nature, and had given them this night...

The last version came over the page.

She says, 'Let us run and if the Bhooth catches up with us, we will tell it it does wrong, but if it does right, then it will eventually die, and be reborn a human being...'

Champa had abandoned the copying of the story at this point. Had she thought life an impossible bargain? Or had she imagined there had been a real *Bhooth* in her life? Or was it Telegram who had become the ghost in the story? Ancient/Ferret would ponder on this for many a long day, reaching into Champa's mind, searching for the reasons.

Champa wrote that she hadn't woken up until midday, when her whole body had been hurting. In the few days before, Emily had been talking of him, still going on about how he took her to India under false pretences and then abandoned her. Same with the other one, the pretty one with his pretty ways and pretty eyes – he had left her too. Champa wrote that Emily should settle down, be calm…

In the last entry, Champa said that she'd told Emily she was going to sleep downstairs, that she couldn't climb the stairs anymore. 'You're as strong as a horse,' Emily had said; but when they were out, Champa had to stop every few steps. Now they used a wheelchair and Emily had to push it. Champa felt sorry for Emily having to do all this work. A boy had stared at them. 'What're you gawping at?' Emily had shouted, 'you snot-nosed shit.' The mother had had a few words with Emily for that. Emily had shouted her down; Emily had said the area was going downhill, they'd have to move.

The rest of the book was empty. Ancient/Ferret held it in her hands. Those who do the cleaning under beds and in dark corners discover the hiding places of secrets. Champa had had a whole collection of diaries, spanning the years. They had become the link between her and Champa, even if Champa had been unaware of the connection.

Ancient/Ferret moved the stool to the wardrobe, and carefully, holding onto the wall and wardrobe, climbed onto it. The top of the wardrobe was laden with old shoeboxes, a small tin trunk, and a pile of romantic magazines, all covered by a thick layer of dust. She pulled at the suitcase and the shoeboxes, lifting them up and lowering them to the floor, holding in her breath to avoid the dust that flew up in clouds. She rifled through the magazines but found nothing hidden among them.

Getting down from the stool, she knelt carefully, for her knee bones could spark with pain. The shoeboxes were filled with Christmas cards. She hesitated, but couldn't resist looking through a few. 'To Christine,' they all said. Some had little messages but others were clearly duty cards, all from people that Champa had worked with. Right at the bottom, and still in its heart-shaped envelope, was a Valentine's card. Inside was a message of flowery compliments, with sleazy innuendoes about a rendezvous behind the works canteen. Ancient/Ferret wondered whether it had been a nasty hoax, and how Champa had reacted to it. The second shoebox contained unused Christmas cards. Champa must have bought them at a jumble sale and stocked up for years. The tin trunk was locked which gave hope. Going over to the dressing-table, she hooked her nails at a section that seemed to be part of the fascia and pulled. The secret drawer slid out, and she picked up a key. Ancient/Ferret knew that the tin trunk contained Champa's precious Indian things that she had hardly worn here. As she threw the lid back, a familiar, yet slightly different sight met her eyes. Everything had been packaged, each item of clothing carefully wrapped in tissue paper and sealed in plastic bags. Ancient/Ferret took them out and piled them on the floor. A small metal box lay at the bottom, a padlock hooked round the handle – Champa's old box of valuables! Ancient/Ferret's memory of it was of something bigger, grander. She remembered how Champa used to count her rupees and then lock them away, always wondering would they be enough?

Ancient/Ferret replaced everything in the suitcase and, with great care, lifted it and put it back on top of the wardrobe. She couldn't risk searching further now. She had one more night. It was unthinkable that Champa could have done anything other than hide them. The diaries were her companions.

Coming out, Ancient/Ferret glanced towards Emily's room. The door was as tightly shut as before. She turned towards the stairs leading up to the old attic bedroom. There was none to witness her foolishness. The door of the old bedroom creaked as she opened it. With the room high, up in the air as it had seemed to her so long ago, it had taken her years to trust this house enough to be able to sleep through a night; haunted by fears of the stairs dissolving and leaving her stranded, or the roof silently caving in upon her, burying her without a sound! Holed up in her eyrie, her memories ran on a loop, creating a yearning for the past that had never existed in her before, and a fear of the future that she had never had before.

She stood against the door. Nothing essential had changed. The curtains, the single bed, and the table in the alcove, were the same. She recognised the old embroidered cover on the bed; remembered standing at the window, mesmerised by falling snow, endless rain, sloping roofs and chimney-stacks. Sometimes she'd smuggled up children's books and practised the writing of ABCs, only to produce deformed, broken shapes. Ancient/Ferret had used to watch in envious admiration all those whose pens raced across a page with effortless ease; knowledge hidden in hieroglyphics, reminiscent of the necromancer's art. Determined to master the intricacies, believing that it would confer a magic upon her, a tool with which to transmute her world, she had gritted her teeth and gripped her pencil ever harder. But when her toiling dragged her down rather than propelling her onwards, she'd felt useless and hopeless. Once she had scored a furious zigzag into the table, holding the pencil with both hands, pushing it through the top layer and jerking it from side to side, breaking it – a little eruption of despair, compounded as much of frustration as an inner desolation.

Layers of dust also coated the table. Ancient/Ferret brushed her hand backwards and forwards across, raising clouds of dust. Peering down she made out faded cup stains, ink stains and other marks; at one end, a faint pattern ran along the side, diamond shaped. Two lines of zigzags moved inwards and outwards, inwards and outwards. Ancient/Ferret stepped swiftly to the door, turned off the light and walked quickly out, ignoring the little thud as the door closed behind her.

They had travelled by ship and had seen the land fall away out of sight. Forever. She and Champa had stood by the railings, Champa gripping her arm bruisingly.

In India, Ancient/Ferret had been used to living on her wits, she had known and believed in reality, a reality in which you can see and hold, believed in the existence of the past and the inevitability of the future. The exile to England had wrenched her from her certainties. Outwardly, The Ferret had continued as before, but her mind became muddy and swampy, a turgid, festering place. However, one day, when Emily sat down at her table to eat, The Ferret was struck by her expression. Contentment! Smugness! Emily was replete. The Ferret had been astounded by this realisation, and a curtain had been lifted on a new landscape. Emily had achieved what she had set out to do. She had ventured forth into the world, succeeded and returned to a self-satisfying conclusion. They had changed places. Unknowingly The Ferret had been happy in India whilst Emily had been bitterly unhappy. She and Emily had crossed the waters and changed places.

From the beginning, when Champa had so passively handed her over, The Ferret couldn't have flouted Emily – that would have been to put herself out in the gutter. 'It is not allowed,' was all that she had managed to say. 'I'll decide what's allowed here! And out there,' Emily had declared, her arm sweeping across the city. It was the Time of the Terror. Like the blood-letting of the French Revolution, India had its blood-letting too.

194

Girl/Ferret didn't know then, that decades later, a young girl would look at books and atlases and realise that the maps of the world are only changed by blood.

Emily had said in a hoarse, strained voice, 'It's chaos out there.' Then speaking with the conviction of an evangelist, 'I'm not going back empty-handed.' Though Emily had been shopping and shipping like an addict, depositing bundles of cash in the bank as if she were printing the money herself, that still wasn't enough for Emily. None of that counted with Emily. It was still far short of what she had been promised. 'Peacock Palaces!' he'd said.

'D'you know what your kind are doing?' she had asked once, bending down to whisper into The Ferret's face. 'They're murdering each other, looting and plundering, even burning holy pilgrims. Here, it's in the newspaper,' holding it up right in front of The Ferret, who couldn't read the print, but couldn't mistake the picture of burnt carts and bodies. 'Returning from a pilgrimage they were,' Emily had continued softly. 'What good did that do them when the mob set fire to their carts? Don't you dare tell me what's not allowed!'

Fifty years ago! Ancient/Ferret had trespassed against herself; the words had never grown old, the act had never faded.

Ancient/Ferret had a couple of hours to wait before she could go to the hospital. She returned to the spare room and started work; methodically and meticulously going through a sheaf of papers, double checking as she went along, making phone calls on her mobile when necessary. She wouldn't use Emily's phone. She wouldn't be dependent.

'The high-powered businesswoman!' Emily remarked from the doorway, freshly bathed, in a soft woollen dress, the light shining on her blonde curls. Along with the beautician, the hairdresser must come regularly too, bringing bagfuls of hair colouring, thought Ancient/Ferret. Emily had the determined glamour of a faded Hollywood star. A part of her admired Emily's persistence in making real her image of what she should have been. Perhaps reality is forged in the mind after all!

'No,' replied Ancient/Ferret, closing her laptop and putting away her phone, 'just a working woman. I'm going to see Champa now. I'll be back later.'

The doorbell pealed through the house.

'I shouldn't think there's any need,' said Emily, 'for you to return later.'

'Do you want me to answer that?' Ancient/Ferret asked, as another ring of the bell snaked through the house.

'Some door-to-door salesman,' answered Emily dismissively, 'he'll go away.' She'd visit Champa herself tomorrow and tell her to get a move on. Tell her it was the cheap season to book tickets, and if they left it any later, they'd end up sharing a flight with the peasant immigrants going back for their weddings and holidays. Champa wouldn't want to travel with a pack of villagers.

The knocker thundered through the house. 'Hooligans,' said Emily. 'I'll give them what for,' she declared, turning round with her walking-stick. Ancient/Ferret followed out of curiosity and an unadmitted desire to protect Emily in the unlikely event that a gang of thugs was actually standing on the other side.

Ancient/Ferret watched Emily's wrinkled and spotted hands grappling with bolts, chains and keys, remembering the days when she had stretched her fingers and the nails had glittered bright red, or when they had clutched at things to make them their own, transferring ownership by the action of her hands. Ancient/Ferret had tried the same trick, but Emily's hands must have had magnetic power for what she gained stayed with her, and whatever Ancient/Ferret gained jumped to Emily. By right of natural law had been the assumption. Emily swung open the door.

Hair swept up and pinned, wearing a cream-coloured coat over a close-fitting red top, tight Indian skirt with sparkling mirror work, delicately carrying a black patent handbag, all she needed were dark glasses and a cigarette to complete the image.

Sita/Ferret had only gone into the shop to purchase one article, one item to help her on her 'scared-as-hell' journey to the Mausoleum, and had found that one item couldn't turn the trick. So she turned herself on the axis of Emily's obsessions, she would meet like with like; and refusing to calculate figures, or dwell on this extravagant emptying of her purse, she made herself anew. Only as she went through the gate and walked up the path did it occur to her that Emily would see only her stolen wealth as having paid for Sita/Ferret's appearance. 'Shit,' Sita/Ferret had thought, but it was too late to run away.

'Well! Goodness, gracious me,' declared Emily. 'I never was one for believing in fate. I'll have to after today won't I, Ferret?' said Emily, opening the door wider, disclosing the woman who stood in the background.

Sita/Ferret and Ancient/Ferret are as startled as each other at the use of the old term, each thinking it applies to herself.

Not till the other woman turned and swiftly ran up the stairs did Sita/Ferret realise that the appellation included them both, and piercing knowledge flooded through her, a lightning knife slicing through. She was rooted to the spot, still seeing a tall, thin, sloe-eyed beauty with white hair framing her face. 'Well, you'd better come in, hadn't you,' said Emily.

The sight of the one who had turned her back on her, had turned Sita/Ferret's blood into lead. Now she knew why Kala hadn't rushed off and flogged his gains to the jewel merchants. When you've waited all your life for something, the idea turns, warps and binds you, so when time erupts, and places it before you, the old you is in danger of being demolished, your known world broken – and no warnings of what new dangers you may be sliding towards. Unalloyed joy is a rare occurrence.

'I'm not going to eat you up,' said Emily.

'How do I know?' Sita/Ferret quipped back, old fears of this house stirring up. But images of the other, the *She*, the other Fe...rushed into her mind in their place. Was she at one with Emily and her house? Sita/Ferret watched as her foot stepped over the threshold.

'Keep your hands in your pockets,' warned Emily. 'And lock the door behind you. I don't suppose you've got anything for me.'

'The shop had run out of red roses,' she retorted.

The desertion of a moment ago brought a new wounding, a welling pain; the image of a moment ago a new betrayal. Sita/Ferret had always imagined a figure essentially like her own, though older and heavier; the distinct differences she had just glimpsed proved false all the assumptions she had held dear over decades, the lean simplicity a rebuke to claims of ownership.

Following Emily up the stairs, they passed along the hallway. The old patterns on the wallpaper became alive again, the high ceilings with their cornicing, the painted fingerplates on the doors bringing back memories at every step. Sita/Ferret saw everything as through a lens, trying to capture a whiff of *She*, to draw her into sight.

As Emily went ahead of her into the upstairs sitting-room, Sita/Ferret lingered behind, trailing her hand along a wooden chest, fearful that the *She* may be inside, with Emily. Then like a guilty child, she sidled in – exactly as she remembered it! She stood by the door, taking it all in. It felt like slipping back into an old self. The divan, made of intricately woven wickerwork with carved wooden sides, was still by the curtains, with little marble-topped stools at either end; a large wooden table was in the middle on which gleamed silver candlesticks and a huge marble bowl, so perfectly oval and cool it was like balm to the soul; in a cabinet against the wall was a set of crystal ware that had mesmerised Sita/Ferret as a child; the tantalising transparency of glass drawing a line across the heart. But an invisible barrier guarded the cabinet. Sita/Ferret had breached it once, and learnt such a lesson from Emily that she knew, for evermore, where the invisible barrier was.

The child Sita/Ferret had been entranced by a pear-shaped crystal ewer with the motif of a plant in the middle, two leopards on either side and a little crouching creature on the handle, as if ready to pounce! 'Carved from a single piece of rock crystal,' Emily had once told her. 'Don't you even let your breath touch it!' Forever afterwards Sita/Ferret had made sure she hadn't, and used to sit a little way away, concentrating on the ewer from there. Admiring from a distance! She could have done the same with *She*, and Sita/Ferret wouldn't even have let her breath touch her.

Emily was sitting down on the sofa, near the fire, where she could stretch herself out, and if she chose, perhaps see herself reflected in the mirror above the mantelpiece. Emily had brought over the mirror frame, a broad band made of brass, inlaid in copper and silver, showing scenes of drinking, music making, and of men on horseback hunting and fighting.

'They say it never rains, but it pours,' Emily said, lifting an Indian fan and turning the handle to and fro, the sequins in the embroidery reflecting the light, the lacy frill flapping with the movement. Emily liked to play the game of memsahib, fanning off a hot day.

'Mutant Memsahib,' Sita/Ferret whispered to herself, stepping gingerly into the room. Why hadn't Emily ever called the police? Sita/Ferret didn't sit down immediately. She roved from one piece of furniture to another, examining each in detail, kneeling down and looking closely at the designs of doors, the shapes of legs; admiring the vases, bowls and figurines, all of them in silver or bronze, occasionally glancing towards the door.

'Can't put those in your pocket and take them,' remarked Emily, breaking the silence.

'Have you any idea how much they're worth?'

'Yes.'

Sita/Ferret sat down on a chair by the table, keeping her spine straight. She had the visual answer to her visit. A face could launch a thousand ships, but could it fulfil a single hope?

'You've made something of yourself, then?' asked Emily.

'Of course.'

'How much? Excluding the smart little fortune you walked off with.'

'I'm a woman of...' she began, shifting her position in the chair. 'I'm worth more than I was in this house.'

Emily threw back her head and laughed.

Ancient/Ferret was at the front door, quietly sliding back the bolt. Hearing Emily's laughter, she paused to listen.

'I'll decide that. Let's have it in plain figures,' Emily stated. Sita/Ferret was listening out for sounds in the house and missed Emily's attack, 'Are you the boss? Or the tea lady? With what you took from here you could have increased it a hundred times over. I bet you haven't made a penny of your own. You've been living away but living off me. It must be in the blood.'

A door banged downstairs. Sita/Ferret was out like a shot. Running, jumping down the stairs, she jerked the door open and rushed down the path. A white car was turning the corner at the bottom of the street. Sita/Ferret stared helplessly at the shadow it left behind. Gone! Perhaps gone forever? Next time she'd tie her down with ropes.

Sita/Ferret went back in, her temperature rising. Emily had knowledge of the *She*, simple things like addresses and telephone numbers. Did Emily have the measure of the knowledge she possessed? What had these three crones been doing all their lives? Mysterious witches from the East!

Upstairs, Sita/Ferret stared angrily at Emily. 'Don't you lecture me. I haven't hurt anyone, I haven't used anyone, I haven't done anything immoral, and I've survived years without asking you for anything.'

'Survival is shit.' A pure Emily answer! 'Anyone can survive. A dog can survive. A rat in a sewer can survive. Lifting yourself up from the dung-heap…'

'And making a million I suppose!'

'Just as I suspected. You're a spineless little wretch. Champa used to say, "she'll make something of herself. She'll come back and show us. After all…" ' Champa's intonation and mannerisms were so perfectly replicated that Sita/Ferret couldn't help appreciating them, ' "…she is England born, England educated." ' Emily leaned back with a sarcastic smile, 'So England-born one, how much are you worth? Excluding the precious items you stole from me.'

'You haven't asked if I've got happiness?'

'I was right!' Emily declared triumphantly. 'The English-born whelp has jelly in her bones. If you weren't going to do anything with your life, why bother leaving this house? If I didn't have a sodding thing, you wouldn't be here, all tarted up and wanting more. If I didn't have anything, Champa would have died years ago, a used-up whore only good for the gutter. I brought her here, I helped her.' Emily ran her world from her mind, her truth the only truth. 'I worked for them,' Emily was saying, her voice flowing hot and rapid, 'and I earned them.' She pointed through the door at the shadow of *She*, '*She* was a gutter wretch. When chaos came, *she* did what *she* had to do. What had to be done!' Emily shook her head, 'You're young, you've had it soft, and you learnt to thieve! That of course is in the blood. I always suspected, and watched you, but you were too slippery for me. I went all the way Over There,' again her arm pointed, this time to that other distant place. 'I went against my own. And d'you think I got off scot-free?'

Sita/Ferret shot back a different reply, as if she had to eject it quickly before it burnt her tongue. 'Who am I? Where does she live?'

'Have you brought my goods back?'

'If you tell me what I want to know, then I'll tell you what you want to know.' Momentous knowledge packed into those thin, quick words that evaporated in the air.

'You haven't brought them,' Emily provided the answer. 'You wouldn't be so stupid as to walk around the streets with them.'

The temptation to tell Emily that that was exactly what she used to do was so overwhelming that Sita/Ferret blurted out a truth that might have been better kept for a later time.

'I've returned them to the rightful owner.'

'I'm the rightful owner!' Emily stood up, and taking her stick advanced towards Sita/Ferret like a lioness on the warpath. 'They were promised to me,' she said, mixing the promises of one man with the possessions of another, 'they're mine!' her hand thumped her chest. 'They belong to me. Here! Inside me! What did you get for them?'

Sita/Ferret stood up. She wanted to follow a white car and have the truth. So she told Emily her truth. 'Nothing.'

Emily's stick lifted and banged down on the table (her precious table with its mirror polish), sending bowls, vases and candlesticks flying through the air. The oval marble bowl hit Sita/Ferret's leg before thudding onto the floor. Emily would never forgive her for this damage to her precious possessions. 'You bring him here. It's a him isn't it? Always is with women who don't know the difference between their cunt and their purse.' Hot, contemptuous words! 'Bring him here so I can see his face. Then you can ask your stupid questions.'

'Deal?' rushed Sita/Ferret, ignoring the pain in her leg and jumping illegally on Emily's words.

'Champa spoilt you rotten. Now she's dying in hospital. But what do you care. The Ferret is a hundred times better than you.' The Ferret would have had an instant heart attack at hearing this praise from Emily. '*She* can swallow poison if she has to.'

'She must be dead already then!' Sita/Ferret retorted. Even then Sita/Ferret would pursue her, make her turn and look at her.

'Get out. Bring him here and I'll show him who's the rightful owner,' Emily snarled, back straight, stick hard on the floor, burning memories inside her.

Chapter Seventeen

Bombay, 1946–7

Gopal's wife came to visit, covered in a veil, clutching the letter that Emily had sent him, and speaking pretty English, like a convent-educated girl. She struggled to be diplomatic but her anger spilled out, and she threatened Emily with the police.

'If you want to ruin him,' Emily retorted.

'If you haven't done it already!' the wife retaliated.

Mutual jealousy governed both. The hostilities between them had begun long before either met the other; the wife had heard of Emily through well-placed snippets of gossip, Emily had heard of the wife through his own voice, lauding her virtues and possessions.

Emily was not visited by the police. The wife's hand was constrained, as Emily had guessed it would be. She could hardly let the world know her husband had been involved in the running of a brothel.

Two weeks later, the wife came back to see Emily, ready to beg. Since the first night he went missing, fear, anxiety and sleepless nights had become her lot. She had arranged for discreet enquiries to be made, had paid private detectives, hired others to follow up rumours, and come up with nothing. Emily didn't welcome the wife's visit, but she was sourly glad to see the change from the pampered creature that had first visited her to this distraught woman who begged for help, and who offered to pay handsomely for it. Emily repeated that she knew nothing and sent her away, watching her walk out of the room; this woman's steps had a ball and chain around them now.

Neither was Emily immune to this grief: Gopal's disappearance had left a desiccated hole in her; she was more alone than the first time, and living with a nightmare fear that she may be next. To silence her fears, Emily not only continued with the business of The English Rose Garden, but also re-doubled her efforts to increase the profits with longer hours, more girls, and more 'shows'. She had taken over the finances of the house: 'Until sahib returns,' she had told his man, 'you can come back then.' Ant had demanded a percentage which was carefully put aside for him. These days he was not a frequent visitor, being kept busy elsewhere and complaining the country was like an inferno. Gathering and accumulating the profits of each day, Emily continued her shopping and shipping to England, becoming more discriminating in her purchases, as well as searching out the more valuable items and making sure that each month, sums of cash went over too. Everything travelled across the oceans in a one-way direction.

The wife suspected Emily. Having already corrupted and fleeced him, she must be after the rest of their wealth. The wife thought Emily wouldn't be satisfied till she'd taken the wife's last paisa, her last trinket, and made her and her son destitute. This business was personal. The wife believed that Emily had betrayed him, and had had him kidnapped, perhaps even murdered. His punishment for reckless foolishness!

Then the wife visited Emily a third time, this time in a furious rage and waving two letters at her. 'How dare you!' she shouted at Emily. 'Demanding more money than we have ever had. You want to throw us out on the street, see us starving. So be it. But first you return him.'

'Let me have a look,' asked Emily, holding out her hand.

'You know what is in it, there is no need to pretend.'

'Please,' Emily moderated her voice and manner. She was in sole charge of The English Rose Garden now and wouldn't want to have that changed. She also needed to know about him for herself. 'Please let me have a look, I may be able to give you some information.'

'If you like to read your own writing so much you should have become a writer,' she said contemptuously, 'but here you are and then we will bargain.'

She handed over two sheets. The first was a letter, written in rough English, demanding three million rupees. Emily gasped at the figure. And looked up at the wife who glared back at her. Three million rupees! The zeros danced in front of Emily. Could anyone possess such fantastical sums? The money she had squirrelled away was utterly paltry and pathetic in comparison. She looked at the wife with another layer of hate. The second letter, which must have been written by Gopal, was short and far too sweet for Emily's liking.

To my dearest wife,

I am well and safe.

I believe you will have to enter into some negotiations. I know that you will use your intelligence and judgement. Be sure to look after the needs of our son. Rest assured I am perfectly comfortable. I shall soon be back with you. To see your lovely smile.

— Gopal

Emily handed the second letter back with jealous spite, 'It's not his writing.' He was hers; he had rested against her soft body. The wife had never been able to keep him. Or satisfy him. Clearly no harm had come to him. The wife could pay and he'd be on his way back. An ordinary case of kidnap and ransom. She need not have suspected anything darker.

'I know his handwriting,' replied the wife, taking the letter, folding it carefully.

'I know it better,' replied Emily. 'I've seen more of it. When would you have seen it? Did he write you,' a pause, 'love poems?'

The wife paled, and stood up. 'This building is in my husband's name and if you ever send me another letter I'll have it taken away from you.'

'A man only writes love poems to the woman he loves,' silkily, sneakily said Emily.

The wife twisted the end of her sari tight in her hand, tearing the embroidered cutwork. 'I'm not paying that ransom. It is a sick joke. Everyone knows that amount is impossible. We do not have it. There are no names, arrangements, instructions in the letter. Which means that you are the one I have to talk to. Let us talk.' Coming nearer to Emily, she whispered, 'Let my husband go, and you can have all this...' Her lips curled in disgust, 'You can have this property and the despica...' The wife stopped, calmed herself, '...the income from it. Plus, one hundred thousand rupees. Which is enough to last you the whole of your life.'

Figures, money, property, security, comfort – she'd never have to worry about a penny again. Desire and reason exploded like little fireworks inside her. How could she deliver? And what would Gopal say afterwards? What would he do? Emily relinquished the idea, like Cartier giving up on diamonds, like Leonardo giving up on the Mona Lisa.

'Believe me, I don't know anything,' Emily asserted. 'We're both in the dark.'

'Do not say "we".'

The wife waited for a second ransom letter. None arrived. She paid for more secret searches and private detectives, but their work was hampered by the need for discretion. How would Gopal live if he came back to social ruin? She didn't go to the police or any of their influential friends. What could she say to them? Toiling with her own anguish, she was oblivious to the profound changes gathering momentum.

Mahatma Gandhi was staying in Bombay. 'A people who want to be free,' he advised the Bombayites, 'should learn to mount the gallows with a smile upon the face.'[4]

One cocky young lad had marched around The English Rose Garden, shouting, '*karenge ya marenge!*' Emily had heard this slogan, almost from the day she had come to India, meaning 'do or die!'

She replied in Hindi, '*Karega ya jayega,*' pointing graphically to the gate. The young lad went back to work. No one could afford to lose a job. India was suffering a food shortage, and as usual, the poor always suffered first. And Gandhi blamed not only the British Government saying that it had, 'denuded India of her vital resources,' but also the people of the big cities like Bombay, claiming that there was far too much wastage.

Emily was like a squirrel, concentrating all her energies on The English Rose Garden, taking everything that wasn't needed for its running and buying up what she could, especially when there was a sale of household goods by those who had decided to return back to the old homeland. The sales increased after news of the Calcutta riots, and the cycle of revenge riots that followed. The story was that the chief minister of Bengal, a keen supporter of Jinnah's demand for Pakistan, told the police to take a holiday, and 'let the city's killers and thugs take charge of the streets' – Murder Unlimited! The Sikhs and Hindus retaliated; between twenty and thirty thousand people were killed. Revenge massacres occurred at Noakhali, but this time not only were people killed but Hindu women were raped. The news of these political rapes shocked the whole country. Women had never been molested before! Hostilities had taken a new and dreadful turn. This hot wind of terror was to spread from Calcutta to Dacca, from East Bengal to Bihar, to Ahmedabad, Lahore, and of course, to Bombay.

Time parcelled into weeks and months, elapsed like a black cloud collapsing silently into itself, like the silence into which he had disappeared, like the silence from which terror would spring.

Then the Rose Garden went up in flames.

Emily was sick with rage, clutching the few things she'd swept up in her arms, before she'd had to run out. She had barely begun to establish her foundations, and the ground was cut from underneath her. Yet again! The tally of what was owed to her grew longer. India had taken two men from her, she had barely begun to build the future, and *suitable recompense* had not yet been made.

The red flames rose in the early hours of the morning. The Rose Garden had held a particularly lavish and splendid party for Holi, the festival of colour heralding spring. The girls had been inundated with bookings for the Holi celebration. One of the girls had performed a dance, not of the seven veils, but of the seven colours: after losing her clothes of the seven colours, a fortunate client had the privilege of decorating her with a colour of his choice. Emily had even asked Champa and The Girl to stay and help, promising Champa compensation for her loss of earnings.

As smoke arose, and the flames lit everything around them with a hellish red glow, useless efforts were made to quench the fire with buckets of water, and someone was sent running for the fire brigade. The women sobbed and cried, looking like wounded birds dressed in their flimsy nightclothes or hugging shawls and sheets around themselves. They looked to Emily for help. Emily stared stony-hearted at the ruin before her. She would take ash and turn it into gold!

Champa took her home. They walked to her rooms on the other side of town, and The Ferret trailed behind. For a week Emily didn't go out, severely inconveniencing Champa's work. When Champa hinted that she might be more comfortable elsewhere, Emily had ignored her.

Emily did go out one day, dressed in one of Champa's saris. Her face half covered, she walked the bazaars, as in the days of old after his death; she walked to the houses of the English, lingering outside their gates, walking around to their gardens, haunting them! Then she walked to the neighbouring colony of well-to-do Indians, haunting them too. A servant had watched her standing by the gate and come forward to shoo her off. Lastly she visited the ruins of The English Rose Garden. She returned to Champa's rooms, exhausted, black circles in her head. The Girl cringed at the fearful sight of her.

'That's right,' said Emily.

The next day Emily told The Girl to get her a dress and hat. At first The Girl didn't understand, neither did Champa. 'Look you,' enunciated Emily, through clenched teeth, grabbing her shoulder fiercely, 'I don't have a rag for my back, go and get me what I need.' The Girl looked at Champa who shrugged her shoulders. 'Little Ferret,' said Emily in a sing song, 'who knows where she goes? Little Ferret who slips and sneaks! Get me what I need or else! Ferret is what you are. Ferret out what I need.' The Girl again looked to Champa for help, but Champa had gone to sit by the window, and was concentrating on threading a needle.

'I don't steal,' she said in Hindi.

'You will now,' Emily replied in English. Emily knew how to make herself understood and The Girl couldn't evade comprehension.

The Girl came back in the evening with a dress that was too large and a hat that was too small. They cut and sewed the dress, but Emily told The Girl to wear the hat on her head till she learnt how to get the right size. The Girl wore it while she did the cooking, serving and washing; the hat kept falling over her eyes or off her head. The next day The Girl 'obtained one' that fitted Emily better.

Emily went to see Ant. Surprised but not delighted, Ant asked how she had acquired his address? Emily told him about the inquisitive habits of The Girl.

'That thin little scrap,' he laughed. 'What else has she told you?'

'Nothing else yet,' Emily had replied. 'She can climb over walls, but she can't walk through them. I'll get her to practise.'

She told him about the fire that had swallowed everything.

'You were on a dangerous track.'

'It was business,' Emily replied crisply. Surely anyone could understand that.

'Not with them.'

'They paid handsomely for it.'

'Can't be done. You don't cross the line. They think the same too. You're for us, not them,' hands on her breasts, digging, mauling.

'I don't give a damn what you can or can't be having,' Emily replied. 'I've got to live.'

'The living may not last that long.'

'What do you mean?' asked Emily, eyes wide in anxiety.

'Pack your trunks, take what you can and go.' Fearful of having her dress ripped, she facilitated the opening of buttons and hooks. He laughed greedily, 'Still got a taste for one of your own? Are you going to run a whore house in free India? You've already been shown what'll happen.'

Deliberate intent! She had suspected it to be so. She'd never know who, or which side had lit the match.

'Help me,' she begged, as she slipped to the floor and Ant pushed into her.

A rock-like thought grew and fixed itself. Emily determined she would protect herself; she wasn't public property, she must be cool and distant, she must secure herself pink palaces, or the equivalent thereof. As Ant banged into her, she fixed her eyes on the guns hanging along the wall, and blinked as a line of cockroaches crawled across them, down towards the floor, one adventurous one making its way towards them. She concentrated her mind on it, watching to see how near it would approach. Sweat was pouring off Ant, dripping onto her, his smell filling the air. She tried not breathing.

She recalled the day when she had dressed in white and walked down the aisle of a church on her father's arm. Ant was on the last lap, hoarse groans erupting from him; she eyed the cockroach, counting the wasted years, her slide downwards, when it should have been upwards. Ant was now shouting and pumping into her, jerking and pummelling her whole body. Lifting her hand, she bashed it down on the cockroach, grinding its body and blood into the floor. Ant collapsed on top of her; she put her hand on his back, tenderly caressing him.

Emily's mind ticked on. The cockroaches have to pay, decided Emily, the ones who had come to purchase their pleasures at The English Rose Garden. They'd want to protect themselves. The Ferret could run the errands. She could wriggle through any closed gate. If they didn't comply, thought Emily, then she would make a few home visits, make herself visible in their residences. Not only morality, but the new public virtue of

208

patriotism to India would be outraged. They'd pay. Let them pay. They could never have had their forbidden pleasures if it hadn't been for her. Emily would send The Ferret to Fat-Slobby first, the one who'd wanted two at a time.

Eventually Ant pulled himself off, their bodies sticky with sweat. She quickly dressed herself, pushing her arms into her sleeves. Perhaps Ant sensed the blood on his back, for he asked, 'Ever think of pretty boy?'

Emily fastened buttons and smoothed out wrinkles. 'Who?' she asked carelessly.

'You know who I mean. Golden-boy Gopal. He's being very useful.' Ant opened his mouth and a sound issued, a sound related to a laugh though it seemed to come from the torture chamber. Emily's blood went cold, her hands shook as she was pinning her hat, so she left it off; she'd carry it instead. Emily remained silent and didn't ask the question she should have. Didn't ask the question she should have and thus sold her soul.

Silence is not empty. Into it went Emily's humanity and out of it came her bondage to Ant.

She turned to leave.

'It's time to return,' he remarked.

'You said that John Company Raj would never end.' She swung back to him, wide spaces in her eyes. If he was thinking of returning then it must really be the end of the world coming. Everyone would scrabble for what they could get.

'Oh,' he replied airily, 'the politicians are giving up, running away. Not John Company Raj.'

On the way back, her rickshaw was held up by a demonstration. Slogans were shouted, fists pushed into the air, Indian flags waved high. Emily stared at them disparagingly: the women in cheap saris and men in dirty clothes. These were the people who were going to overturn an empire, were they?

When she returned, she found Champa entertaining a white gentleman. He turned as she entered: a broad, toughened face, passionate evangelical eyes, a broad white collar around his throat. She almost laughed aloud at this picture of the whore and priest engaged in polite conversation.

'Is he a customer of yours?' she asked Champa rudely.

He stood up and bowed, 'I was informed that an English lady was staying here. I thought I must come and introduce myself, and of course offer any help that you might need.'

'What do you want?' she asked abruptly.

'I come to give, not to take,' he answered earnestly. 'I offer help in God's name.'

'Why don't you go back and do good where you came from.'

God's man was not affected by her rudeness, his mission to save souls outweighing any insult or injury. Emily was in a rage. What did this petty priest think he could do for her with his Bible and talk of riches in heaven? She needed them here, now, in her hand!

'We are all sinners in God's eyes,' he said. 'By asking forgiveness we can obtain absolution.'

'I'm not a sinner,' Emily raged at him. 'I came here in proper wedlock, with a proper send off and I'll return to a proper welcome.'

The Girl, eavesdropping behind the curtain, was awed by this display of power against a man of God. No matter which God they served, all men of God were supposed to be revered. Emily must either be very strong or utterly reckless.

Therefore when Emily told her to do some more 'shopping' for her, The Girl couldn't object, afraid of consequences either way. She suffered them both that day.

The servant woman had caught her from behind, pounding at her with slaps and fists, grabbing her hair and arm, and dragging her along the ground to face the memsahib inside. Both were thin and scrawny, but the strength with which one dragged and the other resisted would have done a sumo wrestler proud. For the servant woman, The Girl was the culprit for all the things that had ever gone missing, or may go missing in the future, threatening not only her livelihood but her home as well. She, who laboured all day at an honest day's work, had constantly to guard against this kind of vermin. Pulling and hauling with all her might, in between gasps and ragged breathing, she let loose a stream of invective at The Ferret, accusing her of every sin under the sun. The memsahib would send for the police, and they'd deal with her as she deserved. Slimy thieves like her put everyone else in the dock. With a gigantic effort, the servant woman managed to drag the struggling Girl up the three steps to the veranda, relishing the screams of pain, the blood and bruises. Only at the top, when she had to take one hand off The Girl to open the door, did her hold falter, a chink of opportunity which The Girl seized. Tearing herself away, she lost her balance and tumbled down the steps, the world whirling around her, her body bumping against concrete and sharp edges, the taste of blood in her mouth, an elbow hitting the ground, and pain shooting through her. Energised by sheer terror, she didn't pause, but hurtled towards an escape, running for her life. Once in the clutches of the law, who'd care for a penniless ragged child. Life would come to an end. She'd been given a chance: she ran, slipping and falling, crying and bleeding, her body full of pain, her world full of fear. But, she'd been given a chance! The greatest gift.

The Girl returned empty-handed and received little sympathy. Emily lectured her and hectored her for being careless; she should have made sure the coast was clear, that someone wasn't lurking around, she'd better be more careful in future. Looking at the broken, bleeding state of The Ferret, Emily decided that God had done some of her work for her. The Girl wiped her face with her torn sleeve, the movements of her arms stiff and hard. Her body throbbed with pain and waves of fear still flowed through her. Champa told her to go and get the evening meal ready. Emily reminded her that she still needed a dress and while she was at it she should get something for herself. The Girl nodded, and obediently went through the curtain into the corner where the cooking was done.

The Girl crouched down and lit the fire, unaware of the smoke stinging her eyes. She dropped spices into hot oil, seeing but not hearing their sizzling; she stirred vegetables, kneaded dough and baked food. Nothing over-cooked. Nothing burned. She didn't feel the hot air or the sweat soaking her clothes. At the end she prepared two thalis, didn't forget the glasses of water or the spoon and fork that Emily always insisted on, and took them inside. She returned, sat on the floor and waited. When they needed more, they'd shout to her and she'd take it in. Normally she might take a surreptitious half meal at this stage; flouting the convention of the servant waiting till last, having to make do with what was left. Not tonight, tonight she followed all the rules. When they finished, she still didn't partake at her allotted time. She collected the dishes, washed, dried and tidied. Then she climbed out through the little window, onto the small patch of roof. The evening breezes ruffled her hair and clothes, cooled the heat in her body. The sun was sinking in crimsons and oranges, yellows and golds. She tucked herself into a corner and watched the everyday transition of day into night. Darkness gradually fell upon her. No one would be coming to call for her, or wonder where she was. She crossed her arms around herself, eventually falling asleep in the cold night air.

The next day she returned with two items. One she hid in the kitchen, the other she gave to Emily.

At night she unfolded her mat, and carefully put the silk dress she'd taken for herself underneath. Silk for a servant's bed. Imagine! During the day she folded it up, inside the mat.

Emily didn't know the ways of moving around in confined spaces: coming out of the little cubby space they used for washing, her foot accidentally kicked the mat.

The Girl hadn't known, till then, that a hand could rock your brains inside your head. 'Enough,' Champa had told Emily for once, 'you can send her out tomorrow to get something else!'

'How dare she steal!' Emily raged. 'She keeps the best for herself and gives me rubbish. This is mine!' Said with the ferocity that lays claim to treasure. 'She's getting above herself. You do what I tell you to do in future, you thieving little Ferret. You bring me what I tell you to bring me. Next time you think of thieving, I'll break your arms and legs. Do you understand.' The Girl's terrified, tear-streaked face nodded. Emily was satisfied. The Girl had been pulled into shape.

Champa was not overly pleased with Emily. She had affected the whole tone of her life: none of the Soiree Sisters dropped in for afternoons of tasty gossip; her usual clientele were wary of her guest; The Girl looked at Champa with hot resentful eyes; Emily showed no inclination to leave; and Champa's money was running out.

'Of course you can have money,' Emily said to her grandly. 'Just wait a while for me to arrange it.' Champa's financial scope ran to the needs of the week, with a little left over; Emily's needs ran to how much she could gather and send. She was building her empire on the other side. Sometimes Emily felt as if she could see money and riches floating just beyond range – if only she could find a particular way of leaning over, she'd be able to reach out and grab them. Champa suggested to Emily that perhaps she would be more comfortable somewhere else. 'Oh, no. I'm quite happy here,' Emily replied.

The Girl hated Emily. Emily saw it and was pleased. Emily was like a volcano on the boil. She went a second time to see Ant and asked for a loan. She'd gather from every side. Nothing was permanent. The money in her hand might turn to ash! Ant owed her enough! Instead Ant gave her some financial advice, told her borrowing was false money, the only way to get real money was to get people to give it you, and they should want to give it you.

'Time's short. You never know, they might manage to shove us out; these days you don't know what goes on behind your back. Fucking bastard politicians betraying us. I'll pay you,' Ant said, 'if you can get a job done for me.' He needed someone to run a little errand for him. Then she wouldn't have any need to borrow.

'Write a letter for the first errand,' he explained, giving her a draft. 'Pretty boy's not so smart these days. Needs a few annas to spruce himself up.'

Each time he mentioned 'pretty boy', he watched her with needle-sharp eyes. She was silent. The past is dead she tells herself. Ash! Suffocating the memory of his body curving around her. 'The wife is desperate,' continued Ant. 'She's been softened up. There's nothing like getting time to do your work. She's not going to resist. She's been selling property and businesses, gathering cash.' As Ant was talking, Emily put a hand to her head, as if adjusting her hat. 'Enclose these,' he said, giving her a few sheets of paper that crackled in his hand. 'If she dithers about meeting the expenses, send a second letter in two weeks' time. With this little reminder.'

Ant was organised. How long had he been planning this? Opening the bottom drawer of a cabinet, Ant brought out a box. Oil had leaked from it. 'She's been waiting for this,' he said, his eyes shining. 'Perhaps she's not the only one,' coming up to Emily, lifting her dress and shoving the cold metal box between her legs. She gasped and tried to move away, but his hand gripped her fast as he kept shoving the box into her, cold metal against her, sharp corners plunging into her softest parts. 'You used to like it. Now listen to me,' he warned, his voice lowering, putting his face close up to her. 'I know where you live, who you're with, and about the girl who brings you goodies from other people's homes and gardens. If I wanted to there're many things I could do. To you. Or perhaps drop a hint to others, who'll want to do many more things. To you. So send that scrawny little bitch to me with my packets and the right amounts on the right days. Understood? Try any dodgy little trick and I might decide to visit you.'

Emily does not look inside the box. That omission goes into the silence too. Ant must have people of his own to whom he could have given this little job. But this is too secret, too private, an even darker shade of Ant. If

Emily chose to betray him, who would listen to the accusations of a failed whore? Furthermore an accomplice would have to reckon with the consequences to herself.

In a corner of Champa's rooms, Emily rewrote the draft letter, increasing the number of noughts; she wasn't cheating him out of his share. Emily started reading the sheets which crackled: *'Sarojini, is this bloody fool chaprassi...'* they began. Then she skimmed them, then she folded them, as soil falls upon a coffin, as a dead bird falls out of the sky.

Emily intercepted the first package and took her share. Whether Ant suspected or not, no wrath came her way. Emily did the same with the second, the final errand for Ant.

Ant never knew that there had been a third errand, that the metal box from which oil leaked had been kept and used for it, that the letters with Gopal's writing, which crackled so ominously, had accompanied it. Women's business! A personal matter between the wife and Emily. For all the years the wife had possessed him, for all the attentions he'd lavished upon her.

The Girl was like beaten iron these days. No words came out of her. When, days later, in the early dawn, The Girl brought Emily a bundle, she was as shocked as Emily, who, impatient in her eagerness, opened it in front of her. Glittering colours spilled across the floor, the red fire of rubies refracting in shining rays, greens glowing with mystery, pearls shining like creamy moonlight, diamonds sparkling like new life, pink opaque ones nestling, like love, among them all. All sorts of necklaces, thick and thin bangles, small earrings, dangling earrings with chains to pin into the hair, gold chains for the ankles, rings – all the ornaments a woman could want. Emily gathered them up, clutched them in her hands, held them to her breast. Now she possessed him all over again. Now she possessed the promises that had been made to her. Emily stroked the metal and stones, and The Girl was reminded of a scene in the grass many years ago. The submission inside The Girl began to unlock.

Chapter Eighteen

London, March 1997

Sita/Ferret heard the door bang shut behind her.

Emily must have watched her walk away for there had been an interval. Sita/Ferret paused outside Emily's gate, looked up and down the road, but there was no longer even a whiff of a white car. She walked on in the direction the car had taken and came to the corner shop. Sita/Ferret stopped by the corner shop. The first time in ten years! Is the distance of time only in the mind?

Time can be bridged by arms that invite, that hug you close. Thirty years could melt into thirty seconds if the other person looks at you, wants you.

Sita/Ferret opened the door and went into the shop. She felt her whole being shiver. Everything had been changed, modernised: fresh organic vegetables, flowers and plants on one side; herbal products on the rack of shelves in the middle; newspapers and magazines on the other side; and at the back, under the counter, fresh soups, tarts and Indian food. An Asian woman with cropped hair and dungarees came forward to serve her. Sita/Ferret asked her about the previous owners, Mr Sanders (or had it been Saunders?) the one who had given her her first job. The woman shook her head and said she didn't recognise the name; they'd bought the shop from a woman, and didn't know of any other owners. Sita/Ferret's history with this shop had gone.

Buying a fruit bar, Sita/Ferret put her change in the charity box and left, unwrapping the bar as she walked to the park. She sat on a bench in the playground where the children played on swings, slides and roundabouts, or romped in the sandpit.

Once Sita/Ferret had read a story about a 'basket baby'; the tale must have left its legacy for an older Sita/Ferret had become fascinated by 'abandoned-in-the-forest/river/desert-and-parents-unknown' stories. From Moses to Mowgli, from Oedipus to Tarzan, literature was littered with nameless, motherless infants. She started to comfort herself with the commonality of her situation till one day she twigged that these babes were all blokes! Girls either didn't get abandoned or they didn't survive.

Would she have preferred that the *She* had remained a mystery than to have seen the distance for herself? The distance of a desert between them.

You can never really possess anything that's alive. The *She* had never been and would never become hers, no matter the shared blood that flowed between them. Blood was only liquid – but Liquid Soul with its own will and voice.

Sita/Ferret imagines the *She* looking upon a lover's face, abandoning herself to an act in which the future is ignited: present love making future love. But neither *She* nor the partner had completed the cycle. When her body had emptied of its baggage, had she wiped her mind clean? A mistake erased? It was too dangerous a question.

Home is where the heart is – home and hearth, home and a burning fire. Is home a place in which the fire is lit like a ritual? Home, heart and hearth! Sita/Ferret must have worked her way through a hundred homes or more. After she had made her great escape from the Mausoleum, Sita/Ferret had at first avoided Indian homes as lodgings. If she inadvertently turned up at one, she'd put on a posh voice and pretend she was something quite different – Italian, Spanish, anything. But when she took on a job that paid pennies rather than pounds, she had had to look for the cheapest lodgings in the poorest part of town, and found them with the poorest Indian family she had ever seen. Yet Sita/Ferret's blood-need would have changed places with the sons and daughters of the family just for the everyday damp, soggy, interwoven intimacy, for the times when the mother and father said 'my daughter', 'my son', 'mine', negligently or indulgently, affectionately or angrily.

However, the desire to be near those from Over There had been planted and she moved from one Asian family to another. From the working class to the middle class, from the professional class to the business class, she sojourned in so many places that she realised there is seldom the ideal place you can call home. Home is what you're landed with. Lump it or leave it! The eternal choice. She had been in homes in which quiet arguments revealed themselves as bruises the next morning; homes in which prayers were recited and serious money pursued; homes in which traditions were revered and enforced; homes in which a middle path was being forged. And underneath it all was the push and pull, the dynamite of human relationships.

Which Champa was about to leave behind? To go across the Styx. Except that Champa would not know of the Styx. She must have another version hovering in her mind. Emily had informed her, in spitting words, that Champa had requested a visit from Sita/Ferret. Sita/Ferret hadn't responded; Sita/Ferret's heart was hardened against Champa. Sita/Ferret's heart was set on *She*, set on entering *She's* heart and tearing it apart – on being enfolded into *She's* heart.

The early evening with its wintry dark was beginning to pull its shadows over the day. Sita/Ferret got up abruptly and started walking to the station. Champa's hospital was on this side of town. Champa of the thousand hopes: Champa who had tried diet after diet to entice back the curves of yore, Champa who only did her shopping in the sales, returning with a motley collection of clothes that seldom matched and always required cutting, shortening, tucking and tacking – thus it was that Sita/Ferret had acquired the maidenly art of plying her needle. Hating the work, she'd indulged in acts of sabotage and found they profited her nothing for the unpicking and re-doing were harder than doing it right first time. Champa had taught her an important lesson about life. She hadn't needed to go to no guru.

Sita/Ferret walked almost at a run, as if she were in a marathon, her temperature rising, sweat starting to form on her body. A car turning a corner frozen in her mind; Champa's request starting to trail her, like a ghost at her back. What are acts of love? From where do they come and what do they want? She'd come from the Mausoleum filled with the image of the *She*, the other Ferret – one name connecting the two, one idea describing both. Sight seen. Image stored. Vacant spot filled! A face to hang betrayal on. Champa included, for she had colluded.

On the open platform of the station Sita/Ferret walked restlessly up and down, looking beyond the station to the night above where a faint moon hung in the sky, a fuzzy halo around it. *'Who goes there under the light of the witching moon?' 'It is I,' replies the Lady of Shalott, in her boat, 'insufficient the reflection I dared to look on my love's face! The mirror cracked, the curse opened and I journey to the next world.'* The train arrived, making Sita/Ferret jump backwards; she had been standing on the rim of the platform for a better view of the moon.

Sita/Ferret's head was overloaded tonight. There was nothing that Sita/Ferret could do or think that didn't have a strand of *She* running through it. Like dye. Like dying, like Champa. Like flying, like fleeing, like fire making. Fire-making K. What place did he occupy that her thoughts connected so naturally to him. The chain had grown, now running from *She*, to Champa and now to Kala. When she got out of the train, she handed in her ticket and went to a phone booth. He had said once he hated surprises. She put her hands on the phone before she picked it up and dialled. The *She* had turned her back. Why shouldn't the K? 'Chaos!' Emily had said, 'then came chaos, and *She* thought she would lose the rags *She* had.' Sita/Ferret might lose the moment. The phone rang. He answered and invited.

Blood-lines etched on the soul! Like the song lines of the Aborigines. The E & C & *She* are in there too.

By the time she got to Kala's building, the wind had increased and was blowing her hair wildly around her face. If there are blood-lines then they must be connected – only then could the electricity fly.

She decided to use her key instead of ringing the bell, wanting to see him before he saw her, to have him all to herself for a few seconds. He had an obsession about his keys, once saying he'd hate to come home and find the unexpected waiting for him. This doesn't count, she assured herself. She knew he was already here for the flat was warm and softly lit. Music came from the little room that he used as his study. She envisaged all the rooms of the flat and knew that she had memories of each, that there was a person here who might welcome her. This combination of memory and reality, and the expectation of being wanted must be like coming home. Near the study door, she paused, telling herself that rivers have many bends, including dangerous rapids.

He was in front of his computer, brandy by his side, and figures on the screen. More figures! She knew better than to creep up on him.

'Hello. Namaste *Sat-Sari-Akal. Salaam Alaikum. Jai Shri Krishna.*'

218

'You survived the journey to the lion's den?'

'This could be a ghost you see in front of you,' she said, and wished she hadn't.

'I'd better check.'

She moved first, meeting him with an emotional giving and openness he'd never experienced in her before. Arms locked around him, her body pressed against his so that every inch of her was touching in a way that was both an offering and a receiving.

'Help!' he cried, lifting his head, like a stone breaking the water's flow! Immediately she loosened her hold and made to move away, but he held her back. 'I thought we should give the air a chance to circulate.'

'Fine,' she said, lifting his hands and putting them back by his body. 'I'll be more considerate to the air in future.'

He started to protest and then stopped. 'Here,' he handed her his glass. 'B for brandy strengthens the blood. You can have a humdinger of a row after a few of these.'

'I apologise for having disturbed you at this late hour of the evening.' She'd murder him with polite words.

'No matter. If you'd arrived earlier you'd have found me in tears. I was saved the humiliation.'

Tears or fears? Disasters or tragedies?

'But it's nice to see you here,' he said from his seat, a distance between them. Could this be the indirect affirmation that she was welcome?

'I didn't get a damn thing out of Emily,' she told him.

'Even though you went dressed to impress?'

'I saw *She*. I saw that *She* is me. I feel as if there's been an earthquake today. There's nothing in common between us. Why would I have found you crying?' she asked, quickly changing tack. 'Or was that another one of your jokes?'

'Oh, that,' he replied, 'was C for comic, a tragi-comic joke. My first goodbye.' *Goodbye!* – a word that slices one into two, separates, a little sound that leaves indelible debris.

'One of many?' she asked, tapping the glass with a fingernail, an improvised rhythm.

'It always takes more than one, doesn't it?'

'What the hell are you talking about?'

'I've sold up,' he said without a smile. 'I'm a free man. Take me.'

'I hate your jokes.'

'Thanks for the applause.'

Time the divider. How much time between him buying a one-way ticket and Champa lying in a coffin?

Emily had gone to bed early. Ancient/Ferret sneaked quietly back into Champa's room. She knelt on the floor, gripped the corner with both hands and breathing deeply, lifted one side of the wardrobe and shifted it forward. Then she went to the other side which was now at an angle and, forcing herself into position, lifted that side a few inches forward too. She knew it would take time.

'What are those figures?' Sita/Ferret asked Kala, pointing to the screen.

'Nothing!' he replied. 'Whichever way I calculate them, they come to nothing.' Switching off, the screen went blank. 'Money! Money! Money! I ain't got none honey.'

'Except a fortune tucked away in a pouch.'

'That,' he said, 'has to go back where it belongs.'

'How do you know for sure?'

'Too late to ask such questions. You shouldn't have been so liberal with your largesse.' At least she was getting equal treatment from all sides, everyone dishing out condemnation. 'I'm going to take them B for back, and give them to my grandmother.'

'Emily wants to see you.' The collision of two worlds! And after that, more change: '*But at my back I always hear/Time's winged chariot hurrying near.*' Whoever said it was a chariot must have been under some romantic delusion: time is a damned pitchfork in the back.

'How nice that will be,' he replied, passing his hand backwards and forwards over the blank screen. 'This was mine. And now, it's as if I've done nothing for the last ten years. And don't tell me it's the experience that counts,' he added, taking the bottle and refilling the glass in her hand.

'You felt you were worth something?'

'What is this? A self-esteem session?' His eyes were hot with sarcasm.

'No. It's what I've had chucked at me. But if there are any of those self-esteem sessions going, then I'll have them today, tomorrow, and the day after. Thank you!'

'So the family reunion wasn't all sweetness and light.'

'We're not family!' she snapped through gritted teeth. Fear most often is the decision maker: what if she didn't see Champa today and she died?

'Temper, temper. Madam has hardly imbibed,' taking the glass from her, and helping himself to a big gulp, 'yet madam exhibits the full influence! It must be in the nature of the personality,' wagging a finger and waggling his head knowingly.

'I hate that fake Indian act!'

'But I am thinking it is very Alec Guinness, very *Passage to India*, very…worth something? You have hit the nail on the head. I worked from the first penny to the last, put in the best years of my life, you could say. I'll take any cliché going, they have that time-worn ring of doom about them.'

Many will smile righteously and judge it to be a fitting denouement for the man who broke into another's marriage vows and stole the merchandise.

'Ten years ending in this, C for chaos,' he said, raising the glass in a salute, and draining it in one go.

'*It was chaos and I had to mould the world!*' Emily used to say, turning it into a knife; 'Chaos,' Champa used to say with a shudder; 'Chaos,' *She* must also have said with her hardened exterior. 'Chaos' had been a word placed in the Mausoleum like another one of the artefacts from Over There. Now he had come out with its twin. If you let the moment of chaos pass, you become its victim, but to turn chaos into your desire, you must first become one with it, reckless, anarchic, chaotic. Sita/Ferret jettisoned discretion and reason to test a figment of her imagination.

'Um, actually,' she said, sitting down on a chair, back straight, legs crossed at the ankles, hands cupped neatly one inside the other, voice controlled to be falter free. 'Actually,' she repeated herself, 'I'm sorry your business has had to be sold. It's very painful to have the efforts of a decade wiped out. A great loss.' She stopped, fearing that she sounded like a glib politician – all words and no meaning. 'I backtracked ten years too today. *She*,' doubly emphasising the word, 'was seen.'

He was concentrating on her words, a frown furrowing that gorgeous forehead, at sight of which she nearly lost her courage. 'Completely different from what I had ever imagined,' she paused, and decided to go no further in trying to describe the effect of *She*. 'It showed that thoughts are useless when tested against reality. Which made me see things more clearly.' If you become one with chaos, do you increase the chaos? 'And the thing that I realised most clearly was that I love you. Very much.' She closed her eyes and let her breath out like a diver coming up from the deep. The sound of her own breathing seemed to fill the room. Nothing happened. No movement or sound from him. She opened her eyes and stared back at him.

'How very English!' he said.

'Indubitably,' she replied.

Ancient/Ferret shone her torch on the area behind the cupboard. The light shook a little. Ancient/Ferret had been tense all day, unusually for her. She focused her eyes on the unbroken condition of the cobwebs and ropes of dust behind the wardrobe; nothing could possibly have been stored here. With infinite patience, little by little and moving from one side to the other, she moved the wardrobe back into place. Ancient/Ferret was becoming a little disquieted. Perhaps, knowing the seriousness of her illness, Champa had decided to do away with her diaries. Ancient/Ferret wouldn't accept it; Champa the hoarder must have hidden them somewhere. 'She's got a little fortune tucked away in her bank account,' Emily had said. How had Emily known that? Were the diaries neatly tucked up in Emily's room having betrayed Champa's secrets? Those little remarks about Emily and her habits, that little drawing in which Emily met the devil and had scared him to hell!

The laundry where Champa worked had bleached her into a worn and faded person but The Ferret had often been surprised by Champa's gumption – like when Champa had started a market stall at the weekends. It had been taken for granted that Ancient/Ferret would help with the driving, fetching and carrying, all the heavy work. Initially Emily had objected to the use of the car, but relented when Champa agreed to give her a share of the profits. In the summer Emily would even go along with them; she'd sit in a chair and fan herself while Champa sold pieces of cloth, now and then informing Champa that she was being too generous in her cutting, or under pricing the material; Champa would reply to her, their sentences going back and forth. At lunchtime, they'd sit side by side, eating their sandwiches.

Champa had stopped doing her stall when it was once overturned by a gang of men who had towered over her, and showered her with insults and abuse, taking delight in dwelling on her colour, gender and sexual habits. 'You too,' they had shouted as Ancient/Ferret had arrived back at the stall with three cups of tea, which she'd then spilt and burnt her hands. Afterwards, Emily had said they should expect that kind of hooligan behaviour; after all, she herself had been thrown out of India. 'It's not the same,' Ancient/Ferret had shouted at her, nursing her hands, but unable to say how it was different. The men had frightened her, the menace and force of their attack had reverberated inside her. When they'd overturned the stall she'd thought they were going to throw it at her.

A few months after that incident, and after she had made a visit to a jewellery shop, she had chucked in her job, demanded her share from Emily, fought with Emily, and had left.

Now, as Ancient/Ferret searches Champa's room, she remembers her first impressions of Champa. She no longer knows if they are truth or fabrication, but the first impressions of a little girl were that she had been brought to live with a fairy queen, and everything sparkled and shimmered around this beautiful being who sings and dances, and is the centre of adoring love from all her visitors.

'Does this require an answer?' Kala asks. Sita/Ferret is still sitting in the chair, convalescing, and has no energy left to reply. 'Can I think about it?' he asks, negotiating the issue. She nods her head, for one must be polite and respond to a question, though the application of a mental process to a declaration of passion is incongruous, if not impossible. If she wasn't personally involved, she would have considered his reaction to be eminently sensible. But as she is the one who has unravelled herself and uttered those tantric words, fabled for their properties to produce happiness and change lives, she sees her moment pass, unfulfilled.

Falling in love must be like winning the lottery, and then finding you've lost the ticket.

'Are you going to sell this flat?' she asked, breaking the silence, initiating the distraction of conversation.

'Hell no. I can't go down in history as the second family traitor.'

'Who was the first?' She should go and see Champa, if only for the sake of safeguarding her future peace of mind – a self-interested act of duty. He didn't answer immediately; he was obviously back to his habit of pausing. Her bruised insides couldn't take silence of any kind so she quickly started telling him about Champa, as if having started on the path of self-revelation, she couldn't stop. He got up immediately, saying, 'Let's go,' took her hand, pulled her up, and propelled her towards the door.

On the journey, he is the one who starts talking non-stop, unrolling time, unfolding the history of his family, sketching in a missing century for her. He speaks of people now long dead, of their connections with each other, what they had done, whom they had befriended, hated, how they had died, what they had left behind, and how their descendants in turn had lived and filled their days. She absorbs his words through every cell in her skin; this amazing possession of a personal history beginning so far before one's existence. It must be this weight of years that gave such people their sense of being placed, materially, psychologically, geographically, historically.

'The so-called family traitor,' Kala continued, like a river running to the sea, 'it seems, was my grandfather. I've already told you about him. The very stuff of melodrama: betrayal, torture, extortion and so on. Now nobody really cares. It was too long ago. My grandmother has something in a B for box. I was sometimes privileged,' a bone-dry word, 'to see it. Floating in oil and spices. In England, they call it "the family jewels".' He's driving therefore he must concentrate on the road ahead.

'Pickling is an art that women know. Do you know your pickling?' he asked. She nodded her head, and then realised he wouldn't have seen it.

'Yes.'

'So, you are a homely domesticated type!' Reverting to his stylised Indian accent, 'Educated to diggree level?' he asked.

'No.'

'But you have a fair complexion. That will do nicely. And how much dowry, I mean, so sorry, of course that is against the law. I was wanting to be asking, how much contribution to the housekeeping? We are simple people, all we are needing is a house-car-furniture-a-few-thousand-in-the-bank-fridge/freezer-washing-machine-TV-VCR-PC-CD...'

'Stop it!'

'I can see you are the dominating type. But that is not a bad thing. One gives the orders, and the other obeys. Life is hunky-dory. OK, B for Boss?' At last, he turned for a quick look at her.

'I hate that ABC habit.'

'Sorry. Flesh…' he said, resuming his story, 'does not look very nice, years after it's been, er, used as an item in the art of persuasion, shall we say? My grandmother doesn't wear a widow's white. A body was never found, a funeral never arranged, so as far as she's concerned, the story hasn't ended.'

The Ferret had a letter hidden inside her clothes. 'Go in the dark,' Emily had said, 'else someone will see you.' Emily was afraid of detection. The Ferret was afraid of danger. A woman child does not traipse through the city streets in the middle of the night, but she couldn't risk saying so for she might have found herself permanently out on those very streets, a prey for the carnivores that came out at night. Moonlight or dense darkness, both were foes. Where she could, The Ferret stayed close to buildings, and when she had to cross an open space, she'd run with her heart pounding inside her. The dark changed the shape of buildings, hid landmarks and created confusion. When she thought she should have reached her destination, she found she'd veered off in a different direction. The Ferret huddled against a wall, fearful and tired; tears ran down her cheeks; the letter stiff against her body, she didn't question the heavens for an explanation of her situation. She'd never owned herself; she had to do the business of the place where she was. She set off again, back the way she'd come. Nearby the yelping of dogs made her break into a run, sweat pouring off her face. Street dogs were the wolves of towns, and whether you met a single snarling one, or a growling pack, you could forget about going home. She didn't know if any had picked up her trail, but as she ran, her chest burning with pain, she looked for places in which to hide. Walls, closed doors and shuttered windows defeated her searching eye. If she were to knock at a door, none would let her in. The Ferret pushed herself forward, towards her destination, trying to evade harm; she didn't want to die. She wanted life. This night (the second of her fraught journeys to that house) would return to her many years later when she would be reminded that she had run to preserve her life; her only possession. The memory affected other decisions, including the birthing of a child. Once begun, despite her forebodings and worry, she had not wanted to stop its life, she wouldn't rob it of its one possession.

'What I shall do is this,' Kala continued, laying out a plan. 'Go back to India, try to land a job as a pilot. I'll have to take whatever comes along. It won't be glamorous. Salary average middle-class, lifestyle ditto. You can have a couple of servants, join the local ladies' charity group, or become a high-powered executive. You can be honest about your dubious origins and be in with the lefties, or do the foreigner-returned act and be in with the snobs.'

As the implication of his words became clearer, she listened in astonishment and anger. For someone who had evaded the answer to her emotional confession, he was rushing madly towards its logical conclusion. Didn't he see the missing step?

The second significant moment! Passing by without unloading itself of its legendary cargo of happy-ever-after promises. This should have been the moment when life delivered, or so it was believed. In contrast to the concentrated intensity of her avowal, this moment was so diluted with flippancy that it must even doubt itself. But neither had risked a straight question. She had made a statement about an act of faith; he had talked about living arrangements. How come she had suddenly got so ambitious? How come he had suddenly become so prosaic?

'Why?' she asked, hugging her arms tightly around herself – in case she leapt off a cliff?

'So you can have many, many in-laws, a dozen sons and a fully functioning husband, we hope.' Dropping his act and speaking normally, he continued, 'Actually there are only two in-laws left. Hadn't you thought about it?' They started passing signs for the hospital.

'I hadn't got that far.'

'Life's short. You can't dilly-dally.'

'Don't you think there's a missing connection?' she hit back, her temper flaring.

For a moment he looked completely puzzled, or pretended to, then his face cleared as if enlightenment had been bestowed upon him. 'I am forgetting...' He was back to his head-wagging routine. 'You are a Western-educated girl. You are requiring wine, music, dance and singsong. Yes?'

'What do you think I am? A bimbo?'

'But I have the most highest regard and respect...' he began, putting on his wounded innocence voice, but she cut into his pretence.

'I am requiring you to tell me...' Realising that she was picking up his accent, she stopped and shot him an irritated look which coloured her next words. 'I have bared, B for bare, my soul, as they say, and need to know from you, if you reciprocate?' Love, the pot of gold at the end of a long hard road – was this to be her reward on the day she had made an emotional gamble.

'Ah yes,' he said, 'that question!' He wouldn't relinquish his hold upon himself. The dead do not go quietly, they lay traps in their wake.

She hated old English hospitals with their yellowed, peeling paint, iodine smells, endless corridors and high ceilings. In her must-do-good days, she'd sometimes been a visitor to those who had no one else to visit them, buying toothbrushes, combs and drinks for them, making conversation; doing caring! She'd forced herself to do it, hating to admit that she wasn't a natural.

Sita/Ferret and Kala followed signs and corridor markings. Her finger sought out a finger of his and held onto it. She couldn't hold hands with him. He hadn't given her a suitable reply.

'Don't leave me alone with her,' she pleaded.

'No promises.'

They climbed stairs, walked through double doors that closed with a swish behind them, the corridors ominously silent – this was after visiting hours but Sita/Ferret had insisted, and been admitted. A fitting place to meet, Sita/Ferret thought, feeling calmer as she saw the ward a few yards away, a place of pain, loss and lost expectations; as well as recovery, healing and hope. Opposites.

'Are you the one she's been waiting for?' asked the nurse at the duty desk.

'Certainly not,' Sita/Ferret stated categorically.

'You'll find she's very weak, a couple of times we thought we'd nearly lost her, but she managed to hang on. She's in Twenty E.'

If the nurse hadn't told her the bed number, Sita/Ferret would have carried on, not recognising the gaunt, wrinkled face that Champa had become; the ragged grey wisps that had once been her luxurious curly hair. Eyes closed, one frail, forlorn hand on the cover, Champa lay sleeping.

Sita/Ferret couldn't bring herself to say her name or touch her. She stood irresolutely by the bed. Kala waited for her to do something, then brought a chair for her to sit on, seating himself at a little distance – granting her privacy or keeping himself separate? A vase of red roses stood on the bedside cabinet. Sita/Ferret couldn't believe that Emily would have spent so much on a collection of plant fibre.

'It's me.' The voice came out in a whisper, then again, 'It's me,' injecting some strength. '*Mein hoon*,' Sita/Ferret said, switching languages.

Champa's eyes flickered, her head moved towards the source of the voice. 'Thoufi?' Her voice was worn to a shred, the bright brown eyes of old now milky and clouded. '*Ainek*,' requested Champa as she started to lever herself up, a sad, laborious process. Sita/Ferret did not help. Kala glared at her; she looked away. Finally, Champa sat up at a little angle, and rested, her chest heaving up and down. '*Ainek*,' she asked again. Sita/Ferret looked on the cabinet and saw a pair of brown-framed glasses. She handed them to Champa who took several faltering minutes to open them and hook them round her ears, and then to stare at Sita/Ferret as if drinking in her face. She lifted her hand to touch, each movement taking an age to complete. Cold, dry fingers rested on Sita/Ferret's face, and then, strangely, a small little smile, affectionate, with warmth in the eyes. Was this love coming towards Sita/Ferret? What secret changes had occurred in Champa? Sita/Ferret looked away. She'd rather have the old Champa with the smart slap. It was unfair of fate to reduce her to this.

'The last one,' Champa said. Champa's hand fell down, exhausted. 'You will be alone.'

'Who's Thoufi?' Sita/Ferret asked quickly; it must be a name familiar to Champa for her to have used it so automatically.

'Toffee. Thoufi. Present girl, *Tofa*. I let Emily have her.' Champa's head shook contritely. Her hand moved towards Sita/Ferret again to touch her sleeve. Making a huge effort Champa heaved herself up a little more, '*She* came back with you not born.' So Champa was the one to give it all in the passing of a moment. Stopping to recover her breath, her eyes closed again, the words requiring effort. 'You will be left, the only one.' A finger flickered up, and Champa continued, more strongly than before, 'Go to sister. Tell her I want the letter.' Kala motioned to Sita/Ferret that he would go. Champa's hand again crept onto Sita/Ferret's arm, her eyes closed behind the glasses, blue veins vivid among the wrinkled skin. The skin that Champa had creamed and fed, clothed and adorned. And now it was betraying her. Mortality!

Never to be seen again! Now Champa's passions had been worked out, her time was used up. But Sita/Ferret was her creature, (and Emily and *She's*). They had ordered the flow of her life as only family can do.

'I hated you,' replied Sita/Ferret. 'All the time.'

Champa's hand patted her arm, 'You had to be pure. And strong.' Champa's voice was a worn remnant of her old musical tones. '*Pani*.' Sita/Ferret looked around for a nurse, wished Kala would come back, and remembered how she had held glasses of water for countless others. Strangers. *'Pani.'* Champa's tongue licked her dry lips; tongues grow old too.

She had never used to touch them, verbal communication being more than enough – till the time Champa had told her to massage oil into her head. After her first fumbling efforts, and a severe castigation from Champa, she'd learnt to warm the oil to just the right temperature, pour it drop by drop onto Champa's head, and massage it in with her fingertips. The whole process could take hours, with Sita/Ferret standing behind Champa, working it in, till her hands and arms ached or till Champa fell asleep. In the summer Champa would find a sunny spot in the garden for this ritual, and sit with her face upturned to the sun.

Sita/Ferret placed her hands around Champa and pulled her further up into a sitting position, heaving harder than was needed, for Champa's plump body had not only wrinkled, but had shrunk to her bones. She held the glass of water to Champa's mouth. Champa drank clumsily, like a child. Her hand lay on her chest, going up and down with her breathing; she filled her lungs with air.

'New child, Sitachild. Everyday I prayed for you.'

'Then why...' Sita/Ferret was about to argue, but Champa held up her hand, a shadow of the old authority still attached to it; Champa had drilled into her, *do not demand, do not ask, take what you are given, do not be selfish.*

Kala and the sister came up, a brown envelope in the sister's hands.

'Is this the one?' asked the sister, pointing at Sita/Ferret. Champa nodded. 'Do you want me to give her this envelope?' The sister wants to be perfectly sure.

'Yes, yes,' replied Champa, nodding again.

'To Sita Bombay. And this is Sita Bombay, correct?' Champa nodded again, and held up her hand. The sister placed the envelope in it, and Champa's shaky hand conveyed it halfway across the bed to Sita/Ferret – like conveying it halfway across the world.

Sita/Ferret wondered what dynamite was contained in the envelope as she gingerly took it. When Champa has gone, what would Sita/Ferret do with her share of hate? Hate, and love its opposite, are immortalised inside us, as she was about to find out. As a trolley passed behind, Kala shifted his chair and the movement caught Champa's attention. She leaned forward, her eyes blinking rapidly. 'Here,' she said, her hand motioning to him, her voice like dry sand. She didn't move her gaze off him as he stepped nearer. Her head started to shake.

'Where have you come from?' she whispered. Her eyes filled and tears slipped down her cheeks. 'And my sahib?' As her glasses began to fall, Sita/Ferret took them off, and placed them on the cabinet. Taking a tissue she dabbed at the tears. Champa's eyes were closed.

'She's sleeping. Let's go,' she said to Kala.

Sita/Ferret placed Champa's envelope in her bag. She'd read it tomorrow. They were waiting by the lift when the nurse came running after them.

Death is not one-dimensional. Not the end. No other event loads time and emotions so heavily. The past swills around in those left behind, emotions veer from remorse to guilt, to fear and loneliness – so that when Sita/Ferret asked the hospital staff to ring Emily and tell her, and Kala said she should do it herself, she meekly acquiesced, only to stumble at a hurdle.

'I've forgotten the number. I was determined to forget it, so I did.'

The hospital staff were wary of passing on telephone numbers, and as Mrs Miller was stated as next of kin, they would take the responsibility of phoning her.

'She's not,' Sita/Ferret had contested hotly. 'How can she be? They're, they're…different for a start, and I'm the same. And I'm…'

The blockage burst inside her, '…I'm her daughter.' Champa had brought her up, although in her own particular way, therefore Sita/Ferret had every right to that claim. Biology wasn't everything. But this newly minted maternal connection cut no ice with the authorities.

She sat next to him in the jeep, clutching a plastic bag containing Champa's spare nightdress and dressing-gown. She recognised them, she'd washed them often enough.

'See,' he said, halfway through the journey, a barbed-wire smile on his face. 'Pimps and murderers. One look at me and she keels over.'

Flesh has a die-by date!

Previously, like disciples of platonic virtue, they'd never undressed before slipping under the sheets. Today she insisted, and also stopped him

230

from switching off the lamp. These are borrowed skins, skeins of life, and subjects of death. Watching the play of shade and light on his skin as he moved towards her, she ran her hands along his shoulders, down his arms and into his fingers, which clasped hers. Her lips licked and tasted his skin, storing it in her mind for memory, for when something may have happened and she would need to draw on it. Did the five senses multiply when two were engaged in this game of pleasure? She nibbled the softness of the skin, then bared her teeth and plunged for that heady taste of sweet blood. He pushed at her trying to dislodge her. Tenacious in her pursuits, she resisted till he abandoned politeness and heaved them both over, pinning her arms, putting his weight on her, and then hesitating. Some steps not only take you further along the road, they change the route altogether.

What would happen if he stopped now? Her fear. Would the world come to an end and start again somewhere else, without the two of them? And yet he had asked her to mingle her living days with his, offered her the shape without promising the substance. Wasn't he old enough and young enough to have a past and a future? They stared at each other like adversaries. His hands began a slow ballet, encircled breasts, moved in soothing, caressing tenderness, like a lullaby; suddenly tightening and crushing as lips and teeth swooped, harshly and peremptorily taking and gorging. Gasping at this treachery, her fingers plunged into his hair and pushed at his shoulders, her efforts to dislodge him only serving to increase his hold on his territory. She retaliated with other weapons, arching her fingers and scoring her nails across his back, breaking skin and drawing blood. He pulled himself up, grabbing her arms and holding them together with one hand, while he moved down, pushing her legs open with the other. She struggled to escape his hand, not to free herself and run but to hunt down spoils of her own. He was not so strong that he could effortlessly contain her resistance; his hold tightened round her wrists, twisting skin against skin. A shocked shiver ran through her as his lips and tongue moved into her, exploring and taking the most private areas, engaging in an intimacy of their own. Distrustful of him, she tried to resist as her senses unrolled under the waves beginning to wash over her, no telling when he would somersault this conjuring of pleasure into a little trick against her. He released her hands and moved himself further inside, then out and around, tracking backwards and forwards, homing in on the vortex gathering inside her. She placed her hands on his shoulders and pulled herself up and away. He looked at her as if he had been betrayed, then she unrolled her body to take him into her mouth as he returned to his own interrupted engagement with her.

Later: 'Sex is a duplicitous agent,' he said.
  A delayed delivery sting.
  Clever.

Ancient/Ferret was still in Champa's room. She had found the collection of Indian music posters spanning the fifties, sixties and seventies; little gatherings which eventually evolved into proper concerts. Ancient/Ferret couldn't remember Champa ever having gone to a concert, or professing to be a music lover and yet the years were marked out by these posters. Ancient/Ferret remembered the hand-distribution system whereby men and young boys would hand out posters on the streets for events and film screenings, or there'd be a pile by the till in the Indian shops. No sight of women in the embryonic businesses of that time. Champa had refused to go to any of the Sunday morning screenings of the Bombay blockbusters, complaining of the type of person to be met there. 'Peasant types from the villages only,' she had sniffed, her city sophistication offended by having to mingle with yokels. 'They don't know how to dress even, they are just working for money all the time.'
  'Aren't you doing the same?' The Ferret had asked.
  She had also gone through a pile of calendars, one for each of the last fifty years, almost as if Champa couldn't let go of time, wanted to freeze it? Ancient/Ferret had even gone on her hands and knees and crawled around the room, pressing her hands on the carpet to see if anything was hidden underneath. Now she sat, resting against the bed, staring at nothing, the sound of the cell door shutting banging in her head, the cursing of the servant woman who had hauled her up the stairs by her hair echoing in her. She must have deserved it even then for sins not yet committed. For she was the woman who only today had seen the face of the child she had birthed. The same child that had taken Ancient/Ferret's revenge on Emily.
  There was that time when The Ferret had become the chauffeur as Emily went on her biannual tours to every branch of her family. Sitting in the back, with her fur stole draped round her shoulders, Emily had done her rounds as regally as a duchess. If she noticed the coolness of her reception at these worker's cottages or the lack of invitations to stay

longer, she never let on. The Ferret would search Emily's face reflected in the rear-view mirror, but no shadows ever flickered through the powder and lipstick, the fierceness of the eyes only shone sharper. When The Ferret first left Simla Sunshine, she also had been as fierce as Emily. Had Emily, quite unknowingly, trained her in this art?

Ancient/Ferret had gone to bed and fallen asleep when the phone rang.

On the first night that Champa had left the house, Emily had been woken by its stillness, the first night in over fifty years that they hadn't shared a roof. Champa would be back, she assured herself, once she'd tired of this poor-me-sick-invalid act.

On the second night, Emily was again woken by the stillness of the house, as if Champa's breathing had somehow filled out the silence. Emily got up and went into Champa's room, leaving the door wide open to release remnants of Champa's breath into the rest of the house, to refill it.

Emily would make Champa return! There was no going away from this house. Sooner or later all would return. No matter how hard they pretended otherwise, they were linked to Emily by bonds of fate. Both Ferrets may have said 'fatal bonds', but Emily saw them as destiny. If he had to leave her and die, then this was the way India repaid. Emily had stroked the down of a folded, fleecy cardigan. She wondered if this was the one with roses embroidered on the front, sequins and beads threaded through. Emily shook it open. A book thudded to the floor. Gathering them in her arms, she took a pile of books back to her room. This was part of the *suitable recompense* – part of the past and part of Champa's secrets. It was meant to be so.

The telephone rang on the fourth night.

Ancient/Ferret held out the receiver to her, 'They want to speak to you.'

Emily shook her head into the phone. 'It's not true,' Emily stated, with absolute conviction. 'I want to speak to a doctor.'

Emotion was not their way. They went back to their respective rooms.

Next morning, Ancient/Ferret went into the upstairs living-room, her bags in her hands. She looked at the room and at Emily. This was probably the last time she would be in this house. Emily was at the table, leafing through brochures on properties in India: seaside villas, 'Western-style' apartments in cities, condominiums in Goa. 'Pah,' she said, throwing the last one aside, 'it'll be full of these made-it-rich-quick upstarts.'

'While it took you decades of hard, back-breaking work,' taunted Ancient/Ferret, putting down her bags, coming to sit opposite her.

Emily was silent for a while. 'It took me! Everything in me.' The voice snaked at Ancient/Ferret and wound around her.

'I'll arrange Champa's funeral,' began Ancient/Ferret, but was interrupted by Emily.

'No. That's my province.' *My possession!*

'I'll help you,' Ancient/Ferret offered.

'No. It's mine to do. Champa came to me!' Her hand banged on her chest. 'Came to me at the Rose Garden.'

Ancient/Ferret held in her breath. It was a great deal to give up. 'Alright. I'll agree. In return give me Champa's diaries.'

'What are you on about?' asked Emily, opening another magazine.

A sound somewhere between rage and grief erupted from Ancient/Ferret. 'You're as relentless as a machine! Do you still visit...'

'Silence!' Emily thundered at her. They looked at each other as if across a field of carnage. 'I've protected you,' Emily claimed.

'Champa protected me,' Ancient/Ferret countered. 'In her own way. Death isn't far from you either, Emily.'

'Be careful!' warned Emily, her voice sharp as a knife. It wasn't the mention of her own mortality that had roused her ire but the use of her name. In decades of living together, quarrelling and fighting, not once had Ancient/Ferret committed the sin of articulating the syllables of her name.

Ancient/Ferret pushed back her chair, got up and picked up her bags. She mustn't get into a fight over Champa's dead body, Champa's belongings.

'Coward!' Emily taunted, banging her stick on the floor. Like a trained dog, Ancient/Ferret couldn't help turning. 'Got no fight left in you, have you? Get my goods off that whelp of yours, and you can have what you want. It'll be your last errand for me.'

Chapter Nineteen

Bombay and England, August 1947 onwards

Emily had returned in triumph! Diamonds round her throat, a fur coat on her shoulders, with two servants trailing in her wake!

'My oriental treasures!' Emily had laughed at Champa and Girl/Ferret as they stood on the English dockside. Champa had been shivering with the cold and looking like a frightened rabbit; Girl/Ferret had stood apart, arms folded, holding herself in, so she wouldn't spill out.

★   ★   ★

Before that, there had been another time. In a frame of fire! It had been a time for the cutting and quartering of hearts, for the vivisection of a country, a time for immortal words at midnight, for the parting of the ways.

History's tragedies are a web woven by fanatics, politicians and the powerful; ordinary people are the ones trapped in its killing strands. Events had begun their irreversible push on the lives of Champa, Emily and Girl/Ferret. Some events were far away, some near, some they never even knew about.

A date had been fixed: Independence was coming, the beauty of freedom itself. Partition had been agreed: division was being fixed, tortuous lines drawn on small, often out-of-date maps – pen lines that are incisions, flooding the map with blood.

The world's great exodus had begun, and a holocaust had commenced its carrion work. Thirteen million people were uprooted and millions killed. Some would later argue that it was far greater than the Massacre of St Bartholomew, profoundly more terrible and immense than the

235

Massacre of the Armenians. The stench of blood and murder swept across the country.

Telegram came to Champa's door, a thick *dupatta* pulled low over her face. 'They are talking of the Englishwoman. Tell her to go.' Champa told Emily there was danger coming; Emily looked at her stony-eyed.

'They wouldn't dare! Suitable recompense has not yet been made. Not by a long way.'

Just before the midnight hour, Nehru, applying poetry to salve a nation's soul, declared: 'Long years ago we made a tryst with destiny, and now the time comes when we shall redeem the pledge, not wholly or in full measure but very substantially. At the stroke of the midnight hour, while the world sleeps, India will wake to life and freedom.' The haunting call of a conch-shell horn sounded...

Bombay went wild! Lights burned, people crowded onto the streets, singing, shouting, crying; in the harbour, ships' sirens hooted, and from the tops of hundreds of temples, clouds of rose petals were cast into the air.

Champa stepped out, but stayed at the top of her stairs, a shawl held tightly around her, watching the excited throng of people in the street. She saw two of the Soiree Sisters with trays of sweetmeats moving among the crowd. One saw her and looked away.

Emily sat inside, sewing up a thick bundle. Girl/Ferret was out on the roof. She had looked out across the other roofs, seen a city lit with millions of lights, heard the excitement rise into the air, heard the cheers and shouts. Now crouching in her corner, she looked up at the sky at the darkening monsoon clouds. If she had been in Delhi, she would have seen something that she could have kept for herself from this night. In Delhi, as the Indian flag unfurled, a sudden shower of monsoon rain fell over the Red Fort, and 'a rainbow curved across the night sky!'[5]

Emily used to go out, taking Girl/Ferret with her. Telegram came to see Champa a second time, quickly rushing up the concrete steps to Champa's door, quickly coming in and closing the door.

'Get rid of the *Angrez* woman. She's trying to buy a house. She says to a Hindu that the Muslim round the corner is selling his much cheaper and he has better manners. She goes to the Muslim and turns her tongue round to say the same about the Hindu. Yesterday she slapped a child selling peanuts for not calling her memsahib.' Telegram's words came rushing out, colliding against each other. 'Something's happened to her head. Take my warning and get her out. Or both sides will come for you. And now we know what they do to women.' The words she had relished took on a new weight, alluded to the horror stories coming out of the Partition where each side reportedly raped the women of the other, or captured them. In one town, captured women had been hailed as prisoners and paraded naked through the streets. The worst imaginings were for those women who were never found, neither dead nor imprisoned – just disappeared! 'I would kill myself before I let them take me. Heed my warning,' said Telegram again. 'The fire will fall on you too.'

Other dangers were being designed. It was in 'Bombay the Beautiful' that a Hindu Mahasabha leader blessed an assassin with the words: 'Go and become famous.'[6]

Champa's life had come to a standstill. Emily was the one who would try and squeeze water out of a stone. Girl/Ferret was morbidly quiet. She knew that Emily was on the prowl, that sooner or later Emily would step on a snake but the fangs would sink into Girl/Ferret's skin. Emily hadn't given up her business of taking payments from some of the old regulars of The English Rose Garden. Instead she had increased the amount, in recognition of Independence; these men had more to lose than ever before, some of them had become powerful bureaucrats or politicians. One of them had been difficult with his payments so Emily went to see him in person. He warned her that this would be the last time he gave her a gift, next time he would have her thrown out, and if she said a word to anyone, she would bitterly regret it. Emily retaliated with threats of her own. Power is the transformer of lives. After Emily and Girl/Ferret left, he had called a servant and sent a message.

These days people would stop talking and stare at them as they walked through the market street and up to Champa's rooms. The English had existed by the rule of force; now that their right to force had been wrested from them, they should be long gone. Emily glared back at them. Years ago, others had tried to send her back to England. They had failed.

That evening columns of smoke spiralled into the sky. Champa, Emily and Girl/Ferret went onto the roof to see. They didn't know what had happened, neighbours didn't rush to give them news of disturbances or turmoil.

'You must leave,' Champa said to Emily. Emily did not answer. Girl/Ferret quickly moved away, to put herself out of reach of Emily's anger.

'Traitor!' Emily spat at Champa.

Calamity bursts through the skin of the present, wrecking, destroying. Champa was sitting, staring out of the window, in a gloomy depression; Emily was writing, her pen scratching on the paper, and Girl/Ferret was cooking. Champa was thinking that the midnight hour of Independence had been like a knife, slicing her life. None would come near her. From her vantage point, Champa saw Acid Eyes come running round the corner, her *dupatta* falling onto the ground, her hair streaming out, and a man running with her. Or was it after her? Acid Eyes veered towards Champa's stairs, the man pounding behind. It took several seconds for the meaning to click in Champa's head. She ran to the door and opened the bolts, quickly flinging it open. Acid Eyes hurtled in; Champa tried to close the door on the man, but Acid Eyes held her back, shaking her head, unable to speak through heaving gasps. The man ran in and Champa banged the door, throwing the bolts. Acid Eyes gestured with her hand, 'Go, go,' the words coming through a tortured throat. 'Telegram...' She shook her head, 'Killings...run...go...' pushing Champa towards the back.

Girl/Ferret came from behind the curtain, fear on her face. 'Listen,' she said, a sound like a strange and distant roar coming ever nearer.

'Whores and English,' gasped Acid Eyes. 'Something stolen from a temple. Run! Go!' Champa was rooted to the spot; Telegram should have been delivering this news. Girl/Ferret pulled her arm, pointed to the kitchen, 'Through the window.' Emily dived into the back room, and suddenly Champa followed her, coming out with her little tin trunk cradled in her arms. Emily had a large bundle she clutched to her chest. Acid Eyes shook her head, her logic unable to understand this. She ran for the back, the howling roars were coming even nearer.

Girl/Ferret helped them all through the window, and just as she was going to climb out, she looked around her to capture the room in her mind, and saw the cooking fire still burning. Picking up the oil, she splashed it around the tiny room and overturned the fire. The flames gushed up.

Girl/Ferret led them, all her wanderings round this city now helping her. She instinctively moved towards the harbour, away from populated areas where a crowd might suddenly come upon them. Girl/Ferret had looked back at Champa's rooms and seen ferocious red flames rise into the air. That was her doing. Their burning home couldn't be blamed on a mob.

Exhausted and dazed, they found themselves at the docks, suddenly in the midst of a mass of people, a chaotic throng desperate to get on board. Many had tickets, but the less fortunate were begging, bargaining and fighting for theirs. The returnees! English civilians, army men, Polish refugees – all were going to Great Britain. There must have been a ship about to leave. Acid Eyes stood still.

'Come on,' commanded Emily, authority back in her voice, as their strange group faltered at the side, looking at the people with their bags and anticipation, people who had homes to go to, even if the homes were far away across the ocean. Manzil, destination, destiny! Acid Eyes, hair flooding round her face, looked at the man who had run with her. The man moved closer to her, a hand on her arm. For years afterwards Champa was to wonder why the man had been there. Could Acid Eyes have had a secret love? But right now Champa was a grieving being, a torn and tortured Telegram fresh in her mind. Girl/Ferret was in an abyss of her own, tortured by images of splashed oil and an overturned fire. Doubt began to eat into her. What if she had been overhasty, perhaps the mob would pass by. She would have made them homeless, beggars on the street, for nothing. But, underneath the knowledge of the fire, she had the knowledge of a theft; of her hand reaching out swiftly; of sacrilege.

Emily was frozen, she'd come to the end of her horizons.

'Him, him, him. Ask him for help,' cried Girl/Ferret suddenly, pointing with her hand, startling their silent group. Her voice must have carried for Ant turned round to look at them.

Impeccably presented in a dark grey suit, a stiff hat on his head, accompanied by a friend, and surrounded by a mêlée of servants and baggage handlers with two Indian men and a veiled woman standing at the side of his circle, the men were dressed in English clothes but looked uneasy, a little desolate.

Emily looked at Ant and her blood boiled. Wasn't he the cause of all her grief? The hidden hand of menace? Wrecking her men, her body and her life!

Ant and his friend were pushing their way through the crowd towards them, intrigued by their motley group. By the time he reached them, Emily was in an unholy rage. Her words lashed at him. He was to help them. They had lost their home, a mob was on the loose, they'd be murdered.

Ant smiled his wolf smile, 'You'll have to take your chances.'

Emily's hand whipped out and cracked across his face. Champa gasped, Girl/Ferret moved nearer to her. Time froze.

Emily words ripped at him, 'I'll destroy you. I know the ones to go to. They're in charge now, and they'll want to drink your blood. They'll follow you to your precious house in Hindhead. And if I go to her, the wife...'

'Enough!' Ant cut across her, a red mark blazing on his cheek.

'Fire,' said Girl/Ferret, who ordinarily would never have dared to speak to him. She merely wanted help so that she and Champa could have another home. In some Indian city. Then she could start atoning to Champa.

'Anthony,' Ant's friend was looking anxiously towards the ship, 'be quick, we have to hurry.'

'Then move,' Ant said to Emily. 'You too,' pushing Champa and Girl/Ferret with his stick.

'But...' Emily began.

'But yes,' Ant snarled at her, shoving them through the crowd towards his group of servants. Then he said, 'Think of them as booty,' and laughed. Emily glared at him but could do no more. What grisly calculations had taken place in his head? 'Stand by the woman,' he told them, a glint in his eyes, and rushed off to the office, barging ahead of other people.

Deck passengers! Each ship going to Britain was frantically overcrowded as the thousands of people who needed to be returned desperately sought places. Champa didn't know how Acid Eyes had melted away from her. Bewildered, grieving Champa hadn't known what was truly happening. Her greatest fear had been that she would lose her little trunk. Girl/Ferret had pulled Champa along, fearful of Ant, still thinking they could start again somewhere in India, thinking she could look after them both, be a servant to other people and earn them money. Emily had not said a word since she set foot on the ship, staring away into the grey sea, hissing at anyone who spoke to her.

As they had waited at the dock, Ant had returned and herded them through the rush and mêlée to the gangplank, using his stick to keep them together. The veiled woman had uttered a little sound and hesitated. 'Help her,' Ant had barked at the two men. Emily had clutched Champa's other arm, perhaps feeling the throng pressing on them.

Five days into the journey, Emily changed her status. She acquired a berth and new clothes; she sat in the dining room for meals and graced the bar for drinks. Girl/Ferret said that Emily had sold something. Champa had merely looked at her uncomprehending. It wasn't till many, many days later, as they both huddled in blankets watching the endless grey sea, that Champa's mind surfaced and she asked Girl/Ferret what Acid Eyes had been trying to say about a temple and the mob. Girl/Ferret had looked out into the endless water; why couldn't her words be lost in it? Ever since

Emily had come into their lives she had been faced with dilemmas, forced to think before she spoke, forced to be silent, or to speak an untruth. 'Don't know,' she replied.

A mourning soughing sigh came from Champa, 'Hardly matters, the fire was waiting to be lit. So much burning already. What matters another little fire?'

The story had run from one mouth to another: a small, solid-gold linga had been stolen from a temple. At first the Hindus blamed the Muslims. But a voice took charge of the milling anger, and said, 'There are many other enemies of society, including the English who're still lingering, wanting their power back. Who would want to steal a sacred linga?' Leaning towards the crowd, voice rising, he continued, 'Only those who defile it, make money out of it. Only those who seduce poor hard working men, and cheat them of their earnings. And those who're not Indian, but are helped by them. Indians betray Indians!' The man's rhetoric was one of general hate; he could edit it to fit any purpose, any master. A murdering motor-mouth for hire.

The crowd were foaming by the time he finished and waved his hand for them to follow. He had a certain destination in mind, and saw this as his way to remove a certain blackmailing white woman and collect a bounty. But the crowd saw Telegram first, who had come out to see what was happening.

Many decades later, a solid-gold linga would be sold at an auction in England, the only piece of Indian religious art owned by an administrator, a man who had worked in the Indian Civil Service. The man had preferred to save his pay, he liked to have cash. But on the return journey, when, unexpectedly, yearning nostalgia had seized him, he had bought a small piece that was being offered for sale.

During the rest of the journey, Emily would occasionally condescend to join Champa and Girl/Ferret, boasting of England's glories, promising them they would be astonished. Champa and Girl/Ferret had listened and remained silent. No matter what their lives had been, both felt as if a song had been cut in half.

Docking at dawn! The cold seeped into their bones. Emily took a taxi from the dock all the way to the deep south of London where her brother, on her instructions, had bought her a house, and placed in it the furniture she'd shipped over. Champa and Girl/Ferret had hesitated before climbing into the car. Neither had ever been in a car before. This, their first journey, was long and cold, through the early morning dark. When they finally arrived, Emily grandly gestured them into her house. Champa and Girl/Ferret were rooted to the spot, their eyes travelling up and up to the chimney pots on the roof, across and across the width of brickwork and windows. Champa's rooms would have fitted into a single corner of this house.

'Look,' Emily demonstrated, flicking the light switch on and off; 'look,' lighting the gas cooker; 'look,' said Emily, 'your own room, your own bed, you can sleep like queens.' Champa gasped and uttered exclamations. The Girl/Ferret had gone mute. 'Look,' Emily did not say, 'be grateful that I have brought you to the land of the sahibs.' A few days later, when they were out and saw the poor in the streets, Emily waved off their questions: 'They're not British.'

Emily had returned to her family in triumph, bearing gifts galore. Passing her old factory, she'd looked down at her gloved hands, rings shining on top. In her old working-class terrace, children stopped their games and ran after the taxi, people on the narrow pavements turned and stared. Others peeked through their windows and doors.

Champa stepped out first, the thin silver border on her sari incongruous in this street, her glinting nose-stud standing out like an exotic tribal mark. Girl/Ferret stepped out in a black dress that was too big for her, her face determinedly stuck in a sullen mood. She'd lifted the dress off someone's line. Emily had thrashed her. Emily's mother quickly ushered them in for fear of the cold. She wondered what to do with the servants, unsure if etiquette allowed for them to sit in the front room, and she hardly possessed a downstairs for them to be sent to. Emily packed them off to the kitchen. The mother squeezed two chairs between the cupboard and the cooker and gave them cups of tea. Not her best china. Girl/Ferret poured hers down the sink.

In the front room Emily asked after Maureen. Her mother shook her head sadly. Maureen had passed away, leaving two little ones behind her. Emily didn't ask her if Maureen had been happy. Wasn't it enough to leave behind a husband and children, people who would use the word love and link it to her name, thus creating posterity? Emily suspected Maureen was having the last laugh. She wouldn't allow it: Maureen must have slaved and skivvied, cooking, baking, cleaning, boiling kettles of water for the washing, wiping the children's snot and shit, encased in a wraparound pinny from morning to night. Maureen could have the posterity; Emily had the property.

Boys had been sent running off to fetch a taxi. Emily had departed in style. Her mother had not asked her to stay the night – they were hardly grand enough for Emily now, and where would they have put the native servants? Curtains had twitched and faces peered as she left. Emily had concentrated on the road ahead, else she would have seen the knowing smile on Girl/Ferret's face.

Girl/Ferret had believed the myths about Great Britain. For the first time she had begun to imagine change. Perhaps the journey across the waters would wash away her sins, perhaps the wrath of the gods couldn't follow her to Great Britain? Girl/Ferret had allowed herself to think of a new beginning. So when she arrived, she had expected a transformation, and found only continuations of the same. She had journeyed from one land to another, crossed the divides of language and customs and landed up in precisely the same place – at Emily's beck and call.

One new dimension did enter. Work! And work of a kind they had never known. Emily said she would take them to factories and help them get jobs, else how were they to pay their way? As they went from one smoke-spewing factory to another, from one machine-rattling place to another, Girl/Ferret refused point blank.

'You brainless little idiot,' declared Emily. 'England is the Land of Opportunity for you. In one week, you can earn more than a government officer in India.' Girl/Ferret had a stubborn, obstinate streak to her.

Those were the days of frugal living and making-do; days when you only lit one fire in the house, washed clothes with your hands, wrung them through the mangle, and then hung them out to dry on a line that glowed white with frost. The frost must have affected Girl/Ferret's brain for she started asking Emily for money.

'I beg your pardon?' Emily had replied, unable to believe what she'd heard. When Girl/Ferret repeated her demand, Emily looked as if she was about to have an apoplectic fit, and told her to go and find out how much a room, food, heating, even water cost. 'You'll come back here with your tail hanging between your legs. I could put you out in the street and you'd die. Be thankful I look after you.'

'I looked after you! And I do all the work.'

Girl/Ferret received a whacking slap that rocked her backwards. 'That's for cheeking your elders and betters.'

Champa started work in the biscuit factory. Girl/Ferret made her an early breakfast, cooked parathas for her lunch, and walked with her to the factory. She watched her going in, covered in the thick coat she'd bought at a jumble sale and which made her look short and fat. Girl/Ferret remembered the gorgeous creature of another age. In the evening Champa came down to the kitchen and asked her not to make parathas again: they smelled and they called her smelly. Champa stayed on in the kitchen, sitting at the table. She had come to England and come down in the world.

At the end of two weeks, a shift in viewpoints occurred. Champa brought home two packets of English biscuits. Fanning some onto a plate, she put them before Girl/Ferret, 'Eat, eat, eat.' Girl/Ferret hesitated, then tentatively picked one up and tenderly bit into it. English memsahibs were eating these very same biscuits while they sipped their tea. Champa then took out her pay packet and opened it. With great concentration, she counted the money. Girl/Ferret stopped nibbling her biscuit and counted with her.

The next day, Girl/Ferret trudged from factory to factory on her own, soon learning to read the 'No vacancies' signs and to calculate hourly rates into weekly wages. She returned jobless, cold and starving. Before she could eat she had to do the cooking, her heightened state of hunger lending an extra concentration. Then she had to serve Emily and Champa. 'Delicious!' they declared, and asked for more. The following day, she started her job-hunting earlier, determined not to return till she had a job. When she came back, she cooked herself a surreptitious meal. She could pay for it in cash if need be. The first time ever!

In the mornings, Emily would watch Girl/Ferret and Champa trotting off with their sandwich bags and thermos flasks, disappearing into the morning darkness. At first she'd been sourly pleased, particularly at Girl/Ferret's capitulation. Now the little wretch would get a taste of real life. As the days passed, and the house was emptied, even of Ferret's busyness in her chores, Emily realised it was the first time in years she'd been alone, without one of them hovering somewhere near her. She decided she'd invite the whole family for Christmas, every far-flung member of it. She'd even get in help for Girl/Ferret so that the whole house would be sparkling and shining. She'd give the family a Christmas to remember. Then they'd really see what she'd made of herself.

The months to Christmas passed, the house was decorated with tinsel and ribbons, a Christmas tree put up, shining baubles hooked onto the branches, and a lavish dinner was cooked, supervised by Emily. As it was

Christmas, Girl/Ferret was allowed to sit with Emily and Champa in the dining room – just the three of them. 'I'm not inviting anyone else,' Emily had declared, 'no need to have the *hoi-polloi*.' How typical of Emily! Emily even poured them sherry and proposed a toast to 'Christmas in England, the best Christmas ever.'

The house ran smoothly, emotions were dormant, everything was in place, each of them living in a tunnel of her own. Then Emily made a mistake.

The mistake that made Girl/Ferret's anger and rebellion solidify into a row of numbers. Emily sent them on an errand to the jewellers. They were told to dress in their best saris, and look 'wealthy'. Girl/Ferret announced that she couldn't, because she didn't possess anything that would make her look remotely 'wealthy'. Emily sighed in exasperation, and told Champa to sort her out.

The tin trunk! Girl/Ferret lifted it down from the top of the wardrobe. Like an excited schoolgirl Champa threw open the lid. Girl/Ferret tried to pretend she didn't care, that she was only enduring another chore. Girl/Ferret had to pretend, because she knew that if you start wanting, you can end up ruined. Champa's enjoyment was bittersweet. The world in which she had worn this finery was far out of her reach. She cajoled and persuaded Girl/Ferret to try some saris, a memory brushing across her of the days when Girl/Ferret was little and Champa adorned her in frilly dresses and shiny ribbons.

'*Hai*, look at you,' murmured Champa in sad wonderment, standing back and gazing at Girl/Ferret. 'Perhaps it's better that you are here,' Champa nodded. 'Perhaps the gods fated it so.' In India, how long would Champa have been able to keep her as a servant? How long before some man rustled notes for this fresh, young beauty?

'No,' replied Girl/Ferret, 'the gods are busy looking after the devoted.'

Before they left on Emily's errand, Girl/Ferret sneaked into Emily's room to look at herself in the long mirror. A stranger stared back at her, glorious in orange and gold. Slowly turning around, twisting her head to keep herself in view, she tried to recognise this other self. Is this how you dress up dross as gold? Is this how you change into something else? Is this how you fool the world?

They were dispatched in a taxi. Girl/Ferret remained quiet, and Champa didn't try to break into her silence; Champa didn't talk as much as she used to. They were to have certain items valued, for Emily could not have peace till she knew the conversion rate in pounds. Solid figures were what gave substance. Emily would not wish the jewellers to remember her, but a couple of oriental ladies carrying a stash of goodies in their bags would be self-explanatory. She sent a letter with the two, explaining, as a husband might, that the ladies were not conversant with the English language and if the Kind Sir would write down the required information, so and so would be extremely grateful.

At the jewellers, one Kind Sir took the goods into the back room, and the other Kind Sir stayed in the front. Champa sat back in her chair and lit a cigarette, a newly acquired habit from her workmates at the factory. Girl/Ferret remembered the reflection in the mirror: hair pulled up into a bun, lips glistening with lipstick, her work-stained nails covered with a red varnish, silk rustling at each step. This was the gilding that made the rich look precious and powerful. As if testing out her theory, Girl/Ferret engaged the Kind Sir in conversation, speaking in prettified broken English. She evinced an interest in some of the display pieces and Kind Sir brought them over. Like magic!

When the Kind Sir returned with the goods and an envelope, he didn't bother to seal it. He hated to be unnecessarily pedantic, neither did he wish to offend the ladies by seeming to imply anything. In the taxi going back, Girl/Ferret ignored Champa's protests and told her to look away if she preferred, which Champa did. Girl/Ferret blinked her eyes rapidly, and shook her head to make space for the numbers as she replaced the paper back in the envelope and sealed it. Once seen, never forgotten. She looked out of the taxi window, her past and her future coagulating. She would die in Emily's house, doing Emily's work.

Girl/Ferret was a very young woman in a foreign land. The outside world was daunting and huge. Girl/Ferret's feet did not know this place as she had known the other one. And there was Champa to whom Girl/Ferret owed. It would never have occurred to Girl/Ferret to take and run, to heist the jewels whose value had made her head spin. She may have laid claim to half Emily's goods, but she couldn't do an appropriation. She couldn't do for herself what Emily had made her do – it would be another sin.

Chapter Twenty

March 1997, London

Visual reality: a long slim body, sloe eyes, white hair and a face that turned away had confirmed the *She*/Ferret's existence. Add a name to a face and you have recognition. Sita/Ferret made a baptism, a naming of her own: the *She* would be Ferret the Foreign till the day she became known, just as Emily was the Mutant Memsahib and Champa was the Dumpa.

Champa the Dumpa: cold chill on the outside, a still heart and still brain on the inside. Still life. Still gone. Gone.

'You've got to start,' Kala said, practically pushing her out. 'Go and make the arrangements.'

'Not my responsibility,' she replied.

'Coward!'

He opened the closet, took out her old fortune-carrying coat and held it out to her.

'Throwing me out?'

'Pointing you in the right direction,' he replied.

'I can bloody well decide for myself.'

'You won't. You'll go by old hates.'

'If you want to preach, go be a preacher.' She ignored the coat in his hand, grabbed her new cheap one, and banged the door hard behind her.

She saw Champa's letter as she took her purse out to buy a ticket. On the platform she stared at the advertisements: from boutiques to boot sellers, from holidays to holy places, the written word cajoled, persuaded and hoodwinked. Why would Champa have written her a letter? More admonitions to ensure her 'purity'? If Sita/Ferret were to be fair, then she must accept that Champa had looked after many of her needs, from baby care to heavenly beseechments for her soul. Then it occurred to Sita/Ferret that Champa may have written such letters to the Mutant Memsahib and Ferret the Foreign too. Taking out the envelope she inserted her thumb under the flap and ripped across, cutting her skin. Sucking at the blood on her thumb, she flipped the letter open, read it and put it away in her bag.

This morning, carrying the first taste of him inside her, making her feel as fiery as the sun and as a fragile as a leaf, her emotions had somersaulted at the words on the page. To lose and to receive! But not to know the meaning of it.

Before opening the door to Sangeeta Rayit's house, she sat down on the doorstep and took out the letter again, to check if the words were still the same. They were. She closed her eyes, as if to think herself into Champa's thoughts. There was a meaning here that she couldn't grasp. In the pattern that the three of them had made (the E, C & F) Champa had included her, while her own heart was set and dry against them. She fooled herself! Her heart was set against them but set on them too. They were the only ones in the world who could be her enemies and the only ones in the world who could be her... Here she stopped as all the relationship words came packed with emotional meanings. Had Champa tried to arrange it so that she could fit into their pattern? If one went then another could slip into her place. Seamlessly. Without them noticing? 'Fat chance!' thought Sita/Ferret folding up the letter, and putting it carefully away – the *She*, Ferret the Foreign, had done a runner at the first glimpse of her.

Sita/Ferret went in. The house was unusually quiet, deathly quiet. For a moment, dread filled her. 'Afraid? No fear! Not me!' Chant a mantra, dispel the evil spell! They must be out, perhaps doing the family shopping, negotiating crowded supermarket aisles with an overloaded trolley, or buying things the girls needed, or socialising, or entertaining themselves. Perhaps they were on a boat cruise up the Thames, or taking in a matinée at the West End, or down at McDonald's, digging into burgers and fries. London town offered a hundred and one delights. For the living!

The living must do their chores: wash and iron their clothes, dust and vacuum their rooms, clean their windows, paying special attention to the historical, original pane of glass through which the world was always a little distorted; and hours later, when the dark comes and street lamps shine, cook food for themselves, although they find themselves disabled, find that all the culinary skills they possess were imparted by the one who now lies as dead and cold as dark ice.

Champa lives in Sita/Ferret's fingers. Sita/Ferret washes her hands, and regards the half-cooked food. Half-baked! Half-done! Doing things by halves! Ferret the Foreign lives in Sita/Ferret's blood; skin and kin, flesh and fierce hates.

The front door banged and Sita/Ferret ran into the hallway to greet Sangeeta Rayit and her girls.

'Wow!' she exclaimed, 'fantastic outfits,' observing their stunning colours, silks, sequins, floaty *dupattas*, shimmering shoes. They came in loaded with bags and boxes.

'We've been to our uncle's wedding,' said the older girl. 'I stuffed my face with ice-cream and jalebis,' she confessed, giggling at herself. 'We've brought lots of yummy things back with us so you can have some too. And we danced *bhangrda* all day. *Dupatta saat rang tha...*' she sang in her child voice, clapping her hands.

'Do you know how to do *bhangrda*?' she asked. Sita/Ferret shook her head shamefacedly. 'We'll teach you,' offered the child, still high on the wedding festivities.

'Come on, let's party,' said Sangeeta Rayit, going into the living room and putting on a tape, turning the volume up high. 'Let the neighbours hear for once.'

Sita/Ferret watched and imitated. The girls giggled at her efforts. Sangeeta Rayit showed her how to lift her arms, turn her hands, shake her shoulders and wiggle her hips, injecting a teasing seductiveness. 'When I first got married,' she said, 'we lived with my in-laws. I had three *nanae*. You can imagine what that was like, three sisters-in-law at various stages of immaturity and puberty. But sometimes we'd really let our hair down. We'd make popcorn, pots of tea, put on our tapes and *bhangrda, bhangrda! Khap pie thi si*. We made a hell of a racket.'

The younger girl was tugging at Sangeeta's clothes, 'Mummy, mummy, the phone's ringing.'

Sangeeta Rayit shouted instructions as she grabbed her keys, opened the door, and rushed out, leaving a stunned silence in the house.

'The bride's fucking run off,' she'd told Sita/Ferret, for once not censoring her language. 'With all the luggage, baggage, money and jewellery from the wedding. Sounds like a fucking heist. Faking it through the marriage ceremony! And I was the idiot who did the introductions, wasn't I!'

Sita/Ferret and the girls looked at each other. The younger one held onto her sister's hand. 'Is this a tragedy?' asked the older one. Sita/Ferret nodded. 'Today we had a new aunty, we sat on her lap, and now we haven't? How can...' How can the world dissolve and leave you stranded?

'What's a tragedy?' asked the younger one.

Sita/Ferret sat down so she could be closer to them. 'When people do really nasty things which hurt other people's whole lives, then it's a tragedy.' (Like not arranging a decent burial?) 'When our feelings hurt, often it's because people have hurt them.' The girls ingested this information, looking at her with wide, serious eyes. 'Your mum said it was time for bed. Let's go.'

Sita/Ferret helped them get ready, brush their teeth, change their clothes, thinking these were the easiest children she'd ever cared for. She went downstairs to fetch water, came back up and found shouting, screaming, sorrow and suffering. She tried to disentangle the claims and counter-claims of who had done what first to whom, in between trying to outlaw such wonderful endearments as 'poo brain', 'monkey face', 'cow-pat' and worse.

Silence. After they'd fallen asleep, she sat on in their room; plump, rosy cheeks, teddy bears clutched in their arms, the stillness of slumber, and behind it, the voyage into another world – like millions of others at this moment. The world is always dreaming, till ye dream no more and no more return from that other shore.

She went up to her room and re-read Champa's letter. The phone rang and she ran downstairs to pick it up, wondering what catastrophe would be relayed through it now.

'Have you decided?' asked Kala: K for the voice in her ear that melted her body, soft and warm; K for the love one-sided, unrequited.

'Tell you what,' continued Kala. 'This is one of those rare occasions when you can A for act first, and regret later, with complete impunity. I'll throw in a bonus. You can put all the blame on me.' Kala had met the demons of death; deny them their dues and they sit in your brain, poisoning you.

'I don't owe her anything,' she argued back, ignoring the moment when she had claimed the closest kinship, of mother and daughter. Sita/Ferret put her hand on her stomach. To hold something in? Her own bile?

'And I'll C for come, come and make my "namaste" to Emily and your mother.'

'The Other,' she corrected him.

'Mother!' he shot back. 'They rhyme. Merely with the addition of one letter, the whole meaning is changed, and in fact the opposite is merged into its apposite, or do I mean the opposite is merged into its opposite?'

'You're being execrable.'

'That is a super-posh English word, containing pot-holes of difficulties to pronounce...'

'Oh shut up!'

'That is a lower-class English word...' He stopped abruptly. 'Shall I leave you alone?' Her body and mind went hollow at the idea.

'*She* might have a whole brood, of, you know, biological descendants. A husband. And other things.'

'What other things?' he asked.

'I'm the outsider, the unwanted.'

Kala remained silent. Then he said time doesn't come back.

Two hours later, Sangeeta returned with the groom who looked as if he'd been hit by a twenty-ton truck. Sangeeta held him by the arm and carefully steered him to a chair in the lounge. Sita/Ferret was about to make a discreet exit when the doorbell pealed. A posse of people came in talking volubly and turbulently.

Sita/Ferret went into the kitchen and put on a pan of water, throwing in cardamoms, cloves and fennel. Suddenly she stopped. On the rare occasions a visitor had come to the Mausoleum, and especially the gentleman visitor, the only person Sita/Ferret had ever seen Emily afraid of, she'd had it dinned into her that she should go and prepare refreshments without being asked. She was doing the same now.

Inside the lounge, the volume of noise rose higher and higher. The lounge door opened, and the shell-shocked groom and one of the young women came out and into the kitchen. The woman opened her bag and gave the betrayed groom a cigarette packet and a lighter. Sita/Ferret knew he hadn't even seen her as he went past her into the dark, night-time garden.

'That smells wonderful,' exclaimed the woman. 'You make the pukka 'cup-a-chai' do you? Look at him,' watching the groom out of the window, 'he gave up smoking. He was going to start a new life. With a new wife! That bitch made suckers out of us. You know what they're talking about in there? The usual. Get out the swords and cricket bats, charge off after the guy she's run off with, break a few heads and legs. Like that's going to make any difference! Revenge is totally stupid, but so satisfying.'

'Why did she do it afterwards?' Sita/Ferret asked. 'She could have run off before the wedding.'

'And miss out on all the dosh? This is the third case I've heard of. They may be Asian on the outside, but they're Thatcher's children on the inside. No scruples and no fucking principles. There's integration for you. They all have blokes on the side.'

'Perhaps it's understandable, if circumstances...' began Sita/Ferret, thinking of a pouch lifted from its hiding place. The woman turned on her with a snarl.

'You don't screw up someone else's life. If you want someone different you should have the guts to see it through. It's a free country and the law's on your side. They used to talk about the "runaway Asian girl running away from an arranged marriage"; believe me, it's taken on a whole new meaning now!'

Sita/Ferret was still reeling from this new outburst when a broad-shouldered young man with close-cropped hair and a wilting flower in his lapel came in. 'Another bloody take-the-dosh-and-run bitch,' he said. 'It's a fucking epidemic. Know what? It's them that wants the dowry. Them that keeps it going. I'm going to India for my wife. Wouldn't touch one here with a bargepole. Twisted, the whole lot of them.'

'That just fits in with your bigoted ideas,' the young woman snapped back at him.

'You tell him that,' he replied, as he went out into the garden.

Sita/Ferret and the woman watched their dark shapes through the window. Emotional embezzlement! And you can't call in the Fraud Squad. Like a Frankenstein parody, the bride and her secret man had stitched together two contradictory ideas, love and the arranged marriage system, smashing the life the groom in the garden had planned. Life is only the next step, seldom the distant future as planned; seldom the destiny to which we think we are entitled. Sita/Ferret put a finger on the window. Transparency! Like putting your finger on something and nothing. She had always felt herself cheated out of a true life, as if such a thing could exist!

'We could get a private detective and flush them out,' the young woman next to her was saying. 'But what's the point. It'll never be right again.'

A group left to go and talk to the bride's family, the 'I'm-going-to-India-for-my-wife' guy took the wounded groom off with him, and one of

252

the younger men went off to fetch cans of beer and bottles of wine. On this wedding night they held a wake. Deaths were of many kinds.

Sita/Ferret wondered what she herself was: did she have a heart that could expand and go beyond her own hates, a soul that could appreciate the intention and forgive the action? She had wanted love but had doubted its existence, a fantasy dreamt up by mad poets, artists and ad-men. And yet she was now one of the many, caught in its madness. She was no more, no less, than any other on this planet. Rationally, she didn't have to do anything beyond fulfilling the needs of her own life, which would be to barbarise herself.

The next morning as Sita/Ferret went to work, she stopped at *Bhagwan's,* the shop of Heavenly Goods. The Hindu deities adorned the window: Ram with his bow and arrow; Sita, her own namesake, twice exiled, suspected of betrayal, cast out; Ganesh, the elephant god, the child-man whose father had cut off his head in anger, not knowing it was his own son, his own blood! No linear routes to love here either.

Sita/Ferret pushed open the door and went in. Cool fresh air greeted her. This shop must have an air-conditioning going all the time. An elderly, bald-headed man was sitting behind the counter tweaking the folds of a goddess' sari. Sita/Ferret asked for information on funerals. The man nodded and bent down to get something from under the counter. Champa had used to say her prayers in the mornings. Once Sita/Ferret had asked the name of the goddess to which Champa prayed. 'Goddess Yellama,' Champa had begun, and then stopped and shooed her away, giving her some chore at the other end of the house.

'Who is the goddess Yellama?' Sita/Ferret asked the man, as he brought up a box.

'I don't have her here,' he answered, as he took out a pile of leaflets from the box and separated them: birth; marriage; death. 'I have written these leaflets,' explained the man of the Heavenly shop, 'because many people are doing things the wrong way, or the English way. That is carrying Westernisation too far. One young man said to me, "after all, we are in this country, integration is necessary." Tell me, what use is integration to the dead? But people live a fast-food life, a quick-fix sex life, and a quick-run-to-the-psychiatrist life. Is this what you are requiring, madam? One pound please.'

Sita/Ferret paid her pound and repeated her question.

'The goddess Yellama,' echoed the man, busily packing his leaflets, 'is the goddess of prostitutes.'

'Thank you,' replied Sita/Ferret politely, taking her leaflets and leaving.

Privacy and the past. Had Champa been afraid of Sita/Ferret's reaction, afraid of condemnation? She began to think about secrets that another would hide as shame. She began to think about the necessities needed to stay alive, dignity being one of them. No body can be sold without a portion of the soul being soiled – unless they can offer themselves as an equal in the transaction. 'Pure', Champa had said, purity for Sita/Ferret. What was it to be at the mercy of others' greed, to be a morsel for them to ravage? Sita/Ferret had left the Mausoleum and been able to choose her own work, her own kind of pay packet. But she knew that throughout the centuries, women have only had one thing to barter.

She dug out her keys to unlock the door to Universal Enterprises and found it already open, the lights on, and Poonum sitting at daddy's desk, a pile of papers in front of her.

'Do you usually get to work so late?' was the greeting Sita/Ferret received.

'No. Normally I'm much later. I wanted to ask for some time off. A matter...' She stumbled on the words – if you use the word of a relationship, does it make it real? 'An aunt has died and I need to make the arrangements.'

'Sure. Has she left you a fortune too?' Poonum accused. Sita/Ferret involuntarily took a step towards her, startled by an impression of damage. Poonum's face was bare of make-up, her hair unceremoniously tied back, and she was dressed in sweatshirt and jeans.

'We're closing the business. Selling the premises. I want to get the accounts finished, cancel consignments. I'm giving you a week's notice. Here's the letter,' taking an envelope from the desk and holding it out to her, 'you won't have to work the whole week, you can use the other days to bury any number of aunts.'

'I've already resigned.'

'Set up elsewhere have you?'

'May I ask why you're closing?'

'No.' Poonum was definite. No breaches of privacy to be allowed here. 'If there's any money owing to you, I'll sort it out. We have your address don't we? Kala's flat?' At this the old Poonum popped out and fired a lethal look. 'I'm sorry if this has come as a shock to you, but I won't grieve too much, you've done pretty well out of us. With your particular skills, I'm sure you'll have no difficulties getting what you want.' No need for Sita/Ferret to become overly worried about Poonum, her claws were as sharp as ever. 'However if you're thinking of putting in an offer for the business, we'll certainly consider it. I'm sure dear-departed hubby would be delighted to know his money was being well spent. Let us know. Through a solicitor. Thank you Mrs Pretending-to-be-Pandey.' Clever Poonum, the only one to suss out a fraud. 'If I need you I'll let you know. Write down the number you'll be at. If you clear out your desk, that'll be a big help.'

'Thank you,' Sita/Ferret replied idiotically. The English language couldn't function without these two words; sometimes genuine, but mostly impostors. Writing down Sangeeta Rayit's number she pushed the paper back to Poonum, adding, 'I believe you know Kala's number.' If you've only got one shot left, you may as well fire it. She was expected to walk away in neutral detachment, to be ended as it had begun. Sita/Ferret shook her head. Changes had occurred which had altered the landscape of her life. Explanations could account for all that had happened without any reference to this place. Explanations have never been a substitute for feelings and belief. 'If there are problems, I would be glad to help out. Without pay,' she offered.

Poonum shook her head, 'Couldn't trust you.'

Sita/Ferret flared up, 'Your father never doubted me,' and stopped abruptly, remembering a broken Krishna and the words of accusation. 'I haven't been caught with my hands in the till. You're just riddled with jealousy!' (*No boasting*, warns Champa, *fate will slap you down*.) 'I've had some things given to me, I've...' She couldn't choose the right word. 'I've enjoyed the work,' she said, settling for a nice, safe word. 'That's why I offered to help. But if you want to go down the drain by yourself, enjoy the sewer.'

Downstairs, she opened her drawers and cleared the contents into a black bag. Old newspapers and magazines, packets of drinks; there was nothing to take away with her. She hadn't reached the stage of personalising her work area: no furry little mascot sitting on the desk, no flowery plants, and the most significant absence of all – no photographs. If there could be a shift in the world and if she could have her time again, she'd have a row of photos in flashy frames, one for each one of them: one for the K; one for the C; one for the *She* who spurns through sloe eyes; and one for peppery Emily too!

Taking her scarf, she wiped the desk clean.

She laboured back up the stairs with her sackful of rubbish, and was greeted by the sight of Mr Steven Singh sitting across the desk from Poonum. Realisation dawned: Steven Singh had at last dug up something to rock the Kalyan clan. 'Firstly hello,' she said, 'secondly goodbye.'

'Goodbye?' he questioned. 'What's this goodbye business?'

'Boss' orders,' she replied.

'Boss knows best,' he bounced straight back. 'But you can't go off just like this. After all the work you've done here. Tell you what, I'll organise dinner. For all of us.'

'You might find you're the main course!' Poonum sniped back. 'I've never doubted her hard work. It's her tendency to run off with the associated personnel that's the problem.'

Better to hold back than run headlong into a swamp. 'I'd like to say goodbye to your father,' said Sita/Ferret. 'May I ring him at home?'

'See what I mean!' gloated Poonum. Steven Singh smiled at Poonum, he'd let her get away with murder it seemed. 'Anyway she has a body to bury, so we'd better let her get on with it.'

Steven Singh expressed his condolences.

'I'll need a pandit. Do you know where I can get one?' she asked Steven Singh. If his family had been here for decades, he must have enough relations and contacts to rival the internet, and would surely know of a holy man to conduct a funeral.

'Make sure he's chaperoned,' cut in Poonum.

'Certainly,' he assured her. He couldn't have been sweeter to her. Then he offered to carry Sita/Ferret's black bag, gallantly opened the door for her, and asked Poonum if she would like him to get a coffee for her. Sita/Ferret was glad she wouldn't be around to see this new relationship in all its sickly-sweet glory. Before leaving, Sita/Ferret turned around to have a final look at the shop and Poonum. Whatever mysterious changes had happened, they had released the last constraint on Poonum. She would now take control.

'What did you do?' she asked when they were outside, wondering whether he'd tell her. Why should she expect him to explain events when she had grown up in a house where the past was always kept securely hidden?

'I slipped up badly,' he replied, shaking his head ruefully, 'and I won't get a penny out of it. Poonum's being nice to me because she needs my help. I know more about the K's "business" affairs than she does. He wasn't exactly the kind to put everything down on paper. And I'm being nice to her because I've learnt a lesson. I've got to play tactics. I've been going round, heart on my sleeve, telling everyone my hard-luck stories, and...' a big smile towards her, 'winning the lottery for someone else. Here we are.'

World's End café: full of steam, heat and the smoke of cigarettes.

'Last time it was a cauliflower, this time I'll treat you to coffee.' C words. They sat down on plastic chairs at a plastic table. She was in no hurry. Her work schedule had just been torn up. Sita/Ferret hated jobless periods. She had to be pinned to work or she'd feel herself becoming unstuck at the seams, or going cold, like a body in a morgue. She'd phone Jeevan, ask her if she knew of any jobs going, and ask to see her. For a chat. A conversation. Simple words.

'The Korrupt K,' began Steven Singh, 'worked very simply. He just used people's weaknesses against them. A lot of people might say, so what? Serves them bloody right! No.' Steven Singh was shaking his head. 'You know what's yours and you know what's someone else's.'

'Knowing's never stopped anyone,' she interrupted. 'Not armies, businesses or the man/woman who wants someone else's man/woman. Everyone pays lip-service to it but few have the guts to live by it. Yet another tragedy for the human race!' She smiled flippantly. She'd find out where Ferret the Foreign lived and give her no peace. Then she quailed and buried her bravado; Ferret the Foreign had known and kept away. How can you make someone want you?

'It is.' Steven Singh answered, deadly serious, moving back as the waitress mopped their table and took their order. When she'd gone, he took out a handkerchief and cleaned the table again, carefully arranging the sugar bowl, salt and pepper cellars in the middle. 'I've been working at the past like a bloody miner, digging it up scrap by scrap. I hit rock, shit and gold. I've criss-crossed this country and heard some stories and seen some sights. The young, the old, the in-betweens. I've seen the ones who've made a little India here and I've seen the ones who think India's a foreign land. I've seen the ones who wish they could live their life all over again. Pitiful. And the ones who've made peace with the past, even if they look battered and worn.'

Two cups of instant coffee slapped down in front of them, the coffee spilling into the saucers. Steven Singh asked for clean saucers and serviettes. The waitress raised her eyes heavenwards at such pretensions, chucked paper napkins onto the table and practically threw two saucers at him. He cleaned the bottoms of the cups and placed them on the clean saucers.

'Now, back to the story of the Korrupt K: our boy K is beavering away at making a million, or getting others to make it for him. Complication. Primeval (pronounced prime-evil) urges strike! The K thinks, "what's wrong with a quick roll in the back room with one of the tenants. Let her off the rent. All's fair and square." But the K didn't reckon on consequences. She gets a samosa in the oven. Now, she's a church-going catholic lass from Ireland, and she's got to think of the family honour, so,' he said, a gleeful grin on his face, 'she gets a posse of "brothers" to use gentle persuasion on our boy K. They threatened to wreck the houses.' Steven Singh's laughter bubbled out.

'The K was forced to do the decent thing. Shotgun wedding and all that. Then, and this is where he gets slippery as an eel, he tells them a pack of porkie-pies as would shame a congenital liar. You know the sort: if his family finds out back home, they'll be shamed forever, his sisters won't be able to get married, family disgrace, and so on. All that crap. So, he says everything has to be hush hush, till the right time comes to let it be known.

'Time passes. Now there are two little samosas running around. Time passes, and she moves back to Ireland. Question is, was she pushed or did she go willingly? He demands a divorce. If he ain't got no options, he ain't got no choices – right? She agrees. Question is, did she agree willingly or was she suitably persuaded? Remember this man tidies up his little messes. Cleans up after himself. What he did was to offer her one of the houses. She probably couldn't believe her luck. This man doesn't leave anything to chance. That's it!' Steven Singh suddenly banged the table so hard everything jumped, the coffee spilt and sugar scattered. 'That's where I've got to start looking!' Steven Singh was ecstatic, as if he'd just seen a vision. 'I've been looking all around him, but not at him. Not at what he does, day by day. And I'm bloody well in the right place to do it now. But I'll have to change tactics, I'll have to be sweet to him too.'

'You mean deceive him?' asked Sita/Ferret, as she quickly mopped up the mess on the table, smiling placatingly at the waitress who was glaring at them.

'No,' answered Steven Singh. 'I'll tell him I want to learn from him and that I still want what we're owed.'

'But what you learn, you'll use against him. It's still deceit.'

'No, my dear. I shall hold up a mirror for him to see himself in.'

'Hair-splitting.'

'Back to the story. Time passes. His bank account swells. He goes to India and comes back with a bride so high up in the social scale they could invite the Queen to tea. Well that's how he puts it about. Thing is, she's a widow with a child. Now why didn't he marry a fresh virgin bride? Answer: he had some dosh, but not enough to zoom through the class barriers. Wife number two arrives here, and learns a few things about reality. Like he wasn't half as rich as he'd made out, he wasn't even a flea on the social ladder, and she didn't have any servants. Had to do her own cooking, with her own hands.

'So now K the Korrupt has wife number two, but still no happy home, and I reckon he wasn't getting any, if you get my meaning. So guess what, he persuades wife number one to come back, and commutes between the two homes. He can satisfy his primeval urges, and work at his social profile. But he reckons without me, the little dog sniffing…'

'Ferret,' she informed him.

'What?'

'Ferret,' explains Sita/Ferret, 'number one: a small animal, *Mustela putorius*, bred for hunting rats, rabbits etc. Number two…' counting them off on her fingers, 'black-footed ferret, *Mustela nigripes*, of North America, weasel-like animal. Number three: often followed by *out*, to find by persistent investigation, for example *to ferret out, to search around*. From the Latin *fur*, thief. The last meaning, which was the original meaning, gives one much to think on,' she finished off.

'Indeed it does,' echoed Steven Singh, in admiration. 'So you know it by heart. Why I wonder? One, you were called by that name at school or home. Two, it hurt…'

'Poonum's waiting for you,' Sita/Ferret interrupted him, pointing to her watch.

Steven Singh looked at her measuringly, 'You don't want me to *ferret out* the meaning. All right.' He had learnt patience. 'Back to the story. It's terrible to break someone's trust, like pulling the rug from under their feet. But then, people give their trust too easily.' Did Ferret the Foreign think that people gave their love too easily?

'Just like my old man. I hope the old man's having a laugh now. We hate the K because he's poison, but,' and Steven Singh paused and shook his head, 'I wouldn't wish that moment on anyone, that moment when your past comes out, when your lying and cheating come home to roost. The K went pale and it wasn't just the face. His whole body sagged, as if the blood was running out of it like a building, a monument, slowly crumbling before you.' Mr Kalyan's blood-lines had obviously caught up with him.

'Life can jack-knife in a second. Scandal and shame. Wife number two is going back. No more powerful relations in India to help him with his "artistic business". He's alone. They'll help Poonum instead, she's taking over the business affairs. Wife number one bit his head off about that one: "why should she have anything, she's not even your flesh and blood." Well, you know Poonum, she went for the jugular. She can rip the skin off you! It's war between them. Poonum gonna take her mother's revenge on the Korrupt K. I guarantee it. I'm there too. We've moved on to the next stage.' He said it wryly; this wasn't how he'd planned the next stage.

She'd been immersed in his words, the blood and gore of ordinary life, immense ideas, dramas, the colour of everyday life. 'Poonum will be wondering where you are,' she suddenly reminded him.

'She'll think you've run away with me. Why would she think that?' he asked, his whole attention focused on her. She was tempted to lie, but decided it would be unfair to this man who was on a mission of truth. Besides, she couldn't risk it with those sharp eyes trained on her.

'She thinks I've stolen her bloke.'

'And have you?'

Stolen love? But she couldn't yet be accused. He hadn't admitted to any loss of the heart. 'I had something that Poonum didn't.' Steven Singh leaned forward. 'And he wanted it. So I gave it to him.' She watched with relish the variety of expressions that flitted over his face.

'Was it information or property?'

'Why should it have anything to do with either?'

'What else is there?' he replied. 'He met you the night of the exhibition. Something happened that night. One, you did or said something to make the connection, or two, he recognised something. Actually, the move would have had to come from him, because you were the one in possession. He must have recognised whatever it was, which means it must have been an object. So, three, he created an opportunity for you both to be together. Four, you were already attracted to him. Five, you handed over whatever it was. I hope it wasn't for the sake of winning his affections. Six, developments occurred.'

'Not the kind you think,' she said, and then added, 'not quite. If you see what I mean?' finishing lamely.

'I'll think about it,' he promised. 'OK, back to the count. Seven, you have a dead husband, and you work in a basement with lifeless artefacts, so perhaps you engineered the whole business, but I don't believe that, because you watch everyone. I've watched you watching,' he said. 'Watching even when I was talking to you, as if life is a Rubik's Cube and, try as you might, you can't click it into place.'

'Talking about life,' she said, thinking about death. 'Pandey isn't my real name and I don't have a dead husband.'

He straightened up, his eyes shining excitedly, 'Why?'

She looked at that young/old face, 'I can't tell you yet. When I know everything I will. Promise.' He deserved the story. He was the one who pried open memories and collected the fragments.

Outside the café, he looked at her as she hugged her black bag.

'You keeping that for posterity?' he asked. 'Give it over. I'll chuck it for you.'

Chapter Twenty-one

London, March 1997

A letter, a goddess, a word, a profession: she has them inside her like the secret contents of a safe deposit box.

The morning is not yet old, as Sita/Ferret sits in the kitchen, reading the leaflet on funerals.

'The dead person…if female should be bathed by females. Sandalwood paste should be applied to the body, which is draped in new clothes.' [7]

To touch the flesh of the dead? Living hands on the dead one? For the final purification. The flesh that had once been in the hands of any man who could pay, whether for a few hours or a night. To be owned from the outside to the inside, to have their hands grabbing their fill, to have the weight of them on top, plunging inside – was it possible to keep the mind secret, private? If she now took on the arrangements and if she did them with her mind locked away, she'd be as guilty of deceit as a fraudster.

The telephone rang. It was Kala on the other end. Sita/Ferret this end. Half a city in-between. Half-unknowing in-between.

'I hear you're out of a job,' he said.

'I ain't got no money either honey.'

'Short rations for us, as the English say.' Us? 'Have you begun the arrangements?' he asked.

'I may,' she replied cautiously.

'You have to,' he replied unequivocally. 'I mean, *you* have to. Otherwise it bugs you, forever.' This was the first time he had ever even alluded to a thought about the one who took herself away in his bed. 'And if Emily wants to see me then let's go tonight.' E meets K? 'Then we can come back here.' Here? Where? Where there's breath on breath and skin seducing skin? Where there's doubt and confusion and fear of the future?

Sita/Ferret put down the phone and looked at her hands. Champa had never had any choices. But she'd given them to Sita/Ferret.

She goes into overdrive: rings the funeral parlour and makes arrangements; rings the hospital and informs them; they inform her that both Mrs Miller and Miss Bombay were going to let them know of the arrangements. Sita/Ferret took a deep breath and told half a lie and half a truth, 'I am Miss Bombay. We're family and I'm taking care of this.'

Sangeeta Rayit came home early to do some studying. Sita/Ferret paid her a month's rent and duly informed her of her unemployed status. Sangeeta said she should get herself trained for a proper career, it was sheer madness for a woman to be without economic prospects. 'The law,' Sangeeta advised her, 'should be your aim. Pays well, and utilises at least some of your brain. Any woman who's halfway intelligent can do it. Lots of men who're brain dead do it already.' Sangeeta Rayit was busy revising for her exams, dark rings under her eyes.

'What does your family think about you living alone like this?' Sita/Ferret asked, thinking of the ones that had filled the house a few days ago.

'I pay my mortgage, bills and pension. I take care of me and mine. If I don't ask them for a penny, they can't ask me for a pound of flesh. Right? And that's the way they like it too. They're busy enough living their own lives. You should get your head straightened out.'

'It's better to have a bacchanalian evening once a month is it?'

'I get my priorities right,' Sangeeta Rayit retorted, taking books out of her bag and going upstairs. 'I don't go running after a man every time he crooks his finger.' She paused. 'See you when I see you then,' she added mockingly.

Sita/Ferret swung off the bus, and seeing a clock, counted the hours, his voice like silk lining inside her. It was a voice as seductive as the saris in 'Chandni's' where she now stood, next to efficient housewives in briskly tied saris, neat *bindis* and weighing eyes. Sita/Ferret averted her face, fearful that mere proximity might telegraph news of her unconnubial pleasures; if they were to mind-read they would brand her not only as a scarlet woman but as sacrilegious too, for her mind should be melancholy and sad. Duty and tradition required it to be so. These women had all married, propagated and behaved as expected. Champa had been their opposite, perhaps their nemesis.

'What kind of a sari is madam looking for?' The shop assistant was groomed to perfection, her style chic punk, her hair in sculpted disarray, make-up in glittery grey and black, and her sari, with its deep slashes, held together with silver safety pins.

'Bird of paradise,' replied Sita/Ferret.

The assistant looked puzzled, 'I'm sorry, I don't think we have that. Though we do stock the traditional and latest styles.' Rows of folded saris stretched out on shelves behind her, round racks displayed them on the shop floor, and fan-shaped saris hung from the ceilings, creating a canopy of delicate materials.

'I meant the colours of the bird of paradise,' Sita/Ferret answered.

'Which are...?'

'I don't know.'

The sales assistant sighed, 'I'll put out a call on the Internet, shall I?' All types came into the shop these days, this one looked dead shifty, she kept dropping her eyes and looking away. She'd bet her last penny she'd left home, made an unsuitable liaison, and was now looking for a way back in. The respectable, well-settled ones would have worked out precisely what they were going to buy and how much they were prepared to spend, before even stepping out of their door. 'What is the purpose of the sari, madam? That may help us to choose the right one.'

For the final passage. For the woman who said she'd prayed for her. For the woman who'd had to take the trade of the streets? How could she and Emily have come together?

She paused; some words were too awesome to be quickly spoken. 'For a funeral, for the person whose funeral it is.'

'For the deceased?'

'I want something flamboyant, vivid, stylish!'

Sita/Ferret raced up the road, her boots pounding on the pavement, her breath coming in short gasps, her wet hair frizzing round her head. She came to a skidding stop outside the tube station and couldn't see Kala anywhere. She looked inside the station, even peered down the escalators, and came out again, wondering if he'd decided to go without her. See Emily without her? Learn the past without her? Live the future without her?

'Hi,' he waved to her from a few yards away where he was kneeling on the pavement, tightening the bolts on a tyre. A young Asian woman, dressed in a leather jacket and blue jeans, crouched next to him.

'I don't know what I would have done,' said the woman, getting up as Sita/Ferret reached them. 'Kala...' First names already thought Sita/Ferret jealously. '...has been so helpful. I had a flat! Those bolts are murder to undo.'

'Oh, yes, he's OK with anything that needs brawn,' answered Sita/Ferret, 'pity about the brains.'

'Who needs brains in a man,' replied the woman, 'brawn will do me just fine.' Kala finished off, the object of two pairs of eyes, put the tools in the boot, and came to the front.

'That was wonderful. Do look me up next time you're in Wembley,' she invited, taking a leaflet from her car, 'I'm an interior designer. I mix the Eastern and Western, I design my own fabrics, tiles, etc. Tara Designs. Give me a ring. I like to repay favours. I'll be happy to do your interior designing.' That's sexual harassment thought Sita/Ferret indignantly. Kala took the leaflet, stepped back and said goodbye. The woman waved and drove off.

'I hope that tyre falls off,' Sita/Ferret said.

'Are you doubting my work?' asked Kala, moving a wet strand of hair off her face. 'Are you always late? Or is it just Indian Standard Time?'

The Mausoleum was always well lit. A light in the porch lit up the stained glass in the door and the plant pots on either side. Kala stopped her as she was about to press the bell, his hand tight on hers. 'Not yet,' he whispered. He pushed her hard against the wall, hands inside her coat, under her clothes, rough on her skin, but there was no impromptu lovemaking here. Instead words tumbled over her, 'People have died, starved, drowned, been buried alive, murdered, disappeared forever and we know nothing; families destroyed and we know nothing; atrocities and torture, and we know nothing. Our family was broken, millions of others have been too.' His hand moved underneath her skirt, settled in the dark warmth – like a homecoming. His head rested against hers, his voice fell into her, 'Wouldn't we die with the grief if we knew? And somewhere it's happening right now, to some man, woman, child even.' He moved back and ran his hand across her face. 'Fifty years! If it hadn't happened, we would never have met.' A greater pledge than she could ever have hoped for! She was silent, fear riddling her heart – what if it proved to be transient, or got taken away from her, got 'disappeared'?

He rings the bell. Sita/Ferret puts her hand on the door. She knows its thickness and solidity well. Emily's determination had spun a web. Sita/Ferret is grateful.

Emily saw their shadows against the door. The girl had flown out of her hands. Emily felt everything slipping away from her. Her fingers itched to hold the cold shiny things, then she could fly away to where her promises awaited her. Emily opened the door carefully; she wouldn't let her eyes see his face till she was ready.

Upstairs, when she was settled in her chair, the stick under her hand, she turned her head carefully and slowly brought him into view. He wasn't the same. The face bore similarities, but the eyes were different. The ones in front of her had a dark, sombre texture to them; the ones in her memory were mischievous, glowing with life.

'I wanted to ask,' Kala began, 'about my grandfather.'

'Who?' queried Emily. She'd kept him inside her, as he used to be. So it was alright, external time only passes by on the outside.

Kala mentioned names, dates, places. Each time Emily shook her head. If he started to dig, what wouldn't he find? It was all The Ferret's fault. If she hadn't produced that whelp, none of this would have happened. Ferret ran from here and started playing at being in love; *Ferret ki bachi* ran from here and did exactly the same. Couldn't mother and daughter keep their hands off men!

'You had the jewels, you're the last link. You must know what happened,' Kala asserted, his voice getting sharper.

'They belong to me. Stolen property should be returned.'

'I agree,' said Kala. 'I'm going to return them to my grandmother.'

Emily put her hands on her stick and leaned forward. 'Determined to outlive me is she? Give her those little baubles and she'll have a heart attack. She looked down her snooty nose at me.' Emily's words dripped with the venom of a viper. 'Thought she was a cut above me. But at the end of the day, she was still a dark little native, and I was a memsahib!' She held her chin high. 'She destroyed him. Didn't she know there were those

266

who did exactly as they pleased and didn't have to answer to anyone. What did she think we were there for? The good of India? Brainwashed she was and didn't know it. First she puts the blame on me, then she starts chucking money, throwing it, trying to buy him back. When it was too late.' Her eyes glared at Kala.

'Yes,' stated Emily tartly, 'take them back to her and she'll throw them in your face. You'd better leave now. I've got to lock the door and make sure nothing else goes missing.'

'So you do know what happened to him?' Kala asked, involuntarily standing up and taking a step towards Emily.

'He loved me,' replied Emily, 'only me. Now get out, both of you.' Back straight in the chair, hands on her stick, skin that was creamed and pink, fingers rich with rings, Sita/Ferret couldn't help looking at her with appreciation. What had she done to make her life come true? Uncoupled her conscience from her will?

'What did you and Champa do in India?' probed Sita/Ferret.

'What we had to, you fool. This is all your doing.'

'Was he your customer or Champa's?' asked Sita/Ferret.

A flush spread across Emily's cheeks, 'Parasite! Living off me. *Namak haraam!* Stealing from me. Champa got soft over you; *She*, Ferret, wanted you adopted. Forgotten. It was Champa who kept you, and look what her meddling has done! He was a hundred times better looking and smarter than you,' she spat, suddenly turning on Kala. 'Gopal the Golden they called him. Whatever he touched turned to gold. And he was mine.' Her words challenged any who would dare disagree, even those who may have been thousands of miles away. 'Now get out.'

'So what happened to him?' asked Kala, taking another step towards Emily.

'She's the one who wants to know, isn't she? She only had him for a few years, but I've got him forever. Are you two going, or do I have to call the police and have you thrown out.'

'What do you mean you've got him forever?' asked Sita/Ferret.

Emily looked at her and shook her head in pity. 'God knows what kind of a man The Ferret went off with. Ferret's got brains. You must have taken after the father. Now out. And if you don't give me back what belongs to me, you remain guilty of theft.'

'B for bargain,' began Kala.

Emily paled. Putting her hands on her stick, she heaved herself up, and moved towards the door. 'Go!'

'I haven't finished,' insisted Kala. 'Who was bargaining for my grandfather? Was it you?'

Emily didn't answer straight away. 'He's gone. I want my goods back. Deal through Ferret, else I'll have the law on you and see you locked behind bars.' Pointing her stick at Sita/Ferret's heart, she accused, 'A jailbird. Like mother like daughter. You've already had a taste of it; she had you sticking out in her belly like an overdone bun when she got banged up.'

Jailbird! Like mother like daughter. Like Ambrosia like honey! Sita/Ferret felt a wall breaking inside her, tears welling up. If they hadn't turned knowledge into secrets, she needn't have turned her heart into hatred.

Her night of hot love! They couldn't stop talking. She started off and carried on, as if knowledge of the jailbird connection had loosened her tongue; he talked in and out of her sentences, their voices plaiting around each other. They lifted the stones over their childhoods, describing the worms and crevices for the other to see. Both had played the game of 'if', had tried to imagine normal life and what they would have been like in that life. She had thought she was base and the other life was superior; he had thought he was corrupt and the other life was pure.

Eyes opening in the early hours, the chill seeped into her mind. Tomorrow, today in fact, she would have to use her hands for the final ablutions. They had never touched properly, never put arms around each other, never poured emotion or sought comfort from each other's flesh. Could her hands move all over that body, in intimate detail? Would Sita/Ferret find imprints on Champa's flesh? Her hands curled inwards. But then neither were these hands accustomed to wandering in free abandon over a warm living body. These hands held their own restraint. Turning round towards the sleeping Kala, she moved her hand under the covers, slipped it down his body. She remembered how Champa would turn her face to the sun. Why had she left her land and journeyed so far? To join her life with one so different? Had it been poverty, that most fundamental compulsion, driving the feet of humans since time began. Had there been no one to whom Champa had said, 'I'll come back for you,' no one for whom she could give backward glances?

'Doing your morning meditation?' he asked, making her nerves jump.

'I was thinking about happiness.'

268

'Dangerous thoughts.' His face hovered above hers, the distance of strangers or the path to the next act? Putting her hands hard around his face, she pulled him to her, drew her hands scrapingly down over his shoulders, and tightly over his flesh, pulling at the skin with her palm. She forced his lips open with her own, her teeth digging into the softness, her tongue moving deep into that delicious darkness, swelling the senses. Putting her hands under his shoulders, she turned him over and climbed on top, imprisoning him by her arms and legs, and with a stabbing pang, she saw the fragility of the body underneath her: hit it and it will flinch in pain, cut it and blood will flow, kiss it and pleasure may embrace you, give yourself to it and happiness may visit you – or grief engulf.

She opened her hand wide, and placing it on the side of his body, moved it in caterpillar waves across his chest. The time-worn method of measuring by hand spans! And now she would always know – three and a half hand spans! Such a small creature for this vast world.

Suddenly she was thrown backwards and they were belly to belly, legs on legs. Then he let go of her arms and looked up, asking a question. Would they always be on this road of 'if'? She put her hands behind his back, and opened her legs wide to welcome him. Their minds melted into the flesh. Phoenix fire!

They woke up late. Frantic rushing! Neither had wanted to separate, and the clock had ticked on, till panic propelled them into frenzied activity. She phoned for a taxi, smiling broadly, her whole body smiling. He scrambled to get his papers ready for a meeting with the new owner. They hurtled down the stairs, laughing.

Feeling doubly alive, a singing in her skin, she carried the bag into the funeral parlour. The bag was full of everything new: towels, soaps, cosmetics, and the fabulous silk sari in its box, peacock blue and scarlet. She was eagerly enthusiastic to get started, to wash away all the men Champa had never wanted, to wash away all the trouble and toil of this world, keen to see how Champa would look in her finery.

A covered body on a cold steel table! Her fear hovered back. To touch death; to see the body without the person, no talk, no flicker, no movement; birth, death and love, the ultimate mysteries. Removing the sheet, for the first time she saw in detail the face that had been Champa. She moved her hand through space, holding her breath, and touched and trailed across the planes of Champa's face. It wasn't true that people had a hundred-and-one faces; the everyday human range was far more limited:

Champa the angry, Champa the tired, Champa echoing Emily, Champa working, Champa glued to *Coronation Street*. Had Champa ever been truly loved, caressed and cherished? Or had her days been ones of endurance and survival?

Splashing water over the body, she rubbed the perfumed soap onto a flannel, and cleaned the face, from the brow to the chin, to the neck; more soap, then across the shoulders and breasts, wilted and thin. Then looked up as if she was seeing a ghost. Ferret the Foreign stood opposite her. Jailbird! The light shining on her white hair, those sloe eyes looked at her from a far distance.

'I'll do it,' offered Ancient/Ferret. A voice heard for the first time! Like bruised blue, carrying a different intonation.

'I'm doing it,' Sita/Ferret replied like a stubborn child.

Sita/Ferret washed hair, hands and feet, and then needed to roll the body to do the back. And twice tried and failed. Ancient/Ferret put her hands on the body and moved it, and held it steady. Head to head over Champa!

Outside the rain lashed down, and they lingered under the porch. Sita/Ferret wanted to stare and gaze and be amazed at Ferret the Foreign; a wonder to think she was here at all. Instead, she looked at her watch.

'You must be busy...' began Ancient/Ferret. 'I will do the rest of the arrangements.'

'No.'

Ancient/Ferret didn't argue, perhaps couldn't argue. 'It is an expensive business. I shall reimburse you.'

'No.'

Ancient/Ferret took out a folding umbrella from her bag. 'Emily would like her possessions back. I can negotiate over them.' Could the voice get any darker blue?

'How dare you?' Sita/Ferret rounded on her. 'I return the goods to you,' her voice rising with each word, 'you return them to Emily, and Emily gives you something you want. What a pretty scheme! I have a right to the past, the truth, without any bargaining – if you've kept your memory in working order that is. Or did you cut out bits?'

Ancient/Ferret moved. A little step, and then clicked open her umbrella, 'There are no "rights" in life. Only what you can manage to do.' Then she took something from her bag and looked at it. 'My card.' Held out to Sita/Ferret – direct access! Was this a door opening or merely a cold calculation? Sita/Ferret stuffed it into her pocket; she'd examine it in minute detail later.

'Emily has asked for Champa to be returned to the house,' Ancient/Ferret said.

'So she can embalm her there!'

Ancient/Ferret's lips twitched.

'I call it the Mausoleum you know.' This confidence burst out of Sita/Ferret.

Ancient/Ferret hesitated on a reply and then said slowly, 'I called it the Black Hole of Beckenham.'

'And you left me there.'

Ancient Ferret said she must get back to work. Sita/Ferret watched the tall thin figure walk into the car park and open the door of the white car.

Chapter Twenty-two

London, March 1997

Sita/Ferret sits alone in the chapel with Champa's body. Her eyes are closed, and at times her lips move. She's not saying her prayers, even in this chapel of God. She's imagining a hot Indian city (which must be Bombay, else she and Ferret the Foreign would not have been blessed with that surname) and a room where a woman plies her trade. Sita/Ferret hopes that the woman feels proud not demeaned. The reality may have been more humdrum, perhaps more grubby and soiled, perhaps more light-hearted. Whichever way it was, Sita/Ferret takes it all inside herself. This is what she will keep of Champa, just as Champa had kept her when Ferret the Foreign would have given her away and cast her out from the configuration of the E, C & F. No blood-lines run between the three of them yet they hold lifelong leases on each other. Her anger against Ferret the Foreign boils and hardens. She'll make her acknowledge, make her see that they were of each other, no matter what they were: the Good, the Bad and the Jailbird.

'Red roses?' questions a voice behind her. Sita/Ferret almost jumps out of her skin. Jeevan stands behind her, wearing a white *dupatta* over a black suit. 'I won't be able to stay so I thought I'd better pay my respects now.' 'Respect' is Jeevan's word, 'respect' for the Rules of Life.

'The red roses,' answers Sita/Ferret, 'are from a Miss T Bombay.'

'I see,' Jeevan nods her head, as if she truly does.

'The white lilies are from me,' Sita/Ferret adds. Jeevan nods at each piece of information. Then she sits down across the aisle. Sita/Ferret leaves her alone.

After five minutes Jeevan was ready to leave. 'Darwin got it right, you know. Life is for the toughs. Want to go to a *Baisakhi Bhangrda* rave? All the top stars, non-stop dancing, *chak de phate* stuff!'

Sita/Ferret confessed that she'd never been to a proper *Bhangrda* rave, and then made matters worse by suggesting that she might be over the age limit. 'It's the youngsters that go, right? Then they go home and pretend they've been at school or college all day.'

Jeevan sighed, and sat back down. 'I forgot you're an addicted reader of the white press. Every society contains the complete range from liberal to lynch mob, and every society changes, is constantly evolving.' She went over to the coffin and adjusted the fall of a rose. 'Nothing stays as it was.' Jeevan put her hands on Champa's coffin. Jeevan had chosen a way of living, and had to stick to it, otherwise she might end up being weak, and that was when danger came in. 'Isn't it strange that a country twenty times smaller than India took it over, and then got everyone thinking what a good thing it was?'

'Yes, isn't it?' said Sita/Ferret, no longer surprised at Jeevan's changes in conversation.

'We've got an Asian girl in the hostel at the moment who's been on the game. One night she got herself a maniac who tried to beat her into the tarmac.' Jeevan put on her coat, ready to go. 'India got itself chucked in the slammer as it were.' Jeevan suddenly stopped, as if she'd just heard the echo of her words. Jailbirds all!

What was the history behind Ferret the Foreign's flight from the Mausoleum? Behind the sloe eyes that were so bleak?

Jeevan, still standing by Champa's coffin, adjusted the fall of the drooping rose again. 'Invasion was nothing new. India had waves of invasions; the Brits were just following in the old tradition of "grab and take over". But might's not right! Just because you can force a country...or a person...'

Her voice dried up and a breath came through her, out of her whole body, like the last breath she'd been holding in; slowly her body sagged and slid down against Champa's coffin. Sita/Ferret went to her, put her hand on her arm, and then, as if her arms had now learnt the art of embracing, put them around Jeevan. But Jeevan did not incline to comfort and rested her head against Champa's coffin.

Sita/Ferret walked her to the door. 'Be seeing you then, Jeevan,' said Sita/Ferret deliberately bringing out the name she refused to use.

'Don't push me, Flotsam, I bite back! If you don't fancy the *Bhangrda* bash, there's a pyjama party at the Eastgrove. If you want something different – young medics who want to hone their skills. Ring me.'

'I'll come,' replied Sita/Ferret enthusiastically. 'Let's go to the dance rave.'

'Dancing? And on whose grave?' asked an acid voice. Emily had arrived, swathed in her fur coat, make-up and jewellery, every inch the Grande Dame.

Steven Singh arrived fifteen minutes later, bringing not only the pandit, but Mr Kalyan and daughter Poonum too.

'We have come to pay our respects,' Mr Kalyan said. 'The older ones are passing on. Soon we will be going too. Life is very short.'

Sita/Ferret caught Steven Singh on his own and asked the reason for this visitation of the father and daughter of the Kalyan clan.

'Dunno. He wanted to come. I couldn't really say no. Didn't think you'd mind too much. Indian funerals are open events, after all. Anyone who wants to can tag along. Perhaps it's his way of doing condolence. For his sins. Like I'll let him!'

Kala arrived with two bouquets of flowers.

'I've done the flowers,' Sita/Ferret informed him.

'I'm doing these,' he replied.

Ancient/Ferret arrived last, not looking at anyone, pushing a wheelchair in which sat a frail old English gentleman. Sita/Ferret glanced at him curiously. Had he been one of the occasional visitors to the Mausoleum? She didn't recognise him. Perhaps he had been one of Champa's hidden admirers? Ancient/Ferret parked the wheelchair in the aisle near Emily, who did not turn to greet the new arrival. Ancient/Ferret then went and sat right at the back, closed off as if still behind her cell door.

Sita/Ferret looked around at this odd collection of people, come for Champa's last rites. Did they think that through her they might find a link with their own lives? The Kalyans and Steven Singh sat across the aisle; Kala sat behind Emily, his eyes boring into her.

Om Trayambakam Yajaamahe Sugandhim Pushtivardhanam
Urvaarukamiva Bandhanan Mrityor Muksheeyamaamritaat.

The pandit began his prayers, majestic syllables sliding over them, weaving a shroud of sound. Sita/Ferret looked at Champa's coffin, and took her last image of her, the blue and scarlet against her skin, a blush on her cheeks, a rich red on her lips. If it were to happen again, would Sita/Ferret want it again? Yes, replied Sita/Ferret silently, but not the secrets, not the assassination of love, not the waste.

Na jayate mriyate va kadachin-	The soul is never born nor dies;
Nayam bhutva bhavita va na bhuyah	Nor does it become only after being born
Ajo nityah shasvato'yam purano	For it is unborn, eternal, everlasting, ancient...
Na hanyate hanyamane sharire.[8]	Even though the body is slain, the soul is not.

Immortality! Eternity! Salvation is to be a particle of the universe. Mr Kalyan had his eyes glued to the pandit. Sita/Ferret turned around and looked across the pews at Ferret the Foreign. She was sitting with back straight, looking fixedly at something in front of her. What did she see?

Jatasya hi dhruvo mrityur	For in that case death is certain for the born,
Dhruvam janma mritasya cha	and rebirth is inevitable for the dead.
Tasmadapariharye'rthe	You should not, therefore,
Na tvam schochitumarhasi.[9]	Grieve over the inevitable.

Grieve for the living, thought Sita/Ferret, the living need the salt tears of pain, the welts across the heart, else they become stony-hearted barbarians.

Vayur anilam amrtam	Let this temporary body be burnt to ashes,
Athedam bhasmantam sariram.	and let the air of life be merged with the totality of air.
Om krato smara krtam smara	
Krato smara krtam smara.[10]	

Champa's coffin shivered; the water in Sita/Ferret's eyes distorted. For the first time a tear for Champa? If the other didn't allow love, how could you give it? All her mixed emotions of hate and anger, waste and ungiven love, so long held under the control that Champa had taught her, slowly coalesced for there would never be another Champa. *Sometimes you have to do a little actressing, a twist of the wrist, a flick of the eyes.*

The pandit invited a family member to initiate the last act. Family? By virtue of coincidence, chaos, or contiguity? Sita/Ferret could not do any more, and waited for one of the other two to press the button that would take Champa's body into the furnace.

Ancient/Ferret still sees an upturned fire that had consumed, and a woman clutching a tin trunk looking back with haunted eyes. Ancient/Ferret had never confessed to Champa.

The silent expectation in the chapel gathered and became overdue. Ancient/Ferret looked at Emily; Emily was looking at the coffin.

'My oriental treasure!' laughed Emily. 'I brought her here. She got him first...' Ancient/Ferret immediately stood up and started towards the coffin to forestall any more reminiscences. As she passed, Emily grabbed her arm, and putting her weight on it, hauled herself up. Accompanied by the tapping of Emily's stick, the two progressed to the front.

An image of these two, cobbled together for life, comes to Sita/Ferret.

Supported by Ancient/Ferret, Emily lifted her hand, looked at the coffin, shook her head as if she couldn't forgive something, and pressed.

They filtered out into the daylight, as if coming back from somewhere else. The flowers had been displayed outside the chapel. Among the roses, lilies and Kala's bouquet, was a large cellophane-wrapped one. Sita/Ferret bent forward to read the card: 'Rest in peace, from Mr Anthony B Child.'

'Where do we go now?' Emily asked her. Sita/Ferret hesitated, thinking Emily was asking a philosophical question about their future.

'Lunch?' reminded Emily, 'the do afterwards.' Emily took in the embarrassed shake of the head and nodded. 'Thought as much, knew the brain cells wouldn't travel that far. Here are the cards with the address. You come after you've handed them out.' In the passing of a minute, Emily could erase the passage of a decade, and reduce Sita/Ferret to a furious wretchedness.

'Why's she doing this?' Sita/Ferret asked Ferret the Foreign, holding out a card.

'She's not, I am,' replied Ancient/Ferret, looking down at the card. 'I am familiar with the address.'

Never had Sita/Ferret seen such a feast in that house. Accompanied by uniformed staff, she saw Steven Singh pick up one of the strategically placed company cards, while Ferret the Foreign quickly gathered up the rest.

'What does it say?' Sita/Ferret asked Steven Singh, sidling up to him.

'Simla Sunshine Caterers.'

'Original with their names aren't they.'

Mr Kalyan was in transports of delight, praising everything he could see. 'This is a treasure house,' he declared to Emily.

'Thank you, everything is an original,' Emily replied, 'and everything is for sale, except of course the recent receptacle. The ashes,' she declared in sonorous tones. 'Those I will take to India and dispose of in the sacred way.' She left a little silence to mark the future event. 'After I have received back what is mine.' Her acid look took in Sita/Ferret and Kala.

'Very good,' approved Mr Kalyan, who'd witnessed the look. 'We are re-arranging our business situation, and will be most interested in such good-quality, top-class items, such treasures.' Sita/Ferret noted that Mr Kalyan seemed to be getting back to normal. 'Will you be arranging the sale on your return?'

'Now, immediately,' said Emily. 'Feel free to look around. Remember that everything here has been extremely well looked after. Left in India they'd have rotted years ago.' Emily should be a national heroine of India at this rate, thought Sita/Ferret. 'I will be going to India on a one-way ticket,' Emily continued. 'Champa and...' And stopped. 'Girl,' she said, raising her voice and summoning one of the waitresses, 'more tea, over here. Look lively. *Ek dum!*'

Mr Kalyan congratulated Emily on her Hindi. Emily was flattered. Kala was in conversation with the elderly gentleman though his eyes were often on Emily. Steven Singh served Poonum with his own hard-working hands. Mr Kalyan, sitting by Emily, was apparently taking dictation. Sita/Ferret saw Ferret the Foreign pick up a jug, give a quick flick of her eyes around the room, and leave. Sita/Ferret followed.

Ferret the Foreign had rounded the corner at the top of the stairs. Sita/Ferret put her hand on the banister and bounded up two at a time. Her flights down these banisters used to be spectacular! Not allowed to play outside, she'd made her play inside. Bloody Cinderella syndrome! And who were the two ugly sisters? Today she couldn't pursue this line of thought, and perhaps never again. But misfortune had struck her banister-sliding the day she'd jumped clear at the bottom, banged into Emily and sent her sprawling. For years thereafter, one of her tasks had been to rub in the polish. She noted that the present cleaner must skim the work, for no reflection came up to meet her gaze. She determined to have a severe word with Emily. Emily was letting the house go to rack and ruin.

Ferret the Foreign was in Emily's room, on her tiptoes on a chair, skimming the top of the wardrobe with her hands.

'What do you think you're doing?' Sita/Ferret asked sternly, arms folded.

Ancient/Ferret nearly fell off with shock, 'You startled me.'

'So sorry.'

'Did anyone see you?' asked Ancient/Ferret.

'No.'

'Good. You can help me.'

'I thought you didn't ask for help.'

'I've only got a couple of minutes,' said Ancient/Ferret hurriedly, getting down, opening a drawer, and quickly searching inside. 'Do you want to bargain?'

'No.'

'I'm looking for a collection of exercise books, the kind children use. Do you know where she keeps the keys to those trunks?' she asked, pointing to the two rug-covered trunks under the window.

'Sure.'

'Could you tell me, please?' Ancient/Ferret slid open the drawer at the bottom of the wardrobe.

'First, you answer all my questions. And tell me everything about my father.'

Ancient/Ferret quickly flicked through shawls and scarves, 'You may not like what you hear.'

'I'll take my chances.'

Ancient/Ferret closed the drawer, 'Please get the keys and search thoroughly inside the trunks. I must go back down now.' She was nearly out of the door but stopped, 'Do you know if he is a danger to you?'

'What?'

'The one downstairs, the man who seems...the one who is talking to...the one with grey eyes. Is he a danger to you?'

'What kind of danger would he be?'

Ancient/Ferret looked impatient and was about to turn away, 'Does he obey the law?'

'I expect he gets his share of parking tickets,' retorted Sita/Ferret.

'Is he a good man?'

'What do you care?' asked Sita/Ferret.

Ancient/Ferret gave up and turned to go, so Sita/Ferret spoke quickly to hold her back another moment, to keep her near. 'Yes, he is a good person.' She was whispering, knowing instinctively that their voices must not travel down. Sita/Ferret was admitting that she trusted, that she was willing to put her faith in another human being. And if Kala were not a good person, then she would have to suffer the consequences.

'But I am not a good person,' replied Ancient/Ferret. 'I have stolen what people believe.'

Faith-stealing thief! This beautiful woman who stands straight, her white hair framing her face, those old sloe eyes which must have bewitched in younger days.

'Find the diaries and I will answer your questions.'

'Why are those books so important?' Sita/Ferret hissed at her.

Emily's voice echoed up. Ancient/Ferret was already at the door.

'They're Champa's diaries.'

Sita/Ferret kicked Emily's bedpost, banging her toes, and bringing tears to her eyes; she'd forgotten she wasn't wearing boots today. Sitting down on the bed, she balled her hands into fists, trying to stop the sobs coming out of her. It was in this very house that she'd been taught not to cry. *Push it back down, that way you can swim in the world, if not, you will drown.* Weighed against her own worth, Champa's diaries tipped the scales. She would never forgive Ferret the Foreign!

Ancient/Ferret looked back and whispered, perhaps unheeded by Sita/Ferret, 'Don't you understand? Champa's diaries have the secrets of who you are, of who we all are.'

After Jeevan had left, Emily and Sita/Ferret had been alone in the chapel. Emily had asked to look at Champa and the attendants from the funeral parlour had removed the lid.

'Pink,' Emily had commented, putting a finger on the lining of the casket.

'I thought she'd like it,' Sita/Ferret had replied defensively, sensitive to criticism.

'I'm sure,' Emily had replied sourly, 'I'm sure he promised her all sorts of pink palaces too.' Emily opened her bag, and removing a little velvet box, took out a locket and chain, and then hesitated. She didn't place it round Champa's throat, instead slipped it into the side of the coffin. Sita/Ferret had watched, surprised at this gesture. Emily didn't let anything go. Emily had opened her bag again and taken out a pile of exercise books which she had arranged at the sides, spreading the sari folds over them. A corner of one of the exercise books had remained exposed. Sita/Ferret's fingers had longed to reach in and filtch, instead she'd twitched the sari fold over it, respectfully. Emily had watched till the lid was securely back on.

'Oh dear,' said Mr Kalyan, peering in from the door, accompanied by Emily. Poonum and Steven Singh hovered behind. 'The sad time has come. The tears are falling out.' He had obviously decided to parade the quaint Indian persona today.

'Bollocks!' Sita/Ferret could see it coming neon-lit from Emily.

'We're doing a tour of the house. To take an inventory,' Mr Kalyan informed her. His voice was thinner than before, as if his blood had weakened. 'This house is like an Aladdin's cave,' he exclaimed, raising his hands in wonder. Sita/Ferret wished he'd drop his stupid act, did he think he could pull the wool over Emily's eyes?

'Mrs Miller tells us you grew up in this house.' The unmistakable voice of Poonum! 'Who was the wicked aunt from whom you ran away to marry your love, who died a swift death, from which you swiftly recovered and swiftly moved into the arms of another, Mrs Pandey? By the way, did you know that was her name?' she said, turning to Emily.

Sita/Ferret brushed a hand sharply across her face and stood up. 'Don't get too carried away with your inventory. Half this house and its contents belong to me.'

Emily sighed, 'Not another one.'

'And I intend to claim every percentage,' Sita/Ferret raged at them. 'Champa left half of everything to me, her will is with a solicitor. Right now! Every transaction will require my agreement. Enjoy your tour!' She strode past them, but turned at the stairs and looked at Emily, 'You must have very cold blood. Be glad. You got your revenge at the end.'

'Seems to me you got yours at the beginning.'

Downstairs, the aproned staff had packed up and were leaving. Ancient/Ferret closed the front door behind them, the stained glass in the door throwing tints of colour onto her hair. She turned and transfixed Sita/Ferret with such a glittering look of demand that Sita/Ferret halted on the stairs, tightening her hand around the banister, counting out the moment.

In the large reception room, Kala was still doing his duty by Mr Child who was criticising the colonial days. 'The politicians never understood the Indian way of doing things. They went in with their hobnailed boots making enemies, getting things wrong,' he was saying.

'You must have been quite a rebel,' commented Kala.

'I did things my way. You can't let clerks tell you what to do. It was like this,' Mr Child lowered his voice, leaned towards Kala, 'one rule for us and one rule for them. That's divide and rule, my boy.'

'What's happening upstairs?' asked Ancient/Ferret, looking at Sita/Ferret with the other question still in her eyes.

'Chaos I hope. I've just laid claim to half the house.'

Mr Child stopped talking and turned to listen. 'Rather soon to be fighting over the spoils,' he admonished in his rasping, old-fashioned voice.

'And the ashes aren't even cold yet,' Sita/Ferret retorted. 'But fifty years isn't too soon. That's how long these three have been at it. I forgot, it's two now, isn't it? But don't forget *moi*, who was dropped in like a bag of potatoes. Back to the magic three!'

'Who is this young lady?' asked Mr Child. Ancient/Ferret moved herself away to sit in a corner. 'You must have been born here? Ah, yes, now I remember, the little girl that Champa loved. Part of the post-Independence generation. British born, a potent mixture. You wouldn't have a roof over your head, if it weren't for them, young lady. You should be thankful. But what do they care?' he said. 'They were born here and got spoilt. I've seen them, going off to discos and dances. They haven't got half the guts of the older generation.' A wracking cough overpowered him; Kala offered him a glass of water.

Sita/Ferret turned on Ancient/Ferret, 'If I tell you where they are, do we still have a deal?'

'Will I be able to read them?' asked Ancient/Ferret. No wonder she's successful, thought Sita/Ferret, she knows what the pertinent point is.

'You can,' replied Sita/Ferret, 'possess them,' gesturing in the direction of the box.

'Possess what?' asked Emily, coming back into the room with her entourage.

'Here's the expert,' announced Ancient/Ferret grimly. 'This is the end Emily.'

Emily grandly ignored her.

The tableau remains in her mind: Kala, the elderly gentleman, Emily, Ferret the Foreign.

Kala offered his hand to the gentleman.

'Don't,' snapped Ancient/Ferret, her voice blue-black. 'Today my errands come to an end. Let me introduce you to Mr Anthony Bernard Child.'

Kala looked blankly at her. Ancient/Ferret's anger rose, 'He brought over booty from India. She,' her finger pointing at Emily, 'knew. She knew and left him to rot.'

'What?' asked Kala, confused. Mr Child's body convulsed in a fit of coughing, the colour came and went from the gaunt face that was now almost like a skull. Perhaps he had always been a thin man. Tears seeped from his eyes and dribbled down his cheeks, his breathing came in rasping gasps, and his eyes closed as if he'd sunk into a coma. Ancient/Ferret took the wheelchair handles and let down the brake.

'I'll complete the errand,' she said. Then, looking at Kala, 'Don't say I didn't give you your chance.'

'What d'you mean?' Sita/Ferret started to ask, but Emily interrupted, swishing past her, picking up the container with the ashes.

'I'll need something better to take these back in. Perhaps that brass box with the lion lock?' She stopped at the door, looking back scornfully, 'The stupid fools panicked, sold things they'd had for generations. They didn't know what it was like to be hungry with time running out. And danger coming in. She doesn't know.' Her finger pointing accusingly at

Sita/Ferret. 'But you know Ferret, you know what it was like. And now you're in charge of your own workers and money. Stick to your business and don't meddle in other people's affairs.'

'You didn't have to destroy them,' Ancient/Ferret flung at her. 'They wouldn't have done you any harm.'

'They were meant only for me. I shall do as I wish with my possessions.' Ancient/Ferret's hands shook on the wheelchair handles, 'They were the only thing I had left. So be it.' Emily ignored her and walked out of the room. Ancient/Ferret pushed the wheelchair after her, still talking, 'Then I'll do what I want with what I possess.' As they came into the hallway, Emily was nowhere to be seen. Ancient/Ferret, still quivering with anger, struggled to manoeuvre the wheelchair towards the front door. Kala tried to assist. 'No,' Ancient/Ferret warned him off. 'You should not touch it.'

'I was only trying to help,' Kala expostulated.

She looked at them before she left, then spoke to Sita/Ferret, 'Because you have met him,' inclining her head towards Kala, 'you'll have to force Emily to do it. She can. Years ago, I used to drive her there, but I always sat outside in the car. Today, I saw.'

Ancient/Ferret's eyes deepened, she moved close to Sita/Ferret, the closest in thirty years. A parcel of knowledge passed from one to the other. Sita/Ferret went cold with shock.

The sound of Ancient/Ferret's car faded away. 'She's gone,' thought Sita/Ferret, Ferret the Foreign, always going away from her. Years ago, in this house, she'd given her her life and left her. Today she'd given her another terrible gift and left her.

As if in an envelope of time, Sita/Ferret takes Kala's hand and traces three letters. He is still puzzled. She goes close and whispers into his ear, so that the words may not escape, may not spread more grief. He refuses to believe, and moves away from her. They stand apart. She wishes she could take back her words. But he moves towards her and asks her to repeat. He staggers as comprehension dawns, they slide against the wall and hold each other. 'No,' he says again. This was not what he'd been searching for, not what he wanted to find, not this unbearable knowledge.

They ran through the house searching for Emily, pounding up the stairs, first into Emily's room, then into Champa's. Further up the stairs, in and out of rooms, and, as if some kind of madness had overtaken her, words hurtled out of Sita/Ferret, explaining the rooms, furnishings, events, drawing him into the history of the house. But still no Emily. They rushed downstairs. Sita/Ferret knew Emily would be somewhere; she'd never leave the place that belonged to her. But Emily wasn't in the kitchen either, and Sita/Ferret started wondering if the unthinkable could have happened – a change in Emily. Then they saw her, coming out of the cellar.

Kala's words hurtled at her, stopping her in her tracks. But Emily was not one to be intimidated. She calmly closed the door, and said she didn't know what The Ferret had been talking about. The Ferret couldn't be trusted, one minute she'd be doing your bidding and the next minute she'd be snarling at you. Uncivilised, that was The Ferret's trouble.

Sita/Ferret said she'd snarl too if she had to; perhaps it was the only way to talk to Emily.

'Ungrateful wretches!' Emily still had the box with the ashes clasped against her.

So Sita/Ferret lied through her teeth, 'Champa told me everything. Everything about what you did in India.'

Emily looked up at the ceiling and ruminated, 'I had a casket. I remember, an ivory casket with a pattern of vine leaves. You wouldn't happen to know where it is, would you?'

'To hell with your caskets,' Kala shouted. 'I want to know...' but Sita/Ferret interrupted him, putting a warning hand on his arm to hold him back.

'How did you enjoy being a...' she gathered the word inside herself, '...a prostitute?'

Emily shook her head, 'Stupid little wretch! Look at you both. Spineless worms! If you were worth anything, you,' jabbing Kala with her stick, 'you would have sorted things out years ago, not waited for Ferret, or Ferret *ki bachi* to get you started. *He* had the world at his feet. *He* was the talk of the town! And you,' turning on Sita/Ferret, 'you wouldn't have survived if you hadn't stolen from me.' True Emily, how true! If she hadn't possessed the jewels, what disastrous paths might she have been tempted to travel?

'Now bugger off,' Emily finished, re-adjusting the box into the crook of her arm. 'You're trespassing in my house.'

My house! My possessions! My world!

So it was Sita/Ferret who, knowing the weave of Emily's mind, realised that only a great desire can be pitted against another great desire.

And so they bargained. And arranged a barter of the most unholy kind.

Chapter Twenty-three

23 March 1997, London

The time in-between.

In a thousand villages they still light *laltens* in the evening because electricity has not yet arrived, or it cannot be afforded. It is the light of the poor. The *lalten* has a thin metal handle, a chamber for oil, and a little door that can be opened for lighting the wick. A door is a door – the link between one space and another, between oneself and the world. A door provides shelter and safety. But doors can be dangerous too, depending on which side the locks and bolts are placed.

The *lalten* needs its door to guard the flame, protect it from the evening breeze or a sudden gust of wind. The *lalten* sheds its shy light on the area around it. Suspended from a hook, it overhangs the talk of evenings when tired limbs rest under the warm night sky; when words take on an intimate quality, an eternal and mythic tinge; when there is talk of the day's events, or last year or long ago, talk of uncles, aunts, strangers, ancestors and others. A cast of hundreds! These are the stories that tell of the essence of power, the power of people over people. The danger from a person could be here, in your house, next door, or on the street. Giants, ghouls and monsters hardly venture into the lives of humans.

Lalten light falls over listening faces, over stories of loves and enmities, luck and calamity, hardships and sacrifice, rewards and loss. Loss! The most tragic word in the world!

The *lalten* glows in the dark. Throughout time, those who must travel have always lit a *lalten* to light their way and to frighten off predators. If there are sightings of tigers in the vicinity, every *lalten* in the village is lit and other lights are improvised, rows of lights on roof ledges and walls.

But will mere light suffice to defend against a tiger's marauding prowling?
What if a tiger comes in the shape of a human?

Those who are caught in the dark can signal with the *lalten* for its light
will carry further than a shout. 'Here I am, come help me, come rescue
me,' it says. But what of those who don't have a *lalten*?

In the evening light, Sita/Ferret hurries across the road. A man on the
other side is giving out leaflets for one of the political parties because an
election is on its way, just as the world is on its way to the Millennium; and
just as Sita/Ferret has come from the day of Champa's funeral, just as the
day of Champa's funeral dragged terrible knowledge from Emily.

Sita/Ferret takes out her keys, and thinks gold could not be more
precious than the possession of one's own key. Sangeeta Rayit and her
daughters are in the kitchen. Books spread out on the table, all are
engrossed in their studies. The older girl has drawn a plant and is labelling
its different parts, the younger one has two plates in front of her and
counts chick-peas from one to the other, then writes down her answers,
Sangeeta is reading a thick law book, and making notes. Work and peace
pervade the room. Tea and snacks sit on the table. Wordlessly Sangeeta
pours a cup of tea and pushes it towards Sita/Ferret. She sits with them,
sipping the warm, comforting brew, feeling its warmth spreading through
her. The numbness inside her begins to shift and dissolve and pain comes
in. Sangeeta frowns over something in her book, the older girl draws rain
over the plant, the younger one colours in numbered squares. Sita/Ferret
takes silent solace from them.

Upstairs, Ancient/Ferret's card is sitting on the mantelpiece and
Sita/Ferret picks it up, touches it, looks on the other side, in case
something had appeared from the last time that she had looked. Where
does Ancient/Ferret live? Does she have solace? Does she have a partner
or children? Sita/Ferret shivers at the thought of others who may share
blood and flesh with her: strangers and siblings in one, to be connected
and not know. Sita/Ferret puts the card back, wedges it in so there can be
no possibility of it falling off, and realises that if she does not make a copy,
she may lose it forever. She writes on five separate pieces of paper and puts
them in different places, and lastly sews the card into the hem of her coat.
Eventually, she drags the old armchair to the window, pulls the duvet off
the bed, and wrapping it around herself, sits by the window, looking down.
Her bedroom door is wide open.

The street lamps are on. She tries not to imagine, but can't help it. *The ABCs have begun...* Kala too will be trying to close his mind, and failing. She goes downstairs, the house is quiet, the girls have gone to bed, and Sangeeta is studying. Sita/Ferret picks up the phone and rings him. His voice comes from far away.

The black, lapping waters of the river make little noise but fill their eyes with a grimy gloom. This is a city river, a famous river – if the river had not been, London would not have been. The village clustering around its watery edges had grown so far beyond itself that it now touched the other side of the world. Sita/Ferret and Kala walk along the embankment. They'd driven past Tower Bridge, but refused to look, else imaginings would have riddled them through. Then they'd parked and started walking. Past the Tate Gallery (Jeevan would have given them the history of sugar-man Sir Henry Tate) they walk up the steps of Lambeth Bridge, their footsteps loud in the night air. Sometimes they look back, checking. They come to the Houses of Parliament – the mother of all parliaments! Gunpowder, Plot and Treason!

Treason on its own is enough, thinks Sita/Ferret. As they turn towards Westminster Bridge, they look up towards Trafalgar Square, dominated by Nelson's Column and the colonnade of the National Portrait Gallery. Beyond is Leicester Square, high voltage and neon lit.

Sita/Ferret and Kala turn left at Westminster Bridge to carry on walking along the embankment. They walk past the tourist boats that cruise the river each day, the restaurant and disco boats that blare out hunky slabs of music; carry on walking till there are fewer people around and office blocks start rising up.

They drink coffee at an all-night café. They aren't alone. Others come in for food and beverages too. Some in evening gear, others in rumpled suits or dirty overalls. The city never sleeps!

Chapter Twenty-four

Kala unlocks the drawer and takes out the jewellery boxes.

Sita/Ferret is thinking of Ferret the Foreign and wondering what paths of humiliation and suffering she'd had to endure. Kala hands the boxes to her and she opens them at the table, lowers the lamp, light refracting in their shining rays. Ice and fire! Beauty that exists by itself!

Kala comes to sit next to her. They are both taken back to the first time they had sat here, side-by-side, the same jewellery displayed in front of them.

'I was different then,' she confessed to him. 'I thought I was the outcast, and had a hard glaze over me. These were the nearest, dearest things in the world to me. When I left them here, I felt as if a part of me had been torn off.' Her voice died away.

'You took half with you,' he retorted tartly, yet his eyes were lost. *What pretty pretty eyes you have!*

A laugh bubbled out of her, a new mischievous laugh, 'Count yourself lucky you got half.'

Count yourself lucky?

' "Stick with me babe, and we'll go places," ' she joked, attempting a Humphrey Bogart voice.

'Babe?' he questioned quietly, a finger on the coral – the stone to protect against spells, to calm storms, to enable the wearer to cross rivers, to staunch the flow of blood, to give wisdom and overcome fear. 'You're right' he said. 'We're certainly going places because of you.' But was it a place anyone would ever want to go?

Guilt skewered through her.

He took her hand, interlocked the fingers, 'There is no blame from me to you.'

Blame by blood connection! Even with Emily. The threads that tied them were interwoven. She'd wanted to know. And now she knew more than she could ever have desired; a knowledge that was shrapnel inside her. And she hadn't yet had her fill. Ferret the Foreign was still a stranger.

Outside it is already light, winter is giving way to spring. She's always hated this season when you must have a spring in your step, an object of desire, and condoms in your purse. They progress smoothly on their journey, with very little traffic to hold them up. She can't understand it, for even on a Sunday, London's roads can be jam-packed, causing tailbacks and delays. The sound of pealing church bells comes to them. When he stops for petrol, she can't help herself, has to get out and buy a newspaper. Bunny rabbits and Easter eggs decorate the front page. Easter Sunday! The day of Resurrection? She folds the newspaper and puts it away. Doesn't want him to see it – for who knows what the truth is?

At first Kala had said, 'B is for believe. C is for con. I don't believe it, it's a con.' But now his eyes are impatiently on the road ahead, his fingers tight on the steering wheel, grimly determined. She moves in her seat to get as close as possible to him; her hand goes under his jacket, slides to the back, pulls up the shirt and makes communion with his skin. A liquid shiver runs through her, as if all her feathers have fallen into place, in perfect sequence, and her blood, at last, flows the right way.

They travel through quiet streets, along roads where the trees are still bare and winter-like, they drive over Vauxhall Bridge, crossing the river, and are glad they have the coral with them. She map-reads and directs as they drive through south London towards the A road that will take them out. After about two hours they should arrive at a small place outside London – a genteel place, with spacious homes and large green spaces where people attend church, walk their dogs, and greet each other as they pass.

A is for arrival. The house has a balcony running along the front, trees dotted in the garden, and flowerbeds near the house.

'There's a whole colony of them here, I've been told,' he said, as they stood outside, looking at the house warily. 'A colony of ex-pats.'

'Living on their memories.'

'If that was all...' he replied, making no movement to go forward.

Something evil in there dwells!

She inserts her hand into his. Unconscious reliance. What if it were suddenly taken from her? He grips her hand with a fierce tightness. She is silent. C is for calamity and catastrophe. She opens the gate. Her favourites are also in C: coincidence, chaos, contiguity. As they walk up the path a branch brushes across her face, and, moving it aside, she sees a gardener, weeding a rectangular patch of ground where the large-bladed leaves of tulips have come up with the stems blossoming into colour.

They halt as they reach the door. 'C,' she says aloud, for her ears to hear, 'is also for confluence. Ready?' she asks, her finger hovering over the bell. He shakes his head. 'Want to wait another fifty years?'

'It's human beings who are demons,' said Kala, reaching forward and pressing the bell. She puts her hands around her bag – not till the bargain is concluded. Another C word.

Emily is at her haughty best. Perfectly turned out, hair folded back to show off her earrings, and wearing a pink woollen dress with a pure white shawl round her shoulders, her mind is perfectly under control. 'He won't be long,' she says, 'so you'd better be quick. It wasn't easy to arrange. He's an unpredictable bastard. A bugger if you ask me.'

'I won't,' Sita/Ferret assures her.

'The Virgin Mary are you?' Emily throws at her. 'He could be back any time. Be quick.' She doesn't want to look at them. 'The Ferret,' Emily says, giving Sita/Ferret a shock, as if she were the one being talked about, 'has concocted this little drama. She was always prone to exaggeration and delusion, wicked ideas. It's nothing to do with me. It's someone else entirely. But a bargain is a bargain.'

Emily is afraid of consequences. Sita/Ferret has never before seen a shiver of fear pass over Emily. So Emily was like them all.

'My grandmother also made bargains,' accuses Kala. 'None of which were honoured.'

'Not my fault if she left it too late!' A shining smile lights up Emily's face, as if a beautiful nugget of knowledge has just entered her. 'She could never have won. She was weak, I was strong. She was inferior, I was superior. That's how it was. How it is,' nodding her head in confirmation of the idea. 'I'll open the door. You can go in, and then give me what belongs to me. We'll go our separate ways.'

'I still own half the house,' Sita/Ferret reminds her.

Emily turns on her with the wrath of a clawing cat, 'Champa was out of her mind. She was a sick woman. And you manipulated her. Ferret *ki bachi*!' This, presumably the highest insult that Emily could throw at her.

'Are you two ready or do you want to wait till Ant gets back and makes mincemeat of you?'

'Ant?' echoes Sita/Ferret.

'Mr Child to you, prat.'

Kala spoke over them, 'Why don't you have this family discussion later...'

'Family?' Both turn on him.

They moved from the hall into a round lobby, and passed rooms with closed doors, walls decorated with rifles, spears, old maps and prints of India. Wheelchair tracks crossed and criss-crossed the floor. This house did not possess the elegance of Emily's; it had a rough, uncouth feel to it. A shallow ramp led into a large kitchen with a fireplace in one wall, a huge table in the middle and French doors leading out to the garden. Emily stopped in front of a door with an electronic lock on it.

'Don't say I didn't warn you,' Emily stated, exonerating herself again. 'They say he wanders out, the person, walks out into the night, gets lost. So he has to be protected.' Not once does she look at them.

Sita/Ferret held onto Kala's coat sleeve. Emily herself seemed to have become immobile till Kala asked her to open the door. Emily's hand hovered, then fingers bashed in the code. Sita/Ferret, hawk-eyed, watched her: A 19 B 46 C 97. More than fifty years!

'If you knew,' Sita/Ferret hissed violently at her, 'and if you knew how to open the door, why did you leave him here?'

'It's not him. I told you,' Emily repeated vehemently. She had repeated it for fifty years. 'Hurry. And return to me what is mine.'

Sita/Ferret opened her bag, and taking out the packet, extended her arm to Emily. Emily had half-turned away, but she put her fingers on the packet, slid it out of Sita/Ferret's hand, and opened it. Her burning eyes looked at Sita/Ferret and Kala. 'It's done,' she whispered. The packet clasped against her breast, Emily left.

Doors are so dangerous. Open them and you may see what you were never meant to, scenes that will breed worms in your heart. Go through them at your peril. Sita/Ferret and Kala stepped through.

What had they expected? A medieval cell with barred windows and chains on the wall? An old but serviceable carpet covered the floor of the room, a low cupboard stood in one corner and a chair in the other. Sita/Ferret put her hand on Kala's arm for support; it was rigid with tension. The room appeared empty. They turned to look behind them, and saw the man who cowered into the corner.

Afraid? No fear. Not me! had been her litany. A childish game! She hadn't known what real fear was. The bleached eyes are dilated, the body shaking; the person is petrified.

He is crouched on a covered mattress, a stained sweatshirt hanging loose from a shrunken, shrivelled body; the face a carved skull with its terrible eyes staring out at them. Kala takes a step forward, and immediately the figure on the bed moves back, arms raised to protect himself, a little mewing sound coming out of him.

'*Dada*,' says Kala, softly, dropping onto his knees, '*dada*.' The figure tries to move further away, into the wall. '*Dada*,' Kala speaks, in a voice liquefied to soothing. '*Mein aapka hoon.*' *Grandfather, I am yours, I am of you*. He inches forward. The person on the bed cowers and covers his face with his arms. '*Namaste...*' Kala tries again.

Sita/Ferret crouches down and whispers, 'Speak in English.' *The long thin one likes to show off his Hindustani.*

Kala begins again, 'Don't be afraid,' repeating it over and over. 'I won't harm you. No one is going to harm you.' No response. As if under siege, he's barricaded himself behind his arms. 'It's alright, it's alright,' syllables softened to reassure, 'no one is going to hurt you, we are not the bad people.' Kala inches forward, stretches out a tentative hand. Sita/Ferret stops him – a hand coming towards him might terrify him even more.

'Tell him who you are,' she suggests in a whisper.

'*Dada*, I'm Ka... I'm Rajesh Gopal, Gopal Sharma, Rajesh Gopal Sharma, your grandson, *Dada*, grandson, Rajesh Gopal Sharma, Gopal...' A hand moves, an eye peeps out. 'I'm Rajesh, your grandson.' The arms lower slightly, the head shakes in a vague way. Could he be saying no?

'*Dada, dada*, you are Gopal, Gopal...' repeats Kala like a mantra. This time a little sound escapes, protesting. There is no such thing it says.

Kala glances at Sita/Ferret for help. She is close against him, kneeling at his side.

'What if it really isn't him?' she asks.

'It doesn't matter.'

'Are we going to take him out of here?' But how can they know what is right? For the ruined man in front of them, this might be the only way to live.

Kala inches forward, infinitely slowly. He can see blotches and discolouration on the thin petrified skin.

'*Dada,* I am your family, your grandson, I am yours. I am here to help you, I will not hurt you, no one will hurt you again. You are safe, *Dada,* safe. *Dada* I love you.' That word at last, like a diamond rolling off his tongue.

But it was the wrong thing to say; it must have meant something awful to the one in front of them for another one of those pitiful sounds escaped him, and his old bleached eyes looked wildly at them, waiting for what was to befall him.

Hardly a thread of a breath left in him, could it be possible that brutality was still inflicted upon him?

'*Dada,*' tried Sita/Ferret, '*dada.* Come with us, we are taking you home. You will be safe, *dada,* safe. Safe, *dada,* safe.' The words couldn't get past his barriers but he looked at her with puzzlement. Where had this woman's voice come from? What did it augur? Sita/Ferret whispered into Kala's ears. He nodded. She spoke in Hindi, '*Sarojini aageyi,*' *Sarojini has arrived.* Sarojini the wife. '*Sarojini ke saat chalo. Aao.*' *Come with Sarojini, come.* Did he remember the wife? Was she the one person with whom he would go? Sita/Ferret stretched out a hand, a feather touch on his arm. As if her words had just reached him, he looked with growing horror towards her. Sita/Ferret cursed herself. She'd inflicted the greatest humiliation. With hands groping against the wall, he raised himself up, and then, before they knew it, stumbled past them and out of the door.

They thought they'd moved fast, but there was no sign of him in the kitchen. They wasted time trying to open the door into the garden, and then rushed towards the main lobby.

'Stop there!'

The command halts them in their tracks. And, just as suddenly, they realise it cannot be for them, they're still in the corridor and no one can see them.

'*Kutti!*' Bitch! '*Kali kutti...*' Kali? Kala? 'You fool of a man! How did you get out?'

As they came running into the lobby, Ant first paled and then reddened, 'How dare you break into my house!'

'Emily let us in, actually,' Sita/Ferret answered him.

'Now you can bugger off!'

'Certainly,' replied Kala. '*Dada,* come with us,' going over to him, carefully taking his arm.

'Unhand him!' Ant's voice reverberated around the room. Gopal removed his thin, shaking arm from Kala's hand and put both his arms around himself, his eyes on Ant, waiting.

'Get out now,' Ant snapped at Kala and Sita/Ferret, 'or I'll call the police and have you done for trespassing and attempted kidnapping.'

'Do it. We're not going without him.'

Sita/Ferret came to stand on Gopal's other side, wanting to take his hand, but knowing she mustn't. Neither Kala nor Sita/Ferret knew what reaction they would get from Gopal if they tried anything.

'He won't go with you.' Ant wheeled his chair backwards a little, towards the wall. 'Ask him! Go on!' Both knew the futility of trying. Ant smiled triumphantly as Gopal moved forward, knelt, then prostrated himself on the floor, at Ant's feet.

Sita/Ferret looked away. This was part of Ant's hidden, silent evil. She glanced at Kala and saw water swimming in his eyes.

'I cheated your stupid, useless Independence!' boasted Ant, 'I don't give up what belongs to me.'

Belong! The word fills the Universe. From possessions to passions, the world has been riddled, ruined and resurrected by it. Belonging is a B word. Longing comes into it, being-ness too. To long and to be? By that which belongs to me?

'Go to your room,' Ant ordered the figure on the floor. 'And you two? Get out, while you can.'

An age passed as Gopal painfully raised his body on his shaking arms and levered himself up; his weight on his feet, but the rest of him bowed, turning to go back towards the kitchen.

'Stop!' shouted Sita/Ferret hoarsely at Gopal, pushing Kala towards him at the same time.

'You filthy bitch! Go with him and do as he says.'

Kala pulled Gopal towards the door and Sita/Ferret rushed forward to open the locks. Ant wheeled his wheelchair and reached for something on the wall.

'Unhand him!' Ant's voice whipped as he levelled a gun towards them. 'I've got every right to shoot burglars and trespassers.' Kala told her to open the door – display guns aren't left loaded. A click and a shot, and plaster showered over them, shocking them into stillness. Through the side window Sita/Ferret saw the gardener pause and look towards the house.

'Here!' barked Ant at Gopal, which was how he must address his dogs. Gopal hesitated, looking from one to the other, then shuffled back towards Ant. The old terrors were safer. 'Now get lost!' Ant ordered, pointing the gun at them.

Kala moved a step nearer. 'You evil old bastard. You've ruined our family and tortured him all these years. You get out of my fucking way. Come!' he said more softly, taking Gopal's arm.

'Take your buggering hands off him. In the old days, I would've shot your head off. I was in charge!'

'Well you're not any more. You were kicked out! Remember?' shouted back Kala, while trying to pull gently on Gopal.

'Then what the bloody hell are you doing here? Get away from him!' Ant threatened, raising the gun in readiness.

'Taking him back, he belongs to us.'

Belong! The word carries wars and battles tucked inside it, from Helen of Troy to *Kramer v Kramer*. Atlas didn't carry the world on his shoulders; he carried the word 'belong'!

'Is that what B stands for?' asked Sita/Ferret, stepping a little towards the side, thinking perhaps it would take her to the other side of Gopal.

'What?' said Ant, keeping his gun aimed at Kala and Gopal. What rubbish was this woman talking now?

'Aaaaaa,' Sita/Ferret dragged out the sound, as if teaching a child, but spoke direct to Gopal. 'Beeeee. Ceeeeee. Did you learn your ABCs?'

For the first time, the voice came out, a sound like ancient honey. 'Anthony Bernard Child,' it said.

'Move away from him, you bitch,' Ant commanded, wheeling his chair towards them.

'That's the wrong ABC. He's been telling you lies. I'll tell you the real one.' She was thinking fast now. 'Asian British Co-operation. That means you can take orders from him,' she added, nodding towards Kala, and starting to rush her words, 'and me. The old ABC doesn't work any more. Our ABC is good; it'll let you out. Outside. Fresh air.'

'Shut up!' Ant wheeled himself in front of her, his gun digging into her stomach. 'Get out, you and your pimp. Out!'

Gopal moved towards the door.

Sita/Ferret ran to open it.

Ant tried to wheel his chair towards Gopal, lifting the gun high in his hand, ready to crash it on Gopal's body. Kala grabbed the wheelchair from behind and dragged it around, as Sita/Ferret and Gopal disappeared through the door.

Gopal was running as fast as his bowed body would allow him. Driven by the intoxication of fresh air? Freedom! Sita/Ferret glanced backwards, as she caught up with him.

'And where do you think you're going?' asked the gardener, barring the way with a spade.

A shot blasted in the house.

Chapter Twenty-five

London, June-August 1997

Sizzling! Scorching! Summer in the city!

London is buzzing! The sun shines with a tropical heat. Sita/Ferret wears flimsy dresses with deep necklines and high hemlines that swish around her thighs, sunglasses and a satin-ribboned straw hat. She melts into the London crowd – but only on alternate days. The other days she wears sheer saris with bikini blouses, displaying her body as never before, revelling in its shape and form, admiring its composition. The body is for display, enjoyment and fulfilment – not for locking away.

She's taken out the little containers and brushes that she'd bought for Mr Kalyan's 'Art Exhibition', and takes delight in colouring herself, magicking herself into more than skin and bone. The art of artifice is the art of the imagination too! She has an array of lipsticks now, one for each different shade; she paints her lips then grins at herself. Life is for conjuring not confinement.

She works in an office for one of the large insurance companies. In the office, the other women talk of families, boyfriends, husbands and children, all the paraphernalia of personal lives. In the past Sita/Ferret would have been reserved, held back. Now she avidly participates in that churning pool of 'he said', 'I said', 'he did', 'I did', 'she said', 'I said...' Sita/Ferret has added her contribution to the pool, and formed their names on her tongue. Emily, Champa, Ferret the Foreign and Kala – she has talked of them all, described them, quoted them, made fun of them, made them her own. Now when she gets into the office, work is not the first thing on her mind; the doings of the night before, or the next instalment in a long-running saga, a good giggle and a gossip is what she's after. She goes for pub lunches, joins in the joking and teasing, laughs as raucously as the others, feeling her belly muscles stirring, her head lightening.

Gopal is the only one never mentioned. His name requires a different intimacy. For this she met Jeevan, and poured the words into her ears; and though Jeevan's eyes grew darker, her arm went around Sita/Ferret. So there is such a thing as comfort!

And there are also such entities as doubting, unexisting and stolen love. The first one is absent, the second turns her sloe eyes somewhere else, and the third had all his loves taken away.

Thoughts of the one in India-land, Hindustan, perhaps never to return to Englistan, filter through her days. Kala has been away in India with Gopal. Since his first letter he has not written. She cannot complain that he is not a more prolific writer; her perspective on time has been turned inside out. She lives with separation and experiences its many layers. She lives with the fear and jealousy that he might already have got himself sorted via the arranged marriage system, its beauty being that you can arrange it whenever you want; you don't have to wait for love to strike you barmy or take lessons in flirting from personal relationship consultants. She tells herself that she will make herself accept anything he decides, whether to live there forever, to live with another, to live without ever seeing her again. On that day of Ant's rage, the blood on Kala's face had run into her eyes. He was alive! Underneath the longings, the doubt and loneliness, hers was a thankful gratitude.

In the meantime, 1st May had come: voting day! Sita/Ferret, who had never participated in the democratic process, made sure she was on the electoral roll, and got up extra early to get to the polling booth. She knew the Labour party were hardly going to be angels of purity, but believed that the Tories' eighteen-year monopoly had to be broken. Even if never properly fulfilled, democracy and free speech are sacred ideas. A half-open door is always better than a locked one. She had seen Sangeeta Rayit come out of a booth, and with a wave to Sita/Ferret, go on her way, trendy bag on her shoulders, lipstick gleaming, permed curls bouncing in the air.

On another day, Sita/Ferret made a journey to an office above a supermarket – 'Mrs Smith's supermarket', the *upmarket* supermarket, the kind where the pasta is hand-made, and fruit nestles in frilly pockets. Mrs Hampton, efficient, intelligent, salt-of-the-earth type, introduced herself as the office manager, and replied, 'I'm afraid Miss Bombay isn't here. Would you like to leave a message?'

Sita/Ferret didn't answer, convinced that Ferret the Foreign has seen her coming and was hiding somewhere. Sita/Ferret looked around her. It was a wide room with two desks at one end, covered with the usual computers, fax machines, telephones. At the other end of the room was a large table with chairs ranged around it, and on the wall were prints of landscape paintings. No sofas or easy chairs, the only luxury seemed to be the coffee filter on a cupboard next to a fridge. Organised and functional!

'Where is Miss Bombay's office?' asked Sita/Ferret. 'I'm an interior designer and she asked me to have a look at it. Tara Designs,' she lied, and was immediately found guilty.

'Miss Bombay doesn't have a separate office,' Mrs Hampton informed her sharply, looking at her more closely, perhaps memorising her features in case she had to give a description to the police.

'Oh no, really? My secretary must have made a mistake,' Sita/Ferret rattled on. 'She doesn't usually, she's very efficient. An MA you know. Far more qualified than I am.' Perhaps Ferret the Foreign would walk in any minute. Wouldn't she get a surprise!

'Would you like to leave a message before you leave?' Mrs Hampton enquired.

'Message?' Sita/Ferret echoed idiotically. A message from the womb? Love me, don't leave me! 'You make her coffee do you?' she asked, nodding towards the coffee filter.

Mrs Hampton opened the door. 'Miss Bombay makes her own coffee. I'll let her know that you called, Miss...?'

'Miss Sita Bombay!' That would give her the jitters! 'In fact I would like to leave a message. Tell her I'll be back.' She'd haunt Ferret the Foreign. Step on her shadow. Invade her dreams.

The separation of fifty years churned inside her too, fifty years when there was a vacancy in the universe. She wanted to solicit something of what has been lost, and make an offering to the spirit of what was stolen.

She mixes imagination and reality, tries to imagine how he would have felt the world, a world that had been so long hidden from him. When she's out, she touches the hedges and bushes, crushing leaves in her fingers, staining her hands, licking the acidic remnants; each day she looks at the sky, takes in the colour changes, the wind, the feel of evening darkness. Instead of just observing people, she begins to greet them, indulge in remarks about the state of the pavements, the rubbish collection, the progress of the new government. Gradually names are exchanged; an invitation to tea comes her way one day. These are all the simple little ways of living that had been stolen. When she bathes, she sprinkles perfumes and bath oils, and allows herself to dissolve into their dreams.

She opens herself out, widens her attention, for if a man smiles, she'll smile back; if he invites, she'll accept. She eats rich, aromatic foods in the latest restaurants; drinks cocktails and wines in the crowded bars; indulges in nights of endless words in the open-air cafés, words that go through smart cerebral to see-through sexy, that delineate desire from the physical to the passionate, from short-term flings to long-term relationships, from confusion to understanding; absorbs the emotional, sexual histories of others and finds her own emotions stretching, deepening. She had thought herself in love, and now realises she had merely grazed the surface; gradually she sees the limitlessness of emotion, its atomic power to create and to destroy.

In all her flirting, she will not step across the 'skin and sin' line, for the flesh is the guardian and the purveyor of emotions, as sacred as it is profane, as faithful as it is faithless.

She visits the museums of London and experiences the changes to the heart that a museum can engender, for they are full of different kinds of marvels, many from nature, many from ancient craftsmanship, many from new technology. At the Natural History Museum, she is awe-struck by the bulk and length of Tyrannosaurus Rex, by the journey to the centre of the Earth, and by seeing that we really do live on a ball of fire, that we are nothing more than mere insects scrabbling on the surface, and yet we look to the stars, and know that we are entitled to justice and fulfilment. As she goes through the evolution gallery, her legs feel wobbly and she thinks that, not so long ago, those legs were probably fins or flippers, propelling her through water as she hunted down her dinner. After she leaves the museum, she passes restaurants and cafés where all sorts of manipulations for other kinds of dinners were being worked out, never mind the nutritional content.

Half the twentieth century missed, one Sunday she went to the Science Museum where a person can be like a child in the latest high-tech playground with its computers, spacecraft, gadgets and knowledge; in the Challenge of Materials Gallery, visitors were building an atomic model of a diamond in order to see both the outside and the inside. She asked if she could add a piece too. She was given a small red plastic tube with a hollow spoke in the middle, and shown where and how to link it with the ones already there. She put it in for Gopal.

She'd stood outside the Victoria and Albert, admiring its Gothic/Colonial façade and then decided not to go in, for it was the museum that contained many artefacts brought over as 'official booty'. And if you can have booty of one kind, why not booty of another kind?

She's become voracious for everything in life. Sita/Ferret can come in from a late night, and immerse herself in a book till the early hours. She used to be a library-book person: borrow, binge and return with nothing to possess. Now she browses the late-night bookshops in central London and comes back with an armful. She takes them out of the bag, smells them, flips the pages, runs her hand over the crisp new paper.

Jeevan rings her at the beginning of August. *(August is a wicked month.)* Sita/Ferret is delighted. A wild night to shake up the blood cells and burn up the nerves will be sheer electric joy. 'Where and when?' she asks before Jeevan has even begun a sentence. But lunch in the park is what Jeevan suggests.

The park was packed out with tourists and office workers taking time out from their hot stuffy offices! Sita/Ferret arrived first, settled into an unoccupied patch in the sun, looked around to make sure Jeevan wasn't approaching, and whipped out her daily tabloid. 'Diana and Dodie! The First Kiss!' she read. Sita/Ferret has read them all and every twenty-four hours rushes to buy the next fix. As Diana and Dodie duck and dive, and the paparazzi pursue them relentlessly, Sita/Ferret and the world watch in vicarious lust.

She tilted her hat further over her face.

'Should have got yourself a proper *topi*,' Jeevan mocked. She herself went bareheaded. 'Memsahib of London, ordering her *nimbu pani.*'

As Sita/Ferret guiltily shoved her paper in her bag, Jeevan asked, 'Want to go to an Independence do? Full of stuffed shirts and expensive saris.'

'If you call me Sita/Ferret. I'm not Flotsam anymore.'

Jeevan thought about it, and then shrugged her shoulders and nodded. She made no reciprocal offer of wanting to stop being called Jetsam. 'I'll get the tickets then. I'm leaving work soon,' she announced quickly. 'I've signed on to study history.'

'The truth, the whole truth and nothing but the truth? You think you'll get it on a history course?' Sita/Ferret asked her.

'Depends on the evidence. I'm learning how to argue my case and I have a good memory now.' When hadn't she had a good memory? 'See you tomorrow evening then.'

Sita/Ferret watched her go. Jeevan had needed a lunch date, a body to sit next to in the hot sunshine, someone to tell her news to. Jeevan's edges were melting.

The following night, at the Independence celebrations, Sita/Ferret was enthusiastically appreciative of the dancers, singers, bands, the traditional and avant-garde, applauding at every opportunity. During the interval she dragged Jeevan off for a drink.

'I hope this clap-happy new you isn't going to be permanent,' complained Jeevan.

'Doubt it, I'm going to see the Mutant Memsahib tomorrow.'

Emily greeted her with basilisk eyes. 'You stole from me once. You stole from me twice. What have you come to steal from me this time?'

'Nothing was ever yours in the first place.'

Emily snarled back, 'I made it come true.' Emily had achieved an approximation of the fantasy first planted in her mind. She had no need for regrets, there was nothing to regret except perhaps trusting too much. *Suitable recompense had been required.*

'Where's lover boy these days?' Emily asked.

'India.' *August is a wicked month!* Was there a separation she didn't yet know about? Perhaps he was India-resident already? Perhaps he had meant to drop her a line, but somehow never found the time...

'Serves you right!' cackled Emily. 'In my day, a man was the one who opened his wallet. Did you have to buy your way into his bed? Or was it to get rid of the one already there?'

Sita/Ferret didn't rise to the bait, 'Why was everything in Champa's name?'

'None of your business,' Emily retorted.

One by one they had refused to come for the Christmas dinner. Time after time they had refused invitations, and not extended any to her for weddings, christenings or funerals. She had buried their rebuffs, made regular visits, till her brother asked her to discontinue her interest: 'Too much of the tar brush on you!' he'd said. He'd failed twice to be chosen mayor. An accident on the way back in which the car had been severely dented, had only served to enlarge her fury. She had blamed Girl/Ferret for not driving properly. But money has no past and if she died, she doubted they'd spurn her pounds and property. So Emily made a visit to the solicitor's office, accompanied by Champa, and changed the names. Now she was safe.

Decades later, illness must have deranged Champa's mind for she had written on a piece of paper, witnessed by a nurse and a doctor, and split along the middle. 'Typical!' Emily had fumed, 'didn't have the guts to go this way or that. Fudged everything. Surprised she didn't leave the rest to The Ferret!'

The accompanying letter had explained that Champa had already repaid Thoufi. Champa had done her balance sheet.

Sita/Ferret wanted to ask why The Ferret had left them; instead she asked why Emily was going back to India. Emily looked at her with pity – when was this girl going to get wise to the world?

'Because then I'll have what I want. Servants to look after me day and night; I'll live by the sea and think of you shivering in the snow. Here,' she said, giving her an envelope, 'you can take care of these, my instructions. Follow them to the letter. Is that understood? Of course you will. You're too soft not to. You didn't have to do it the hard way like us.'

'Thank you. I shall do my very best to make up on the blood, sweat and tears I've missed out on.'

'You'll have to if you want to buy my share. Every penny is to come to me. Miss Kalyan will see to that.'

Sita/Ferret groaned. Poonum muscled in on everything, determined to create her own empire, considered her father to have too many scruples. 'Why don't you let the solicitors deal with it? Or me?'

'You!' Emily snorted, 'you'd hock the lot and pocket the money.'

'You got back what you wanted. Nothing was missing,' Sita/Ferret reminded her, 'you're losing your touch, Emily.'

'Mind...' A danger-filled warning from Emily! Her name was not for usage by the likes of Sita/Ferret.

'Emily,' Sita/Ferret repeated calmly, 'you're going to get done. And don't say I didn't warn you.'

The emotions towards Emily weren't hate any more, neither were they love. She hadn't yet found the right words, but inevitability seemed to be part of it, inevitability and belonging were the same.

'Why did you abandon him, Emily?' She could ask such questions now.

Emily twirled the handle of her fan, the frills thwacked through the air, raising a hot wind between them. Sita/Ferret thought she wasn't going to answer, and opened her mouth to ask another question but was forestalled by an admission that made her sit back.

'I didn't have enough power.' The wind died down, stillness filled the room. 'Possessions are not power. I didn't know that. We were both his prisoners.'

Sita/Ferret leaves her chair and pulls up a stool in front of Emily, to view her as if for the first time.

'Shouldn't love protect?' she said, asking a question for Gopal, seeking an answer for herself?

Whatever she was hoping for, she certainly wasn't going to get it from Emily. The new Emily didn't linger longer than a snowflake in a heat wave. 'There is no such thing,' Emily announced. Adamantine. Hard and rigid. Her will is her hatchet and reason.

How could there ever be a meeting point? They looked at the world in different ways. For Emily the world was something to be hacked and cut into the shape she wanted. For her, the world carried fulfilment for those who had the guts to carve out chunks of it for themselves. Just like Poonum Kalyan! But for Sita/Ferret, the world was a mystery to explore and solve.

Emily changed tack. 'What do you think is happening Over There, eh?' she taunted, her stick pointing through the wall to the ever-mythical Over There. 'Happy Ever After? I should think she's had a heart attack by now. I'll bet you she's fallen down flat and given up the ghost.'

'How would you know?'

'I know her. I know my enemy,' Emily asserted, nodding her head. 'If you live by the emotions, then you die by the emotions. She ruined herself and her family. Destroyed the work of the generations before her.'

'So she shouldn't have given in to your blackmail?'

'It wasn't. And I didn't. As for him, he's frightened out of his wits. You didn't know when to leave well-enough alone, did you?'

'You got back what you wanted!'

'So? They belonged to me.' Emily put her hand on her chest; whenever those items were mentioned, Emily did that.

'He belongs to her,' Sita/Ferret stated, watching Emily.

'Prove it!'

Sita/Ferret left with the promise of a last return. Emily did not look overjoyed.

The once-a-month ritual at Sangeeta's Rayit's house was in full swing. Some of the faces had changed, but the pattern was the same. Sangeeta asked her if she was going to be staying put, staying in or staying out? Sita/Ferret assured her she'd be staying in her room. 'I've got a headache,' she said.

'Gone off with someone else, has he? Into the black hole of the nineties. That's where they all go. And never to return. Black, brown, white, they're all the same – no balls, just sperm.'

'I'll make myself a voodoo doll.'

She closed the door of her room tight. A shrouded noise from downstairs seeped up, but not enough to disturb anyone. The neighbours could happily watch their TV without danger of the partying from this house disturbing them. The group downstairs went wild, within confines.

Sitting on the bed, she studied a file forwarded by Steven Singh's friend, the estate agent. He'd done a valuation on Simla Sunshine and its contents. The figures were nice and rounded, pleasantly pleasing to any owner – but clearly showed that she couldn't afford to buy out Emily.

She looked up, straight into the distorted effect of the original glass. Mrs Sangeeta Rayit must have used it as the selling point for every lodger: 'If here ye shall lodge, through the looking glass of history shalt thou peer.' But if money was the only obstacle, she could mortgage herself to the hilt, work double time, overtime, shift-time and spend the rest of her life paying it off. She could ensconce herself in the heart of Simla Sunshine,

and never again call it the Mausoleum. Eventually she could become a
replica of Emily, fluffing her pride with her possessions, checking the
polish on the banisters and the shine on the tiles. Or she could haggle with
Miss Kalyan, get a good price for the whole job lot, and buy herself a
smart flat in Fulham. Or she could haggle with Miss Kalyan, get a good
price for the whole job lot and give it to charity, which would give her
enough moral superiority to last a dozen lifetimes. Going over to the
window, she took a tissue and wiped the window-pane. Streaks of black
appeared on the white. 'You're a real little survivor,' she remarked,
running her fingers on the cold surface, 'and you'll continue to exist
whether I live in this room or whether Sangeeta Rayit owns this house.'

A for-sale sign could be nailed to the gate of the Mausoleum, an act to
relinquish the combination of memory and place, and put her past into
the narrowing perspective of distance on a painting till it was nothing
more than a dot.

Binding herself to the fabric of the past was no romantic fantasy: she
would have to work for the rest of her life to pay for it, to meet the monthly
payments, bills and necessary repairs. She'd have to lavish the attentions
of an Emily upon it.

A knock on the door startled her. Sangeeta's ironic expression greeted
her. 'Some people use the telephone. Some people make arrangements.
Some people don't like to be disturbed. He's downstairs!'

They went through the door into the room where he'd first told her the
story of the one who'd concocted a cocktail of love and poison. She kicked
off her shoes and sat cross-legged on the bed. He sat down in the chair at
the furthest point from her. She couldn't see the scar from where she was
– it ran all the way up his cheeks. *Not so pretty any more!*

'It was a fiasco!' he said. 'Either I'll have to live there, or I'll have to keep
going back. The slightest chance, and he shoots out of the house. One day
it took us hours to find him, and then he did a runner that night. The next
night I had to lock him up. I mean, I locked the door.' As if there was a
difference? 'Even worse than that. What I actually did was to lock both of
us in so he wouldn't be alone. Well that was a lousy mistake. He was
terrified of me. So another night, I put up a bed for him on the roof so he
could be in the open. He stared at the stars and the moon all night. He
loved it and stayed put. The next night, I dropped off to sleep, and he
wandered off again.' Exasperation stretched his voice, 'Our area doesn't
have street lighting. It's not a rich area. Anything could have happened to

him. I hunted through the streets, and eventually I found him with a night-watchman, sitting near his fire. Trying to smoke a bidi,' Kala laughed; the middle of the laugh was made of mourning. 'I stayed with them, I didn't have the energy to make him leave. So that's what I arranged. The night-watchman suggested the two men who could help to look after him; older men, who have patience, and,' he shifted in his chair, 'and compassion. Strange isn't it? People who have the least have this empathy.'

'The noble poor?' she mocked.

He chose to ignore her interruption. 'Perhaps it's because they've given up hope of having a share of the pie. They're so far removed from it, they may as well forget it. No need for them to join the rat pack and sharpen their claws! Once they've shelved that idea, they can be lavish with their affections. What is madam's opinion on this thesis?'

They were awkward with each other; not like those who have just met, but like those who have delicate questions to ask of each other.

'Seems like a convenient idea for the ones who have, and want more.'

'I'll have to consider it further. Shall I carry on?' Did he want to start a cat-and-mouse game? To delay the point where the past ended and they would need to meet?

He is more afraid than her. Perhaps because he hasn't seen what she has – blood pouring down his face! Sita/Ferret had thought his skull had been blown away. Kala doesn't know about the gratitude that her heart is now made of. Sita/Ferret doesn't know that Kala has other memories in his head: raging anger, wanting to smash the head of a crippled man who'd been thrown to the ground, to swing the gun and smash it into him, again and again.

'Please do carry on,' she replied politely.

'If you're sure.' He could be polite too. 'Where was I...?'

'Compassion.'

'Thank you. They'll look after him. Taking it in turns. Be with him all the time. This way, he can tramp around the city, be out as long as he wants. I had to...' He paused, regarding his hands intently, 'I had to insist that they always have a rope tied between him and them. It's been...how long have I been away?'

'Five months,' she told him. She could have told him the days as well.

'Well, of course,' he said, conversationally, 'there was my grandmother's funeral to attend to also.' Emily, Emily, the prophesier!

She slipped off the bed, and warmed his hands with her own. Kneeling in front of him, she started a story of her own. 'I've eaten at her table, Miss T Bombay's,' she told him. 'Sitting all by myself. I did think of not paying and claiming a maternal IOU.' The possibility of Miss T Bombay denying the connection in public had instantly withered the idea. 'I've had a "natural" beauty treatment, at her Clarice Beauty Salon. Why does she use an English name?' she questioned.

'Who wants to come out looking like a "wog",' replied Kala.

'Perhaps I should become fabulously rich and buy her out!'

'Would that make you happier?' he asked, moving his hand through her hair, taking off the hairband.

'It would even the score.'

'To give her a big fat cheque?'

'I'll find a way to break that cast-iron shell she has around herself.'

'That's how she is.'

His hands press hard on her shoulders. She fingers the buttons on his shirt, and looks at him for permission; permission is not denied, neither is it fully granted. She has to take advantage.

'If Ferret be my name, then Ferret out The Ferret I shall. She could have treated me like one of her businesses. Taken a gamble, put in some hard graft, then reaped the profit.'

'What profit?' he asked, sliding the zip at the back of her dress.

'I could be an extension of her.' Like mother, like daughter – the umbilical chord all over again!

'It won't be easy,' he said, changing the subject, sliding cloth off her shoulders, bending down to taste the warm skin. Her hands undid the buckles of his belt. 'Either I have to live Over There or visit frequently, or...' She pushed back his shirt, skin and veins and pumping blood! Alive and working! Mouth open, she lifted herself and took his lips.

They landed on the bed with a thud. To create your own chaos! To take another unto oneself, to give oneself! Without thought for the past or the future, for right or wrong, for morality or immorality! To be blessed with this gift of another. To behold and be beholden. To belong!

'Or?' she reminded him, a long while later.

'You relentless woman. You must have the memory of an elephant!'

'You're lucky I happen to like elephants, else I'd have taken that as an insult. Emily had an Indian punishment for me. Do you know it? You have to bend down, arms go backward through the legs, and then you have to hold on to the ears. It's murder: you get neck-ache, backache, knee-ache, the lot. But it "makes you a good Indian" she used to say.'

'But you are talking tradition!' He was back to his gimmicky Indian accent. 'Everyone in India is knowing it. It has been proved to be the most effective tool in learning. Accelerated learning, in fact. You see, when the head is down, the blood is rushing to the brain, and when pain is put on top of it...' He paused. 'Do you want me to answer your question?'

'If you please.'

'Such a polite, well brought-up young lady! Not so young actually. Mature, shall we say? Well.' He sat up and moved away from her. First establish distance. 'Or? Or I'm not going anywhere without you.'

A raft upon the ocean! An oasis in a desert!

She was glad he'd put distance between them; she needed to be careful with these words, to be sure that they were what she had heard, to let them root inside her, for they changed her world. Ordinary words. Wish-fulfilling words!

But a raft can flounder! An oasis turn into a mirage!

'Elegantly put,' she praised him.

'Indubitably,' he replied. Now he waited.

Mischief stirred in her, but mischief can turn into misfortune. 'OK,' she replied, 'that's cool with me,' nodding her head.

'The first time I came to England,' he reminisced, 'was today, on the thirtieth day of August, twenty years ago, give or take a few absences.' She should be grateful to August. And no longer call it the wicked month.

310

'I'm going to buy out Emily,' she told him. 'I can't let the Mausoleum go. The past has to be linked to a place, as well as people, and that's my past. So I'm going to keep it.'

'Don't. It'll bury you,' he warned.

'No,' she says laughing. 'I'll follow the well-worn path of Asian entrepreneurship. I'll rent it out! Mr Kalyan can give me his expert advice. Then, in terms of further expanding my business empire, I think I'll open a nightclub, and call it Scarlet Sitas! Or Kala's Kinky Klub?' She suddenly stopped. Some things are not to be said, even in jest. Then she resumed, 'I'll appoint Steven Singh as the overall manager, no detail will escape his attention, and put Sangeeta Rayit in charge of entertainment. Charge Poonum Kalyan double... Oops! I forgot you have a tender spot for her, don't you?'

'Getting tenderer by the minute. She didn't keep me awake with wild schemes.'

'Ouch!'

'Say sorry!'

To emerge from sweet oblivion! He sleeps. She leaves the bed, and pads out to the kitchen where she opens the curtains, makes herself coffee and watches the street below. She now recognises the shops and houses in this street. In this early morning dawning, Ferret the Foreign sleeps in her bed, perhaps Steven Singh dreams of finding the hidden clue, perhaps Poonum Kalyan devises strategies for survival and ambition, hopefully Sangeeta Rayit is sleeping the sleep of the just, Jeevan might be lying awake, thinking, but not Emily. With a time difference of five hours, Emily must be basking in the morning sun. Sita/Ferret switches on the radio, turning down the volume, and goes back to stand by the window. Morning light is creamy and soft, tender on the heart. For the first time, she tries out the words, 'we', 'us', till the sombre tones of the radio presenter make their way into her. She listens for several minutes, not wanting to believe this news of a car crash in a Paris tunnel. She picks up the radio, and cradling it in her arms, listening to every word, goes back to the bedroom, touches his chest, checks its rise and fall, puts her fingers in front of his lips, waits till they are brushed by warm breath. August is a Wicked Month. Living is a dangerous occupation.

'Afraid? No fear. Not me.'

Notes

1.   Quoted in *The Illustrated Weekly of India*, January 1940.

2.   *Reporting India*, Taya Zinkin (Chatto and Windus, 1962).

3.   From one of Sir Josiah Child's dispatches in 1687, quoted in *British Dominion in India and After*, V B Kulkarni (S Ramakrishnan, 1964, executive secretary, Bharatiya Vidya Bhavan).

4.   Quoted in *Gandhi and Bombay* (Bharatiya Vidya Bhavan, Bombay).

5.   *The Last Days of the Raj*, Trevor Royle (John Murray, 1997).

6.   Story reported in *Gandhi and Bombay*.

7.   *Funeral Service of Hindu Rites*, by kind permission of the Indian Funeral Service, London.

8.   *Ibid.*

9.   *Ibid.*

10.   *Ibid.*

Bibliography

The author is grateful to the following publications in the researching and writing of this book:

Libas Vol. 3, 1990, issue 3
The Illustrated Weekly of India
Reporting India, Taya Zinkin (Chatto and Windus, 1962)
Gandhi and Bombay (Bharatiya Vidya Bhavan, Bombay)
The Last Days of the Raj, Trevor Royle (John Murray, 1997)
A New History of India (4th edition), Stanley Wolpert (Oxford University Press, 1993)
British Dominian in India and After, V B Kulkarni
    (S Ramakrishnan, 1964, executive secretary, Bharatiya Vidya Bhavan)
The Funeral Service of Hindu Rites, The Indian Funeral Service
August is a Wicked Month, Edna O'Brien (Simon and Schuster, 1965)

RAVINDER RANDHAWA

A WICKED OLD WOMAN

Rejected by her family, Kulwant chooses instead her own identity, and masquerades as an old woman decked out in Oxfam garb. In such guise she befriends a series of unlikely characters and uses her new-found freedom to come to terms with the disappointment of the past. For Kulwant has come to understand what those around her fail to see.

A Wicked Old Woman is a poignant and heartfelt look at an Asian community living in Britain.

OTHER TITLES BY RAVINDER RANDHAWA AVAILABLE DIRECT FROM HOUSE OF STRATUS

Quantity	£	$(US)	$(CAN)	€
☐ A WICKED OLD WOMAN	6.99	11.50	16.95	11.50

ALL HOUSE OF STRATUS BOOKS ARE AVAILABLE FROM GOOD BOOKSHOPS OR DIRECT FROM THE PUBLISHER:

Internet: www.houseofstratus.com including author interviews, reviews, features.

Email: sales@houseofstratus.com please quote author, title, and credit card details.

Hotline: UK ONLY: 0800 169 1780, please quote author, title and credit card details.
INTERNATIONAL: +44 (0) 20 7494 6400, please quote author, title, and credit card details.

Send to: House of Stratus Sales Department
24c Old Burlington Street
London
W1X 1RL
UK

Please allow for postage costs charged per order plus an amount per book as set out in the tables below:

	£(Sterling)	$(US)	$(CAN)	€(Euros)
Cost per order				
UK	2.00	3.00	4.50	3.30
Europe	3.00	4.50	6.75	5.00
North America	3.00	4.50	6.75	5.00
Rest of World	3.00	4.50	6.75	5.00
Additional cost per book				
UK	0.50	0.75	1.15	0.85
Europe	1.00	1.50	2.30	1.70
North America	2.00	3.00	4.60	3.40
Rest of World	2.50	3.75	5.75	4.25

PLEASE SEND CHEQUE, POSTAL ORDER (STERLING ONLY), EUROCHEQUE, OR INTERNATIONAL MONEY ORDER (PLEASE CIRCLE
METHOD OF PAYMENT YOU WISH TO USE)
MAKE PAYABLE TO: STRATUS HOLDINGS plc

Cost of book(s): _____ Example: 3 x books at £6.99 each: £20.97

Cost of order: _____ Example: £2.00 (Delivery to UK address)

Additional cost per book: _____ Example: 3 x £0.50: £1.50

Order total including postage: _____ Example: £24.47

Please tick currency you wish to use and add total amount of order:

☐ £ (Sterling)   ☐ $ (US)   ☐ $ (CAN)   ☐ € (EUROS)

VISA, MASTERCARD, SWITCH, AMEX, SOLO, JCB:

☐☐☐☐☐☐☐☐☐☐☐☐☐☐☐☐☐☐

Issue number (Switch only):

☐☐☐

Start Date: **Expiry Date:**

☐☐ / ☐☐   ☐☐ / ☐☐

Signature: _____

NAME: _____

ADDRESS: _____

_____

POSTCODE: _____

Please allow 28 days for delivery.

Prices subject to change without notice.
Please tick box if you do not wish to receive any additional information. ☐

House of Stratus publishes many other titles in this genre; please check our website
(**www.houseofstratus.com**) for more details.